The
SELECTOR
of SOULS

A Novel by

SHAUNA
SINGH
BALDWIN

ALFRED A. KNOPF CANADA

PUBLISHED BY ALFRED A. KNOPF CANADA

Grateful acknowledgement is made to reprint from the following: Rao, Velcheru
Narayana. *Hibiscus on the Lake.* © 2003 by the Board of Regents of the University of
Wisconsin system. Reprinted by permission of the University of Wisconsin Press.

Library and Archives Canada Cataloguing in Publication

Baldwin, Shauna Singh, 1962–
The selector of souls / Shauna Singh Baldwin.

Issued also in electronic format.

ISBN 978-0-307-36292-6

I. Title.

PS8553.A4493S44 2012   C813'.54   C2012-902052-4

Cover images: Shutterstock.com

Printed and bound in the United States of America

2 4 6 8 9 7 5 3 1

FOR

Ena
Kimberley Chawla
and
Cindy Birks Rinaldi

who give me shakti

PART I

Dil hai chhota sa, chhoti si aasha.
My small heart has a small hope.

(Song from Hindi film *Roja,*1992)

Gurkot Village,
Himachal State, India
October 1994

DAMINI

DAMINI SITS CROSS-LEGGED ON HER ROPE-BED, HER week-old granddaughter wailing in her lap. A bukhari glows in the corner, the shallow basin of orange-grey coals warming the room. Her son-in-law and grandson sleep in the men's quarters next door. Her daughter, Leela, still unclean from this birth, is sleeping in the birthing room beyond the men's quarters. The baby's older sister, Damini's granddaughter, sleeps on the floor below in the cow's room. *Hé Ram!* How can any of them sleep through this child's crying?

Damini shelters the infant beneath her sari-pallu and opens the child's swaddling. .

She is so beautiful.

Yet tonight Leela turned away from her again, and bound a long dupatta about her breasts. And despite Damini's pleading, her son-in-law, Chunilal, is making no preparations for her naming. She isn't worth naming, he says.

Damini extends her legs and lays the small bundle in the groove between. She strokes the baby gently from head to toe. The wailing becomes crying, the crying turns to sobs, then at last quiet.

Damini touches the baby's tiny eyelids with her fingertips, and strokes outward to the temples. With the balls of her thumbs, she gently pushes up on the bridge of the girl's nose then down across those soft cheeks. Lightly, she traces a smile on the baby's upper and lower lips. Tenderly, she massages the backs of the baby's delicate, shell-like ears. Now up under the baby girl's chin till her jaw relaxes. Then down—her hands seem huge surrounding the drum of the baby's torso.

Again the creature begins to cry, as if for the suffering of all worlds. She's so hungry, poor thing. No baby can live on sugar water and ghutti for more than a few days.

Carefully, Damini cups the baby's cord stump and rolls her over to compress her hunger. She turns the girl's dark feathery head outward. Already she's holding her head up a little—she's strong, like her grandmother.

Slowly, Damini's hands swoop from the girl's neck to her small buttocks. Holding the baby's ankles in one hand, she massages with the other, all the way down the baby's legs. Her fingertips inscribe circles, moving down the baby's back. But the baby still whimpers.

Damini unhooks her sari blouse and positions the child in the crook of her arm. Tiny lips pucker and pull at her nipple as Leela's once did.

How quickly the girl has learned to suck—such a needy child.

Damini strokes the baby's black hair. She traces the whorl of those delicate ears.

They would look so pretty with earrings.

Tears are drying on the baby's cheek. She's asleep. But when she wakes, she will need milk.

Leaving the small bundle on the bed, Damini rises and lights a Petromax lamp. She removes the sari, sari-blouse and petticoat she's been wearing since this baby's birthing began and steps into a fresh salwar, shivering as she pulls a kameez over her head. She drapes a thick brown shawl over her shoulder, knots it at thigh level.

When she opens the puja cupboard, Lord Golunath's clay eyes bestow his blessings on her. When her husband was alive Damini would return the gaze of the god of justice with worship, but if a widow performs puja at home, she brings bad luck on her family.

What are the gods asking? She should try and see with her third eye. Damini turns from the cupboard, gazes at the sleeping child.

And maroon velvet jewellery boxes spring open where the child lies. They display glittering 24-karat gold necklaces, finger-length gold earrings, gold cuff-bangles, uncut diamonds, nine-jewel necklaces. Leela and Chunilal must buy jewels like these and more for the Ganesh puja, and the sangeet, mehndi, chura-kalire, and saptapadi ceremonies to dress this girl as a bride.

Beyond Damini's reach, goldthread-bordered silk saris in plastic wrapping are stacked all the way to the ceiling, along with more jewellery and garlands made of hundred-rupee notes—presents Chunilal will give with this girl, to the groom's family. At the end of her rope-bed, a TV set is playing an advertisement for yet another TV. Beside the TV sits a two-in-one, a radio-cassette player.

Moonlight washes the room, expanding it to ten times its size, lining it with red-gold cloth: a shamiana. Chunilal will have to rent a shamiana as large for relatives and friends invited to this daughter's wedding.

Men in red coats and white trousers playing golden trumpets, shehnais and drums march past Damini and mount a marigold-garlanded bandstand. White-gloved men array silver tureens on long tables draped in white. They lift the lids, releasing aromas of paneer shahi korma, makhni dal, chicken floating in creamy tomato curry, saffron lamb biryani, potato gutke, bhangak khatai, madua roti and cumin-spiced raita. Guests flash their cameras. Video-wallahs zoom in, zoom out.

A shiny red motorcycle stands on a rotating platform for all to see. A wedding cake appears—white as the ones in movies. Chunilal is presenting his son-in-law thousands of rupees for a honeymoon in Shimla. On the TV a four-door Gypsy with black-glazed windows is climbing the Himalayas. A gold pennant flutters from its antenna, with a 125,000-rupee price tag emblazoned on it. The TV flashes pictures of the cows, quilts and bedsteads Chunilal will have to give.

Plus a Timex, a wall clock, a Godrej steel cupboard and a refrigerator. And there's the bride—grown up, caparisoned in red and gold silk. Rose petals fill the air as she is given to her new family and sent where she may never see snow peaks or her parents or Damini again.

Damini gazes down at her sleeping granddaughter. An ojha or a doctor might take thousands of rupees to cure her son-in-law's ailment; who knows when Chunilal will drive his truck again. Then how will he and Leela afford such a wedding—and after they've already paid for Kamna's? They'll have to sell the truck, the cows, and the land, and become labourers.

Damini's children were larger than this little girl at birth, so were Leela's two, Kamna and Mohan. This infant feels little more than 2,500 grams. How much will it cost to feed her? From the third child onward, babies are always sickly. What kind of work can a sickly little body grow up to do?

Women's work. Servant's work without a rupee of pay. A tiny step above sweeper-work, if she has good bhagya. She'll become like Leela, tired out before she's ever seen New Delhi.

The baby's lashes lie so gently on her cheek. Perhaps she dreams.

Last night Damini dreamed she was in her father's home, a girl before marriage. She was back in a village that clings to the edge of the Thar Desert between Jaisalmer and Bikaner. Sandy scrub, hot as the coals of a bukhari, beneath her thin sandals. And she was hungry, so hungry. In her dream, her eldest sister, Yashodra, went away again. Not to be married, no. That year, hunger felt like rats' claws in the sack of Damini's belly. So Damini's mother and Yashodra said they were fasting and gave food to the little ones from their share. Gave to little Damini, mostly—she was youngest of five.

Yashodra's eyes are before her again—black as jamun-berries. Her sister's petal-like eyelids are beneath her fingertips—closing, closing. A death of normal causes in that time in the desert. No violence to be seen, just a quiet release from the punishment of living. Yashodra's spirit is peaceful, since she never appears, even when Damini asks her advice or begs her to return.

The baby begins to sob, as if expecting no one can console her. Damini picks her up, rocks her, pats her back till she quietens again.

No one should know such hunger, not even an animal. If you're someone, you may survive the hungry times. But the word for someone, *koi*, is not for girls. So girls and women—even women like Mem-saab—can only borrow and use it with permission from men. So girls and women are no one.

Naming this baby will proclaim her a girl. From that moment, she'll know herself weaker and smaller. She'll be like a roti, a chair, a sandal, a pencil, a dhurrie, a rope-bed, a furrow, a lentil seed, a small box, a pot.

A pot. Yes.

Damini places the baby on the bed and wedges a quilt all around. She takes her towel, steps into open air and descends a steep stone stairway to the lower terrace. Beyond the latticed cement parapet, forested ranges and distant snow peaks of the upper ranges of the Himalayas are tinted blue. It's Amavas, the time of the growing moon, auspicious for offerings. Fireflies spark on terraced fields below her. A few lights wink in the valleys.

Damini fetches a shallow basket, lines it with the towel and returns to the baby girl. The child shifts, tiny lips yawn, but she doesn't wake as Damini lifts her into the basket and covers her with the towel. From her bedroll, she takes a paper-wrapped cone of rolled beedis and slips it between her breasts.

Damini jams her feet into her boots, lifts the basket to her hip. Lamp in hand, she leaves the house, climbs the steep stairway up to the road. She places her lamp on the stone parapet, stiffens her neck muscles and lifts the basket onto her head. The lantern swings as she picks it up and continues uphill.

The energy of all souls, atmic energy, exists long before the moment of birth. This child's jee was already here, everywhere—Lord Krishna tells Lord Arjun so in the *Gita*.

Why did this atman incarnate? Only the gods know. Jee doesn't ask for birth. The purush-energy of fathers like Chunilal pulls it into existence. And so this soul came, bringing all the desires of a being. Because it became a girl, along with it came all the expectations and demands of her someday husband and family.

There's the minibus sign, beside the storage sheds, at the mouth of the ravine. That's where the ghost-trail descends.

Damini gave her jee to Leela, as did all her ancestors. Chunilal's ancestors passed their jee to him and through him to this baby. Every element combined to form the girl now sleeping quietly in the basket. Damini watched the moment this soul entered existence, with her first breath and cry, opening her eyes in this world.

Damini stops, sets her lamp down, shifts the basket to her right hip, takes up her lamp again.

One misstep . . .

The tree-lined abyss yawns beside her. Her toes scrunch as the path steepens. Down, down.

Leela needs me, I must not fail.

The lamp creaks as it sways, creating shadows. She keeps her gaze on her trudging boots. Her shoulder brushes the mountainside. Small things loom, dark shapes brighten.

Edging downhill in the dark, Damini takes much longer than the usual two hours to reach the flag and trident that mark the cave of the goddess who has no name. As she enters, bats flutter. She places the basket with the sleeping baby before the huge clay pot of the unnamed goddess. Anamika Devi, namer of all the gods, namer of the unnamed, protector of Gurkot. Painted snow-leopard eyes look upon Damini and the baby, as from a place beyond karma.

Oil in a clay diya flickers as Damini holds its threaded spout to her lantern flame. Cave paintings are illuminated. Damini draws back the towel. Infant eyes turn toward the light.

Small arms rise. Little fingers clench and unfold. The crescent lines of the newborn's lashes part. Brown eyes, twin fireflies, gaze into

Damini's. An open gaze, as if the child sees. As if the child sees her.

Damini turns away. She must become a stone to know what a stone feels like. She must become a mountain to know what a mountain feels like. She must become ice to know what ice feels like.

Only six more days to the baby's naming day. A name will bring her inside language, inside family. Something must be done in these fragile days, before the girl's mind blooms, before she begins to show like and dislike, mother-love, father-love. Before sensations of this life lure her into forgetting lives past. Before anyone begins to enjoy her helplessness, her sweetness. Before her punishment for living begins.

Damini draws the paper-wrapped cone from between her breasts, takes a beedi in her mouth and bites down. Feels a jolt as raw tobacco crosses from membrane to bloodstream. She removes the soft brown wad from her mouth.

Lord Golunath, you who bring justice: allow the merits of this deed to cancel any demerits. O spirits of the prêt-lok, come and receive this atman, this jee become matter, that mistakenly entered this world.

Anamika Devi, overcome the hungry ghosts that will haunt me if this deed be wrong. If this be wrong, let me, not my Leela, take my next birth in a sweeper's hovel. This is my role in the movie of Leela's life.

When Lord Arjun could not find it in him to draw his bow against his own blood on the battlefield, Lord Krishna told him about the oneness of jee. "Knowing this is indestructible, constant, unborn, immutable, how does a man kill anyone . . . who does he kill?" And Lord Arjun followed his dharma, played his role as a warrior, regardless of consequences.

Return this atman to your realm, O Krishna.

With her forefinger, Damini pushes the tobacco into the tiny mouth.

The baby's tongue emerges. She gags, then gulps but does not swallow. Damini wipes drool from the tiny mouth.

Release this atman, girl-body. Let it return to the place that continues long before and long after this world. Let it take shape when this world is a better place for girls.

Damini leaves the infant in the cave with the goddess and the lamp. She squats outside, waiting, breathing hard in the swirling dark. The baby begins crying from the pit of her tummy.

If this deed were right, the spirit of my dear husband would be here with me now. Maybe even Yashodra's spirit would come.

Damini's mother is the only familiar spirit who joins her. *Stop your crying, Damini, she says. Chunilal will get better soon. They will have more children, maybe a son. He will not refuse to name a son.*

Make her crying stop, Ma-ji. Make the crying stop.

Damini shivers and shakes, unable to call on other spirits, gods, men or women for help. She cannot leave—let Anamika Devi witness Damini's suffering with her grandchild.

Shadows move across the screen of trees, and the bulk of the mountain is a darkness behind her. Leaves whisper to the spirits that an infant girl will soon join them.

None but earth, sky and forest have witnessed Damini's deed, and if this was predicted by the lines of her hand, or the movements of the stars, or written in her bhagya or kismat, then no other could have happened. And though no one else knows what happened here tonight, Damini knows.

How will she ever again be the woman she once was, who arrived just two months ago as Leela and Chunilal's guest? This stain on her karma is to spare Leela's. But before she dies, Damini will, she must, balance this deed. She will find the courage to do it.

She can barely see the path homewards. It turns and turns, rising up the moonlit gorge.

Damini tents her shawl over head and shoulders, and clutches it tight. She lays her head on her knees. Her tongue is dry, swollen, and tastes of tobacco.

Daylight is so very far away.

PART II

For years and years, your mother longed to have
a tiny boy in her womb, and you came, so now
she lets you do just as you please.
VISWANATHA SATYANARAYANA

Song of Krishna (5)

New Delhi
May 1994

DAMINI

AMANJIT SINGH HAS ARRIVED ON A PRE-DAWN FLIGHT from Bombay to find the speared iron gates at the foot of the driveway locked. He's shouting, "Open up! Open up!" and swearing. His taxi driver's honking, the neighbour's dogs are barking, and mynah birds screech.

Damini snatches up her dupatta and drapes it across her chest, slips into her rubber sandals, and rushes downstairs. As she runs down the driveway, she yells again and again that she's coming, she's sorry, it was her fault for sleeping so soundly. As soon as she unlocks the double gates and pushes them open, he strides past her, bounds up the driveway, dashes upstairs and begins shouting at his mother.

Mem-saab is standing at the front door of her apartment, fumbling with the zip of her dressing gown. Confronted by her son's ferocious look, she gazes first at Amanjit's lips, then over his shoulder at Damini, her eyes huge and questioning.

This turbaned man, who Damini knew when he was still coaxing his beard with coconut oil, towers over his mother and shouts, "You knew I was coming, and you locked me out of my father's house!"

Aman could be yawning or yelping for all Mem-saab knows. He should speak slowly. He should remember Mem-saab can't lip-read

13

properly through a moustache and beard—even a tidily rolled, hair-netted beard such as his.

Damini ducks past them through the doorway, and takes her place behind Mem-saab. She lays her hand gently on Mem-saab's shoulder. "Be more respectful, Aman-ji," says Damini, her respectful "ji" coming with effort. "No one was trying to lock you out. See, everything is open." She needs an excuse to come between them—she takes a dupatta from its hook behind the door, and offers it to Mem-saab to cover her head. "She's old and left without a man to protect her."

That should shame him. He should remember his duty to protect his mother. But there's no shame in the look he flashes at Damini. That look says she may have been his mother's ears since he was twenty-two, but she is only that pair of ears. "Go, Damini-amma." His thumb jerks past her eye. "Go sit in the kitchen."

Damini ignores that thumb as she used to ignore his tantrums, and helps Mem-saab to her room instead. Mem-saab's grip on her arm is tighter than usual.

Aman is now shouting down the stairs for Khansama, the cook who is probably still in his servant quarters. "Bring my suitcase," he yells. The Embassy-man, his wife and children, who rent the five bedrooms on the ground floor, must be well woken up by now. She hears the cook's sandals slap-slap on the driveway as he runs to the gate.

Damini fetches Mem-saab's silver water glass and her pills. Mem-saab says, "Tell Aman I am not signing any more papers. I already gave him twenty-five percent of this house last time he came." She makes her way to the bathroom and closes the door.

Water purrs into the plastic bucket. Mem-saab's preparing to bathe, without taking a single cup of tea.

Damini goes to deliver Mem-saab's message but Aman has pointedly closed the door to his father's room. She can hear him inside, unpacking. She could shout or write a note to slip under the door, but Mem-saab's message might make matters worse. Soon he will want breakfast.

Mem-saab has begun reciting the Japji aloud in her tuneless chant—she must have emerged from the bathroom. The prayer takes about twenty minutes. Mem-saab should eat breakfast immediately afterwards, to avoid further argument.

Damini opens the screen door to the kitchen and pops her head in so she doesn't have to remove her sandals. The rail-thin cook looks up from his cane stool, his face grey-brown as a potato. Why doesn't he just wear a moustache and beard? Then he won't look like a parched lawn every morning. Hairy forearms poke from his sleep-rumpled kurta and rest upon pyjama-clad knees. Even his toes look like small potatoes.

"Khansama," says Damini, severely enough to pull him together, "Serve Mem-saab her breakfast."

Back in Mem-saab's room, she squats in front of Mem-saab's chair and enters the chant with her. When the prayer is over and Mem-saab opens her eyes, Damini mouths soundlessly, "What does he want you to sign?"

"He wants me to give *all* of this house to him and Timcu."

"Will they live with us?" Damini mouths. Khansama will need to know—he has four children and a wife in the one-room servants' quarters behind the house. As for Damini, she has a son; she will never need to go begging. Unless Suresh has somehow learned disrespect, like Aman.

"No, they want to make condos in its place," Mem-saab's voice swoops like a bulbul bird ascending. Damini gives a hand signal for her to lower it.

"What is 'condos'?"

"Tall buildings."

Damini can tell Mem-saab doesn't quite understand the word either, though she has two more years of schooling than Damini, having studied up to Class 10. At sixteen, the chauthi-lav of the Sikh marriage ceremony ringing in her jewelled ears, Mem-saab came from Pari Darvaza, her village in the part of Punjab that was cut away to make Pakistan. Came wrapped in red silk to ornament Sardar-saab's home in Rawalpindi as his second wife, to birth the sons his first wife couldn't. There was one daughter who died early. Then Devinder, pet named Timcu, then Amanjit.

So respectful was Mem-saab, she never used her husband's real name or called him the familiar *tu*, even after his first wife died. Always, she called him Sardar-ji. After their home in Rawalpindi was abandoned to the Muslims of Pakistan in August 1947, they fled to Delhi and built their lives along with the city.

Until Sardar-saab's demise, Mem-saab needed only to know to pray, decorate the house, shop and give orders to servants.

It's about thirty rains since Damini came from Gurkot in the hills to live here—perhaps more, perhaps less, for sometimes the rains desert the land, sometimes they are ceaseless. And the saab-log have the abroad calendar, ordinary people have the harvest and temple calendar. But for about thirty years, Damini has only needed to know the art of massage and the timing that turns flattery to praise.

But now . . .

"Where will we live?" she asks Mem-saab.

"Aman is concerned about me here . . . such a big house . . . alone . . . with my poor health."

Aman's concern is like a farmer's for a crop of jute—how much can be harvested and how much will it bring? And Mem-saab is not alone. Damini is here. And Khansama, the driver, two gardeners, two sweepers, a daytime security guard, the washerman, the Embassy-man's servants—each looks after her as if she were his mother.

But we are nothing, no one for the saab-log.

"He says a smaller house in Delhi would be better, or that I should go to the hills and live in the Big House in Gurkot." Mem-saab means the estate Sardar-saab received as compensation from the Government of India for the loss of his home and villages in Pakistan.

"The snow there gets this high," Damini says, bringing her palm level with her midriff. "Too cold for you. And me. Though the first year I came to Delhi, I thought I'd die of the heat."

That year began auspiciously enough with her success in giving birth to Suresh, after only one daughter, Leela. But then Pandit Jawaharlal Nehru died, and the whole country mourned. Then her Piara Singh was electrocuted while working and Damini consigned her marriage collar to his funeral pyre after less than five years as a wife. In Gurkot, in those days, everyone did *khuss-puss, khuss-puss* whispering Damini must have done something terrible in a past life to give her widowhood in this one. That Piara Singh's death was foretold, that Damini's bhagya in this life was to be a living ghost. And far away in New Delhi, young Mem-saab's ears stopped speaking to her. So at the end of peach season, Sardar-saab hired Damini to replace those ears, and Damini left Suresh and Leela with her in-laws and became an amma in Delhi.

Mem-saab sighs, "Money—the expectation of Sardar-ji's money—is changing my sons."

Changing? Damini remembers the first time she saw Aman: home from university hostel for the winter holidays, whipping a tonga horse who could go no faster. And his elder brother Timcu, not re-straining Aman, just letting him do it! She remembers Aman a few years later, laughing when a barefoot beggar dived into a ditchful of slime to escape the swerve of his car. And Timcu in the front seat with him, estimating the amount they'd need for a police bribe to forget the poor man's life, should it come to that. A good amma needs to forget much more than she remembers.

"How true, how true," she replies, hanging up Mem-saab's dress-ing gown.

If Amanjit and Timcu still had a sister, maybe they would be kinder. And if Aman and Timcu had been younger when Damini came, maybe she could have taught them more gentleness. But like Mem-saab, she gave these little maharajas too much love, too much forgiveness.

She passed down their clothes to Suresh and gave them all the blessings and hopes she should have given to her own children.

Leela understands. She knows that but for their fear of Sardar-saab, Piara Singh's brothers would have thrown Damini out. But here, an amma gets chai in the morning and two meals a day.

Damini chooses three salwar-kameezes from the cupboard and shows them to Mem-saab, along with chiffon dupattas. If the salwar, kameez or dupatta is a slightly different shade, Mem-saab will look bad.

Piara Singh's brothers were a shade different from him—just enough to make the whole family look bad. But their karma caught up. They had many misfortunes, while Damini has survived when so many said she would end up selling her body for money. She has her ears, she has strong hands and bhagya.

Mem-saab points to a rose and grey silk. Damini lays it on the bed.

Aman has a business that exports fine silks like these. And women's clothing that would barely cover a child. Another business sells plywood, furniture, crates, cricket bats, hockey sticks, cedar oil and varnish. And Timcu—instead of becoming a doctor so he could cure the pains that strike his mother every time she climbs the stairs— Timcu is an astrologer in Canada, divining if prices will go up or down and will there be too much of one thing and not of another. Even his Damini-amma knows prices go up and there is never too much of anything in this eon of greed called Kalyug. So much money spent on Timcu's education, and the man cannot even tell Damini if Suresh will love her when she can no longer give him money.

Foolish mothers like me make astrologers rich.

A knock at the door—Khansama's standing outside, steam rising from the tray in his hands. He has changed his kurta.

Damini takes the tray and elbows the door shut. She places it on a small table in the sitting area and helps Mem-saab to her sofa-chair. Damini adjusts the table before her, pours milk into the bowl of oatmeal, adds raisins and honey.

Mem-saab's spoon stops halfway to her lips. "Where's he now?"

Damini can hear Aman opening and closing drawers, then a creak as Sardar-saab's mirror tilts for the first time in seven years. He's trying on a dead man's silk ties and turbans. "Unpacking," she says.

"Stand here while I eat." The order is a plea. There are things Aman cannot say to his mother in the presence of a servant.

When she has finished, Damini helps her to dress and then calls, "Khansama, tell Zahir Sheikh to bring Mem-saab's car." Her driver will take Mem-saab shopping before the May sun beats down at full strength.

Damini takes her towel upstairs to the terrace. She uses the squat-toilet in her wash area behind the half-wall, and then sits before the tap. She pulls a basin of soiled clothing across the floor, and waits for a thin stream of water.

Aromas of scrambled egg-bhurji, toast and butter rise up the stairwell as she kneads Mem-saab's heavy silk salwar-kameezes, then Mem-saab's transparent dupattas. Rising, she moves past the half-wall to hang the clothes on the line.

Returning to the wash area, Damini half-fills a plastic bucket, pulls her kameez over her head and steps from the legs of her salwar. The water, sun-warmed from the tank at the other end of the terrace, wakes the skin of her forehead and shoulders.

Piara Singh never lived with these rounded shoulders, this slight pot-belly, these grey strands between her legs. But those legs are as lean and strong as when her husband was alive, her breasts still heavy, sagging only a little.

Somewhere below the canopy of gulmohar trees that screens her view of the driveway, Aman is shouting for Khansama to stop a taxi on the main road. Damini towels dry.

The taxi-man honks as Damini steps into a clean salwar and ties its cord at her waist.

Aman clatters down the stairs, shouting at Khansama. Why hasn't the cook placed his ice water Thermos and his briefcase in the taxi yet? How many times does Khansama need to be reminded?

She pulls a clean kameez over her head and smooths it till it falls below her knees.

She can't see Khansama or Aman. "Answer me, don't just stand there—are you or are you not a moron?"

Some English words require no translation.

Khansama, have a thick skin.

Aman leaves. The house crouches in waiting silence.

"That suitcase was heavy." Khansama takes a stool beside Damini, and leans back against the red gas cylinder of the two-burner hotplate.

Damini chews slowly on her morning roti, then takes a sip of chai. "How much did he pay you this time?"

"Full five hundred rupees." He fans himself with the notes.

Just for carrying a suitcase? Payment to forget Aman called him a moron.

"You've forgotten your cap. Mem-saab will find your hair in the curry tonight," says Damini.

Khansama rises and rummages in a cupboard as if he hasn't heard her. He forgets sometimes that he is just a servant. He forgets even more often that there can be honour only from serving those who have honour.

When Sardar-saab was still in this life, Khansama made rogan josh and chicken jalfrezi swimming in layers of pure butter-ghee. His curries, Sardar-saab used to say, were better than those in five-star hotels. And sweet rice, and phirni fragrant with rosewater. He should have been told, "Hmm, these are good but you can do better." But Mem-saab gave him so many compliments, now everyone has to suffer his swelled head. He sits idle most of the day now, and describes flavours and dishes he dreams of cooking—since she became a widow, Mem-saab doesn't order meat or sweets unless she has guests.

Khansama places a small steel bowl before Damini—sugar for her second cup of tea. Damini swirls the square granules with her forefinger.

She lost her sweet tooth a year and a half ago on a December day when she saw Suresh on TV. There was her son—or someone just like him—at the birthplace of Lord Ram in Ayodhya, clambering up the half-demolished sides of a masjid. The masjid was built by Muslims recently, only seven centuries ago. Who but his mother could have recognised that beloved face twisted with anger, those hands wielding a metal truncheon? Certainly no one in Ayodhya.

Suresh had been transported from Delhi along with 200,000 others by leaders in Nehru caps and sadhus in saffron robes. He looked fearless and brave on TV, shouting slogans as he and his fellow pilgrims leapt into the fray and tore down the Babri Masjid. As if fighting the whole Mughal Empire, more than three hundred years after its collapse.

But later, shame churned in Damini's stomach like the milky ocean that birthed the world. Such disrespect for a sacred place. Had she taught him that? Had she forgiven him too many small paaps along the way?

She should, she could, she will, one day, ask Suresh if he was there. Can a mother mistake another woman's son for her own? Impossible. But if he was there, Suresh had committed destruction that is only the right of Lord Shiv.

At that moment her taste for sweetness vanished.

Khansama raises his rupees to a shaft of sunlight that knifes through the chic-bamboo blinds. The notes are worn in the centre, but acceptable.

"Only a fool accepts dirty money," says Damini—then regrets speaking so sharply to a man who has already been called a moron today. He may not be a moron, just a witless donkey.

"He says he will bring his wife and daughter and they will move in here too," says Khansama.

"Here?"

"Where else? You too are becoming deaf."

"Get a few years and some wisdom and your ears will ignore echoes from empty vessels: there are only two bedrooms on this floor. The second is not large enough for three people. If Aman moves in downstairs, Mem-saab will lose her income."

"Aman-ji says he will build more rooms upstairs."

On the third storey? Then where will Damini relieve herself? Where will she bathe? She'll have to share the wash area with Khansama's family. Or will Mem-saab allow Damini to share her bathroom if the sweeper cleans it afterwards? After all, Mem-saab's Japji prayer says there's no high-up, no low-down, all equal-equal. Damini may not be saab-log like Mem-saab, but she is a kshatriya. A warrior descended from rajas, not a sweeper. So maybe she can share Mem-saab's bathroom. That is difficult to imagine.

Much has changed in thirty years—people in towns and cities eat from chai-stalls and in restaurants and who knows if a brahmin, kshatriya, vaishya, sudra or outcaste cooked their food or ate from the same plates, or drank from the same glass? Respected people use public bathrooms that might have been used by lower castes. Newer buildings don't have two doors into the bathrooms, and outcastes enter from the same door as Hindus with caste.

But even in this Sikh household, where caste is banished by decree of ten gurus, when Timcu cut his hair and stopped wearing a turban to marry a no-caste gora woman in Canada, Sardar-saab would not write to him for several years.

Mem-saab, a generation younger than her husband, is a better Sikh. She wouldn't treat Damini like a sweeper. Damini has accepted the ten gurus as her gods and become a Sikh for Mem-saab's sake. Damini's husband's name, which she writes as her second name to get his pension, was Singh—just like a Sikh. And a few times, when

Mem-saab had no appetite, Damini persuaded her to eat a little from her own plate, as sisters do.

Hai! Sometimes Damini needs more gods than one, and more than ten gurus for inspiration; maybe she should become a Hindu again.

"Are you finished?" Khansama says, pointing to the steel bowl with the sugar.

Sardar-saab used to say never trust a clean-shaven man. Potato-face looks happy; to those who follow him, Aman can be the smile of Lords Ram, Krishna and Ganesh in one.

"No," she says, pouring her share of sugar into her tea, though she cannot taste it. She will not share anything to sweeten his life. And no more of Mem-saab's salt than she can help, till she knows the price of Khansama's heart.

Mem-saab returns from her shopping without parcels or bags, eyes red and swollen. She stops several times to rest as she climbs the staircase.

Damini calls for Khansama to serve lunch. She stands by Mem-saab as she eats and then prepares her bed for her afternoon nap.

Damini had a sleeping mat on the floor in a corner of Mem-saab's room until the anti-Sikh riots ten years ago. That night, Prime Minister Indira Gandhi was shot by a Sikh bodyguard and Congress Party officials used voter lists to lead mobs of angry young Hindu men to Sikh dwellings. Mem-saab's Sikh driver was going to risk his life to inform the well-informed police, but Mem-saab ordered him not to go—if she hadn't, he might have been arrested and shot with the rest. As it was the police seized licensed weapons from Sikh men, even veterans, then stood by as mobs burned homes and smoked out Sikh men, women and children. For three days and nights, Mem-saab kept her Sikh driver safe behind her gates, as Sikh women and children fought alongside their turbaned menfolk. On the third day, he begged to come out of hiding. He said he had to protect his family. Mem-saab told him to take her car so he'd look like a saab. But a Hindu mob tore him from the driver's seat, hacked him to pieces, and set her car alight.

Madam G.'s son Rajiv became PM overnight, and promoted the police officers who allowed the massacres. And decorated the Congressmen for their role. So Mem-saab continues to fear Hindu men will come to break down the gates and she will not hear them. And Damini sleeps even closer, on a woollen foot-carpet right beside the bed—and tries to forget she is a Hindu.

Mem-saab lies down for her nap, and Damini does too, waiting till Mem-saab's breathing becomes regular and even. Then she slips out, climbs to the third storey roof-terrace, rests her elbows on the latticed concrete balcony and waits.

A round face appears at the iron gates. Yes, those are Suresh's bright black eyes, his beard and moustache like a close-trimmed hedge. Damini rushes downstairs to meet him. Her son has travelled three hours by bus to touch her feet in greeting, and it will take him three hours to return to the fly-bitten servant's quarters he shares with five other men. He washes at a row of community taps, and lives on plates of pakoras and samosas from roadside chai-stalls, because he's saving to get married as soon as he can find a girl.

Still he comes to see me.

Damini takes the roll of rupees she's been saving for him from between her breasts, unclenches his fist, and slips it in. Mem-saab would say she shouldn't give him everything, and make Suresh fend for himself. But he's a good son—he attends prayer and exercise classes of the Rashtriya Swayam Sewak every morning. And he doesn't shout at his mother like Aman does.

Suresh dips his head in thanks and counts the money. His eyelashes are almost as long as his father's.

"Do you have any more?" he says. "I was saving for a TV, but instead I donated the money."

"To your swami?"

"And the Bajrang Dal, and the RSS."

"No, that's all I have. Don't you donate it as well."

"I tell matchmakers I'm descended from hill rajas," he says, squatting beside her at the edge of the Embassy-man's lime sheen lawn. "And here you are working as a maidservant." Gladioli and begonias offer some shade from the sun. He lights a beedi and flicks the match into the flowerbed. "You need a better job."

Damini shrugs. Everyone needs a better job. Suresh never has suggestions as to what she can do instead. His own job doesn't pay enough even for one person, leave alone a family, but he must find a wife and become a man. "The gods give highborn and lowborn whatever we deserve," she says, eying his beedi.

He laughs and takes a puff. "The gods didn't stop you from leaving Gurkot—you should have stayed there until I grew up," he says, meaning she should have claimed his patrimony by her presence.

"If I had stayed in Gurkot," she says, extending two fingers, "I would be ashes now."

He places the beedi between her fingers and looks through the speared gates to the road. He never believes his uncles would have killed her.

"And you would not be in Delhi," she says.

"Then I would never have gone to Lodi Gardens, never have heard Swami Rudransh."

Damini takes a long, deep drag. She doesn't want to hear how the swami has opened Suresh's eyes to India's real history, or how the swami is Suresh's second father. If Suresh tells her all that again, she'll say one father is enough—you don't need two—even if Suresh doesn't want to hear that.

"*You* should get a better job," she says. "Your eyes will roll round like marbles in your head if you spend more years minding those copy machines."

"I don't watch the copy being made," he says. "One video makes another inside a box."

"When I carried Leela and you, my stomach was like that. A dark box. I couldn't watch either one being made. Most of life is like that only—important happenings are mostly unseen."

He grunts. Maybe she's told him this before.

Doesn't matter. He should hear it again.

She passes him the beedi. "But birthing! It made me feel alive— rohm-rohm." Through every pore and crevice of her body, as never before. Back then, she thought if she could survive childbirth and birth a son, everything else would be easy. Ha!

Suresh blows a smoke ring, and waits respectfully enough, but she knows he doesn't want to hear how painful it was, or how she nearly died to give his atman flesh.

"I don't have to do much," he says, passing her his beedi. "Every videotape comes out the same."

"How do you know?" says Damini. "Maybe each video copy tells a slightly different story—it depends who is telling, who is watching, who is listening, when the tale is told, and where." She holds smoke deep in her lungs, feels it hit, and exhales. "I thought Leela would be my copy and that you would be just like your father. But you aren't even like each other."

"I should be like a woman?"

"I mean she's so trusting and hardworking,"

"I'm not hardworking?"

"*Arey!* One word and you get angry. I only wish I knew how you and Leela grew inside me. If I had gone to college like Aman and Timcu and Kiran, I might know."

"They know? Ha!"

"I saw a doctor on TV pointing to pink and white pictures.

Bapre-bap! How much that man said happens inside a woman—but how does a man know? Only a woman can feel and tell what happens inside her."

"Ask Mem-saab to read you her magazines."

"I can read them myself, slowly, but lady-doctors don't tell about giving birth, even in the new glossy-glossy ones. TV is better—because when I hear something, I don't forget."

"TV is bad for women."

"Bad for us but not bad for you? Why were you saving to buy one, then?"

"To watch Swami Rudransh," he says.

"Ha! You want to watch movies."

"So? You should listen to the radio."

His protectiveness is a comforting omen for her old age, but she says, "I can't, now. Amanjit-saab is visiting." She can't tell him how afraid Mem-saab looks, or that she has a feeling trouble is coming. He'll just say Sikhs are known to be troublemakers. He thinks Sikhs should be given a chance to revert to Hinduism or be told to leave India.

He'll never know Mem-saab has made Damini a Sikh—boys and men seldom learn anything unspoken.

All too soon, Suresh folds his hands in namaste and rises. Damini aims her last puff at the gladioli and stubs the beedi out in their bed. Mem-saab will smell tobacco though Damini only smoked half, and say she must give it up to be a better Sikh.

In blessing and farewell, she rests her right hand on Suresh's dark curly hair for a moment. Then she returns to Mem-saab's room.

Mem-saab has woken from her nap. Aman is still gone.

"I will give you a massage; you will feel better," Damini offers.

She draws the curtains and brings a steel bowl of warmed mustard-seed oil. Sweeping the line of Mem-saab's back, Damini's fingers seek

and press marma points where seen and unseen energies unite. Then
with Mem-saab facing her and watching her lips, Damini talks about
old times, golden times—eleven thousand magical years of Ram
Rajya—when Lord Ram ruled, and children lived with their parents,
and parents with loving, caring children and grandchildren. Her massages take a long time; anything important should be done slowly.

Damini helps Mem-saab to be beautiful, though she is a widow and
her ears hear no sound. Mem-saab applies her foundation and powder
on a face the colour of milky chai, not deodar wood-brown like
Damini's. Despite daily applications of Orange Skin Cream, Mem-
saab's wrinkles trail across her forehead and bunch at the corners of
her eyes. Though twenty years her junior, Damini's look almost as
deep. Damini stands behind Mem-saab, and Mem-saab takes black
kajal pencils from Damini's hands to make eyebrows. Damini regards
Mem-saab in the mirror and mouths how beautiful she looks.

Mem-saab's hair, resting in Damini's palms as she braids it, is the
colour of spent fire-coals. Damini's hair, which went white upon widowhood, looks flame-red in the mirror. For hair dye, she buys an egg
each month and mixes its yolk with dark henna powder and water
that has known the comfort of tea leaves.

Mem-saab goes to the door of her husband's room and sees the
padlock. She weighs it in her hands, then tugs it. She looks over her
shoulder at Damini.

"Did he say when he would be back?"

"No, Mem-saab."

"Tell me as soon as you hear him arrive."

"Will you have dinner together?" Damini mouths. Mem-saab can
pretend she knows the answer; Khansama will need to know how
much food to make.

"Serve enough for two," Mem-saab says.

Around five in the evening, when the fiery heat has tempered to
sweat-crawling haze, Damini leads Mem-saab to her Ambassador
car for a ride to the market.

"Hilloh," she says to the Embassy-man downstairs, trying to sound like Timcu calling from Canada on the phone. He takes the word as Mem-saab's greeting, but Damini enjoys that in Hindi it orders him to move.

The gora man—beardless, moustacheless, pink as Himalayan salt—folds his hands strangely, lower than his heart. Today he forgets to speak to Mem-saab in Hindi and Damini cannot help much, though she understands most of his English words. Mem-saab and he stand for long minutes, smiling, with Zahir Sheikh holding the car door open.

At the market, Damini guides Mem-saab out of the way of tooting three-wheeled scooter-rickshaws, and tells her the prices the fruit-sellers ask. When she turns her face away so that she cannot read Damini's lips anymore, it is Damini's signal to say: that is Mem-saab's rock-bottom price. Mem-saab has very little money with her—just a few notes tied in the corner of her dupatta. Always thrifty, so Aman and Timcu will inherit more of their father's wealth. Even so, she always gives Damini a fifty-rupee note to buy a marigold garland at the Hindu temple. And she waits outside with Zahir Sheikh, in the hot oven of the car, while Damini rings the bell before Lord Ganesh's raised trunk, offers him the garland, and asks his blessing upon her children. The liquid sound of a voice intoning Sanskrit verses circles the inner sanctum with Damini. For a few minutes, she leans against the welcome cool of a marble pillar and listens to a pandit, sitting cross-legged in his corner telling the *Bhagvad Gita*. She takes a few marigolds with her as blessing and braves the dull burn of the air outside.

Mem-saab offers her usual gentle admonition as Damini takes her seat in front, beside Zahir Sheikh, "Amma, remember Vaheguru also answers women's prayers."

"We prayed to Vaheguru this morning," she reminds Mem-saab.

Returning home, she helps Mem-saab put colour on her cheeks and paint her lips hibiscus-red, making her ready to receive relatives.

Ever since Mem-saab lost her hearing, she has been too ashamed to go visiting relatives herself. Sardar and Sardarni Gulab Singh, Sardar and Sardarni Sewa Singh—people her husband helped when their Partition-refugees' application was all that lay between them and the begging bowl—are the only ones who still come to pay her respect.

They touch Mem-saab's feet in greeting; she represents her husband for them. It's been a long time since either Aman or Timcu touched Mem-saab's feet—or Damini's, who also was considered their mother.

"Damini-amma," they call her, with respect because nowadays only higher-caste families have servants who live with them.

Today Khansama's white uniform jacket is crumpled and he wears its Nehru collar insolently unhooked, but Mem-saab does not order him to change it before he wheels in the brass trolley-cart crowned with a wobbling tea cozy. She talks to her relatives in English about his "stealing"—threatening with a laugh to send him and his family back to his village.

When they leave, Damini brings Mem-saab's prayer book. Mem-saab removes it from its silk pouch and Damini joins her in chanting the *Rehraas*. After the evening prayer, Mem-saab tells Vaheguru she was ashamed to tell her relatives about the lock on her husband's room and the suitcase that says Aman is staying for as long as it takes.

It's 10 p.m., long past Mem-saab's usual dinnertime. Khansama's sweet white rasgullahs still wait in the kitchen. Not for Mem-saab, who ordered the dessert, but for Amanjit. Listening to him now, Damini thinks she should have made him eat them before the meal to sweeten his words.

"You are getting so old, you cannot make up your mind about anything." Aman has switched to Punjabi and remembers to speak slowly, but it is still difficult for Mem-saab to read his lips through his beard.

Damini leaves out the part about being old when she repeats his words for Mem-saab.

Mem-saab gestures for Damini to offer Aman more curry.

"Your father told me never to sell or move from this house," she says in Punjabi. "You know, we built it together, selling the jewellery we escaped with during Partition. I still see him walking with me through these rooms—there were only wood beams then, to mark where the walls would rise. This house and the estate in Gurkot, he said, would replace all he'd lost."

"Certainly not all," says Aman. "The government didn't give Sardar-ji any compensation for so many of his villages. They were lost to Pakistan."

"We escaped with our lives—so many didn't."

"Yes, I know. Haven't I heard it, and heard it, and heard it from Sardar-ji and you? He looked backward to Rawalpindi the rest of his life. But Mama, we must look forward. It's a new world now—why don't you decide to live in it?"

Even with the air conditioner going and Khansama's curry steaming, Damini can smell Aman's exotic cologne.

"I do live in it, Aman—maybe you haven't noticed. Perhaps you are right that I cannot decide anything, but . . ." she smiles apologetically, "your father always decided everything for me."

Aman scrapes the serving spoon around the bowl, retrieving the last morsels. He is too old for Damini to tell him not to be greedy.

"If your businesses are not doing well, Aman, I can help. How much more do you need?" As always, she is too mild with her youngest.

Amanjit rocks back in his father's chair, taking her measure through half-closed eyes. "My businesses are doing well, Mama—not that you and my father ever had confidence in any of my projects when I really needed the investment. But one must grow—no limits."

Mem-saab holds up her hand to stop Damini from repeating—he has enunciated clearly enough.

"You're competing with something, someone?"

"There's no one I want to compete with in India. No, it's time to scale up, think bigger, aim higher. All I want is more."

He lets the chair legs thump to the carpet, and shifts.

A mongrel, kicked away once, will attack afresh. And from behind.

He mouths without sound, so that Damini too must lip-read his words. "Today I made arrangements with a construction company. Tomorrow they will begin building bedrooms on the terrace. Kiran and Loveleen and I will move from Bombay and live here with you."

Mem-saab looks at Damini; Damini shakes her head as if she has not understood, so Aman has a chance to change his words. Building on the terrace would make his share far more than a quarter of the house. But Aman mouths it clearly again, just as before, so Mem-saab cannot mistake him.

She gestures for Damini to offer him a chapati.

"Why do you need to move?" she asks, a little too loud.

Aman's strong dark hands close around the softness of the chapati. He tears a small piece from its slack circle. Then another and another. Intent as a counterfeit yogi, he tears every piece smaller and smaller.

"I will look after you in your old age, Mama," he says.

She reads the words from his lips. Reads what she wants to read, but she cannot hear the threat that vibrates in the promise. Her breath comes faster. "It will be nice to have company. I have felt so alone since your father left us."

She doesn't mention Timcu's rights; Timcu's not the son sitting before her, taking far more than he was given. White shreds of chapati grow to a pile before Aman. The handles of a silver salver Damini holds out to him feel as if they will burn through her serving cloth. She comes level with his eyes. They are the grey-white of peeled lychees, with beetle-back brown stones at their core.

Damini returns the salver to the sideboard with a clatter. She will just forget to serve Aman the rasgullahs. She will give them to Khansama's children instead.

The next morning, Timcu calls from Canada and asks in halting Hindi about Mem-saab. Damini tells him Mem-saab is well and not to worry, though Mem-saab breathed heavily through the night.

That evening, Sardar and Sardarni Gulab Singh come to the gates and find them locked, though Damini has made Mem-saab beautiful and she is waiting upstairs. Damini hears Khansama tell them that Mem-saab went to tea at the Delhi Golf Club with Aman. She starts down the stairs to correct him.

"Looking after his mother. Such a fine son." Sardar Gulab Singh's voice travels down the driveway. Damini opens her mouth to yell, but already his scooter is putt-putting away, with Sardarni Gulab Singh seated erect and sidesaddle behind.

Khansama wears a half-smile as he turns from the gate. He glances at a new watch on his wrist. Aman does not like poor relations.

"What a misunderstanding," Mem-saab says, when Damini tells her what happened. "I'll tell Aman he must phone them and apologize for Khansama's mistake." And when Damini tells her about Khansama's new watch she says, "Aman has always been a generous boy." She turns her eyes away. "Put on the TV, Amma—tell me what other mothers and their sons are doing."

On TV you can see past, present, future, upper, middle and lower worlds at once, as Lord Arjun could, but you can't smell or feel them. Damini places the marigold blossoms from the Ganesh temple at its base. She presses the right buttons. An actor's deep voice booms as the *Ramayan* begins, guiding her back to the time of Lord Ram and Sita Mata, and Lord Hanuman. When Lord Ram and Sita Mata were married, two great energies collided. Purush the masculine,

shakti the feminine, the same that create the world. The Aryans of
the day make sacrifices and get attacked by dark demons . . .

Today on TV, Lord Ram and Sita Mata have been banished for
fourteen years to save Ram's father's honour, and have arrived at
Chitrakoot. There is Lord Ram, placing a clod of earth wrapped in
saffron cloth on a mantelpiece very much like the one in Mem-saab's
drawing-room. And he prays to that clod of earth, to the earth of his
birthplace, saying its presence has purified his camp.

"See," says Mem-saab, who doesn't need Damini to explain or tell
her this story, "he's forgetting his mother and thanking a clod of
earth for his life. And he's forgetting Sita Mata, the incarnation of
Earth. Ha! He should be praying to her, begging forgiveness for
bringing her into the jungle! Where is she?"

You can't stop a TV story to ask the storyteller such a question;
his tale is shaped long before it is shown. Sita Mata must be praying
and doing puja somewhere—she's so good.

The story moves on when it moves on, and then it stops.

Each god and goddess's face is being shown up close, with a short
sharp trumpet blast.

Damini turns to Mem-saab. "Why is Ram's birthplace more important than any other place?" she mouths, "The whole world is
Lord Ram's to take birth in anywhere he wants, isn't it?" The question has bothered her since her glimpse of Suresh on TV.

The gods and goddesses are all having similar reactions of shock,
as if they weren't gifted with any foresight. But they never disagree
with each other. Or at least, not for long.

"He can come as Ram-ji, he can stay as Vaheguru-ji," says Mem-
saab. "This is just a TV play, Damini. You know this is an actor, not
the real Lord Ram."

But even when you know the actor is just an actor, Lord Ram's
name and crown make him seem larger than the TV. And even when
you know Sita Mata will be abducted by the ten-headed Ravan, and
that Lord Ram will go to Sri Lanka with the help of Lord Hanuman

and burn Lanka to the ground and rescue her, you have to watch out
of respect, though this *Ramayan* is taking weeks and weeks to tell.
The Punjabi song-story version Damini's mother taught her takes
four or five hours to recite, and she can recite the Hindi telling she
learned from her father in eight hours.

Maybe Leela and Damini's grandchildren are watching TV right
now. Once they've seen this show, will they need her song-stories?
Mem-saab has not felt well enough to spend summers in Gurkot, and
Damini has not seen her daughter or grandchildren for five years
now. Who knows when she'll see them again.

Even if TV is just illusion, it's what Mem-saab calls a 'time-pass.'
And Lord Ram, Sita Mata and Lord Hanuman are familiar, serene
and soothing. By the end of this week's episode, Mem-saab seems to
have forgotten her son's slight to their relatives.

"It's only three weeks since Aman-ji began construction, but I can
already see the new walls from down here," says Suresh. He's hunkered down beside Damini, both balancing on the low wall of the
Embassy-man's lawn. Gulmohar trees give some shade, but the sun
still burns through the back of Damini's sari blouse. She draws the
end of her sari around her, mops her face, then covers her head
with it.

"It's good that Mem-saab can't hear the construction workers, but
she feels the vibrations."

"Do you still bathe on the terrace?"

"Not anymore. I told the women who carry the bricks and cement
upstairs they could use my wash area to keep their babies safe. I have
been washing Mem-saab's clothes in her bathroom, and bathing
there after Mem-saab has bathed."

"Toilet?"

"Khansama's, in his quarter."

"Where do you dry the clothes?"

"In the back garden." She can't tell her son how much it bothers her to hang Mem-saab's undergarments where any passing man can leer at them. Or that she's been watching Aman every day, but he hasn't called Sardar Gulab Singh to apologize. Sardar Gulab Singh ventured to visit twice more, but Khansama turned him away.

"Cement dust is settling everywhere," she says. She wants to tell Suresh that she ordered the sweeper to use a wet rag to wipe the painting of Aman's late father above the mantle twice a day, hoping the old man's steady gaze from beneath his white turban and bushy grey eyebrows would shame his son, but last night, when Aman was drunk enough to think no one was listening, he raised his glass, and said, "Hey, Sardar-ji"—he still wouldn't dare call the old gentleman Papa or Dad—"What does your widow need with all this money?"

But if she confides this, Suresh will say, "Sikhs are so greedy."

"You are serving Amanjit and Kiran at table?" he asks.

"No," she says. Because not once since Kiran and Loveleen arrived has the family sat at table with Mem-saab. Khansama has orders to serve Aman, Kiran and Loveleen morning tea in "their" bedroom. "They're often out for lunch, cocktails, or dinner."

Every morning, Kiran wraps her satin dressing gown over a bosom as buxom as that new actress Madhuri Dixit, sits at her dressing table, and preens before the mirror as she applies a mask of gora-coloured makeup. Her sunglasses balance on her nose ring all day, even indoors. She looks petulant and irritated whether she's talking to Damini or any other servant, and only smiles when Amanjit holds up a camera.

"What does she do all day?"

"She takes Mem-saab's car and driver shopping. She likes to shop. I helped her unpack, and even her handbags and high-heeled shoes have saab-sounding names: Kochar, Fear-raga-mo, Hurmeez. Mem-saab gives Zahir Sheikh money for petrol and tells him to treat Kiran with respect, though after so many years of marriage Kiran still has no sons." Mem-saab even admonished Damini, though gently, when Kiran squealed that Damini broke the plastic half-circles in her brassieres when she washed them.

"They must be meeting Mem-saab at chai-time?"

"They are too busy to sit with Mem-saab and talk." Amanjit is not too busy to sit in his room with a newly installed air conditioner and talk on the phone to Bombay. He's not too busy to pay a Chinese yogi to tell him where to position his bed for maximum energy flow, or a Hindu jyotshi to draw up a horoscope for a new business. And he's never too busy to entertain, buying whisky by the case on his mother's account at Malcha Marg market. Bills come, but Mem-saab doesn't give them to Aman. She takes a taxi to Punjab National Bank for money to pay them.

Sometimes after dinner, Amanjit orders Khansama to bring Mem-saab's best crystal and he and Kiran put their feet up on Mem-saab's polished teak tables and her sofas. Sometimes he and Kiran sit in Mem-saab's drawing-room with their raucous pink friends—he calls them "buyers"—long after decent people go to bed. They spend money on electricity the way rajas and ranis once did, keeping the air conditioner running all day and all night. Once he persuaded a buyer to stay two hours longer just because Kiran gave a bad luck sneeze as the man rose to leave.

"Mem-saab doesn't use the drawing-room unless they are out. She watches for their arrivals and departures. Whenever Aman-ji is home, they argue."

"What about?"

Damini sighs. Mem-saab wouldn't want her to tell anyone but it angered her so . . .

"Yesterday Aman-ji said she hadn't done anything useful her whole life. She said she brought him into the world, that she was a wife and mother and gave him love. But he said now that he's in the world, he needs to live and she should give him the rent money."

"If he wants it, how can she stop him?"

"I will stop him."

"You? Ha! So what does Mem-saab do all day?"

"She watches TV and I tell her the story, the lines, and the songs. Today I sang 'Chal, chal, chal mere haathi, o mere saathi . . .'" She claps, urging him to join.

He sits silent, glowering.

"You always loved this song," she protests. "You used to play the elephant, remember?"

"It reminds me of the new party for sweepers. The elephant is their symbol. Splitting the Hindu vote so that Muslims can take control of India."

"Suresh, what are you saying? An elephant is also Lord Ganesh, and Lord Ganesh is Brahma, Vishnu and Shiv together . . . come sing, sing!" Damini rises, covers her head with her dupatta, half-veiling her face. She steps in and out of an imaginary circle singing, "Chal le chal ghatara kheechke . . ." The song lifts her spirit and eventually lightens his expression of discontent.

When she gives him her usual gift, he says, "I should be looking after you. If I still had my father's land, I would be giving you money."

"Don't worry, beta. More will come." It's a line from the movie of another woman's life—Damini once heard a saab-woman say it on TV. But no god is manufacturing any more land for people in India. Besides, if Suresh still farmed Piara Singh's land, it would be mortgaged for Leela's dowry.

It's better this way.

When Suresh is gone, Damini returns upstairs to find Mem-saab sitting before martyr's pictures: of Guru Tegh Bahadur, the guru executed by that mad Mughal emperor Aurangzeb for defending the right of all Hindus to worship, and of Baba Deep Singh, who carries his severed head aloft in defiance as his tortured bleeding body straddles a white steed. Her lips move, soundless, before the martyrs' images, repeating her one god's name: "Vaheguru, Vaheguru . . ."

Images and idols may be forbidden to Sikhs, but even they sometimes need a photo to witness their tears.

"You have Dipreyshun," says Damini.

"No, my chest is hurting."

"We should have gone to Gurkot for the summer."

"Maybe next year."

"Every year you say, 'next year.' It's been five years since we were in the cool mountain air."

"I said next year! Don't you think I too yearn to be home in the Big House? But Aman doesn't want me to go."

Damini drops her gaze to the marble floor to show respect. After a minute, she says, "Shall I bring oil for your massage?" It's all she has to offer.

"Not today, Amma."

And not the next day or the next.

When Kiran breaks a glass bangle, Amanjit buys her a new gold one, saying, "Don't bring me bad luck by breaking bangles."

A carved ivory tusk disappears and a leopard skin is removed for reasons of 'Feng Shooey.' Fine vases find their way to 'their' room; a china rose Sardar-saab brought Mem-saab from abroad is no longer in the sideboard. A set of silver candlesticks vanishes. A mirror with a golden frame is replaced by a Rajasthani silk painting smelling of the street-hawker's bundle.

Around the first week of June, an ivory miniature departs in a gift-wrapped box for a buyer. Mem-saab says it must be Khansama, stealing again. Then she turns her head away so she cannot read Damini's answer.

"Go away, Damini-amma," she says. "I am going to write to Timcu."

ANU

A FEW KILOMETRES AWAY ON THE GROUND FLOOR OF
Kohli House, a three-storey mansion in the Lutyens-designed area
of New Delhi, Anupam Kohli is standing in her daughter's room,
fists clenched at her sides, gazing at Chetna's neatly made bed,
Chetna's little white desk and chair under the window framed with
pink polka-dot curtains.

Only fatherhood has saved her husband, Vikas, from being murdered by his wife many times over. Chetna is the sweetest little
daughter in the world.

A Punjabi bride doll Vikas bought for his daughter sits on the
windowsill. A red silk salwar covers the doll's legs, her kameez cas-
cades over bulbous breasts. A transparent red gold-fringed dupatta
covers her long black hair. Anu looked like that doll, even to the
shade of her lipsticked smile, the day she was married off to a man
wearing a diamond tie pin and a Gucci charcoal pinstripe suit to
whom she had spoken ten words at most.

Now Anu lives in this Taj Mahal of a home with her husband
and in-laws. With a cook to help her, with servants to clean, to wash
her clothes and tidy her cupboards. She's wearing a muslin salwar-
kameez and has many saris bordered in gold. She can get a facial
and have her makeup done at the Taj Palace Hotel whenever she

needs to cover up a swollen or purpling eye. She has pants and matching shirts, embroidered kurtas, pashmina shawls, embellished slippers, and many pairs of high-heeled sandals. She has 24-karat gold and diamond bangles, an array of earrings and necklaces that cost Vikas a fortune. If no one else needs them, she can use the family cars and drivers. She is a Hindu-Christian who has accepted Lord Jesus as her saviour and propitiated god, and all the gods and goddesses as well.

But right now, breathing hurts.

Anu sits on the bed. She has been awake all night, afraid to move in case she woke Vikas.

Nancy Drew . . . Malory Towers . . . the *Mahabharat* . . . the *Iliad* . . . the *Ramayan* say the rainbow of titles on the bookshelves. A cricket bat stands in the corner.

Anu stands, grabs the bat, raises it overhead. *Thwack!* She smacks it on the bed.

That's the sound it would make coming down on Vikas's head.

She's trembling, and has to sit down, holding her ribs.

Sitting hurts. She holds her ribs, takes a deep breath, stands.

A bulldozer seems to have crushed her inner space, thrust each organ into the next. Maybe a rib is broken but getting an x-ray will notify the world—beyond your beautician, nothing is confidential in the capital city.

This pain is nothing—the pain of childbirth is still sovereign. No—maybe the pain after her car accident.

Chetna's scent is still here, as if Chetna had just risen from the white painted desk. Anu sits at the desk. Here's sketch paper, a tin box. Inside the box, coloured pencils point at her sharply, a quiverful of arrows.

Arrow number one is red. Colour of twenty-year-old Anu's virgin blood. Colour of her fault for agreeing to marry Vikas and his family. Not that Mumma presented her with many choices that season—eligible bachelors were already selecting younger women.

Anu's pencil digs a vertical line in red on the page, then another. A few branches, fibrous roots. She realizes she's drawing the day of her "Showing." Here's the table under the banyan tree at the Gymkhana Club, laden with all the Indian, Chinese and Continental dishes Dadu ordered. Here's Vikas's father, Mr. Lalit Kohli, leaning forward as he talks to Anu's father, Deepak Lal. Here's auburn-haired, sleek Mrs. Pammy Kohli, with her perm, her permanent smile and her permanently startled look. Mrs. Kohli, who produced Vikas, is revered and indulged for that achievement, and needs no other evermore. Mrs. Pammy Kohli clasps her elbows beneath her shahtoosh shawl, smiles, and evaluates Anu.

Here's glamorous fine-boned Mumma, her hands darting and waving like intelligent animals in rhythm with her non-stop patter. An anxious look on her sparrow face because her daughter was nearing twenty-one and had been rejected twice. One family said Anu was "not homely enough" for their son. Meaning she wasn't domestic enough. The other said she was "too-much-educated."

Anu draws herself sitting under the banyan, too. Freezing, she recalls, in a chiffon sari borrowed from her cousin-sister Rano. And white platform sandals that were so in style in 1985. Yearning to imitate her friends, most of whom were engaged or married. Wanting so badly to please her parents that she only took a few sidelong glances at Vikas to verify he would be taller than her in high heels. She assumed she could love him. Marriage, she had thought, would free her from the need for chaperones, and worrying about who might see her looking at or talking to an unrelated man. And Mumma, Purnima-aunty and Rano all assured her that marriage would fix her. That afterwards, she'd want—need—children.

Here's Vikas. In those days he had a curly lock of black mane that would fall across his forehead, not the slick-gelled cut he has today. Then as now he had a bow-shaped moustache and a square close-shaven chin. Right arm strengthened from swinging a polo mallet, and the left from neck-reining. Thighs accustomed to gripping the flanks of his ponies. He smelled of leather, horses, and power. Anu gazed shyly at his knee, for most of the Showing.

Ambitious, well-mannered, well-educated, he'd flashed her his movie-star smile. Only son and heir to an entrepreneur much-demonized under Nehruvian socialism, but well-protected from foreign competition. Vikas entered his father's printing business, Kohlisons Media, at twenty-five, the year Madam G.'s son Rajiv became prime minister. When India liberalized and multinationals and private companies began wooing the government for entry into India, the Kohlis were right there to help them advertise to the masses.

The advertising and packaging boom cushions mistakes. All Vikas's decisions are right. Even those to come. He is corrective and combative with waiters in five-star hotel restaurants, ushers at movie theatres, his personal barber. He admonishes his gardener, his security guard, his drivers—whom he now calls chauffeurs. No one challenges him, no one protests, so he brings his public imperiousness home.

Lord, give him a heart attack. Maim him before I sin.

"What matters is who you know—not what you know," Vikas often says to Anu. A member of the Old Boys Associations of Sanawar School and Hindu College, the Delhi Golf Club, the Habitat Centre and the India International Centre, he is proud to be even a Dependent Member of the venerable Delhi Gymkhana Club thanks to his father. He works hard to keep up with the party circuit. "We must attend," is followed by, "I invited about eighty guests for cocktails and dinner, maybe fifty will turn up." Which launches Anu into a frenzy of purchasing and cooking, and ordering shamiana-tents and caterers, flower arrangements and musicians, leaving no time to read or implement her own ideas, or even help Chetna with homework.

Nightly, Vikas makes shows of plenty to people who undertake fasts and pilgrimages and spend lakhs of rupees—no, crores of rupees—on religious ceremonies, weddings and birthday parties.

Nightly he exchanges gold-embossed invitations, floral arrangements and shiny wrapped gifts with people of high blood and low
competence. They drink Dom Pérignon and eat canapés while the
poor go unnoticed and unfed. He's entangled her in a new version
of colonialism.

Arrow number two: pale gold—colour of caution, colour of all
those could-haves.

Could Anu have written to Vikas and confessed her feelings about
children before the wedding, feelings everyone assured her would
pass upon marriage? No. Vikas could have jilted her and left her
reputation in tatters.

Could she have realized that Vikas was comparing her to someone?
Anu writes the numeral one in gurmukhi script, then a three as if
beginning an "om." She extends its tail up, and over to join the beginning. One more arc jumping from there, and it becomes "Ik Onkar,"
symbol of the Sikhs. There must have been more to his first fiancée,
besides her religion.

And now Arrow number three: Green for Chetna—colour of
movement, change, and growth. With the green pencil, Anu draws,
then colours in a telephone receiver.

Anu had been on the phone with Rano late at night. Vikas was
travelling. Rano was on her lunch hour, as lonely in Toronto as Anu
was in Delhi. After the usual discussion of family members, Rano
said her period had come again, and she'd cried, and so had her
husband, Jatin. Six thousand dollars worth of fertility treatments, all
for nothing. Two little blocked fallopian tubes and she just cannot
conceive.

Then Rano had asked delicately about Vikas, and Anu began in
a falsely bright tone. But she soon faltered, tears came, and she whispered to her cousin, "You know how it was, Rano. I never wanted this
child." And Rano said, "*Hai*, don't say that, sis. Listen, Anu. Listen
very carefully. If you really don't want her, send her to me. Jatin will
be delighted, I know."

And the next moment, a click on the line. Had Vikas come home early and heard her? She hung up quickly and walked into the kitchen. There was Chetna, receiver in hand, tears plopping into her Ovaltine-laced milk.

"You never wanted me, Mummy, you don't want me."

"Oh, no darling," she'd said. "It's just that I'd promised myself I'd never have a child—any child." How could she explain that at twenty, she walked around looking like a woman, feeling feminine—attractive, caring, kind, able to feel for the aged or sick without reserve, feeling no distaste for children, overflowing with love for parents, relatives, fiancé, country—but failing to need a child of her own?

Maybe one day Chetna will understand Anu's promise to herself to remain childless. When Anu was growing up the US Agency for International Development, World Bank, Rockefeller Foundation, WHO, Swedish International Development Authority, Population Council, UNFPA, IMF and Indian Government all tutt-tutt-tutted that Indian women were having far too many children. Restrain yourselves! they said. It's an explosion, said European experts, even as their armies pointed missiles at one another. You're procreating too often, they said, even as the Pill bifurcated procreation from pleasure. Control your breeding, they said, and there'll be more water, food, land and brotherly love for each man, woman and child in India. Back in the early seventies the slogan went, "India was Indira and Indira was India," and Madam G. loomed on billboards at traffic intersections, berating Indians for having more than two children. The year India managed to sterilize six and a half million men, a younger Anu told Rano that having children was a selfish act of self-perpetuation, an imposition on India's resources, and a sacrifice of a woman's independence. She would have self-control.

But Rano just laughed and said Anu would feel differently as soon as she was married, that love would come and hormones would kick in and that having a child would make a woman of her. And to believe anything else was abnormal.

Chetna will never understand how naive her mother was. How could Anu have expected her parents to find her a man who would love her for being herself, not because she was equipped to produce babies? How utterly stupid, how clueless she was to believe she could remain childless in the face of her husband's expectations, and her in-laws' expectations. And Vikas's prodding to produce the son he needed to carry on his family name, and the family businesses. Otherwise, he had demanded to know, what was he working for?

"If you didn't want me, why did you have me?" wept Chetna.

"Because . . ." Anu couldn't tell Chetna the whole truth. Never, ever.

The act that conceived Chetna was rape—even if the police-woman with the black leather chestband said, "Such things don't happen in India. Only abroad." She cocked her cap over her sleek coconut-oiled hair and said, "If somehow it happened in India, it is not a crime," and refused to register Anu's complaint. It was rape, even if Pammy Kohli denied it happened, and then said Anu had brought it on herself by saying No, and now doesn't remember any such incident.

Chetna was born of Vikas's disbelief that any woman would not want a child. She was born of violence, and Anu's lack of contracep-tion. She'd fully intended to use the rhythm method.

Raping your wife is not a crime. Killing your husband is a crime.

And premeditated murder is an even larger crime, which would lead to years in prison.

Now a green cord grows from the receiver on the page. Anu curls it up into white space.

A partial truth came out that night, as she attempted to reassure her crying daughter: "Because once you were coming, I couldn't . . . I mean . . . I began to want you." A child Anu once saw as theoretical moved into her body, its very real hunger causing her nausea, its will to survive competing with her body's early desire to expel it. But once Anu felt Chetna's first fiery movements in her belly, she could not bring herself to extinguish a life-spark, and allowed the baby to use her body as incubator. Rano had counselled that a woman is incomplete without the experience of children. That if she had one, she would see.

"Then you were born," Anu said, taking the phone from Chetna and choosing her words for an eight-year-old as she hung it up, "And I fell in love with you. That's why I called you Chetna—it means self-knowing—do you know that?"

Anu could not refuse that tiny hand groping for her breast, laying claim to her body. You will love me, said that gesture, and incredibly, mother-love came like a life-jolt from heaven. The moment she named Chetna, Anu connected with a force much stronger than herself. She was responsible for a life, this one life, and time could never again be linear. She wanted to strain the world through her fingers for Chetna. She found herself petitioning god and all the gods and Lord Jesus to hold her daughter safe.

Vikas's first words when he saw Chetna two days after she was born were, "I wanted a boy." A boy, a boy, everyone wants a son. An heir and a spare, if your wife does her duty. Unless she's as "unnatural" as Anu.

And if the sight of Chetna sometimes brought memories of violence and pain, she tried for the child's sake to pretend to like motherhood. She even went so far as not to hire a maid, though as her mother continually reminded her, all her school friends had. Soon she was charmed by Chetna's tiny hands in hers, asking to be lifted, carried, changed, bathed, and fed. She caught Chetna's first steps, first words and small joys on camera and videotape. Along with the authority of motherhood, Anu discovered patience, a quality she never knew she had. It bloomed from guilt, she knew, guilt that she could not feel total and utter love. "You'll see," said Rano, "It will come." As a mother, Anu has tried to be firm, consistent, awe-inspiring and funny. It helps that her little girl is easily delighted by songs, stories or coloured pencils like the ones rolling back, rolling forward in Anu's palm.

But the night of the phone call, Chetna was not persuaded. The overheard conversation loomed larger in her mind than all Anu's protests. A week later, she came to Anu. "Mama, please send me to Rano Aunty," she said in her high solemn voice. "She wants me."

Anu outlines an airplane, jet streams shooting from its engines. She draws a maple leaf on its tail, and colours it red.

Chetna badgered Anu and Vikas to send her to Aunty Rano for a visit. And Rano helped, gaily reminding Vikas that Anu could get a discount through her employer, a travel agency. She sent letters addressed to the Canadian High Commission certifying her sponsorship for Chetna's visa. She did everything but mail Chetna a ticket—that might imply Vikas couldn't afford to send his daughter abroad.

And as soon as he realized Anu didn't want Chetna to go, Vikas was all in favour. Of course his daughter must go after the school term ended. So with an "unaccompanied minor" sign around her neck, Chetna left three weeks ago in May to spend a summer in Canada.

Anu's pencil line connects the curly telephone cord to the airplane's jet stream. She brushes away a drop that has somehow landed on the paper.

What would Vikas look like bound hand and foot? How wonderful she'd feel standing over him, weapon in hand. A gun? A knife? Maybe poison.

Clap-clap. Vikas's Peshawari-style sandals on the marble staircase. Nerves pulse and skitter beneath her skin. *Calm down, calm down.*

He must be climbing to the guest apartment and air-cooled yoga chamber on the third storey. There he'll pay his respects to his mother's guru Swami Rudransh.

Arrow number four: Anu takes a saffron pencil from the tin and draws a circle, two beady eyes, a pleat between them, and a moustache. Here's the swami's round face and double chin. Two black dots for eyes, eating up the adulation of his devotees. And between them, a large red bindi. Her mother-in-law's precious Swami Rudransh.

Here's his bare chest, the brahmin-cord draped across it. Darken the cord till it's black.

Like god, the swami has no fixed address. Like god, he can arrive anytime at his devotees' homes, and stay as long as he likes. And does. A house guest who expects and receives special vegetarian meals, who must be entertained in air conditioning and given a sheepskin to sit on as if it were a throne. Who spent the whole of last evening preaching against ego for his followers, yet expected his hosts to bow low before him.

"To meet him is a blessing," Anu's mother-in-law insists. She counts herself in the swami's inner circle of disciples. "He only meets those *I* bring to his attention. So many yearn to be in his presence and are never as lucky as you. His blessings have brought all our good fortune."

In the swami's presence, Vikas tempers his Punjabi swagger, turns charming, even obsequious. He who has a B.A. (Pass) Second Division degree in Applied Science from Delhi University, and who finds fault everywhere, can find no illogic in the swami's claims that every important idea in the world was conceived by Aryans of Vedic times. Hindus, before Hinduism was named, from a pre-colonial, pre-Mughal India.

Last night before dinner, Vikas led the swami into each room of the house and the swami raised his hand in blessing. When he entered this one, Chetna's, his presence felt like a desecration.

And Anu just followed along behind Vikas and her in-laws, stomach churning with self-loathing, smiling a don't-notice-me smile.

The sumptuous dinner Vikas and his mother ordered had kept Anu, the cook, two bearers, two maids and three messenger boys in the heat-hazed kitchen the whole day, chopping, frying and roasting enough to feed a hundred beggars. But all Vikas said was, "Where is the paneer? I told you Swami-ji likes paneer." Hot-cheeked, Anu explained that the health ministry had banned the sale of cheese throughout Delhi until the June heat abated.

And the plates—why had Anu laid the table with china? She should know that pure silver platters were to be used for grand guests, grand occasions. Anu dutifully cleared away the plates and asked the cook to bring in silver platters. Then before everyone, Vikas upbraided the cook and Anu for the tarnished silver.

When everyone was seated again, the swami held forth in English from the head of the table. What is required, he said, as if speaking to multitudes from behind a podium, is an awakening of national self-respect. "Hinduism," he said, "is thee only releejun in thee world to which you cannot convert. It has thee most toleration, never insisting on only one god."

He informed the family that Ayurveda can cure cancer, heart disease, diabetes and glaucoma. "And obeesity," he said, tucking in.

Anu values all aspects of the eternal. She has nothing against scientifically proven, harmless and curative Ayurvedic remedies. But last night, the swami's perversion of Hinduism burrowed beneath her skin. "Read thee ancient vedas," the swami said to Vikas. "Pranic healing, kundalini, reincarnation and karma have now been proved by pheesics and biology. Vedic pheesics is only now being discovered by thee West."

Such rhetoric had fuelled the nationalism of freedom fighters against British rule in the 1930s and 40s—but the swami had updated Sri Aurobindo and Vivekananda's ideas with pseudo-science. "Read *Thee Bell Curve?*" he told Anu. "Now West has proven in this book that thee highest intelligence goes with thee highest caste with thee lightest skin." He didn't seem to realize he was emulating British colonialists by dressing his prejudices in scientific conviction. "See, Western scientists too are finally learning thee value of classifeecation by varna. You understand *varna?*" he said, patronizingly positive she knew no Sanskrit. "It means *complexion.* Hinduism understood this long long ago, and this is why Hinduism is superior to every other releejun. Now you see why we must change our schools, libraries, newspapers—all influence of thee West must go from India. Including English."

Vikas nodded, and so did his parents. But if English goes, the Punjabi they speak, and about three hundred other languages, might be next.

For the swami, being a Hindu and being Indian had somehow become the same. The Christian side of Anu was affronted. "English is an official language, ji," she ventured, in a voice delicate and shivery as a spider strand. "Gandhi, Nehru, Rammohan Roy, Aurobindo, Vivekananda, Dayananda Saraswati, Tagore . . . all of them were Hindus. But they spoke English as you do, and wrote very well in English." Her voice strengthened into the coaxing tone she used with Chetna. "Besides, if you banish foreign languages we won't be able to read Voltaire or Shakespeare's plays. Or Darwin. Or the philosophy of Locke, Kant, Jefferson or Franklin."

"Foreign writers." The swami waved them into non-existence. "All making a separation between matter and thee spirit."

"We'll have to give up cricket and polo and all learn to play kho-kho!" Anu said with a laugh. No one else laughed with her, Vikas only laughs at his own jokes, anyway. She should have noticed the thunderous anger gathering behind her husband's eyes. Should have noticed the pleat between the swami's brows deepening, the expression of disapproval changing to affront. And she should have changed the subject. Instead she blurted sweetly, "If you want to remove all foreign influence, we should all leave the country to our tribals."

As if she'd pressed a button, the swami launched into a bizarre version of history: "Hinduism and the vedas were always here in the sacred motherland. Aryans were always here—don't let anyone mislead you with migration and invasion stories. Foreign invaders— Muslims and the British—built thee cities of Moen-jo-daro and Harappa in the Thar Desert, covered them up and then 'discovered' them to make us believe there was a civilization before Vedic times. Tribals and low-castes are Hindus, too—at least for voting. Real Hindus are not willing to turn thee country over to Muslims. Real Hindus understand what thee vedas say, 'Everyone has his dharma.'

You understand *dharma?*" he asked. "Thee duties of his caste. This is thee correct definition of the Sanskrit word. And thee vedas say 'Everyone has his ashrams.' You understand *ashrams?* His stages of life."

Mrs. Pammy Kohli closed her eyes and smiled blissfully, as if a woman's duties and life stages were just the same as a man's. Anu, now trying to steer the conversation back to the future, asked, "How will we learn medical science or genetics without English—so much research is happening in English."

"All matter, living and non-living, is essential energy. What we call brahman. Foreign scientists make a separation between science and releejun, spirituality and science. But science is just an instrument, thee weapon of spirituality. Do you know, aeroplanes are mentioned in thee *Rig Veda* from 23,720 BC? And in thee *Ramayan.* Divisible and indivisible atoms are in Shrimad Bhagwat, written in 4000 BC. Nuclear energy and black holes are described in thee Mundakopanishad, gravitational force is in thee teachings of Shankaracharya. Foreign scientists do many years of research and spend millions of dollars to conclude what we already know. They suffer from illusion."

Suffering from illusion seemed more attractive to Anu last night than the swami's religiosity. Yet why did his faith ring false? She believes in the Christian god plus all the gods. She's a baptized Hindu-Christian complete with all the contradictions of faith and reason. She too has stated belief in a divine human god-man, Lord Jesus Christ. At five or six, Mumma taught her the yoga poses she does each morning. Dadu read Krishnamurti, Tagore and many other Indian religious philosophers.

It was the moment the swami whispered: could she please confirm the food was cooked by a brahmin, before he tasted it? Feudal disgust of lower castes still fogged the swami's mind. Socialism, Marxism, democracy, the Indian constitution—all had passed him by. All he had gleaned from his piety was respect for genes, bloodline and ancestry. "Yes," she told him. "The cook happens to be a brahmin."

Yet Kohlisons Media will be recording Swami Rudransh discourses and duplicating the swami's videos and CDs. They will package them and print flyers, posters, banners and magazine advertisements to sell them. And soon large billboards on rooftops and small billboards on city lampposts will be plastered with Swami Rudransh's baby-faced grin, and Vikas's new cable TV station will broadcast the swami's self-righteous ego-disparaging voice, and Vikas' magazines will publish sponsored "articles" about the swami's ashrams.

She should destroy Vikas just for promoting this caste-ridden ignorant rubbish.

Anu draws the swami's lower half; she colours in the legs of his dhoti. Meanness wrapped in saffron—colour of Hinduism, colour of martyrdom. Then his sandals. Certainly not Gandhi-sandals.

Anu draws rockets shooting from those sandals. On paper as in life, Swami Rudransh levitates above reproach, accountable only in the cosmic ledgers of karma.

"I will do a very special ceremony for you to have sons," the swami promised Vikas at the end of the evening, pocketing an envelope of cash. He didn't look at Anu who would presumably produce those sons, or thank her equally for the donation. And she just stood there smiling, a walking uterus cocooned in a sari. She, a normally competent graduate of St. Anne's Convent, with a First Division Honours degree in Science from Delhi University.

When Vikas's parents and the swami had retired upstairs and Anu was getting ready for bed, Vikas said, "What eyes! Those are the eyes of an enlightened man." His own were starry, though he'd foregone his nightly whisky to teetotal with the swami. He went into the bathroom, leaving the door half-open.

Anu, remembering how she had trusted Vikas's droopy dark eyes before they were married, muttered that she didn't see anything special about the swami's eyes. That *Health* magazine says you can hypnotize anyone by holding his or her gaze for several minutes.

"What an angrez-ki-aulad you are!" Vikas said, dubbing her a descendant of Britishers. "What was your problem," he said making rummaging sounds in the bathroom, "that you had to bring up all those foreign philosophers? Don't you have any respect?"

This, after a whole day in the smelter-oven kitchen in June—June!—cooking the feast he and his precious swami had just consumed. Oh, she should have reached for a cut-glass vase and smashed his head right then. Well, at least her anger goaded her to say what she shouldn't have, and in a much stronger voice than at the dinner table. "How much respect would be enough for you and your swami?"

He didn't answer. After a moment, he emerged from the bathroom, holding up a silver strip in one hand. Her Ovral pills. "You dare talk about respect?" he said. She had no time to swallow her heart back down into her chest, no time to lie or deny. The pills dropped to the floor as he raised his fist.

It felt as if a comet had landed upon her. Then more were falling, pummelling her body. Shame crawls through her muscles, shame that she could not fend him off. She is unworthy of her two running trophies, her frequent walks and cycle rides. She should have fought back harder, screamed louder. But a part of her understood his anger. She wasn't the woman he really wanted to marry. And she understood herself as deserving punishment for some mutation that expressed an urge for extinction in place of an urge to breed.

Anu rises, goes to the door and presses her ear to it. By now, Vikas must be complaining about her to his parents, who must have been sleeping with the air conditioner on High Cool not to hear her screaming bloody murder last night till Vikas tired, flung himself on the bed and slept like a baby. If they did hear her, and ask, Vikas will tell them she provoked him. He will say she *knows* he has a short temper, and she shouldn't have tried his patience.

And tonight he'll watch characters in a Hindi melodrama on videotape and need a tissue for his tears.

Anu returns to the desk and her drawings.

Mr. Kohli says Anu's irritations will all go away if she has a second child. Another child whose welfare will demand her presence, curtail her independence even further. A trap she avoided so far, god forgive her, by using Ovral pills.

When Anu complains about Vikas's shouting and brutality, his mother just smiles and says, "Oh, Anu, he doesn't *mean* anything. Why do you take him so seriously? He loves to tease you—he loves teasing everyone. It's all bombast. I've given him a shouting. I've told him he shouldn't hit you. He said he'll try to control his anger. But you know men are like that only, dear."

Anu grips the red pencil again. To become used to living with Vikas requires a full frontal lobotomy. Nothing changes by accepting it. In twenty years she'll be like Mrs. Kohli, a perpetual smile carved into her face, curiosity and critical thinking banished from her brain, impervious to violence or evidence, a silver flask and three Calmpose pills at her bedside. And she too will seek comfort by doggedly performing every ceremony prescribed by Swami Rudransh, no matter the cost.

Words appear on the wall of Anu's mind, too shocking to speak: *I want a divorce.*

Women from "good" Hindu families don't divorce. Nor should Indian Catholics divorce or annul their marriages. Women staring boldly from covers of English-language magazines get divorces. It's a European tradition.

Anu plays with the black and gold beads of her mangalsutra, the marriage necklace she has worn for nine years. Which is worse—being in this jail or in Delhi's Tihar Jail with other women? And which is a lesser sin—divorce or taking a life?

Divorce will hurt Vikas's parents and her own. It will hurt Chetna. It will hurt Vikas. And though he has worn Anu's initial willingness to love down to a nub of despair, Vikas is Chetna's father. When he raises his hand against Anu, surely it's because of other frustrations . . . he was the husband she was supposed to fall in love with, to honour as a god. All those old old old ideas . . .

Once Anu was strong, confident, always improving, always learning. Today she can't make a sandwich without Vikas sneering that she's prepared it wrong, or that he's tasted better. How has she allowed this to happen?

She lifts the necklace over her head. It pours to the table with a rattle that startles the stillness.

If she stays, it's suicide. Is that better than divorce or murder? More of a sin or less?

Women commit suicide, literally or figuratively, everywhere. In Bollywood movies, tele-serials, novels. At the end of the *Ramayan*, when Ram rejects Sita Mata on suspicion of adultery, she asks the earth to open and swallow her. Real women did it en masse when the enemy was at the gate—her own grandmother, Dadu's mother, joined eighty-four women and plunged down a well during Partition. Dadu says she was a woman of courage, but if that's where courage leads, Anu wants less, not more.

If she stays, she'll be as pitiable as those women. And what kind of example will that be for Chetna?

What kind of example will it be if Anu commits murder?

Anu leaves the four pencils on the table and closes the tin box over the rest. She studies her doodles before crumpling and throwing them into the wastebasket.

In imagination, Anu has left Vikas a million times. The first time she felt ready to leave him, she discovered she was pregnant and stayed. The second time, his driving landed her in hospital, scarred for life. But now, with Chetna safe in Canada she can make it happen.

Anu consults a calendar on the wall. It's flipped to July, when Chetna is scheduled to return. Anu cups her hand over her swollen eye: she must act before then. And before she does something worse.

DAMINI

In Mem-saab's drawing-room, Damini's damp cloth arcs across a table flanking a gold, raw silk sofa, picking up a layer of morning dust. A little girl in a sky-blue cotton dress and matching hair-bows dangles bare legs from the sofa.

Damini's sandals scrape trails in the cement dust on Mem-saab's marble floor; the sweeper doesn't seem to be doing his job, but Damini's not going to wipe the ground for him. Everyone has his dharma.

She crouch-walks to the next end table, momentarily obscuring the view of the pink people on TV. She could have walked behind the sofa, but it amuses her to distract Loveleen.

Nine years ago, Mem-saab sent Damini to Bombay to help Kiran when she was expecting this girl. Damini made khichri and fresh yogurt in Kiran and Aman's apartment kitchen, filled a large tiffin and took a bus, as directed, to the hospital. There she sat on a cane chair, waiting till Aman brought his pregnant wife in a taxi.

As soon as Kiran arrived, doctors and nurses began doing things to her, making decisions for her. And normally assertive Kiran just lay there as she was told—flat on her back with her heels in cups. They didn't give her more than an hour or two without their medicines. Kiran didn't know the meaning of the words they used any more than Damini did, though these words could affect her life, and the life of her baby. Peeto-shin, fee-thal montor, see-sex-shun. After those medicines, Kiran's contractions looked as if a demon was attacking her from within.

She expected to massage Kiran to help the baby come, but the nurse, who spoke strange Hindi, acted as if Kiran was sick instead of pregnant. Soon she called a doctor-saab who made Kiran lie curled up on her side and gave her an injection with a long needle. After that, it was impossible for Kiran to move or position herself and the baby at all.

Kiran lay like a pale candle and refused to allow any doctor to bring a razor near her. Not to shave the mound of her belly, or the hair on her yoni, because of being a Sikh. She ordered Damini to guard her to be sure no one shaved her if she lost consciousness.

A nurse asked Kiran if she felt any pain.

Kiran said, "I feel nothing."

Two nurses came in: a fat, short, smiley one in a white dress, stockings ruched up in her sandals, and a sweet-faced South Indian one in a white sari and starched white cap. Kiran let them tie leather straps across her wrists. They attached a tube to the back of her hand with a needle, and hung a clear plastic bag from a pole beside her. Damini asked the South-Indian nurse if the bag was filled with Ganges-water. The nurse said no, and pointing at Damini's tiffin carrier, admonished her—kindly—not to feed Kiran.

Damini had given birth twice but felt so ignorant. She, a kshatriya, a warrior-woman, was told to hunker down in the corridor beside a mop and bucket of phenyl, and wait. Obviously the nurses thought her as dirty and unclean as any sweeper-woman.

Another doctor-saab appeared, dressed head to toe in green, hands gloved in plastic, wearing a white mask that made him look as monkeyish as Lord Hanuman.

The ammonia smell from the bucket was sharp in her nostrils. Looking upwards, she could see everything the doctor was doing reflected in the glass upper section of the door opposite Kiran's bed.

She watched helplessly as Doctor-saab cut into Kiran's abdomen, as metal clamps spread her wound, and then sutures tied off bleeding blood vessels.

So this girl Loveleen came out covered in a chalky fur, instead of blood and stickiness, simply lifted between the clamps through the gaping hole in Kiran's stomach. Born without struggle. Maybe this is why the child has so little sympathy for those who do struggle.

After the baby came a plum-coloured thing taken from Kiran's stomach. It must have been the Lotus. Damini watched carefully in case the force left in the Lotus rose up to strangle Kiran, because the doctors didn't seem at all concerned—the Hanuman-faced one even turned his back to it!

The child was scrubbed and washed quite roughly, and not given to her mother for hours, though Kiran ordered Damini to ask the nurses every few minutes.

Kiran looked so unhappy. It was two days before she could walk and she didn't remember the birth at all. Most of the time, she just wept because she had made a daughter. Damini hushed her, saying, "Don't let anyone see tears. Some might say your husband can't afford this girl's dowry. And don't worry, next time you'll have a boy."

She gave Kiran sponge baths and fed her, yet despite what they had done to her, Kiran only trusted the men and women in starchy white. Damini called the nurses when Kiran asked for them and didn't complain to Aman when he came at visiting hours—because what does a man know about how a birth should or shouldn't happen? But her disapproval of the doctors and hospital must have shown because Kiran hired an expensive nursemaid very quickly. Instead of allowing Damini to massage Loveleen's baby limbs or feed her gripe water, Kiran sent her home a week early, saying Mem-saab needed Damini's skills more than she did.

Which was true.

When Damini returned to Delhi, Mem-saab rewarded Damini with a pair of solid gold flower-shaped earrings to mark the girl's birth. When Amanjit and Kiran visited Mem-saab for Loveleen's naming, Damini took the girl baby in her arms and showed her to Suresh, through the gate.

Suresh said, "The way you're looking at her, anyone might think she were your grandson." Damini has tried to restrain her feelings since then, but Loveleen knows she is soft.

Once, while visiting Mem-saab, the little girl fell—children do. And Damini had swabbed Dettol on the wound. Direct from the bottle, as she had for Timcu and Aman to make them tougher. Loveleen howled and was inconsolable. Kiran confronted Damini, bottle in hand, scolding that she would kill the child with pain. Didn't Damini know Dettol must be diluted with water?

Usually the most powerful antidotes are required to vanquish threatening unseen energies. But, Kiran explained, there are also threatening unseen energies called germs that attack babies, children and adults. She reminded Damini of how many times the nurses in the hospital washed their hands, how the doctor wore plastic gloves. When dealing with germs, she said, handwashing and Dettol-adulteration with water are required.

But how could Damini have known? The directions were written on the white label in English, not Devanagari script. If she wanted Damini to follow English directions, Kiran should have translated them into Hindi and read them aloud.

Kiran had taken Loveleen from Damini's arms, and set the child down before the TV.

And here the girl now sits as though she'd never moved, just grown in these nine years. She gets two whole months of holy-days each year at this time. She could memorize the *Ramayan*, she could learn to cook, she could jump rope with Khansama's children. Instead this little girl needs videos, maybe the ones Suresh copies, to tell her stories of pale women and clean-shaven pink men. If she doesn't have her videos she gets Bore, a saab's disease like Dipreyshun.

Loveleen does not rise as Mem-saab enters her own drawing-room. "Darling," says Mem-saab. "Go tell the driver to bring my car."

Loveleen turns to face Mem-saab so she can read her lips, and shouts, "Damini-amma, tell Zahir Sheikh to bring the car."

Mem-saab says gently, "No, Lovey, darling. You go and tell Zahir Sheikh to bring my car. The video can wait."

The girl turns her head, but does not move. "You can't order me around," she says.

Offspring of a snake! Damini stands silent with shock.

Mem-saab is looking at Damini, "What . . . what did she say?"

Damini turns to her and mouths the words slowly.

Mem-saab comes around to face Loveleen. Her small hand grips the child's arm above the elbow. "I said, go and tell the driver to bring my car. Damini-amma has to get ready to go with me."

The child shakes off her hand, but goes. Damini fetches Mem-saab's handbag and glasses.

The sun whirls like the brass disc behind dancing Lord Shiv. The car's back seat burns Damini's fingertips and thighs. The fan blows hot air as soon as Zahir Sheikh starts the car. In a few minutes, her bra is a wet cord beneath her breasts.

Outside, tree branches are ridged where leaves have dried and fallen. Park fountains at the centres of roundabouts are dry. Every bright white street, every red sandstone monument seems to pulse with yearning for the monsoon.

Mem-saab says, "Damini-amma, we are going to meet a lady-lawyer."

Arriving at the lady-lawyer's office, Damini helps Mem-saab from the car, then to a one-car garage attached to a bungalow home. Inside, indistinct cries from the nearby market and rumbles from the dusty street compete with the rattle of a window-box air conditioner.

A starched white tie dangles lopsided on a soiled string above the plunge of the lady-lawyer's sari-blouse. Her skin would spring to the touch like Leela's—she seems too young to have read all the maroon books that line the walls.

Damini sits on a cane footstool while they sit in chairs, and she massages Mem-saab's leg through her salwar as she speaks so Mem-saab will know there is someone who cares.

The lady-lawyer listens to Mem-saab with weary though gentle respect; too many women must have cried before her. Mem-saab speaks in Punjabi, because private matters must be said. She ignores Damini's hand signals to lower her voice; her outrage assaults them. Damini contents herself with interjecting a word or two in Hindi occasionally for the lady-lawyer.

I am still her ears, but Mem-saab has seen much that I thought she denied.

At last, Mem-saab has no words left.

The lady-lawyer sees Mem-saab's embroidered hanky has turned to a useless wet ball, and offers her own. She tells Damini to tell her, "Be strong. I will try to help you."

Mem-saab's hand seeks Damini's and grips it. Her fingers are cold despite the close heat.

Now the lady-lawyer talks directly to Mem-saab. She tries to speak slowly, but Damini has to repeat her words sometimes for Mem-saab to read them from her lips.

"You say your son now owns twenty-five percent of your house?"

Mem-saab looks at her from beneath her black-pencilled arches, expecting reproach. "Yes."

"Then, legally, he can occupy the premises."

This is not what she wishes to read, so Damini has to repeat it.

The lady-lawyer continues, "We can charge that he gained his rights by putting you under duress. If you wish to stop him from building, we can ask the court to do that."

"Nothing more?" says Mem-saab.

Damini wants to tell the lady-lawyer to make Aman and Kiran and Loveleen evaporate like the first monsoon rain on a hot tar road, but she is just a pair of ears for Mem-saab, and this is Mem-saab's family matter. The triangular exchange soon falters, then stops.

Nothing more.

Mem-saab writes a cheque and signs a vakalatnama appointing the lady-lawyer to begin her court case.

As Damini leads Mem-saab out into the white flood of sunshine, she leans heavily on her arm.

A tall slender woman in a rose pink sari is sitting on a cane chair in the single car-length driveway, waiting for the lady-lawyer. In profile, her eye is as almond-shaped as an awakened goddess. Her loosely braided black hair is waist-length, thick and shiny as Rekha's in the movies. Very dark sunglasses swing from one hand. As they approach, she turns and hurriedly puts them on, but not before Damini notices the other eye, swollen large, and another swelling above the ridge of one cheekbone. A leaf-shaped scar droops down across the woman's cheek. In this searing heat, the woman wears a long-sleeved sari blouse. There's a bruise at her clavicle.

Hai, what bad bhagya she has.

ANU

SITTING BEFORE SLIGHT, INTELLIGENT-FACED MRS. Shruti Nadkarni in her garage office, Anu feels strangely light after hearing herself say "divorce." She practised the word on the bus, and walking from the stop.

All the way here, people averted their gazes from her bruised face, her swollen eye, her throbbing temples. Everyone but the two old women she had seen leaving the lawyer's office, whose problems were probably worse than her own.

Lord Jesus, help them.

Anu keeps her gaze on the leather-bound books behind Mrs. Nadkarni's head. She feels for her sunglasses, folds them, opens them. Mrs. Nadkarni extends a large printed handkerchief. She seems a couple of years older than Anu, perhaps in her early thirties.

Anu dabs at her scar. Tears on that cheek still feel different from those on the other.

"Did you call the police, Mrs. Kohli?" Unfamiliar with Anu's comfort level in English, she repeats the question in Hindi, without a trace of impatience or condescension.

"Vikas might have beaten me again if I had," Anu replies in English. "And which police officer would believe me? He went to school with the local superintendent of police. The local officers know him. His usual tip is higher than a constable's monthly salary." Besides, Anu doesn't say, her visit to the police after Vikas raped her led nowhere. And if she had gone to the police for slaps, kicks or beatings since, she would have shamed Chetna along with the Kohlis. Shaming the family, she has been brought up to believe, is well-nigh a crime. Even now, before Mrs. Nadkarni, she is compelled to mention that Vikas never wanted to marry her.

"How do you know?"

"My mother-in-law told me. He wanted to marry a girl from a Sikh chieftain family whose land grants date back to Maharaja Ranjit Singh's empire."

"Early 1800s?"

Anu nods. "And that girl's parents said they wouldn't even discuss a marriage proposal from a Hindu family. They had been forced into hiding in a gurdwara during the anti-Sikh riots in 1984."

"Yes, colonial logic—two or three thousand must die for the murder of one of 'ours.'"

"And when they lost their home, they blamed all Hindus."

"Collective responsibility—the same-same thinking that had just been used against them."

"I suppose so. When they heard Vikas's roadster had been seen outside the girl's college, they made her confess: yes, she had gone to a movie with him. She had walked among the monuments in Lodi Gardens with him. Yes, he had held her hand. The very next month, that girl was married off to a much older Sikh man. And Vikas's parents found him a substitute—me."

Hearing this in the first few days of her marriage, Anu wondered what That-Girl was like and how can she try to be like her? But then she heard Vikas shout at his mother, "No one can replace her!"

But was he talking of That-Girl? She wasn't sure, because he's never mentioned That-Girl's name to her. No one has. His mother told her he'd carved their names into a palm tree in Lodi Gardens, but Anu never found it. Maybe That-Girl doesn't exist, never existed. That's why she's nameless. She's too perfect to exist.

"But even so, Mrs. Kohli," says Mrs. Nadkarni, "most men marry the girls chosen for them, even if they liked other girls. Marriage is by caste. All those men don't beat their wives."

"I think running the family business is too much for Vikas. Things might have been different if he had been a civil servant, or started his own company, rather than carrying out his father's ideas. He wanted to be a physicist," Anu says. "But he ended up in advertising."

"Many men his age have gone into a family business." Mrs. Nadkarni is gently insistent. "Many men don't do the work they wanted to. How come they don't all beat their wives?"

"Maybe he believes it is all right to take it out on me."

"He could use a pillow or a punching bag, instead," says Mrs. Nadkarni. "Still, since you never filed a police report, there is no evidence of violence. What kind of wedding ceremony did you have?"

"A very large one," Anu replies. What relationship can that day have to this?

"I mean, did you take the saptapadi around the fire?"

"Yes. Seven steps, the usual ceremony."

"So Hindu Law applies."

"But I'm also a Christian," Anu says. "Lord Jesus has given me the courage to come to you today, while my child is safe in Canada with my cousin-sister."

Mrs. Nadkarni shakes her head and closes her eyes, smiling at Anu's naiveté. "Law," she says, opening her eyes, "only allows one religion: Hindu or Christian. You cannot be two-in-one like—like a radio and tape recorder."

"Women can be two in one," says Anu. "Sometimes even more."

"Personal law is not about persons—it's really . . . well, it's actually about families. Tell me—did you convert before or after marriage?"

"My baptism was after marriage, and I never told Vikas."

Mrs. Nadkarni scribbles on a pad before her. She looks up.

"We will proceed as if you are still a Hindu—i.e. under Hindu Personal Law." It takes Anu a moment to understand what Mrs. Nadkarni means by "eye-ee."

"Where was your marriage registered?"

"It wasn't. Vikas became impatient after hours in line at the registration office."

"How many hours?"

"Seven."

"Only seven?"

"Maybe more—I don't remember. He just stomped off."

Mrs. Nadkarni's hand covers her pinked lips for a moment. "This is not good, not good. Only photos of the ceremony will show you're married if it was not registered."

Anu takes an envelope from her handbag, opens it, and lays six black-and-white photos on the lawyer's desk. "Five hundred guests saw Vikas and me circle the fire seven times at the Ashoka Hotel."

"This is good—if you want to remain married. But you don't. Maintenance and custody are the issue. Without registration, even if you have photos, a man can say he was never married."

If the court grants Anu maintenance, she explains, it will only be Rs. 500 per month, but legal costs might be anywhere from Rs. 5,000 to 500,000, and the cost of Chetna's wedding and dowry could be far greater. Maintenance is an anti-joke.

Anu has grimly hung onto her travel agent job to get out of the Kohli household every day, attend mass, and maintain the illusion of independence. But as Pammy Kohli often reminds her, "It's almost a volunteer job."

"How long would I spend in jail if . . . if I kill him?"

"I hope you are joking, Mrs. Kohli, but seven to ten years. And not in some jail like they show on TV and Bollywood movies, cells with beds and desks and chairs. Women's jails in real life are stinking holes. A woman of your background would go mad in a matter of months. Activists and the new inspector general of prisons are working to change this, but . . ."

"I see. And my child?"

The child, Mrs. Nadkarni explains, is the property of her father. "Women's organizations are working very hard to change this law," she says, "but it will surely take them till the next century. So even with grounds of mental and physical cruelty, you must expect that Vikas will be granted custody of a child over the age of five. If and only if he wants it."

Anu folds, smooths and unfolds the handkerchief upon her sari-pleats, reminds herself that Chetna is safe in Toronto. "I don't think Vikas will ask for custody. How long will it take me to get a divorce?"

"Not you. Your family—if your family persuades your husband to come to a mutual agreement and negotiate a financial settlement, then only a few weeks from the date we draft a divorce petition. If he contests it, minimum seven years.

"Seven years!"

"That's if I fight your case. If you go to other lawyers who don't fight as hard, then ten or twelve. The *Guinness Book of Records* says that one case took seven hundred and sixty-one years—oh, not here in the capital. In another town."

"So if he contests, I'm expected to live on five hundred rupees a month and support my child for ten or twelve years? That's impossible."

"The way you're talking!" says Mrs. Nadkarni. "Maybe the father will support her. Some men do, na? And this is not New York or London—we can rely on family. Actually, who else can we rely on? Your father is alive—that is lucky. Do you have brothers?"

"No—I mean, yes—I had one. Younger. But he is no more."

"Oh. Very very sad."

"Yes, and I don't want my parents to have to look after me—they have been through enough."

"Of course. Extended family, i.e. brothers-in-law, uncles, cousin-brothers?"

Anu shakes her head. Dadu lost his immediate family in the violence of Partition, and was raised by a cousin-uncle. Mumma's older brother is estranged, thanks to his disapproval of Mumma's marrying down-caste. He and his wife have never called, sent sweets for a birthday or festival, or dropped in. Mumma didn't invite them to Anu's wedding.

Her extended family members are her Purnima-aunty and Sharad Uncle. She and her little brother, Bobby, lived with them so they could attend English-medium schools in Delhi while Dadu was transferred across India on government postings.

"Can you rely on them?" says Mrs. Nadkarni.

"How do you mean, 'rely'?"

"I mean financially."

"Well—only on my father and my Sharad Uncle. And I don't know how long I can impose on them. Especially if Chetna could be fifteen or older by the time my divorce is final."

"Could your father or uncle persuade your husband to sign an amicable agreement of separation, guaranteeing payment for his daughter's education and wedding?"

Anu's bruised clavicle throbs. "I'll ask them, but . . ."

"No? Okay," says Mrs. Nadkarni. "Then we should hope that by the time your divorce comes through, your daughter will be grown up and your husband will have paid for her wedding."

So the molasses-flow of divorce cases through the courts can benefit Chetna, so long as Anu remains technically married. And keeps herself from killing Vikas.

"What if Chetna doesn't get married?"

Mrs. Nadkarni laughs. "No, no!" she says, as if the very possibility is just a mother's silly nightmare.

She asks more questions about Anu's salary, Vikas's wealth and income, company names, organizations to which he donates. "Has he applied for one of those new cards the banks are offering? Credit cards, yes?"

"No. He only uses cash."

"Black money, yes? Difficult to trace."

Cars—makes, models? Several, but the one that comes to Anu's mind is the cream and maroon Cord Roadster, gone for two years. Her hand rises involuntarily to her scar.

And she's back in the tobacco-brown passenger seat of that '37 convertible, holding her dupatta across her mouth to filter dust. The car he had in college, refurbished with the money his parents gave him to spend on a puja ceremony for the birth of his son, after he learned Anu had produced a daughter.

Wheels squealed as the Cord careened around the pedestal where Queen Victoria's statue once gazed down its stoney nose upon New Delhi. The parade lawns flashed past as Vikas shot off toward the massive archway of India Gate racing a biker on a motorcycle—black as the lampless night. Up Raisina Hill, the floodlit pillared domes and ramparts of the Presidential Palace silhouetted themselves against the night sky. Up the sand-bordered pathway of kings and viceroys they zoomed, as if all of Delhi was still and only the car flew in the breath of a lion.

Vikas drew closer and closer to the motorbike as if he were riding a horse off on a polo field, trying to scare him. One swerve too close and the motorcyclist peeled away to the sandy shoulder. The wheels of the motorbike jumped the low chain secured between cement posts to cordon off the lawns and sped on, but the Cord rammed straight into the post.

. . . A web of stellar streams above . . . a blade of white pain in her skull . . . Hot hot hot screaming hot screaming . . . blood-red veil before her eyes, as on the day of her wedding . . .

She can't remember scrambling out, just staggering away, and looking back at the shattered windshield. Blood on each palm. Hot hot hot. The screaming in her ears was her own.

The Cord ignited in a halo of saffron. Vikas was a black silhouette against the crackling flames and petrol smell. Feinting like a fencer, getting as close to the car as he dared. Then he doubled over, weeping.

For his car.

The lawyer is still talking. She's telling Anu that since Vikas would be assumed to be the primary member at the Gymkhana Club, the Delhi Golf Club, the Habitat Centre and the India International Centre, it could take from fifteen to forty years on each waiting list for Anu to become a lady-member.

"Vikas's father is the full member, not Vikas," says Anu. "Vikas is a full member only of the golf club. He's so proud of that. I always felt out of place there."

"I will draft the divorce petition and file it in the court. Notice will be served by registered letter, then by dasti. By hand." She translates the Mughal-era term. "And if that is not possible, a copy will be affixed to the door of his home. My assistant will let you know the date of your first hearing. You should pack a bag with your clothes and all your papers and valuables." Mrs. Nadkarni nods at Anu's bruised face.

Most of her pants and shirts are still in her old home at Purnima-aunty's, along with several saris and salwar-kameezes, her books, and piano—Vikas's Ralph Laurens, Burberrys and Calvin Kleins occupy the closet space in her marital home. If Anu had produced a son she might have earned a little closet space.

"Find a safe place to stay. Friends?"

Names pour through a sieve in Anu's mind. Who will value her when she has lost so much worth in her own eyes? Close friends from college have changed last names, moved away to their husband's hometowns. Several are in Bangalore, married to software engineers who are coding away to save the legacy systems of North America from the meltdown expected on January 1, 2000. Some, like Rano, married into families that moved overseas during the brain drain era.

You go to school with other girls, share meals, ideas, books, games, jokes, struggles, and then you get married off, and your name is changed. They change their names too, and you never see most of them again.

The few attempts she'd made to keep up with classmates or make new friends failed—"She's too dark," Vikas would say of each one. Or, "She has such a screechy voice."

"Why doesn't your friend Shalini wear a sari like a decent married woman?" he once said. "She secretly wants to live in London. She'd move tomorrow, if she could take her servants."

But even if she had kept up with Shalini and other friends from school, their husbands wouldn't want a divorced woman staying with them, and for who-knows-how-long.

She may not be able to heal herself, but the world needs healing. She may not be able to heal her family, but her existence should do some good for India, for the world. All ambitions too grandiose to mention—especially with her aching ribs and shoulder.

"I'll find a place," Anu says to Mrs. Nadkarni. "I'll phone and tell you where I am." She writes a cheque and signs a vakalatnama appointing the lawyer to begin her divorce.

Anu takes a taxi back to Kohli House. She downs two Naprosyn and a Crocin—her second round of painkillers today. Then she fills her largest suitcase, humming a hymn she used to play in church when she was . . . oh, fourteen.

> *If you've courage to give, give it now,*
> *If you've kindness to share, share it now.*
> *If there's hope you can raise or someone you can praise,*
> *Do it now, do it now, do it now.*
> *Now, before it is too late.*
> *Now's the time for every good deed.*
> *Do not wait until tomorrow.*
> *For it may be just a little too late.*

She takes only the jewellery she received from Dadu and Mumma, a few everyday salwar-kameezes and dupattas, socks, underwear. Five pairs of thin-strapped high heels, her Bible, her copy of the *Bhagvad Gita*, the rosary Sister Imaculata gave her at graduation. All the money she can find, including some change from Vikas's change-bowl.

Hurry, hurry.

School records, her science degree, driver's license. Photos and videos of Chetna, her baby girl—*this is NOT the time to linger over them!* Chetna's birth certificate, school certificates, Punjabi bride doll.

On second thought, not the Punjabi bride doll. Toss her away.

At noon, she phones for a cab herself, but allows the cook to help her load the suitcase into it. "I'll be home tonight," is all she says. She doesn't volunteer and he doesn't ask where she is going—Vikas haranguing him for complicity would be far harsher than for ignorance. She hopes he won't tell Vikas she has taken a suitcase, but it wouldn't be fair to ask him to keep it secret. Besides, security guards watching from pillboxes in the street could tell Vikas. Any neighbour might tell as well.

Pray.

She works the second half of the day at the travel agency, suitcase under her desk, starting to her feet every time a customer walks in. Her boss, Mr. Gurinder Singh, recognizes the trauma of domestic terrorism when he sees it—this tubby Sikh man survived the anti-Sikh riots by cutting his waist-length hair and shaving his beard. He has a permanent limp from breaking his leg jumping from a balcony, but managed to escape being doused in kerosene and set on fire by the mobs. Noting her suitcase, he presses his handkerchief and a hundred-rupee note into her hand. "Talk to your family, find a place to stay," he says, "I'll send the suitcase wherever you want." Then he shoos her into the baking streets.

Where to stay? Anu lived with her parents during her three years in college when Dadu was posted in New Delhi. Three years of alternating dread and an almost painful desire to please. At the time, if her mother, Indu Lal, loved cheese soufflé or hated karelas, Anu was loyal enough to do the same. At the time, if Indu Lal felt an instant of sadness, Anu's eyeliner could run.

Back then, Mumma's wounds, her hungers, her personal gods were also Anu's. Mumma could read Anu's mind and diary, and to disallow her was ungrateful disloyalty. What Mumma valued was the only value that excited; Mumma pities those who don't see that. Always the teacher, report card in hand. A report card that reads for every area of life, "Could do Better."

Did she regret marrying down? Anu had been prepared to climb the caste ladder and raise the family's profile. At Anu's wedding, Mrs. Lal wore a cyclamen lehnga with a gold border, twice as expensive as her daughter's salwar-kameez. Several guests mistook her for the bride, Mumma still likes to recall.

The thought conjures up Mumma's voice, "So? I wanted you to have the respect I lost by marrying your father. Your father acts like a marriage gets arranged by magic, but it doesn't. I had to arrange it. Did I get any thanks? No. And you liked him immediately, so it is all your fault."

She had liked Vikas. The first few days, she'd liked everything from his lop-sided grin to his affectionate-sounding insults to— Lord, forgive her—his jokes. Every one of them, she later realized, at someone else's expense. She had loved his long fingers and the arrogant grace of his movements. Twenty-year-old Anu had wanted never to make Mumma's mistake, marrying for love. She wanted what arranged marriages promise: the soothing story to be lived, never worrying that your husband will choose someone else, or that you'll be shunned by either family. Many other lives might have been Anu's but for Mumma's choice of husband for her.

Dadu . . .

Had Dadu been posted to the national level of government in New Delhi instead of state level, maybe Mumma and he would have encountered more families like Vikas's. Maybe they wouldn't have been so easily impressed. Love, promises—swept away like ants before a sweeper's broom.

Living with Mumma again, flattering Mumma, competing with Mumma again in every area of life—that's unthinkable. Watching Dadu pander to Mumma in incessant guilt for his slightly lower caste and want of patrimony, apologizing for his too-honest use of his position so that Mumma has to give private tuition in English. Mumma couldn't wait for Anu to be married so that Dadu could centre his attention completely on her. She can't live with Mumma again, she just can't.

But for Chetna's sake?

She cannot subject Chetna to Mumma's pretentiousness, or her Victorian ideas about young women's reputations. Chetna shouldn't make the same mistakes. Chetna needs to grow, to develop separately from Mumma and Anu. If Chetna lives with Mumma, the only language she'll ever know is English. And if Anu and Chetna were to live with Mumma, Anu's mothering, cooking, weight, attire and makeup will be constantly critiqued and found wanting.

Anu can return to her aunt and uncle's home. But how can she impose again, and this time along with her daughter? She buys a newspaper from a street urchin who looks far worse off than she. The ads for furnished rooms will move her forward.

Inquiring about a fanless room on the baking top floor of a home in the Karolbagh area, she is told, "The room is rented."

"A single woman trying to rent a room can only be a call girl or a madam," a prospective landlady informs her, squinting at Anu's sari-clad breasts as if they were offensive.

The next landlord's stomach pops over his lungi. Desperate, Anu manages to give the impression that her husband is out of town on business, and returning soon. The landlord flings his arms skyward and gives her a smile like the laughing Buddha. "Please bring your husband or father," he says, "so we can talk properly." Then he quotes a rent equivalent to two months' salary from Adventure Travel.

So many people, so few houses and apartments. She knew rents were high—but this high? With so many searching for living space, anyone with a few square metres of India is a lord. No wonder two or three generations live together, put up with each other.

She can't. But if she can't look after herself, how will she look after Chetna?

Anu's head pounds. She runs to catch a bus and go "home."

"Anupam," Vikas says from the head of the table that night, "can't find one good thing to say about Swami-ji. All she can talk about is foreign philosophers, foreign books, foreign music. No pride in Indian culture, none at all."

"Convent schooling," says Lalit Kohli from the other end of the table. He glares over his glasses at his son's wife. Can he really not see Anu's black eye and bruises?

"You chose me as Vikas's bride because I was convent educated," she mutters.

Burd-burd—that's what Vikas calls her muttering. The first time he ever raised his hand against her was because of burd-burd. They were leaving the premiere of a new Bollywood film, along with the collected glitterati of New Delhi, so many of them his school friends. Vikas said the theatre should have played the march "Vande Mataram" with the lights on so people could see if Muslims were singing in praise of the slayer-goddess Durga Devi. Under her breath, she said, "That's just a song, not the national anthem. And you can't tell a Hindu from a Muslim man by sight. And if you saw a Muslim woman singing, you'd say she wasn't singing loud enough, or that she didn't feel the words." Vikas's backhand hit her so hard across her chest, she fell to the carpet. People backed away and stared blankly. Vikas said to them, "She has fainting spells." And to her, "Get up. Smile." But even after that, Anu still does burd-burd. Right now, Vikas is pretending not to hear it.

Mr. Kohli, too. He continues chewing his mutton-do-piaza as if she has not spoken. He takes a chapati from the container proffered by the manservant.

"Swami-ji has taken his dinner in private and is leaving by the morning train," Vikas is saying to his mother. "He's offended . . . He'll get someone else to package him and it's all Anupam's fault . . ."

"Vikkoo," his mother replies in a high tinkly voice like Lata Mangeshkar. "Anupam doesn't understand the business. It takes practice." Her eyes sidle to a gilt-framed mirror, and she examines her taut skin and symmetrical features. She lifts a languid fingertip; the manservant refills her glass of Cabernet.

"Everything is my fault?" says Anu.

"Sport, Anupam, your *sport*—that's what Vikas needs." Mr. Kohli means her unstinting support of Vikas's objectives, not Vikas's of hers. "Don't think Vikas is some ordinary man," says he, staring owlishly at her. "I spent years apologizing to the West for being from a poor nation, for India's so-called backwardness. But Vikas—his very name means progress!" Lalit Kohli's forefinger traces the rim of his glass, lifts and wags at Anu. "Anupam, do less 'me-me' and more thinking of the *en-tire* family."

"Family, Dad," says Vikas.

"Don't you correct your elders." Mr Kohli swivels back to Anu. "And you, Anupam, you be more adjustable."

"You can see that your son hits me, but you're saying *I* should be more adjustable?"

"How many years will it take before you learn how to please him?"

"Come, we'll go shopping. I'll buy you some makeup, a few new saris," Pammy Kohli says, as if she's talking to Chetna. "I have a lovely pendant for you. It glitters just like your eyes."

If Anu hadn't visited the lawyer that very day, she would have given way to an urge to scream and scream. She, Anu, who volunteered for national social service instead of the Cadet Corps in college, who vowed to live a life of service, is being placated with jewellery. She should have become a nun when Sister Imaculata offered the chance in school. Then her parents couldn't have married her to Vikas and this wouldn't be happening.

In the master bedroom, Vikas takes her in his arms, takes her chin between thumb and forefinger and apologizes. He tells her he had to shout at her to please his parents—he didn't really mean the things he said, he was only trying to explain why the swami had not graced them with his presence for dinner. He releases her chin.

Lord Jesus and Lord Ram, give me strength.

She does not run but walks to the bathroom, with as much dignity as she can muster. She collects her toilet articles. She walks to Chetna's room. Slowly. Puts them down. He has not followed. She returns to the master bedroom to collect a salwar-kameez. *Don't look, don't look at him.*

One sideways glance. He's lying across the bed, head propped on one hand, paging through *Hindu Society Under Siege*. He looks up, a wounded expression in his murky eyes. "Oh, she's sulking!" he says. "I know you can't resist me, darling—you'll be back soon."

A valid assumption—she has returned before. For Chetna's sake.

Vikas sniffs as if at the scent of her fear. He puts his book down and reaches for the phone. Anu dodges, in case the receiver sails through the air. Vikas laughs and waves it at her before thumbing it.

In Chetna's room next door, she locks herself in. A locked door and her rosary have often helped her make the best of things. She lies down fully clothed, Chetna's cricket bat at her side.

She prays with as much faith as Father Pashan, but in a Hindu way.

Our father who art in heaven, hallowed be thy names . . .

Dadu brought Father Pashan to her bedside two years ago, after her accident. The doctors had said she was dying, and Purnima-aunty and Sharad Uncle had come to Holy Family Hospital to say their last farewells. Mumma was trickling Ganges-water over Anu's bandages. Her father invited Father Pashan to say the rosary. Restore her to us, Dadu said, and you can baptize her.

Between Hail Marys, Father Pashan would comb through his hair with his fingers. And after many repetitions, she was no longer looking up at him doing that, but felt herself floating, looking down at a priest praying at the bedside of a woman. She remembers feeling enormous, skinless. And wondering how she could ever squeeze herself back into her tiny body. The next moment, her consciousness felt linked to an unearthly power. She was moving towards a bright warm light in the distance. But the priest's voice and the refrain of the rosary penetrated her consciousness, tearing her from the lure of that mysterious light that offered comfort and loss in the same instant. To this day, she would give anything to reunite with the light—whether Christ, Shiv or Krishna.

Then came the weight of gravity as never before, and her huge gasping whispers, "Chetna! Chetna." Later, another image—the six-year-old screaming at her first glimpse of her mother's unbandaged face.

Anu's thumb passes the bead for the Lord's Prayer and she begins ten Hail Marys.

Vikas is still on the phone. Probably to an old school chum or a relative. That do-it-as-a-personal-favour-to-me tone, the because-you-love-me tone that gets everything done. Nothing much happens in New Delhi offices, he always says—negotiations and bargains take place after 8 p.m., at parties and over the phone.

Such persuasiveness must be balanced in his next call, to some poor fellow who can't tell the boss not to call this late. Vikas is losing control, letting himself go . . . There are those who manage others and those who are managed, he always says.

Hail Mary full of grace, the Lord is with thee . . .

As long as his shouting continues, it's safe to fall asleep, and she is so tired . . .

Blessed art thou amongst women . . .

Remember how blessed, how very very blessed.

The next morning, knocking penetrates a dream—Vikas is spread-eagled on a white sheet, a stream of red oozing from a slit in his kurta-clad chest. Anu is leaning over him, a long curved knife in hand. He will now beg for mercy.

And she, a caring, kind person, does not care.

The knocking continues. She gets up, opens the door. The cook stands before her with a bouquet of narcissi and carnations.

"From Vikkoo-saab," he says with a tiny bow.

DAMINI

MEM-SAAB IS LYING ON HER BED. GETTING DRESSED
seems to have exhausted her. "It's the heat," Damini tells her. "And
your air conditioner is a little old and tired, too."

Amanjit shouts from the drawing-room. Damini crinkles one eye
shut and presses the other to the peephole in Mem-saab's bedroom
door. He is waving a sheaf of papers.

"This is the thanks I get for giving up my business in Bombay, for
moving my family to Delhi to live with you. How could three people
live in Sardar-saab's old room? If you didn't want me to build, you
should have told me so."

Damini turns the door lock so carefully it doesn't even click.

"I'll never try to help you again, Mama. You just wait and see. I'm
going to have to defend this case and *you'll* be the one to be sorry."

"Khansama," Damini calls. "Mem-saab will take breakfast in her
room."

A weight tests the door. Then Aman says, "Damini-amma, tell
her she has made a mistake, bringing this kind of money-hungry
woman into our private business." He means the lady-lawyer.

Damini turns from the peephole and mouths his words for Mem-
saab, without sound.

Mem-saab turns her head away, seeking refuge in deafness.

Sometimes I think the old custom of burning surplus women on their husbands' funeral pyres spared widows like us from the dangers of living unprotected.

Mem-saab is breathing fast and hard again. Time is not on her side of the locked bedroom door.

ANU

When Adventure Travels closes for lunch at 2 p.m., Anu wakes Rano in Toronto with a collect call.

Rano doesn't sound surprised to hear Anu's marriage is about to be blown to pieces like a seed head before a puff of wind. With so many divorces in Canada, maybe she's accustomed to it. "Do you have a plan?" she asks. "In Canada, there are agencies that spirit you away to a safe house, change your name and give you a whole new life."

"I don't think we have safe houses," says Anu.

"Shall I tell Chetna?"

"After the divorce petition is served. Rano, listen . . ." Anu can barely get the words out, "The lawyer doesn't know how long this could take. Maybe even five to seven years, maybe ten. Can you keep her for me?"

Silence prickles up and down the line.

"Are you serious?" Rano says slowly. "Don't joke with me on this one, Anu."

Anu wishes she could see her face.

"I'll keep her as long as you want—always if you want—you know that." She realizes that Rano is crying.

Anu is crying. It feels as if they have been headed to this moment all their lives.

"What about Jatin?"

"He'll be thrilled. Chetna looks enough like us. And she's not a boy, so we won't have to wrestle with the question of wearing or not wearing a turban in Canada. I put off having a child for years—though you know how much I wanted one—because I had nightmares that I'd have a boy. And Jatin and I would discuss and discuss—would we keep his hair long, or cut it and break my in-laws' hearts? If we kept the boy's hair long, how would Hindu me learn to tie a turban on a little Sikh boy? Which god or goddess do you think would help me? And if we cut one inch of the little boy's hair, I can tell you my in-laws would forgive Jatin, but never forgive me. So I've been terrified even as I'm stimulating my ovaries with a diet of hormones and paying out of our savings for treatments that only give us a seventy-five percent chance of conception! Don't you worry, Jatin will feel as I do, that we have been offered a gift."

A metric tonne seems to lift from Anu's heart—every woman should have a cousin like Rano.

"Don't let her forget her Hindi or Punjabi."

"I promise she'll speak both just as if she lived in India," says Rano. "But Jatin'll expect her to become a Sikh and attend the gurdwara with us—that's not a problem, is it?"

"No, no—light comes from many sources," says Anu. "It might be a problem for Vikas, though."

"If so, he can always ask for his daughter—then she'll have two fathers, and two mothers, like you."

If I had never had Chetna, I wouldn't be losing her now. If Chetna had never been born, she wouldn't be faced with losing her mother. What a selfish mistake I made by not having an abortion.

And just as quickly as this thought passes through her mind, Anu is ashamed of it.

What a selfish mistake it would have been to have an abortion.

She hangs up, feeling a strange blend of elation and depression. She is doing the best she can for Chetna—she believes this from the core of her being. But the rest of the day, she feels like a bag of broken glass, and finds herself weeping at the slightest frustration.

Another strained dinner. Vikas talks to his parents, not looking at her even once. He makes no attempt to invite her back to the master bedroom—probably feels that might show weakness.

Afterwards, knees knocking against the centre drawer of Chetna's white painted desk, Anu tries several beginnings for a letter to her parents. When she succumbs to the allure of the blank page, the letter writes itself; it is difficult to stop.

Early tomorrow, Saturday, before the true heat of the day, Vikas will be mounted on the white-painted wooden horse at the centre of a cement bowl, thocking a bamboo ball around in weekly polo practice, Mrs. Kohli will be in the bridge room with her friends, sipping her first rum and Coke of the day, deciding whether to take the finesse or play for the drop, and Anu can take the cordless into the bathroom and call Purnima-aunty.

"Namaste, Anu Miss-saab!" The cook greets her affectionately as he unlocks the French doors to Sharad Uncle and Purnima-aunty's whitewashed home in South Delhi. Her eye must be less swollen now and her makeup adequate because he doesn't give her a second glance before dropping his gaze. He ushers Anu past the divans in the gloomy seldom-used drawing-room to the sun-glare of the central courtyard. She requests a glass of iced nimbu-pani; he leaves. She continues down the courtyard gallery, her large handbag clenched beneath one arm, the free end of her sari in the other.

She and Rano used to play hopscotch here. Her brother used to lean against that pillar, pouting when they told him, "Only girls play hopscotch." Purnima-aunty used to stand here every morning handing out school lunch packets: paneer parathas for Rano, chutney and Amul cheese sandwiches for Anu, lamb samosas for Bobby. Her piano still stands here, the one her two fathers, Sharad Uncle and Dadu, bought for her. And Bobby's twelve-string as if he is about to snatch it up and play her Bowie's "Loving the Alien."

Between signature campaigns to amend the Dowry Prohibition Act and meetings to prevent the chemical sterilization of Indian women, Aunty drove Rano to sitar, Anu to piano, and Bobby to guitar lessons. She attended Rano's sangeets, Anu's concerts and Bobby's jam sessions. When Rano took swimming and riding classes, so did Anu and Bobby. Yet Rano had always wanted to leave, as her older brothers had. "No one in this house is going anywhere," she said. Anu had loved feeling that Purnima-aunty, Sharad Uncle and this house wouldn't leave her.

She stops at a screen door. She discerns a triangular shape—her aunt is sitting cross-legged on her bed, her usual mess of *Manushi* magazines, cookbooks and papers spread around her.

Anu pushes through the door, slings her handbag onto a chair and surrenders to Purnima's greetings and embraces.

Her aunt's cinnamon skin glistens and her kameez is sticking to her back, despite the ceiling fan toiling above. Wisps escape her grey-flecked bun. "My glasses!" warns Purnima. "Don't sit on them." She scoops up the forms with a swoop of her arm. "Funding applications. To international aid agencies. Must have filled out fifteen or twenty in the last six months. For my friends' NGOs, you know. I'm going to start a women's organization of my own, too."

Anu perches in a half-lotus beside Purnima, and rests her cheek on her aunt's shoulder for a moment. Purnima yells for a glass of nimbu-pani. Anu assures her she has already requested one.

"Aren't you hot in that sari?"

"No, it's fine," Anu straightens, adjusts her pleats, smooths the free end over her sore shoulder.

Aunty moves a roll-pillow behind Anu, rummages in her nightstand for Odomos mosquito cream and a hand-fan, and offers them. Anu declines the cream, but welcomes the fan.

"The cooler's fan belt broke." Purnima-aunty wipes her brow with a handkerchief. "Maybe we shouldn't replace it. Get an air conditioner, now that waiting lists are gone. Wondering if we can afford it."

Purnima and Sharad Talwar can afford an air conditioner, given his bank manager's salary and the money her three engineer sons send from Canada, but Purnima guards each rupee like a blood relative. In her early sixties, she's ten years older than Mumma so she was fifteen when her parents fled the formation of Pakistan. She still keeps a few thousand rupees, a water bottle and a tin of biscuits in a kit bag in the cupboard in case a band of marauding Muslims break down her doors.

"So? What's all this you're talking on the phone this morning?" she says. "Not enough that you want a divorce? Now you want to become Mother Teresa? Your uncle will not like this. You've been talking to that hospital padri."

"Yes, I met Father Pashan again," says Anu. "Remember when you and I went to the Canadian High Commission to apply for Chetna's visa, and they told us we had to wait a few hours?"

"Hmm," says Purnima. "Sat on the grass. Finished a whole Danielle Steel."

"Yes, and I went for a walk . . ."

Embassies flanked the broad boulevard. Soon she was passing the gleaming blue dome of the Pakistani High Commission and the towers of embassies. Walking, thinking. Walking, thinking. That it was her birthday, and Vikas and his father were away for four days at a packaging convention in Singapore, to find a source of abrasion-resistant gloss. That the house would be wonderfully quiet without their constant checking and correcting, and she'd have only Pammy's drunken vagueness to deal with. That Chetna would be so happy if she came home from school today and learned she was going to spend the summer with her Rano-aunty in Canada, Rano-aunty who won't be reminded of violence and anger every time she looks at the little girl.

On her way back, Anu took a parallel street, so as not to return the way she came. Through gaps in compound walls and gates, she saw larger embassies. She walked briskly, her salwar scuffing pavement, and encountered a crowd gathered before a huge wrought-iron gate.

Rich, poor, dark-skinned, light-skinned. A few men carried briefcases, as if they were on their way to work. Some women were wearing skirts and dresses—probably Christians. A few carried babies, so they couldn't be working inside. It was too early in the morning for so many to be embassy employees.

A coiffed nun in a brown and white habit joined the crowd. People turned, greeted her with deep namastes. The gate opened, the crowd filed in. Surprisingly, no one was pressing too close or trying to jump the queue. Greetings in English, Hindi, Tamil and Malayalam filled the air.

Drawing closer, Anu read the brass plaque affixed to the gate-pillar: *Vatican Embassy in India.*

"Anupam!" One blue eye, one black, like David Bowie. Both set deeply above an aquiline nose. That quick boat-shaped flash of a smile against clay-toned skin. No moustache, just a triangular beard that matched the India-shaped lock of hair coming to a point at the middle of his high forehead. Father Pashan. Wearing a stiffer collar and whiter cassock than he had the last time she saw him, at Holy Family Hospital.

He opened the gates, "We're about to celebrate mass—come!"

She had an hour or two. Yeshu, that half-man son of god, had helped her so many times, even brought her back from the void. And so she entered, genuflected, kneeled in a pew as she used to in school.

"The gods don't mind what we call them or how we worship," Dadu used to say. "They only feel the love with which we do it."

Kneeling, standing, sitting in the cream and gold opulence, Anu sang and prayed and listened to Father Pashan's sermon.

"Every day," the priest said, "I meet men and women who question if it would have been better if they had not been born. But know one thing: every child who comes into this world was meant to be here.

"When the person who gave us life cannot or will not give us approval, or when the person we should be closest to spurns us, we can despair. We can descend into a deep depression. But think of what St. Paul said, 'There is no longer Jew or Greek, there is no longer slave or free, there is no longer male or female, for all of you are one in Christ Jesus.' That means god believes everyone is worthy of being loved. High caste or low, rich or poor, deserving or undeserving—even you."

Practical Purnima nods at Anu's account. "Unconditional love. Maybe only god can give it."

"He said a lot more, but those words broke me apart. They reminded me of the light I saw when I was almost dead. That same connection, attraction. He was saying *I* was intended to be here. That *I* was worthy of anyone's love. I sat in that pew long after the service was over, just sniffling. It felt as if something had shifted inside me."

Purnima puts her arm around Anu and rocks her gently.

"And I remembered something you said when you came to see me in the hospital. You said, "A face is irrelevant, Anu. The shape of your eyes, the length of your nose, the curve of your lips, these tell me nothing about you. Or you about me. Only deeds truly speak, and leave traces on the planet.'"

"I don't remember saying that," says Purnima, squeezing her shoulders. "But yes, I believe in being a karm-yogi. Deeds are all we have to go by. In your next life, you'll live with the result."

"I feel Lord Jesus and the gods saved me for a reason after my accident, but I haven't done anything in return. Nothing for others, I mean. I went back to work once my scars were healed enough not to scare away tourists—but does travel help anyone, change anything?"

"Did you pray to Shiv-ji?"

"Of course. I said, *O Lord Shiv-ji, you who have the power to destroy me. Let me live and I will be a better mother, a better woman. You who tread upon Apasmara, that demon of fear and ignorance—tread on my fear, tread on my ignorance.* But I haven't done much to be that better woman."

"So then?"

"I began attending mass at the Vatican Embassy chapel whenever I could slip away. I left as soon as Vikas left for work, got there an hour before I had to take my seat behind my terminal at Adventure Travels, and sometimes in the evening on my way home. And after mass, I spoke to nuns who worked in hospitals, old age homes, clinics, libraries, schools, and centres for the disabled."

"Oh, they do good work no doubt, but what do you know of their lives?"

"One said, 'We serve god by helping those who really need it.' A cloistered nun from a contemplative order said, 'We touch every person in the world through constant prayer.' A very noble selfless nun from an active order said, 'We touch a very small number of people in the world by our deeds.' I talked to Paulines, Sacred Heart, Maryknolls, Dominicans, Order of Jesus and Mary, Order of Loreto, but familiarity and nostalgia brought me back to St. Anne's and the Order of Everlasting Hope. I think joining them is the perfect solution."

Purnima-aunty doesn't look convinced.

"Better than suicide, better than murdering Vikas and being sent to prison," says Anu. "Better than begging Mumma or you to take me in."

Purnima waves this away as hyperbole. "You can always stay with me—us—we're your second parents."

"Yes you are. But you've done so much."

"Why not volunteer in a women's organization. Non-governmental, if you don't like government ones—every new NGO in Delhi needs English-speaking volunteers to write project reports, apply for funding or translate interviews into English. I can find you one—I can find you ten."

"No, I promised . . . well, let's just say something is calling me to do this. It doesn't matter if I am pulled to do this or have been pushed—I'm going to do this. I need to do this."

"Have you watched *The Sound of Music?*"

"Not recently."

"Rent it. Julie Andrews is too thin, but she has a voice like The Nightingale." She means Lata Mangeshkar to whom all singers are compared. "Does Vikas know?"

"Not yet." The thought makes her breathing come shallow and quick. "I'll be untraceable before the divorce notification is served. And the rest is none of his business."

Anu dips into a quilted cloth bag in her handbag and removes three kundan necklaces, several gold bangles, a nine-jewel necklace, a pair of ornate gold anklets, a pair of gold jhumka earrings. They glitter at her fingertips. "Dadu and Mumma gave me these at my wedding," she says.

"That's all?" says Purnima.

"Mumma married for love. Your parents didn't give her these— Dadu did. And Mumma didn't buy more for me, because Vikas's father didn't ask for dowry.'"

"Huh! You're not supposed to *believe* the boy's side when they say such things. But to me, it seemed Vikas was really in love with you."

"He was probably like me," Anu said, "wanting to fall in love to please our parents." She could add what Vikas told Anu the first week they were married, that an alliance with a government servant's family would assure Kohlisons Media a limitless future, but she doesn't. Anu's father failed to bring Kohlisons Media the expected government contracts, or nudge a single multinational towards them. Vikas mentioned this often, as if Dadu was the only honest government servant he had ever met.

"Please, take these to the jeweller, sell them and send the money to Rano for my Chetna."

"Nothing doing!" Purnima's hands are up, palms outward. "That's family jewellery, not *yours*. I'll keep it for Chetna's dowry and we'll have to buy her more. Can't let the same thing happen to her, na?"

The silhouette of a tall stooped man in a white pyjama-kurta appears at the screen door—it's Sharad Uncle, clearing his throat and removing his sandals in the courtyard outside.

"Come in, come in," says Purnima.

Veins on Sharad Talwar's forehead stand out. "So here you are. Purnima told me you're considering . . . divorce?" He makes the word sound like a synonym for a career in prostitution.

"Not considering, Uncle, I've decided."

"Decided? When did you talk to your parents?"

"Uncle, I'm twenty-nine. I have decided what I need to do."

"Who are you to decide? Have you ever made choices for yourself before now?"

His normally mild voice has risen.

"No, Uncle, no." She cannot bear more shouting. Why can't she just make a decision? Why does she have to defend it? Why does it have to be a family decision?

"And not only divorce. What's all this other nonsense? You have been tricked by that padri! Can he and his convent look after you in some way your family cannot?"

"I don't want to be taken care of. I want to contribute."

"You have a child—you have contributed," says Sharad Uncle. "Rano can look after Chetna. She'll be happy to do it. She will be her second mother. But you—you're still my responsibility. I can't allow you to enter any convent-shonvent. Your parents will say . . ."

Anu interjects, "Uncle, you don't need to allow or disallow, it's a personal decision."

She doesn't want to be rude. Sharad Uncle was always anxious to do his duty and more. He opened bank accounts for Anu and Bobby at his bank, saying, "Remember the power of compound interest." There he deposited the cheques Dadu sent every few months for their care, though he could have cashed them as Dadu intended. Anu owes him so much, but . . .

"*Hein?* I'm your uncle and you're a Hindu. I know what those Christians do. Brainwash you and feed you beef, first thing!"

"Where are they going to find beef in India?" says Anu, trying to deflect his ire with a laugh.

"From old cows," says Purnima. "Muslims slaughter them, tan their hides. But I'm not really worried about beef. Rano eats it in Canada, I'm sure, even if she doesn't tell me. Our three sons probably eat it too. I don't know how they can eat the flesh of an animal whose milk they drink, or why they don't think: oh, all three hundred and thirty three million gods are in my stomach at the same time and I might explode from eating so much power. No, my problem is different. Anu, I'm sorry to say this nun-shun business seems like a cult. Maybe two thousand years from now, people will call swamis like Osho, Baba Ramdev and Swami Rudransh 'son of god'—how do we know? But today they are cult leaders, like Lord Jesus Christ was when he began his magic show. They're not for educated people like us. They're for the gullible."

"I'm gullible," says Anu. "I married Vikas, remember?"

"Oh, you had nothing to do with that—we married you to him. We all thought two science graduates would have something in common." Purnima rolls from one buttock to the other, draws up one knee and clasps her arms around it. "Lord Jesus may be calling you but you are going to answer to the Catholic Church—that's no different from being in an ashram with one of these swami-types."

"So should I go to an ashram? I'd have to prove my devotion with years and donations before I could learn anything. Only the deserving are taught by those gurus—that's the brahmanical way. I need a more egalitarian community."

"Okay, okay," says Purnima. "Don't go to an ashram. But mark my words, I went to convent schools too, and I don't think you'll find the Church any less authoritarian than our guru system."

"I have freedom of thought, expression, belief, faith and worship." Anu alludes to the words of the Indian constitution. "I can convert three times a day if I want. Aunty, I just want to be with people who have principles."

Silence. Purnima seems to be considering this. "You said you'll be untraceable. Will becoming a nun make you untraceable?"

"I hope so," says Anu.

"Find some work the Kohlis wouldn't dream you would do. You aren't dark enough to be a maid. Too bad you can't go back to school at any age, as Rano did in Canada—my sister always wanted a doctor in the family."

"Mumma wanted Bobby to be a doctor, not me."

"Become a nurse then. Some are quite fair."

"Go home," Sharad Uncle growls. "Your dharma is to be with your husband." He doesn't understand. He doesn't see. He doesn't want to see.

Anu rises to her feet and lets her sari slide from her left shoulder.

Sharad Uncle's eyes widen—he holds up his hand, palm outward. *"Arrey! Arrey!"* He looks around, either to flee from her immodesty or to verify no other man is looking.

Anu unbuttons the top button of her sari blouse. Comprehension and dismay chase across Sharad Uncle's face at the sight of the purpling stains on her skin. "Look, both of you, look." Anu's voice feels thick and strange. "Is it not enough? When will it be enough?"

Aunty embraces her, holding her fiercely. "That bastard! I'll take a stick and beat his brains out. And to think he comes from such a good family—who can believe it!"

Sharad Uncle wipes his sleeve across his forehead; Purnima offers him a box of face tissue.

"So this is why you're talking about divorce and convents-shon-vents? Come, button up, Anu. I'll talk to Vikas—I'll tell him you're a good girl. I'll tell him he shouldn't get so angry with you again."

"Sharad . . ."

"We all fight and make up—koi baat nahin! Come, I'll persuade him to take you back."

Purnima withdraws the box of tissue just as Sharad Uncle is reaching for one. "You can't send her back to that man."

"He's not 'that man'—he's her husband. He is Lalit Kohli's son, not some uneducated hooligan off the street." He resorts to his sleeve again.

"Sharad, I'm telling you—" his wife warns.

"Softy ice cream, you are. That boy is brilliant. BRILL-iant! Topped his class, could have gone abroad for higher studies like others but he stayed in the motherland. He's grown his father's company to five times its size with only a few crores of rupees from our bank. And he donates to Hindu schools and ashrams, doesn't let them go begging to foreign agencies. You women—a man makes one mistake . . ."

"It's *not* the first time . . ." says Anu, touching her scarred cheek.

Sharad Uncle sits down at the other end of the bed. "An accident is a different kind of mistake," he says. "Didn't he apologize?"

"Yes, he did." She doesn't add, *As he did for the night Chetna was conceived.* Both times, he had taken back his apology, insisting later that it was her fault.

"Then? What else do you need?"

"Each mistake is a different kind, ji, but his are too-too many." Purnima-aunty leans forward, takes her roll-pillow from behind her and propels it across the bed like a missile.

Sharad Uncle catches it deftly and secures it behind his back.

"Why didn't you tell me?" she says to Anu.

"I did," says Anu.

Purnima opens her mouth, thinks better of it. She tries again, "These things . . . well, they don't . . ."

"Don't happen to people like us? Shouldn't happen to an educated woman?"

Purnima's eyes fill. She dabs them with her dupatta. Anu offers her the box of tissues, and hugs her. "Okay, okay." Purnima blows her nose loudly. "I must have been blind or didn't want it to be true. What can I do now?"

"I'm not staying with Vikas." Anu's voice is firm and quiet. "I can't meet his standards. After my accident his mother suggested I leave so he could take another wife. Someone with no scars."

"Huh, as if Pammy Kohli's surgery has made her any prettier!"

"She wants Vikas to have a wife who can produce a son."

"Only natural." says Sharad Uncle. "How can you have a business named 'Kohli and Daughters'?"

"How? You make a sign that says 'Kohli and Daughters,' and you hang it on the front door of the business, that's how!" says Purnima.

Sharad Uncle turns to Anu as if struck by a new idea. "Have another child. Pregnancy will cure you of these . . . these hysterical wishes."

"Even if I wanted one," says Anu, "or wanted Vikas to ever touch me again, there's no guarantee it would be a boy."

For a moment, Sharad Uncle holds his head in his hands. Then he looks up. "There is, there is—nowadays you can check with what is it . . . amnio-something?"

"That's old. You mean ultrasound," his wife says.

Anu shakes her head. "Ultrasound should be used to prevent disease or cure it. The sex of a child is not a disease. I wouldn't abort a girl or boy even if I did know."

"No one is saying to abort a boy."

"I know." She holds her uncle's gaze till she feels him release the idea.

"Anu—Vikas's family—are not small people, you know . . ." Purnima says.

"If I don't ask for money," says Anu, "the Kohlis won't care where I am."

But Vikas? He only wants things when they're beyond his reach.

I am not a thing.

"You may not want money from them for yourself, sweetheart," says Purnima. "But there is Chetna to think about."

"Each nun is paid for her work. I will save for Chetna's marriage. I'll get her married myself."

"On a nun's salary? Don't be so foolish, Anu. And also think— Vikas Kohli's daughter should live as well as her father," says Purnima.

"Well Chetna can't, if Vikas doesn't want her."

"Don't worry, my Rano and Jatin will spoil her completely," says Purnima.

"Ladies, ladies!" says Sharad Uncle. "We don't know yet if Vikas wants Chetna or not. You can't just decide where his daughter will go. All this is not right—bilkul not right. Not right at *all*. Purnima—milao the phone! Your father must be told what you're up to, Anu."

"He knows—I wrote to him and Mumma."

"Achcha. Good-good-good. Let's see what he says. 'Personal decision'—ha! You've been reading too many English novels, watching too many foreign movies. You make your personal decisions when all of us are dead and gone, my dear. Not before."

Purnima makes the call to Anu's parents, using her new cordless.

"Good that Chetna is with Rano," says her husband, pacing the room, hands behind his back, "if this is the kind of example Anu is setting."

Anu says, "Uncle, please don't talk about me as if I'm not here."

Purnima puts her hand over the mouthpiece and hisses at her husband: "And what about Vikas? What kind of example is *he* setting, you please tell me?"

He opens his mouth to retort, but Purnima is now talking to Dadu's manservant. She taps her foot, waiting for Dadu to come to the phone.

Deepak Lal, round-shouldered from daily hunching over government files. Living in a government bungalow in Allahabad and dealing with hot-potato issues. Nomadic as all civil servants, saving to build his dream house after retirement. His worried expression must be even more pronounced today.

Purnima remembers the speakerphone, presses the orange button. She asks her brother-in-law if he received Anu's letter.

"Yes," he says. Which is all he can say before Mumma takes the phone. Purnima-aunty listens to her sister with a "haan-haan" or "yes-yes" and a leftward tilt of her chin. Sharad Uncle folds his arms across his chest and closes his eyes as he listens. Mumma soon forgets she's on speakerphone.

"You're the one to blame, Deepak," she says to Dadu in cutting tones. "You gave your daughter these ideas. Don't think you can blame this one on me." The cook in the kitchen must be able to hear her. "And you, Anu—you're just going to abandon your daughter for your own convenience? Just send her to her aunty? What kind of mother are you?"

And Anu can't say, "Maybe a bit like you, Mumma." Because she doesn't want to hurt her Purnima-aunty by implying her care was worth any less than a real mother's.

Mumma is soon reminding everyone of the butter chicken and mutton curries served at Anu's wedding, the expense of the Ashoka Hotel even with Dadu's government discount, and how she'd haggled with bootleggers for each bottle of Johnny Walker, both Black and Blue Label. Then Mumma is quoting the price of Anu's gold-crusted red salwar-kameez. "How will it look?" she keeps saying, "How will it look?"

Dadu interjects at last. "Sharad," he says, "We thought we chose well, but I see from Anu's letter that our choices were not auspicious. She writes, 'I am not living with him in that house; I am dying.' I don't want her to feel that way."

His middle finger will be jabbing at the black-rimmed glasses that are always sliding down his nose.

"I would have preferred she didn't want a divorce—separation is better for both. I know people who have been separated for years. I know one couple who live in different cities rather than get a divorce. Too much stigma, na?

"We can ask for an amicable settlement, but I think Vikas will not agree. What we must negotiate is for him to pay for Chetna's education and wedding. But let Anu go ahead."

"I have to bear the shame," says Mumma's waterlogged voice. "Because you've made your father look so bad. I hope you realize what you've accomplished, Anu."

Sharad Uncle leans close to the microphone as if to shield Anu from her mother's voice. "Rano and Jatin will have to adopt Chetna legally so she can go to school in Canada."

Dadu says, "The school term in Canada begins in September—we have time. Governments require paperwork; paperwork can be done. And if at any time Rano wants to send her to us, Chetna can always live with us too—every home in this family is her home. The problem will be the same as for Anu and Bobby—no good English-medium schooling available here. English is still only taught in private schools, and they're only in larger cities. So it is best for the child if Rano keeps her in Canada and she studies in English. Come what may, she must learn in English."

"And what do you think about this nun-business?" says Sharad. He draws himself up and away from the speaker as if readying for a flood of invective.

"It may be better than trying to live alone and bear what people say," says Dadu. "When the padri saved Anu's life, I promised she would worship Lord Christ, who had spared me from losing a second child. And he said Anu must have been saved because she was special. I don't know what did he mean—because how can we all be equal and special at the same time for his god?—but maybe Anu can do some good deeds with the Christians. I certainly have no objection."

"Oh, Dadu, thank you!" Anu sounds juvenile to her own ears, but she hopes her voice truly conveys heartfelt gratitude.

"This is not some industrial project getting a no-objection certificate from your office." says Mumma. "Father and daughter both think they can just do what they want, no consultation, no discussion. Typical, typical! My family would never allow such dis-res-pect."

A corner of Purnima's mouth rises.

Mumma's sister never brags about her ancestry—Purnima has enough accomplishments of her own. Whereas Mumma—! The wound of her only son's untimely death has given her a license to say whatever she wants, to anyone in the family. Dadu's no-objection certificate will cost him several months, if not years of rebukes and reprimands—but his solidarity is so comforting. Mumma is still scolding when Sharad Uncle sets the receiver back in its cradle.

Mid-July 1994

DAMINI

AT THE COURT HEARING, DAMINI PLACES A CUSHION behind Mem-saab and takes a seat near her, keeping her distance so everyone will know Mem-saab to be born high on the ladder of karma.

Mem-saab's lady-lawyer is wearing a black robe that covers the swirl of her sherbet-pink sari. Two other lady-lawyers standing in the side aisles are wearing white saris. They look too young to be widows, so their saris could be a uniform. Mem-saab's lady-lawyer's voice, in English, is shrill and indignant.

The judge is called Milord, just like in Hindi movies, but the people in his court are not as respectfully absorbed in the proceedings the way actors are in those movies. He listens more attentively to Aman's lawyer, a ponderous man with spectacles and plenty of uniformed peons to bring him notes and files, than he does to Mem-saab's.

Milord should give his English talk with Hindi subtitles.

She counts eighteen fans humming on long slender stems, flowers twirled between unseen fingers, cooling the crowd in the high-ceilinged room. Mem-saab is waiting for Aman to come to her, put his arms around her, say he really will look after her, say he and Kiran will be kind . . . but Aman's jungle-green turban never turns toward her.

No one can churn butter from soured milk.

Afterwards, the lady-lawyer comes to Mem-saab and takes her hands.

"The judge has decreed there will be a Stay Order. Status quo," she says in English.

Mem-saab looks at Damini but these words are too difficult for Damini to translate and relay. Mem-saab turns back to the lady-lawyer and offers her a notepad and pencil so the lady-lawyer can write them down. Then she reads the English writing and draws her eyebrows together. The lady-lawyer writes some more. Mem-saab repeats the words aloud, in Hindi. "He cannot build the rooms but I cannot tell him to go back to Bombay?"

The lady-lawyer nods. "His lawyer said he has no place to live in Bombay. Mr. Amanjit Singh said you gave him part of your house as a gift to entice him to Delhi to look after you."

Mem-saab puts the notepad away in her purse. She shakes her head slowly. She does not have enough breath today to discuss Aman's lies.

"What has been gained for Mem-saab?" Damini asks.

"Time," says the lady-lawyer, who holds out her hands. Mem-saab grips them to pull herself up from her chair. Damini follows them outside.

Thunder bursts and grinds as if the universe were reconstructing itself. Sheets of rain are pouring over the High Court. The pavement hisses and steams. Street children are already running and splashing in puddles.

Rain, deliciously cool on her hot cheeks, her neck. Across her shoulders, her dupatta feels warm and wet. Mem-saab's is getting wet too, but there's a lift in her gait as Damini guides her to the car.

Rain is a blessing. Divine essence, nectar of the gods.

And Aman will have to find himself a taxi. In the rain.

VIKAS

A WELCOME BLAST OF CHILL AIR ENVELOPS VIKAS KOHLI
as he enters The Claridges' coffee shop. He's early because it doesn't
look nice to be late for a meeting with elders, particularly one that
includes his father. The white kurta-pyjama he's wearing was starch-
scented and crisp when he left home, but has wilted in fifteen minutes
of monsoon mugginess. He dangles a khaki envelope from the thumb
and forefinger of his left hand.

Only a few half-naked foreigners. Tourists who can only afford
this four-star hotel.

Anu won't be coming. Women don't face the music for all the
trouble they cause. Her father will show instead, and her uncle, the
banker who was matchmaker for this marriage.

Dad better get here soon. Dad always sorts things out.

The head waiter doesn't leap to greet him. Still Vikas's air of
command soon results in the requisite obsequiousness and a table at
the centre of the room. He starts toward it, then recalls his reasons
for choosing this old hotel instead of his club. A word to the head
waiter, and he switches to a corner.

Seated, he opens the envelope and reads the divorce papers again.
"Mental and physical cruelty . . ." He is wounded anew by the
accusation.

He called Anu at the travel agency right after he got the papers. "I apologized, didn't I? Sent you flowers, didn't I? This is the thanks I get for working day and night for your every need? What have you ever ever *ever* had to complain about?" Silence. He hates her silences almost as much as her burd-burd. She hasn't been home since. Her clothes are missing. So damn underhand.

In the coffee shop, he crosses one ankle over his knee, and leans back.

When he first met her, he had been attracted to her kindness and gentleness. Such a good listener. The day of the Showing at the Gymkhana, her little foot with its white platform heels swinging so close to his shin. How she teased with a toss of her head, smoothing her long black curls behind those pale ears. He still remembers her cleavage as she leaned toward him, the shy flirty-flirty glances from her huge eyes. The way her red lips promised all the delights of the *Kama Sutra*. What had he wanted that was so unusual? A son. Sex whenever. Doesn't every husband? Unless he's some hen-pecked runt who's married above his caste, doesn't every real man?

He examines a scuff on his shoe. The sweeper isn't polishing properly at all since Anupam left. He picks a speck from his sleeve.

Oh, he didn't let Anu make a fool of him. He got over her maidenly objections. Calmly, firmly, saying please at first, and when that didn't work, without please. It was time; she had to be broken. How was he to know she'd fight with fist and knee and insults and pleading or that her bleeding wouldn't stop for three days? It was awful, but it had to be done. And it made him feel larger—powerful—wonderful.

For a while. He did know that what he did to her was unforgiveable. But any woman except Anu eventually would have forgiven him. She just isn't as sweet, kind, generous or smart as he thought.

If not for the accident with the roadster, he'd have a son by now . . . but ever since Anupam wrecked his car, the sight of her rouses a current of irritation. A sensation that amplifies in his veins like a drug, then explodes. Gives him a greater high than hitting a ball with a mallet.

And a very bad feeling afterwards.

Less and less bad, though, as Chetna gets older and there's still no son.

At first he thought it was the accident. Some women's wombs are so bloody delicate. But now he knows it was the pills—sneaky little bitch.

The parents always said he could educate his wife, correct her thinking. Mistaken. As they have been about many decisions in his life. Still, if he wants to be recognized on sight, or ushered everywhere when he name-drops his father's name, if he wants to live in Lutyens's New Delhi, if he wants a well-tended life full of servants, if he wants to inherit a mansion worth more than three hundred crore rupees, the parents are always right.

"Dharma," he mutters through clenched teeth, a son's role being so demanding. "*Hé Ram!*"

His lawyer says he has options. Anupam, on the other hand . . . well, she's about to find out who's smarter. And here's Dad, at the door of the coffee shop.

Vikas waves, and soon his father is seated beside him, ordering tea and pineapple pastries.

"Not to worry, beta." Mr. Lalit Kohli pats his son's hand. "Not your fault."

"Yes," says Vikas. "You chose her—ji."

"Well, we thought she would be better than that . . ." His father trails off.

"Just as you thought it would be better for me to run Kohlisons Media than get a Masters."

"Then what? You were going to be another Homi Bhabha, hmm? *Arrey!* The nuclear programme has already been founded."

"I topped the class in physics, even though I got a second div overall."

"You've always topped every class. You used to catch the teachers' errors. But remember how many M.Sc. seats were left for us Forward castes after the quotas for Backward caste people were set? Five— just five. I would have needed lakhs and lakhs of rupees as 'donation' for your admission. I told you you could apply to study in England or the US. Less competitive."

Vikas shakes his head. "Cook, wash dishes and clean my own toilet in some student apartment? Not my style, Dad."

"Ah, here are the pastries. Vickoo—have one."

Vikas cuts through foamy cream and crushed pineapple to the layer of plain cake, and takes a bite. "Not as good as at the Taj Hotel."

The tea steeps in silence.

Eventually Mr. Kohli pours, adds milk to his own cup, then Vikas's. "I say Vikas, what's that around your neck?"

"Photo of Swami Rudransh. His society ordered ten thousand medallions for his All India campaign. Devotees will buy them along with his bottles of energized water and vials of herbal medicines— we're designing and printing the labels."

"Very good, very good." Mr. Kohli leans forward to peer at the swami's bindi. "Did he tell what his problem was with the last advertising chap?"

"The fellow didn't like his calling Partition 'the truncation of India.' Wanted him to call the murder of Gandhi an 'assassination.' Didn't like him talking about minority appeasement."

"That chap will remain a two-bit operator forever. One day he'll wish he could ruddy *influence* things. Sugar?"

"No, ji. Playing a match tomorrow morning. Better not eat too much, too." He pushes away his half-eaten pastry with more force than necessary. He looks around.

Couples all over the place. Gora men take their blasted wives everywhere they go.

"Come, come," his father is saying. "Not the end of the world. Hurried too much, last time. Should have checked the femily history."

"Not femily, dad, *fam-ily*."

"Bloody English language specialist, you've become? Vikas, this is good in the long run—pay her off, marry again. You're worth at least fifty lakhs—this time we won't be shy to ask."

Vikas's fist crashes to the envelope. A couple of tourists look around in consternation. He lowers his voice to a hiss. "Don't you marry me off again right away, even for a nice dowry. I'm going to contest this."

"Look here my boy, if you don't settle we'll be in court for years, and you can't marry until and unless you're divorced. No good family in Delhi is going to give you a girl before that. Why waste money on lawyers?"

"I can't let her think she's beaten me."

Mr. Kohli dabs whipped cream from his moustache. "True. I'm not saying you can't have a floozy or two in the years you're in court, but these days you have to worry about AIDS and herpes and syphilis—remember: no foreign floozies!"

"I've time for floozies?" says Vikas. "Have to run the company, remember? So that my six cousin-brothers can be paid both over and under the table?"

"Cousin-brothers, brothers—same thing, Vikas. They also have to live."

"Their club bills tell me they live very well."

Mr. Lal and Anupam's tall stooped uncle Mr. Talwar have arrived at the table. They have a sheepish, apologetic air—as they should, as they should. Vikas rises to greet them, then more tea is ordered, more pineapple pastries.

All they want, Mr. Lal begins, is an amicable settlement. His middle finger jabs his black glasses up the slick slope of his nose. "Best for both families," he says. The three older men nod at Vikas.

Vikas adopts a tone halfway between businesslike and deferential. "Your daughter," he tells his father-in-law, "thinks she can do whatever she likes. No concept of family—no concept at all. Never satisfied. Did you know I told your daughter to quit her silly job but she wouldn't?"

"I always told her to be independent and strong."

"Independent? Day after day she's sitting at Adventure Travel, enticing goras and Muslims to pollute India with their presence. After all the trouble we Hindus went through to get Independence."

"Then what should she do?"

"I told her, 'Come and work at Kohlisons Media,' and she asked how much I would *pay?*"

Actually, Vikas only read the question on Anupam's face. She hadn't said it, but meant to, he could tell.

Mr. Lal looks confused. "Anu volunteers whenever and wherever people need her. But even if she did say it, what's wrong with paying family workers in a family business?" His middle finger rises into view, jabs at his black-rimmed glasses and subsides. "Family businesses don't all rely on slave labour."

"Slave labour! Huh." Mr. Kohli's index finger taps the table. "Your daughter should be grateful she wasn't married to a Muslim, Lal-saab. They have exported legions of Hindu slaves to the Middle East."

His father sounds as if the Mughal slave trading of the sixteenth century were still in progress, but Vikas isn't going to object.

"No, sir," Mr. Kohli continues. "Instead the slave is my son, working and working all the time."

Dad's right about that. Time to go on the offensive.

"And I ask you, does a man pay his *wife?*" says Vikas. "You might as well ask him to pay his son. If it was for tax reasons, certainly—but to *demand* it?"

"I hear you hit her when she wouldn't quit her job."

"All I said was: out of one pocket and into another." His tone says if he hit Anu, he was justified. "She just wouldn't understand simple arithmetic."

"Accounting is always at femily level, Mr. Lal," Mr. Kohli intones. "You never taught her that?"

"Even if *he* never taught her, I did," says Vikas. "Told her many times. But she doesn't have much of a brain that she can learn."

"I hope," says Mr. Lal, his middle finger slowly rising again, "for Chetna's sake, that one day you won't find yourself trying to be polite to a man who hits your daughter and thinks you'll agree that she deserved it." The finger jabs again at his spectacles.

"I have consulted my lawyer," Vikas says. "I will countersue. I have complaints. Frigidity, for instance."

"Women need persuasion, Vikas," Mr. Lal's hand hovers as if he's about to reach for Vikas's cuff.

Vikas recoils. "I have been very patient, ji," he says. "But your daughter has a kink in the brain. Don't think I'm joking. You should have her checked by a psychiatrist. Maybe she's bipolar."

"Shhhh," Mr. Lal's gaze caroms around the room. "She's almost twenty-nine, ji, I can't 'have her checked' by anyone."

"All she ever said was No. That's not a normal woman. You should have named her Anuchit—abnormal."

"Her name is Anupam, meaning special."

"Your so-special so-educated Hindu daughter got the idea she should refuse to have even one," Mr. Kohli says, leaning closer to Vikas. "We Hindus are a dying breed, Mr. Lal. Because we do just what the government slogan says: 'We are two, we have two.' But Muslims and Christians say, 'We are five, and we have twenty-five.'"

"Who is using such a slogan, ji?" says Mr. Lal. "It's all in your mind."

"In my mind? At the Muslim and Christian rate of multiplication, we Hindus will be outnumbered and outvoted in just a few years time. Chunks of the country will become majority Muslim, or majority Christian."

"Then what will happen, ji?" Mr. Lal has the temerity to look amused.

Mr. Kohli continues, "Then they will secede as in '47, and we'll lose more chunks of the motherland."

"Why should anyone secede nowadays—unless we treat them badly?" says Mr. Lal, looking mystified.

"Because both the Kaaba and Rome do not lie in India," Mr. Kohli slurps his tea. "Only Hindus consider India both fatherland and holy land."

"So said Savarkar, yes, but I wouldn't quote that warmonger," says

Mr. Lal. "I consider India my motherland and the whole world as holy."

"The whole world does not consider India holy—all the whole world has ever done is colonize us. First the Muslims, then the British chaps, now the American guys. But it's all enslavement. Your kind of thinking," says Mr. Kohli, tapping his temple, "has allowed this to happen. And your kind of thinking is your daughter's."

"Anu has ideas of her own," says Mr. Lal.

Mr. Talwar's lips purse in agreement with his brother-in-law.

"Ideas come from somewhere, no?" says Dad. "Nothing in the universe is original."

"Do you tell your clients that?" says Anu's father.

"No, we say our advertising is completely original. That's what foreign companies expect us to say, so we say it. But you know what we find, Lal-saab? Genuine Indians want the old traditions and the same old stories, dressed up in technicolour."

"Who is this Mr. Genuine Indian?"

Mr. Kohli reaches around the teapot and helps himself to more sugar. "I made a Himalayan blunder by marrying your daughter to my son. You should reread the vedas. Tell your daughter to do so as well."

"We must abandon Manu if we want to progress," says Mr. Lal.

"Why latch onto that? Read and understand *all* the vedas, sir, not only the Code of Manu about women. The vedas are beyond progress."

"Only god is beyond progress, Kohli-saab. The vedas are man-made and as flawed as all of us—even you, even your son."

His father turns to Vikas. "If this is the kind of argumentation you have had to put up with, it shows how misguided your wife has been." He rounds on Mr. Lal. "Sir, you encouraged your daughter to believe she could shirk her duties and live a man's life. If this is what convent education does, then I say your mistake lies in educating her. Tell me, sir, what would happen if every daughter-in-law in every femily said she doesn't want children?"

"Chaos," says Mr. Talwar with a head-tilt of agreement.

Ah, dissension. Anupam's father quells his brother-in-law with a glance.

"This is a matter of two individuals, Anu and Vikas," says Mr. Lal.

"No sir." Mr. Kohli sounds as if his collar is too tight. "People have roles in their families, people have obligations. A man can't fulfill a woman's obligations and a woman can't fulfil those of a man." He takes another slurp of tea. "So we must follow nature."

"We don't follow nature in all ways, Kohli-saab. We don't stay il-literate, or run around without clothes. I'm saying each person should follow his or her *own* nature."

"If a woman wishes to belong to a femily," says Dad, "she will follow the nature of the femily, she will adjust."

Mr. Talwar's head is tilting again, but Vikas's father-in-law bristles in defence of his daughter. "She did. She had a child, just as you wanted. And we must discuss that child."

Mr. Kohli waves this away, "A daughter—very sweet girl, pretty child." He pauses, studying his gold watch meaningfully. "But I'm talking about sons, Lal-saab, sons."

Mr. Lal is going on now about how daughters and sons are the same. And once they are born, you have a duty . . . etcetera etcetera.

Chetna—another duty.

A nauseating feeling of helplessness comes over Vikas.

He'll have to be both father and mother to Chetna. He's not fit for motherhood. He'll lose his mind. He could hire a few maids, ammas, ayahs, nannies, tutors. And those servants require supervision and become his responsibility even as they grow old and die—along with their families.

He closes his eyes.

Be practical. The law gives custody but how can he look after a child, run an advertising empire, and play four to six chukkers twice a week? And golf whenever he must entertain foreign clients.

Boarding school, like his alma mater? Waste of money. A girl doesn't have the intellect. She doesn't need life-long membership in an old boys' association.

Dad is saying his wife's meditation sessions with Swami Rudransh cannot be disturbed by looking after Chetna. But Vikas knows that his mother's almost continuous state of blissful inebriation makes her unsuitable for looking after Chetna. He loves his mother, of course he does, but she is—always was—so inconsiderate. If she had made a brother for Vikas, he could park the girl with his brother's family.

No, let the Lal family look after her. Let pushy Rano and her impotent husband keep her. Canadians now, they can afford it. "The girl should remain where she is," he says aloud. "I have other priorities."

"If you want her back," says Mr. Lal, "All you have to do is ask."

Anger streaks through Vikas's veins. Why should he have to ask anyone for anything? Aloud, he says, "How do I know?—she may not be mine."

Mr. Lal immediately offers to have Chetna's DNA matched to Vikas's. The two DNA labs in the country are booked till next year, but after that . . .

But Vikas cannot stand entering a hospital. Being vaccinated turns his stomach. Once in bio class, he was reading about mucus and disgust so overcame him, he almost passed out. Another time he gave blood after every classfellow had volunteered, and felt weak for days. When Chetna was born, he didn't want to see her till all the body fluids were cleaned off. "I don't have to submit to any such test," he says.

Mr. Lal is looking as if Vikas's refusal resolves the fatherhood question.

Such a fool. But if he weren't such a fool, he'd be in business not government.

"You're a dutiful father, you must be responsible for Chetna's wedding." Mr. Lal is leaning too close. Does his father-in-law think he can't afford a wedding, today or ten years hence?

His own father's restraining hand weighs on his arm but Vikas ignores it. "There's no *must* about it," he says, "but I will."

"I will also ask that you not try to see Anu until that wedding. She has suffered a great deal. If not, I will request the court for a restraining order."

"Request whatever you like," says Vikas, baring his teeth in a smile. "I too have suffered. Am suffering."

Mr. Talwar's oily voice says, "Both families are at fault, ji, both families."

Vikas purses his lips. Fuckwit. Probably worried Kohlisons Media will move its accounts to Citibank, HSBC or Scotiabank. Serve him right if he did, but how can he think a patriot would move from an Indian bank, even given the circumstances?

Mr. Lal says, "Your family should also have tried to adjust to Anu, not only our family trying to adjust to you."

Vikas snorts. "Why?"

"Because she is a person."

Vikas doesn't need to respond—his father is wearing a castor-oil face.

Mr. Kohli pulls a paper from his coat pocket. "A list of jewellery our femily gave yours at the wedding. Almost twenty lakhs worth of gold. Your femily must return them."

Anu's father takes the paper. "Her marriage necklace, of course. But the rest? These were wedding gifts to Anu. She told me she left all the jewellery she received from your side at your home. I said she shouldn't have and that her personal jewellery is hers by law!"

The outrage and surprise on his father-in-law's face sends a jolt of irritation down Vikas's spine.

Pretending he doesn't know wedding gifts are for show.

Mr. Kohli says, "What law? Marriage ends: you take back the girl, we take back the jewellery. Tell her she's lucky. Because this is what would have happened to her in my day . . ." His forefinger forms a pistol barrel, and arcs over the table aiming at an absent Anu, "*Phatttt!*"

Lal and Talwar recoil.

Does he think anyone gave gifts especially for his daughter, when all they knew of her was her name? Vikas rises to his feet like a coiled spring. Mr. Kohli follows.

The Lal family can foot the bill.

DAMINI

FOR A WEEK AFTER THE COURT HEARING, MEM-SAAB
asks every day if there is a letter from Timcu.

"No," says Damini, "no letter." And since that call in May the day
after Aman arrived, almost three months ago, when she told Timcu
Mem-saab was well, no phone call either. Damini considers writing
to him but she cannot form English letters and is not sure he remembers how to read Devanagari script. And how can she write complaints against his brother?

Today there is a square envelope from the Embassy-man. Mem-
saab reads the English note—it asks if he may come to tea with
Mem-saab. Mem-saab sends Damini downstairs with a note
saying yes.

Damini tells Khansama to make cake and jalebis, and knows this
means Amanjit and Kiran will be notified as well.

It takes Mem-saab most of the morning to dress and prepare; she
rests often to ease the pain in her chest. All afternoon, she sits watching the downpour and waiting for tea as though the Embassy-man
were one of the relatives.

Khansama wheels in the trolley as usual, but he doesn't leave the
room afterwards. He stands by the door, hands clasped before him.
He must have to report back to Aman.

The Embassy-man asks for tea without milk. In English. Damini pretends not to understand.

He should learn Hindi if he wants me to help him talk to Mem-saab.

Mem-saab pours milk in the Embassy-man's teacup.

"As you know—" the cup is small in his large hand. He gazes at the pale swirling surface, "my lease is till the end of this month."

Mem-saab bows her elegant head and smiles. His lease has been till the end of each month for four years now.

"I have been told I will be posted back to Washington after that." He takes a sip, puts down the cup.

Mem-saab smiles again. "How nice."

She has not understood. "Posted back to abroad?" asks Damini.

He looks at her then. "Yes. Tell her I will be posted back to Washington—say, to America—after this month."

Damini mouths his words to Mem-saab. Mem-saab smiles again, her expression tinged with dread. "I see," she says.

He accepts a piece of sponge cake but declines the crisp tubes of jalebis oozing their red-gold sugar water.

Now who will stop Aman—or Timcu, if he arrives—from putting their belongings or padlocks downstairs? The judge said everything must remain the same, but change cannot be decreed away. Four years ago, Mem-saab could ask her English-speaking sons to place an advertisement in *The Pioneer* saying "foreign embassy people desired" so she didn't have to lease to an Indian tenant. Indians can rarely afford to pay the rents embassy people pay and it can take a generation in court to evict them if they refuse to leave. But now . . . ?

Newspaper saabs won't listen to this old amma. How can I ask them to write in their English paper that Mem-saab doesn't want an Indian for a tenant?

ANU

MONSOON RAIN MUTES THE CLAMOUR OF STUDENTS ON their midday break in the quadrangle as Anu climbs the stairs to Sister Imaculata's office on the second storey of St. Anne's Convent. Sister was welcoming on the phone, but Anu's mouth is dust-dry; she can't even murmur namaste.

What if Sister says she's not serious or faithful enough? That she should find an agency—governmental or non-governmental—to take her, or go home. Anu has no home.

"Anupam, dear girl." Sister Imaculata takes Anu's hands in greeting. Her pale skin is almost translucent over her angular features. Those blue-green eyes twinkling from beneath sand-blond brows, are as kind as Anu remembers, her gaze as direct as a sunbeam. The puff of hair between her square forehead and her veil is grey, now. She exudes poise and dignity. No one would ever hurt, hit or rape a woman like her.

A prickly flush suffuses Anu's neck and face. Will Sister Imaculata see any use for her?

Imaculata looks lit from within. "The good Lord has shown you the way here," she says.

After she spoke to Vikas from Adventure Travels, Anu spent two nights in a guesthouse near the airport, checking in with her aunt every few hours. Then she called Mr. Gurinder Singh to say she was resigning. He said, "I hope you will return after your baby is born."

"Sir, I'm not expecting," she said. "I just have to leave work."

Mr. Gurinder Singh's voice dropped to a whisper, "Your husband is not allowing you to work, na? Please send a relative to do your job." He seemed to believe data entry skills were genetic.

Anu didn't have time to correct him. "If my husband calls," she said, "please say you do not know how to reach me."

"I will. Call me if there is anything I can do."

Now she's here in the same office where she first met Sister Imaculata. In the sixth standard, condemned by another nun to writing 'I will not read poetry in Geography class' one thousand times, Anu had, in a tiny act of rebellion, omitted the *not* on the 554th line. Which brought her before Imaculata, who could not hide her amusement and simply told her to memorize Yeats's "The Second Coming" as her punishment. And who listened, enchanted with nostalgia as Anu ploughed through the poem, accenting all the wrong syllables.

"What have you done to your face, my girl?" Imaculata's white skirt and stockings swish as she crosses over to a rattan-back chair before a coffee table. She turns her back to the walnut desk that takes up half the room and angles her chair beside Anu's. "Was it an acid-attack?"

"No, Sister—a car accident." Anu touches the leaf-shaped scar that sits across her right cheek. "What's an acid-attack?"

"Our sisters in Bangladesh and Pakistan say they've been treating women burned and blinded by sulphuric acid flung in their faces. Mercy me, but it's a cowardly way to take revenge on women who refuse or challenge men. It hasn't happened in India—that we know of—but they say it will."

She leans over and slides her fingertips down Anu's face from temple to jaw.

"When did this happen?"

Anu's cheek tingles—she pulls back instinctively, then submits to the caring gesture. "Two years ago."

"Plastic surgery can do wonders these days. I'm surprised it still shows."

"I think this is the best that can be done right now in India, Sister."

Following Anu's accident, Deepak Lal sold half the parcel of land on which he planned to build his dream home, to pay for Anu's surgery. Vikas, the modern Mughal, took full advantage of the old custom of accepting periodic "gifts" from a wife's family. Once Dadu's money ran out, and Indian surgeons were unable to go beyond the standard facelifts his mother required, Vikas didn't offer to take Anu abroad. Anu knew better than to ask. Feeling has never completely returned to her cheek, and her face is still slightly asymmetrical.

A nun with Goan features pushes open the door with the edge of a tray. Imaculata greets and thanks her as if receiving a favour from a friend. She introduces her, but the nun's name sails through Anu's agitated mind as if it were foreign. A flowered china teapot, cups and saucers, a milk jug, a sugar pot and a tray of Marie biscuits array themselves before her.

When the nun departs, Imaculata says, "The good Lord must have saved you for a reason."

"Yes, Sister." Anu lapses into schoolgirl response. She is calm. Really.

"I was so surprised to hear from you. And that—"

"That I want to be a nun?" Saying her wish out loud may create the possibility.

"Well, yes. I didn't know you'd been baptized. But praise be," the sister says, crossing herself. "Lord knows how many times I wondered how your life was going, how often I prayed for your soul. We did discuss your becoming a Christian before you graduated from school, and as I recall you said you were not ready, then."

"Yes, Sister." Not ready, not yet, not now—diplomatic refusals, copied from her father's bureaucratese. How she used to try to please.

Sister pours. "Sugar: one or two?"

"Two, please."

Sister adds sugar and milk. "Father Pashan seems to have opened your heart to the Lord. You met him at Holy Family Hospital?"

Anu accepts a teacup and saucer. "When I was recuperating. And then at the Vatican Embassy."

"Lovely man, Father Pashan. His heart is exactly in the right place, you know. He's been assigned to the hills, I hear. Setting up medical camps, clinics, and dispensaries for the poor. Quite a change from the Vatican Embassy . . ." She offers the biscuits, Anu takes one. "And does your family accept your conversion? Sometimes there are problems . . ."

"Yes, my father was present." At her hospital bedside, making his bargain with the priest.

Sister Imaculata raises her teacup, toasting Anu. "And how long have you known."

"Known?"

"Known you have a calling."

"Since my accident," Anu says. "Father Pashan said I'd been saved for a higher purpose, and I began to wonder what that might be . . ."

Imaculata puts her cup down, and joins her fingertips as if holding a sphere. The ring on the fourth finger of her left hand catches the glow from the window. "And?"

"I heard the call, Sister."

Oh to enter the convent and disappear—sweet revenge. *Give me distance, give me separateness. Give me a second virginity and I will make of it my fortress.* Subtract the whole burden of desire and creation. Become unreachable, unknowable. No longer be anyone's wife. Liberate herself from this woman's body. Shed this bruised and broken skin. Hide her face. *Hide so no one will know what a failure you are.* Yes, that too. Especially as a mother.

"What form did your call take?"

The gap between experience and explanation yawns. "A yearning, Sister. And then I met Father Pashan again."

"God seldom summons twice."

"Yes, Sister." Anu nibbles her dry biscuit.

"Why do you not seek out an indigenous order? Why an international order?"

"Familiarity with this congregation. Your example inspires me, Sister." The four Irish nuns who founded the Order of Everlasting Hope a hundred and fifty years ago also inspire Anu. She should remember their names, but today she just can't.

"I would rather the Lord inspired you. But faith, it seems to me, strengthens as we do god's work. We're apostolic—that appeals to you?"

Anu gives Sister Imaculata a questioning look.

"Meaning we live a life of service, not contemplation and prayer."

"That is what attracts me most."

"Did you consider working in Calcutta? Mother Teresa's Missionaries of Charity are very fashionable at present."

"I did, sister. But simplicity in Mother Teresa's order doesn't mean doing without luxuries. It means often doing without food, clothing and even shelter. I can't imagine owning only one sari. Or carrying all my possessions in a bucket."

"Can't live as the real poor do—yes. And I hardly think Indians need to be reminded to be fruitful and multiply, despite decades of Indian government family planning urging smaller families. We haven't followed Mother Teresa in that, because the Earth must also be considered. But like her and the Holy Father, we hold life holy and condemn contraception and abortion."

"Yes, Sister." If she joins the Order, Anu won't need contraception again, and certainly not abortion.

"Mother Teresa's nuns don't receive much in the way of old age pensions. Our nuns do—something to consider." Imaculata takes a sip, returns her cup carefully to the groove of its saucer.

"I hadn't, but I'm glad to know it."

"So am I, these days. I mention it because my Provincial tells me I should groom a successor. Young women these days don't seem to have leadership qualities. Oh—and another thing—you're not a harijan, are you?"

Surprise silences Anu. Sister Imaculata has used the old term coined by Mahatma Gandhi for the lower castes. Anu would have expected her to use the term *dalit*, or oppressed—the term preferred by dalits—but Sister Imaculata is Irish and may not understand the distinction.

"It doesn't matter to me, of course," says the nun, "but it does matter to others sometimes, so I need to know."

"I—I'm a kshatriya."

"I thought so. Then let me stress that if you're looking for a life of ease, this is not it. You will be required to clean your own toilet, wash your own clothes, make your own bed, cook when it's your turn. Nuns do not have servants."

"Yes, Sister." Over the rim of her teacup, she searches Imaculata's face for a clue to this detour.

"And as I tell women from lower castes, if you're looking for someone to tell you what to do and how to do every little thing, this is not a place for you."

"Yes, Sister."

Sister Imaculata cannot know she's describing paradise. It will be like joining an ashram or a hippie commune from the sixties. Without men. Except Lord Jesus.

Imaculata reaches for a biscuit, munches slowly. "We're in a time of flux, you know—or more so than usual. I've spent fifteen years at this school, and now Mother General has given me a new role." She gives an elaborate sigh. "Teaching young novices."

"Congratulations, Sister."

"Yes. Well—I'm leaving Delhi soon to become Provincial at our Shimla convent. Unfortunately, there are few novices and postulants to teach, these days. Four last year, only one postulant this year. You will be the second." She picks her cup and saucer off the table and balances both on her knee.

"So I'd be living in Shimla." Bobby's accident was in Shimla. Bobby lay in a coma for a week in Shimla's Snowdon Hospital. Anu's hands go cold.

Imaculata nods. "To begin with. Then let's see where the Lord's work takes you."

Obedience, obedience. You can't refuse your first assignment!

She has already scaled the mountain of her marriage. God is giving her another to climb. And if he's doing this, he'll also show her the path.

"It's almost impossible, now," Imaculata is saying, "to find young Irish women with the commitment to serve god. Frankly, I'd like to find more young Indian women—they can stand the heat better—but most don't have that fire in the belly we had."

"Yes, Sister."

"Always the distraction of family."

"Oh, I have no family distractions," says Anu.

"Anupam, in a country of nine hundred and fifty million people, everyone has family, and extended family and relationships and obligations—you don't even have to be Catholic. I've been serving god in this country for nigh on thirty years and I am not stupid."

"No, Sister. Of course, not." Anu winds a corner of her dupatta around her finger, takes a deep breath, "But you may remember that my younger brother Bobby, my only brother, had an . . . acc-accident . . . while I was still in school." She still has trouble saying it.

"Oh dear me, yes. I remember now." Imaculata's pale hand brushes Anu's shoulder. "We said a special prayer for him at Assembly. And what of the rest of your family? Your father—wasn't he posted in different towns?"

"Yes. Dadu kept pulling strings for the poor but wouldn't pull strings for politicians, so he kept getting transferred."

"Your dear mother would write to me every time she moved, to explain why you would be remaining in Delhi."

"They had one posting of three years in New Delhi, and my mother is still hoping my father will someday be transferred here again."

"Remind me—who did you live with here?"

"My Sharad Uncle and my Purnima-aunty."

"Yes, I remember your cousin-sister, Rano Talwar—bright. Volleyball player. Not as studious. Your senior by a year?"

"Two, Sister."

"Lovely girl. Last time she came to India she visited and told me how she met her husband. You know they used to meet every morning at the school bus stop?"

"Yes—we all rode together. He attended St. Anne's School for Boys. I never spoke to him."

"No, you weren't as mischievous. Rano said they used to pass notes back and forth in the bus. And then his family emigrated to Canada but he kept writing to her saying, 'Wait for me.' And when his father asked him if he had any preferences, he told him only one girl would do and so his father sent Rano's parents their offer— so romantic!"

Sister Imaculata is stirred by romance? Well, why not?

"Did Rano convert to Sikhism?" says Sister Imaculata.

"She added the ten Sikh gurus and their holy book to the Hindu pantheon," says Anu. "Now she's a Hindu-Sikh." Just as Anu is a Hindu-Christian, but Sister Imaculata may not understand that.

"You're almost thirty now—you must have been married," the nun says. "If not, you must be one of the very few single women your age left in India. Excepting widows and abandoned wives, I mean."

"I was married. But Father Pashan says canon law doesn't recognize my marriage to a non-Christian."

"Hmmm. He means a marriage between a Christian and a Hindu. Most marriages in India are between non-Christians, and the Church doesn't consider those invalid. When you married, you were both Hindus, surely."

"Yes, Sister. But . . ." Anu dips into her purse for her special dispensation order.

Imaculata holds her reading glasses halfway between her eyes and the dispensation, lowers them and looks at Anu. "And are you legally divorced?"

"Yes," says Anu, and is instantly struck with guilt. She is mentally divorced, but not *legally* divorced. She may not be technically divorced for years. But there's no going back without changing Sister Imaculata's impression of her.

"Find a safe place to stay," Mrs. Nadkarni said, *"and not with your family."*

The divorce action will continue for years. Anu's savings account at the bank where Sharad Uncle works, now a substantial amount thanks to the power of compound interest, will be used to pay Mrs. Nadkarni to appear at court hearings on her behalf.

"Children?" Imaculata is asking.

"One. My daughter, Chetna." Soft cheeks, those bow-lips just like Vikas's. The little girl fills Anu's vision. Her laugh, her high-pitched voice runs through Anu's head and recedes, leaving her hollow with loss.

"And where is she?" Imaculata looks around as if the child might be hiding somewhere.

"Canada—Toronto. Rano has adopted her. You see, Rano—well, she can't have her own."

"Ah. I remember now. She asked me to pray she would have a child."

"Yes—Rano always wanted children. And it seems best for my daughter."

Does she sound uncaring? Will the child's very existence disqualify Anu from entering the convent?

Imaculata drops her gaze and closes her eyes. The pause in conversation grows from semibreve to breve. Anu begins praying too, to Lord Jesus and all the gods. Because what can Anu do if Imaculata refuses to take her in?

Imaculata opens her eyes. Anxiety ripples through Anu.

"God answers prayers in ways we least expect," says Imaculata. "Rano will be good for the child. I always liked her. Perhaps your daughter will be good for her as well. I like that children belong to all relations here, not only their parents. We were twelve, and my dear departed mother could have used a bit of co-mothering."

She puts on her glasses, writes on a notepad, then looks up. "Father Pashan has also requested a dispensation from the Bishop of Delhi for the virginity issue related to your candidacy. These days, I'm sure that won't be a problem—some of our most dedicated nuns enter our order after raising families. It's rare in India, though." She clears her throat and gazes at a spot above Anu's head.

"So. Assuming he receives authorization for you to enter your Juniorate, Anu, I will say to you what my Mother Superior said to me so long ago: If you have some glorified notion of what it means to be a nun, this is not the place for you. You have probably read novels or seen films with singing nuns, beautiful nuns, magical nuns. None of these give you the slightest idea of what it means to be a nun. You will be tested."

A boulder rises off Anu's heart. Imaculata is no longer probing but instructing.

"After five years," says Imaculata, "you can take your final vows of poverty, chastity and obedience. I emphasize obedience—which I do recall was your one failing as a student."

"Yes, Sister."

They all demand obedience—first Mumma, then Vikas and his family—let the Catholic Church do so as well. How difficult can it be to follow the teachings of Christ, the rules of the Church? She has a mind and a will, she tells herself. Both are her own again.

"In fact, let me show you something." Imaculata rises and turns to a cabinet behind her. She retrieves a large cardboard box. She beckons, and Anu peers in. Imaculata peels back tissues to reveal a starchy black mass of fabric.

"My old habit," she says, taking it up and holding it before her. It falls like a burqa, almost to her toes. "I entered the convent just before Vatican II. I wore this for two years. Today, I cannot imagine myself wearing it. But I keep it to remind myself of the nuns I've known who wore it willingly and with pride."

"Yes, Sister."

"You are asking to enter a stream in progress. It flows where it will, changes direction in its own time. You will be required to adjust."

"I'm an adjustable woman, Sister."

DAMINI

THE EMBASSY-MAN'S WIFE HAS BEGUN TO PACK. EVERY afternoon this week a white van—like the ones Madam G. sent to kidnap men for vasectomies during the Emergency—backs up to the gate just as it begins to rain. And every afternoon Khansama has splashed across the lawn carrying cardboard boxes back and forth, emptying the downstairs a room at a time. He could advise them to order the van in the mornings to avoid the rain, but then he might get a lower tip.

Mem-saab receives a note from the lady-lawyer; she reads it aloud to Damini, the way she reads the newspaper or a magazine. Aman has requested the court to restrain her from renting the downstairs "until a family understanding has been arrived at." The judge has granted his request.

"What will I live on?"

"You are a rich woman, Mem-saab. You have money at Punjab National Bank."

"But that is stridhan—just mine on paper, for my lifetime. I use only a little for my needs, Amma."

Like Damini, Mem-saab was taught widows hold their husband's wealth in trust for their sons, that a woman's bhagya dictates if men be kind. But this is Kalyug, and in this eon of greed her men have forgotten *their* duty to be kind to their mother.

"Mem-saab, your husband would not want you to live in poverty. Poverty is for women like me—we are accustomed to it. Besides . . ." and here Damini performs a joker's mock pout like Amitabh Bachhan in the movies, "if you become poor I'll become even poorer. If you get Dipreyshun, I will get even more Dipreyshun."

Mem-saab manages a smile, and says, "Don't worry, Amma. It is my duty to look after you." In Punjabi, the language her mother spoke, and Damini's too, her words sound sweeter, more intimate.

Damini brings her palms together and raises them high to her forehead. She calls on all her gods to bless Mem-saab. She mouths the song "Dum Maro Dum," lip-syncing to invisible music like the actress Zeenat Aman, then prances across the room tossing her dupatta back and forth like Helen the Vamp. In total silence, she enacts slapstick from the movie *Johnny Mera Naam*, then whirls and simpers like Rekha in *Umrao Jaan*. In gestures that have no high and low, no he or she, Damini can reach Mem-saab's blood memories.

If only Mem-saab could hear all the voices she has inside her. Damini can even mimic Mem-saab's tone, which bounces up and downhill because she cannot hear it. Sometimes she even uses that voice to give herself orders.

A laugh—finally!—Mem-saab laughed a real laugh.

Damini turns on all the lights and lamps in the room, to remind Mem-saab: though she cannot hear, she can still see.

This is my role in the movie of her life.

August 1994

A KRISHNA-BLUE NIGHT SHARES HIS SKY WITH THE MOON. Damini wraps them away behind curtains; the deaf must banish all light to find sleep. She turns off the TV and its news of flag-hoisting ceremonies, speeches, marches and rallies for Independence Day.

August heat coils round Mem-saab's bed. Both the air conditioner and the fan are stilled by another municipal power cut, the third in the three days since the restraining order. Still Mem-saab complains she is cold—so cold. Damini brings her sleeping pills and shawls and then blankets, but she can find no rest, no peace.

Mem-saab cries that a train is roaring through her head. Damini flicks a flashlight on and points it at her own lips to tell her that is impossible. It's good that Mem-saab cannot hear Aman or Kiran's party laughter or the tumult in her candlelit drawing-room.

At dawn, Damini brings a glass of warm water with lemon juice and honey, as she did for Mem-saab's sons when they had fevers.

Mem-saab asks for more pills. Damini brings the light blue tin with its picture of Durga Devi, the eight-armed many-weaponed goddess astride a lion. "Are you sure you should . . . ?" she mouths, knitting her brows and raising them.

Mem-saab turns her head away and closes her eyes till Damini gives in.

Mem-saab tears at the plastic wrapping of the pills, trying to find the kernel. She holds them in her palm, examining the red, pink and white granules in the capsule-skin as though trying to fathom their power. She lifts one to her mouth, sets it delicately within the fold of her lower lip.

She turns to Damini and asks for water, and Damini offers the silver glass. She watches the kernel pass Mem-saab's throat, then another and another. Mem-saab's head is tilted upwards, eyes closed as if in prayer. Damini has never seen her taking so many pills, but then she has never been so sick.

When the pills are gone, Damini waits a moment with her.

Mem-saab hands the silver glass back and drops the capsule wrappings in Damini's upturned hands. Silver foil and plastic with English writing on the back. Letters that sit squat, round and comfortable, unlike Gurmukhi and Devanagari letters, which hang like kameezes fluttering on a clothesline.

Mem-saab lies back and closes her eyes.

"Shall I bring oil for your massage, Mem-saab?"

"Not today, Amma. Stay with me."

I am getting too old for such sleepless nights.

Damini takes her place on her foot-carpet. She takes Mem-saab's soft hand in her calloused ones and begins to rub gently. "I am with you, Mem-saab, Amma is here. I am with you, na. I am here. Amma is here." She recites the Sukhmani prayer in ancient Punjabi, then enters the suspended time of the *Bhagvad Gita*, reciting in Sanskrit . . .

A dying fragrance from the kitchen recalls the turmeric Damini rubbed on her Leela's arms before she entrusted her daughter to Chunilal. Damini has two grandchildren, but at this moment, she cannot recall their faces. Sleep-summoned images dance across her inner eye: Suresh's long lashes—or were those Timcu's? Sardar-saab's haughty gaze, Aman's eyes downcast before it. Fragments of soft chapati fall from Aman's hands and shrivel before Damini can reach them. Her tongue seems afire with hot chilies. If she does speak, in which language of the few she can speak, will anyone listen to her?

People's voices in her ears. *Aman, shouting, "Damini-amma, tell her she has made a mistake . . ." Kiran shrieking: "You fool!" because I cannot read English. The lady-lawyer: "Be strong. I will try to help you." Loveleen's voice: "Daddy says you are nobody . . ." Khansama: "You too are becoming deaf . . ."*

I am becoming deaf, too.

There is silence. Inert silence—a constant silence she thought only Mem-saab had ever known.

Damini stops massaging. Mem-saab's arm droops, heavy over the curve of the bed. She puts her hands to her ears. She shakes her head. She hears no sound. There is no sound.

No breath, no sound.

Peels of Mem-saab's pills scatter from Damini's lap as she rises.

She is weeping. She must not weep. *Krishna, Ganesh, Durga Devi, Vaheguru, Guru Tegh Bahadur . . . someone . . . a poor woman begs you, give me strength.* How could she have let her spirit wander in dream? How could she have let Mem-saab be alone as she went to her next life?

Damini brings Mem-saab's kajal pencils and draws her eyebrows, dark above her closed eyes. She brings colour for her cheeks and lipstick to make her lips hibiscus-red. She takes Mem-saab's hair in her hands, hair the colour of spent fire-coals, and she braids it for her though she is a widow.

When she is beautiful, Damini covers her face.

"Begin your journey, Mem-saab," she says aloud, in case Mem-saab's spirit, waiting for cremation in the plane of prêt-lok with all the other spirits, has gained the power to hear.

But even if Damini had been awake, even if Aman were the best son in the world and at his mother's side, you are alone when Yama the green-skinned god comes for you.

Damini washes her hands, using water sparingly from Mem-saab's bathroom, till she remembers Mem-saab doesn't need water anymore. And Mem-saab no longer needs a pair of ears.

DAMINI

SIX DAYS AFTER MEM-SAAB'S PASSING, MORNING IS ripening from a mango-blush sky. Across the market, the narrow caverns of shop stalls are still closed, their rippling silver garage doors padlocked to the ground. Only a flower-seller plies his cart, offering marigold and rose garlands for Lord Ganesh. But Damini doesn't even glance at the temple as she alights from Mem-saab's car.

Lord Ganesh is deafer than Mem-saab ever was, and today she refuses to spend a single rupee on a god like him—or Shiv, or Krishna, or Vishnu. Sky gods have forgotten ordinary people like Damini, these days. They don't deserve bowing or praises or invoking them with mantras. But what can you expect? It's many centuries since they were human.

Still—first they took her kind, hardworking Piara Singh when she was only twenty and left her a widow, and now they have taken away her almost-sister, her mistress for the past thirty years. And how can Damini know if Amanjit and Kiran drove Mem-saab to take those pills, or if she made a mistake and took too many, or if she wanted to take them?

Zahir Sheikh lifts her canvas bedroll and khaki shoulder bag from the trunk and carries them to a row of scooter-rickshaws parked beneath a mango tree.

Like Khansama, Mem-saab's driver is staying to serve Aman, as if he were an inherited chair or table—how can either do any different? They have children to support and Aman needs their skills.

"Khuda Hafiz," he says, in his courtly Muslim way.

Damini makes a quick namaste and they exchange polite wishes to meet again if it be written in their bhagyas. A promise to phone if ever she is in need. And someone she has known almost ten years vanishes.

Damini sits down on her bedroll for a moment, the mango tree at her back. Deep breaths will keep her tears within. Sometimes a woman needs to be accompanied just a little further.

She would have liked to accompany Mem-saab a little farther, at least to the cremation ground. All Damini could do was wash Mem-saab one last time, and massage her with sandalwood paste and turmeric.

Mothers, daughters, sisters, daughters-in-law, friends—all these are useless at the hour of cremation. Only sons can light a funeral pyre, and lead a parent's soul to the path of the sun, that path of the gods on the way to brahman.

The *Bhagvad Gita* says, "For death is certain to one who is born; to one who is dead, birth is certain; therefore, thou shalt not grieve for what is unavoidable." But how can she not grieve?

Damini visited Lakshmi Devi, serene in her temple, and tried to send her wishes with Mem-saab. But those wishes didn't know where they were going. When Damini tried to see Mem-saab's cremation chamber with her soul's eye, all she saw was a place like abroad, where shadow people exist in darkness while she moves in sunlight, and where even the names of the gods are forgotten.

If only Timcu hadn't told her Mem-saab's cremation was nothing like the ones in movies, or her husband Piara Singh's so many years ago. Nowadays in Delhi and other cities, he explained, it's done with electricity. A father is put in a box and his eldest son presses a button and the flowers of his ashes come out in a few hours. A mother is put in a box and her youngest son presses a button and the flowers of her ashes come out in a few hours. And the person who has no sons—he or she must find a brother, an uncle, a nephew, some man to help or their souls will always wander without rest. So, he said, Mem-saab was lucky Aman had moved to Delhi to look after her.

Timcu had arrived the day after the cremation, without his gora wife or Mem-saab's Canadian grandchildren. India is too hot, crowded and dirty for them, he said. He was staying a week, but brought enough baggage for months and moved into the Embassy-man's vacated residence. All he did was loud talk-talk in English with Aman. "Sell the house . . . pay me my share . . . sell it . . . pay me my share." How could Damini interrupt their haggling to ask whether the goddess of fire received your soul more kindly if your son pressed a button or if he applied a flaming torch to your pyre?

Surprisingly, Kiran raised no objection when a few hours before the body was taken away for cremation, Damini lit cotton wicks in shell-shaped clay diyas and placed them all around Mem-saab, as if she were celebrating Diwali. Maybe Kiran also remembered how much Mem-saab loved light.

Maybe Kiran was celebrating because Mem-saab's lawsuit died alongside Mem-saab.

And on the fifth day, after the final prayers were said and all the mourners were gone, it was Kiran who gave Damini her last pay and a bonus for her years of service—far more than Damini expected. And she also gave her the smooth steel kara Mem-saab always wore on her right wrist, a beige everyday shawl, a thick brown shawl, a grey cotton salwar-kameez and a white one that Mem-saab had worn to bed a few times. Kiran ordered Khansama to help Damini pack her bedroll and shoulder bag, and asked the driver to take Damini as far as the market.

The question of her staying on did not arise—it was the Dettol, it was the broken brassieres. It was the brown triangle Damini burned on the front of Kiran's best silk kameez the night Mem-saab's atman began its journey again. It could be her age; Kiran didn't want to be responsible if she got sick.

Or maybe it was that Damini had noticed the black and grey photo of an unfamiliar man tucked in Kirin's dresser drawer and asked Kiran who in her family had cut his hair and did not wear a turban?

Or it was that Damini can only understand English, not speak it. Or that Kiran doesn't want a maidservant who can understand any English. Or maybe it was that Kiran does whatever Amanjit wants done, that's all.

Sardar-saab would never have let Damini leave without asking where she was going, or how she would live, or whether she had a man to escort her while travelling. He would have provided her with a pension or a gift of saleable jewellery for her years of service. He would have told her to bring Suresh before him and formally entrusted Damini into the care of her son. He would know it was his duty to look after all women from his village, and found her another job.

Damini should have asked Aman if she could stay on. Maybe Damini could have asked Kiran to find her another position with a saab-type family like this one. But why should she have to ask for what Kiran should have offered?

Always too proud. Too much ego, her father always said. Even at this age, she could end up selling her body in a brothel somewhere.

Never!

But everything in the last few days is happening so suddenly, Damini keeps having to stop and breathe. She must stop turning to Mem-saab and repeating what everyone says. Mem-saab isn't here.

Of course, she has with great confidence told Kiran that Suresh will look after her, but a scream of panic is rising inside her as if she were a child just arrived in the world. She called the factory number twice, and left messages, but maybe the woman with the air-conditioned voice never told Suresh.

A rain-soaked branch brushes her shoulder, a black insect dangles and wriggles a few inches from her cheek. A caterpillar is sprouting from its armoured cocoon, splitting its skin. It too has no choice but to change.

Damini should be thinking of her future, not the past. Her bhagya is good—she survived when no one wanted her, and has never had to sell this body. She isn't like Mem-saab. She isn't like her own mother. Both had Dipreyshun. Damini doesn't get Dipreyshun. She is accustomed to work, has a sound heart, and is still young. When she was younger, she was never so afraid of change.

But what is my role now, and in the movie of whose life?

If Mem-saab were here, Damini would tell her that neither Timcu nor Amanjit embraced her when she took her leave. If they had, Damini would have given them her blessing in memory of their original goodness, and because Mem-saab was no longer there to do so. But they know exactly what she thinks of them. And what she thinks doesn't matter. Their forefathers well-nigh owned her husband's family. They are saab-log, she is not.

Yet Loveleen had surprised her—she came running to Damini, wrapped her arms around her waist, and said a tearful goodbye.

Mem-saab's spirit came through her grandchild at that moment.

The scuffed black shoulder bag beside Damini contains three saris and two salwar-kameezes along with those Kiran gave her. And a sequined dupatta Mem-saab gave her in celebration of Timcu's wedding, the violet-blue phulkari shawl Mem-saab gave her in celebration of Aman's wedding, her plastic painted gods, a water bottle, a cloth-wrapped bundle with a stack of stuffed parathas, and a tiffin-box of mutton curry cooked by Khansama.

He didn't want any curses from an old woman.

Aman and Timcu are not planning a trip to Kartarpur where Mem-saab wanted to be strewn on the fields along with her beloved gurus. No. Both are planning to take her ashes to Hardwar and drop her off in the sacred water with everyone else and all the fish.

It isn't as if Mem-saab had expected or asked them to use sandal-wood for her cremation—so couldn't her sons have honoured that last wish? And Mem-saab often spoke of donating to build a new gurdwara in Gurkot. And for a girls' school, and a clinic, but . . .

No one listens to women's wishes.

Mem-saab might have wanted Aman to give Damini more, for instance, might even have specified her wishes in writing. But even a rich woman can't keep her promises, should the men in her family decide otherwise.

Mem-saab, may you be a human in your next life.

Damini reaches under the canvas roof of a scooter-rickshaw to shake its sleeping driver by the shoulder. She climbs in to its gold gondola and settles back in the passenger cabin.

The scooter driver stretches, yawns a "Namaste, ji."

He clambers out to hoist her bedroll into the seat beside her. He hefts her shoulder bag on top of the bedroll. He pours a soothing libation of oil into the tank, and winds a scarf about his neck with a flourish like that new actor Shahrukh Khan. He steadies the eager bounce of the scooter's green plastic-tasselled handles. "Where do you go, ji?" he shouts over the engine.

Her destination comes to Damini in a flash. "To Rashtrapati Bhavan," she says. The Presidential Palace, the Secretariat and its surrounding Houses of Parliament lie at the heart of New Delhi. Parliament is where all big decisions are made. That's where positive and negative energies resolve into intention.

Suresh is her son. She is his responsibility; this is the way.

But Suresh shares a fly-bitten servant's quarter with five other men—he has no place for her. No, this is not the time to go to Suresh. Not every son is kind to his mother in her old age—and at this moment, does she have the energy to test her own?

The scooter putt-putts around the arch of India Gate. Damini squints at the eternal flame. It's for an unknown soldier, Mem-saab once explained, "a warrior who may or may not have been of the kshatriya caste. We don't know. All we know is that he—or she—was there when his country needed him."

Suresh doesn't need her. Leela may need her, her grandchildren may need her. Some other woman like Mem-saab may need her. She must be useful.

Wind whips Damini's cheeks.

"So, today you're invited to the president's home?" the scooter-man shouts over his shoulder, as they vroom down the ceremonial boulevard.

"What's it to you if I am?" Damini retorts. Every man in this city must volunteer his opinion about where a woman is going, where she should be, where she should live . . . maybe she *should* go and ask President Shankar Dayal Sharma where can a woman like her live in old age? Maybe he can tell her how to live without an income, without begging, or selling her body.

Leela lives in Damini's old home. The house she and Piara Singh built stone by stone with their own hands for his parents and themselves. The house Damini no longer owns, that became Leela's dowry. Damini's inner ear conjures up Leela's warm-toned voice, honed on mountain ridges. Her little girl who danced and sang as if blessed by snakes. In all of Gurkot, Leela is one of few women her age who lives alone for long periods. Chunilal plies a truck through the Himalayan passes, rarely going as far south as Delhi. He comes home monthly, for a few days at a time, and leaves Leela his gun to scare away monkeys.

Leela is strong today because I left her in the village with her grandmother. Everyone said she would grow up wild, but I could see no other way.

If she goes to Leela, there will be scornful comments in the village about a woman who takes from a daughter's family, just as there were hurtful comments fifteen years ago when Chunilal came to live in his wife's village. "Not our reeti," said the villagers of Gurkot. Not our way.

They said Chunilal should have taken Leela away to his parents' home to live with his elder brothers. And Suresh, who was only sixteen at the time, said dowry is illegal and Chunilal shouldn't have asked for one, and that Chunilal had taken Suresh's patrimony. But Chunilal just laughed and said a trucker lives anywhere.

Damini's scootie passes stacks of dismantled tents, flagpoles and crowd barriers that had been erected for Independence Day celebrations and nears the crossing at the base of Raisina Hill. Leaning out, she can see the massive red stone ramparts and cupula domes of the Presidential Palace. At the centre of the intersection, the Dancing Policeman stands on his traffic island. As Damini's scootie approaches, he snaps to, both arms extended in perfect Kathak alignment, palms up. Pataka mudra: Stop.

Living with a daughter, taking from a daughter.

She can't live with Leela.

The Dancing Policeman holds his position, with a brilliant smile, for more than three minutes, though it's still so early, only 6 a.m., that Damini's scootie is one of the few vehicles at the intersection. Then one forearm swings up and drops across his chest. His head moves left with a roll of his eyes, then right with an eye roll in that direction. His hands rotate slowly till the very last instant, when his thumbs snap up. Ardhachandra mudra: Go.

Damini can tell people it is only temporary.

The three-wheeler advances across the huge expanse of Victory Square toward the palace.

The Dancing Policeman changes position again. Stop.

The scootie rocks back on its hind wheels like a reined-in pony.

How will she contribute? She must. She must pay for taking from a daughter's family.

Her widow's pension is two hundred rupees a month and she has her bonus after so many years' work. Paying will also save face for Suresh.

The Dancing Policeman changes his pose again. Go.

The scooter advances.

When has she ever had a chance to be with Leela? She has seen Suresh in Delhi over the years, but Chunilal has never brought Leela to the city. Damini saw her grandchildren at birth when she went to help Leela with their deliveries, and on her visits to Gurkot with Mem-saab. Leela's baby girl, Kamna, is fourteen now, and her boy, Mohan, twelve.

Damini has been among too many walls and too few windows lately; her inner body feels shrunken and withered. Her blood is tied to the depths and heights of the sacred Himalayas. There the devtas and devis—earth gods, gods of the hills—may heal her.

The black and yellow scootie zooms up Raisina Hill like a bee about to sting the mammoth red sandstone face of the Presidential Palace. Damini reaches out and taps the driver on his shoulder.

"To the railway station," she shouts.

The scooter-man grumbles louder than the engine-din, but veers into a sharp U-turn, and returns downhill. This time, the Dancing Policeman's hands and arms are in position to guide Damini down Janpath, the People's Way. Damini braces against her bedroll.

Leela will be surprised to see her.

PART III

Deeds not Words

ST. IGNATIUS OF LOYOLA

August 1994

DAMINI

SINCE NO ONE IN DAMINI'S FAMILY KNOWS SHE IS coming and no one in her almost-family now wants her to return, she has all the time in the world to get a railway ticket. But even at this early hour, to buy an unreserved third class ticket she must queue and push and shove, as about fifty people are doing before a ticket counter in a corner of the station.

Damini shoulders her bag, clutches her ticket money, and uses her bedroll as battering ram through the press and hubbub of sweaty men already in the queue. She must make the 8 a.m. train. An elbow pokes her breast, a shoulder presses against her ear, a bony arm is wedged into her lower back. An hour later, she is no nearer the counter. And now a man returning with his ticket pushes past so hard he swivels her around to face the rest of the crowd.

"Ladies line here," she shouts, with sudden inspiration.

The wriggling mass before her stops for an instant as three women slap away pinching fingers, glare at unrepentant men, and extricate themselves. Damini, now first in the ladies line, bangs on the glass of the ticket agent with her fist—"Ladies first!"

The agent doesn't look up, but two fingertips appear beneath the small plastic arch, and her money disappears. Damini waits, her eye travelling to a large pink poster on the wall. The three

143

women queuing behind her draw closer against the mass of men.

A woman in a sari is sitting on a European-style chair. One bare foot touches the floor, one rests on a footstool. She's facing a TV, and a couple of pages of a newspaper have fallen on the floor beside her, but there she sits, letting the papers lie on the floor. There's an empty glass on the floor too, but she's not reaching to pick it up. There are two plants, but she doesn't seem to notice how dark and parched they are. *Lazy woman.*

On a low table beside the woman is a cup. It must be full of tea. The woman's chin is raised. She's smiling as if enjoying herself. *Saab-log. English-speaking woman.*

No, there's a book in her hand, and she's reading in Hindi because Damini can just make out Devanagari script. And her cast off shoes are sandals, not high heels. The women behind her follow her gaze, and two of them begin to giggle.

"A woman with nothing to do but drink chai, put her feet up, and read books and magazines—*khee, khee!* This cannot be," says the one in the magenta sari.

"Look," says the other in the green and mustard print salwar-ka-meez. "Must be having two-three children by now. Still she's laughing—how embarrassing for her husband."

The third woman looks too tired to care.

The fingertips appear again, this time pushing a third class ticket out to Damini. She snatches it and uses her bedroll again to fight her way out of the crowd.

Why carry her own bedroll and shoulder bag to the train when there are strong young men around? She spots a good-natured-looking man about Suresh's age, who doesn't look as if he speaks English or is a saab. She calls him son and asks for help. He seems amused or bemused by his sudden adoption, and from respect for an elder, carries both all the way past the air-conditioned first- and second-class sleeper and chair cars to general class. He even hoists her luggage inside, leaving with only her heartfelt blessings as payment.

Inside the carriage, Damini slides her shoulder bag under the wooden bench. She settles herself with the bedroll at her back, drawing her knees up, encircling them with her arms so as not to take up too much space—so many are crowding their way in.

Opposite her, a bride examines her henna-curlicued hands. Then she twirls red and ivory plastic bangles about her wrists. Her groom has a droopy moustache, and sits beside her dressed in shirt and tie.

Damini congratulates the bride, who appears too shy to respond. The groom informs her they are going to Shimla for a honeymoon.

Young couples need to go somewhere the moon is sweet. For us, everywhere the moon shone was sweet.

A South Indian man closer to Damini's age opens a chai Thermos wedged between his knees and unwraps a packet of Parle biscuits. Four hardy-looking men a few years older than Suresh are arguing in Maithili. They must be going north looking for work.

Three little boys surround the woman in the magenta sari from the ladies line; she lets everyone know she is on her way to meet her husband. The woman in the green and mustard print salwar-ka-meez has spread her bedroll on the floor between two benches. She lies down and begins patting her infant to sleep. A grey-bearded man wearing a round Himachali hat and carrying a pilgrim's staff has closed his eyes in the hubbub to meditate himself into peace-filled detachment.

At the compartment door, a beggar cocks his head at the passengers and raises milk-white sockets; he is cataract-blind. Damini's rupee coin passes from passenger to passenger, into his outstretched bowl. Next come three hijras, giving passengers a second opportunity to improve their karmas. The transvestites wheedle and cajole, and make lewd gestures and movements at those who ignore them. If she hadn't been born purely woman in this life, she might have been given into their keeping and joined them in begging. That might be more humiliating than going to live with a daughter. Not as humiliating as selling your body.

Damini donates a five-rupee coin.

The air is vibrating with heat at eight o'clock when the train moves reluctantly from the station. Soon it's chugging and swaying past the outskirts of Delhi, then north, its movement wicking sweat from Damini's skin. A ticket inspector seals the third class carriage off from the rest of the train.

Outside the window, men and women carrying litre-size mugs and pots are emerging from a sprawl of tarpaulin-covered huts, on their way to relieve themselves along with dogs and cats behind rubbish heaps, and in fields. Damini will have to re-accustom herself to that. And she may have to give up her toothbrush for a datun-twig and her bra for a choli in case women in Gurkot think she's putting on airs.

Washermen slap sheets and saris against stone. Vendors are mounting bicycles, filling tricycle-carts, loading handcarts and honing their penetrating cries. Two serious-looking boys in crisp tericot uniforms stand at a bus stop.

A group of girls in navy salwar-kameezes, white dupattas draped across their necks, file into a government school. A couple of boys run barefoot, chasing bicycle wheels so close alongside the train she can see their teeth flash as they laugh. Two boys in shorts—about six years old—are helping men unload a truck. They balance shiny machine parts on their heads, and become specks as the train races forwards.

The city gives way to mud villages, and fields turning a lush green in the monsoon. Damini turns away from the window.

A man seated on the next bench, wearing a white pyjama kurta, looks ordinary yet somehow familiar—she realizes he resembles her father. The thought brings her father's spirit, and a moment later, he's sitting cross-legged before her, picking at paan-stained teeth, his chin cupped on the heel of one hand, the other forearm resting across his knee. Seventy years old, and still no son. He tried valiantly to the end, though, dying in the arms of a twenty-year-old wife bought from a smaller village—Damini never met her. His spirit is restless because his pyre was lit by his brother. It reveals itself whenever she asks, and even sometimes when she doesn't.

Whoever heard of a woman living with her daughter, says his spirit. *Did your mother teach you this? Because I didn't.*

True. When he died last year her father had never visited her or her sisters' homes for more than a few hours. When he did, he would only take water.

It is only for a while, she tells him.

Ha! You could become comfortable and forget you are a guest. Then what will people say?

They will say I wanted to see my daughter.

No, they will say, this is a family who takes from their daughters.

He's still the family guardian; it's his job to warn her. As always, he wants his fears to become hers. Respect for an elder compels her to listen. He carried out his duty, paying for four daughters' weddings on the erratic income of a small-town wholesale flower-seller.

Always, he knew everything—or pretended he did.

And now her mother is sitting at the other end of the bench, in that indigo-sprigged sari she wore to her self-cremation. Her covered head is turned away. Is she ashamed? Weeping? Angry? Who can tell? Her mother's spirit is younger, and will never ascend beyond the prêt-lok, so it is often visible. She should advise Damini but she is as silent as she was when she had a body, that body that bore so many daughters and walked so many miles each day for water.

You were always willful, says her father. *Because you were the youngest.*

And Damini explains why she needs, why she wants, telling them what has happened.

Yehi to baat hai. Damini's father wags his forefinger before Damini's closed eyes. *Always you want, just like your sisters.*

What did I want? she challenges. Chai, dal and roti, a place to sleep, a kind word, a beedi once in a while. Safety in my old age.

Too-too much you want, says her father.

Didn't you want such things when you were alive? Why shouldn't I have such wishes too? And where else can I go—your village? It's no longer mine. It was not mine from the day you told me not to become too fond of it because I would be leaving as soon as you could arrange my marriage. It's no longer mine since you broke the twig at my wedding and gave me to my husband.

Your uncle is there, maybe he can . . .

I have not seen my uncle in years. When you died, he never gave me or my sisters one paisa—said there was no police or power to make him give us anything.

Her mother seems to be gazing at the distant mountains. She always wanted to be elsewhere.

Where are you, now, mata-ji?

But of course, her mother's spirit doesn't reply—can't reply—to such questions. And Damini has more. The same she will ask Memsaab's spirit when it reveals itself.

Was it an accident, or was it your wish? Did you do what you felt everyone wanted? Why was there only one way? Could you not find any other way?

But she does not want to know the answers right now. Maybe someday.

Some Krishna-inspired musician is playing the flute in the next bogey—how amazingly beautiful is each note. Nothing like filum songs that are sung by boys and girls who are smitten with love even before they're married.

I command you to listen to me, her father's spirit interrupts. *Return to our village; your uncle will do his duty.*

If I went grovelling to him, I would just become his servant, Damini tells him. I've been a servant for thirty years. I will find something better, with your blessings or without. Her father subsides into hurt silence. But whether she closes her eyes or opens them he doesn't go away; he still has something left to tell her.

Steel giants stride past the tracks, carrying their load of current downhill to cities hungry for power. Piara Singh used to know each pylon, from below and above. An electrician, he was climbing one of those ladders to the sky, providing a connection for those without connections, trying to bring a little light to a tiny village, when the gods struck him down for his temerity. Damini has the khaki envelope they found in his pocket. She has never spent the three hundred rupees he was bribed. His spirit will come too, sometime. He knows her intentions, knows her so well.

The young bride's eyes are closed, her head rests on her husband's shoulder, and his on her head.

How lucky she is.

Damini gazes through her parents at the reclining torso of the Shivalik Hills. They seem to loom larger than five years ago.

Does her father know beauty now? The flowers he sold to temple-goers were just names and prices for him when he was in the physical world. When she was a little girl, if she found a single date or coconut she'd place it on her father's hammock chair. Never did he mention her gifts.

Oh, she knows—he didn't want to feel affection for a daughter who would be leaving him as soon as marriage turned her into a woman. Loving a daughter, he used to say, was like watering your neighbour's garden. Unlike other fathers, he never beat her—maybe because she never did anything that might bring shame to his name. Instead he allowed her go to school till she was fourteen, almost to the week before her wedding. Without the gift of that schooling she couldn't have written messages in Hindi and Punjabi for Mem-saab, and Sardar-saab wouldn't have hired her.

Now her father's second wife is a widow. And without even one son for her old age. Can she read and write in any language? Mem-saab used to say a woman who can read and write can always do and learn enough to feed herself. And one who can act and tell stories may find new work. But still—her father's widow is only twenty, as Damini was when Piara Singh died.

At twenty, Damini could have become a living ghost.

Dayan! whispered villagers, calling her a witch for bringing her husband terrible luck.

And when Damini claimed a share of the land from her brothers-in-law for Suresh, they were outraged. *Haq-lene-wali!* they called her, for asserting her rights.

At first they said Damini could live with her in-laws. But then they said an astrologer had foretold that if even one square metre of land was given to Suresh, it would be lost to the family forever. Astrologers! Who believes them? And then they warned that Damini was unlucky. They said more accidents could happen. So Damini's mother-in-law, Ramkali Bai, said, "Damini, better that you leave us."

So it was that she left her children in Gurkot and made her home with Mem-saab in the city. For that opportunity, she will always be grateful to Sardar-saab—a Qutb Minar towering above other men—who gave a widow a second chance.

Her father looks up—words have arrived. *You should have planned for this, knowing Aman, knowing Timcu. You should have . . .*

Planning is for saab-log, she tells her father. Can I predict my life as they can? And why didn't *you* come and tell me what was going to happen, ji? Can my third eye see everything? If you can't even come in a dream and tell me something will happen, how can I plan?

Damini had imagined riots, floods, famine, sickness and drought, but not this. But now that she is on this train of events, she must go where it is going.

"Kalka! Kalka Station!" A railway employee appears at the door between carriages.

Damini has arrived at the end of the line, in a city baking in the shade of the foothills. From the window she sees porters—gunny-sack pads over their kurta-clad backs—besieging first- and second-class carriages. One has grabbed a suitcase before its owner can fix a price and is arguing to shame the passenger into payment.

Her father, her mother? Their spirit-energy has faded.

The bridegroom rises and collects the couple's luggage.

"May you be the mother of a hundred sons," Damini says to the bride as she passes. The centuries-old blessing is powerful enough to serve this shy, smiling girl-woman as well.

The woman in the magenta sari gathers her brood, smiling farewell as she transfers a sleeping boy to her waiting husband's arms. The woman in the green and mustard print kameez covers her head with her dupatta, draping a corner over her infant's face to fend off mosquitoes, then steps onto the platform. The muggy warmth of the platform in the midday sun envelopes Damini.

The man who resembled Damini's father helps his karma by carrying Damini's bedroll and shoulder bag from the train. He even guards her luggage amid the jostling sweaty crowd while she uses the station restroom—Damini sends his mother mental energy as blessing for raising him well, and brings her palms together to thank him.

The cloth-bundle of parathas and mutton curry Khansama provided as his parting gift should be saved for her Leela and her family—they can so rarely afford meat. She can't arrive empty-handed. In fact, she should arrive bearing gifts.

She browses the stalls. A peacock-feather hand-fan for Leela.

The shopkeeper proffers a tray of goldthread bracelets for the Rakhi festival tomorrow. Damini shakes her head, "I have no brothers." No brothers on whom she can tie a rakhi. No brothers to whom she can give milk sweets. No brothers to whom she can turn instead of going to a son or daughter. Damini's misfortune, and her mother's failure. She moves to the next stall to avoid his look of pity.

Something for Chunilal, but what?

A spider-limbed man squats amid stacks of books and magazines and urges her to purchase his bestseller in Hindi. A gora with a vertical bar of a moustache gazes from its cover, under an untranslated title, *Mein Kampf*—the bookseller says it may mean "my trembling."

Trembling is not a good sign in a man, unless a god is vibrating him. This one looks angry and powerful. Asuras could be vibrating through him—a demon-man.

Damini buys a carved metal rod that Chunilal can use to thread cords through his pyjama waistbands. And for thirty rupees, a cassette with songs from the hit movie *Hum Aapke Hain Koun* for him to play in his truck.

For Kamna, who adores the *khun-khun* sound of glass bangles, she buys a maroon pair studded with paste diamonds—they sparkle enough to pass for real in a dowry. For Mohan, a bamboo flute in honour of Lord Krishna. Maybe he can learn to play.

Chai and a suntra orange cost five whole rupees at the chai-stall.

"Only chai," she calls to the man simmering tea leaves. Anyway, it's best not to eat before a bus ride through the Himalayas. She checks her bedroll, to make sure she has her water bottle.

Two women who also seem to be travelling without relatives to accompany or greet them are standing a few feet away, waiting in an imaginary queue for tea. Damini recalls seeing them emerge from a second-class carriage. A red-shirted porter lifts their two suitcases from his head to the platform, and wipes his brow with the dangling end of his turban.

The older one is a gora, as ghost-pale as the Embassy-man. She must be a Christian from abroad. Her sashed grey frock only covers half her legs, as if she is still a girl. The younger one is Indian, but isn't dark enough to be an Indian Christian—most Indian Christians Damini has ever seen are southerners. She turns, and Damini sees the leaf-shaped reddish-brown scar that spreads across one cheek, from eye to chin.

It's the unlucky woman she saw at the lady-lawyer's office, just four weeks ago, the one with the bruises. No wonder her almond eyes dart left and right. No wonder she glances over her shoulder at the stationary train as if a demon might jump from it. She's tall—definitely

Punjabi. She's talking with the older woman in English, answering "ya-ya" and "no-no" as little Loveleen does.

She must have been very beautiful, once—definitely saab-log. She must have had an amma who pressed and pleated her frock for private school and whitened her tennis shoes with chuna every night. She probably wore a checked wool skirt in winter, the kind with the large diaper pin. She probably went to an English-medium college.

But she's wearing an unprinted grey salwar-kameez and white muslin dupatta—colours more appropriate for someone twice her age. A plain steel watch on one wrist. No bangles on the other. No henna designs, no tattoos. No nose ring, though her nose is pierced. No earrings, though her ears are pierced.

Like a widow. Like me.

No mangalsutra necklace or marriage collar, not even a wedding ring—did her husband cast her out?

The tea leaves come to a rolling boil. The tea-seller adds milk and returns the pan to the burner.

She's a Jesus-sister. Both are sisters. But they're dressed differently—old and young. No husbands, poor things.

The chai comes to second boil, the pan is removed from heat.

They don't seem unhappy, though. In fact the younger one seems excited, despite her fear.

The tea-seller pours three tan streams from his pan to the tiny glasses before him. Damini reaches for the same glass as the Indian nun, and stops. The nun stops too, gives a hesitant puff of a laugh, and reaches for the next glass in line. For a moment, guileless brown eyes gaze into Damini's. Kind, questioning eyes.

As they sip their chai, the gora nun asks—in Hindi!—where Damini is going.

"Gurkot."

"I was there a few years ago," says the gora nun, still in Hindi. "Our priest held an education camp and a few medical camps there, and our sisters served there for a few days."

Damini listens carefully, amused by the gora nun's accent and attracted by her effort.

"Now, praise be to god, a politician finally gave a permit for a paved road, and there are plans to open a permanent school and clinic there soon."

"Do you live in Gurkot?" asks the younger one.

Damini shakes her head no, then wobbles it—yes. Then again, no. A film is rising before her eyes; she looks away quickly. She doesn't know yet if she lives in Gurkot. The Indian nun doesn't press for an answer, but her large-eyed gaze seems to plunge to the core of Damini's being. She takes another sip, then turns to the tea-seller and requests three oranges. He pops them in a newspaper-bag and hands them to her. She presses one into Damini's hand.

Damini's cheeks warm—the nun must have overheard her asking how much it cost. She searches the young woman's face for any hint of condescension, but senses only the kindness most people reserve for blood relatives. Perhaps the nun's wound opened her to those of others. Maybe she too remembers Damini from the lady-lawyer's office. Damini's heart is too full to ask.

"Dhanvaad," Damini thanks her in Punjabi. She wedges the orange into the side of her bedroll and follows them through an archway.

A cream-coloured jeep is waiting for the nuns in the golden afternoon light. The driver, a Muslim, judging from his karakuli cap, stands beside it. A dignified man of about sixty with a salt and pepper goatee, he wears navy blue pants and a matching jacket with epaulets. He makes a quick namaste and loads their bags.

Damini narrows her eyes and looks around, a little unsure.

The older nun glances at Damini and then turns to her driver.

"Shafiq Sheikh, inko bus par charda do." She sounds accustomed to giving orders. She nods farewell to Damini and gets in the jeep. The driver approaches Damini, and reaches for her shoulder bag. He slings Damini's bedroll over his shoulder, as if he was ten years younger than her, and beckons for her to follow.

Surprised, Damini rushes after him down the street to the ele-
phantine horde of trucks and buses gathered at a crescent-shaped
motor stand. Then she stops and turns to give the nuns a parting
wave and smile.

The Shimla-bound bus is not scheduled to leave for an hour, but
it's already half-filled with passengers and if she doesn't take her seat
now, she might have to stand all the way. While she buys a ticket,
Shafiq Sheikh brings himself merit by climbing the ladder to the roof
of the bus and tying her luggage to it. She nods farewell and he trots
off down the street, back to the nuns' jeep. A few minutes later, the
jeep passes by. The younger nun looks up and smiles as if Damini is
no longer a stranger.

Christians are good-hearted people.

Grey clouds arrive, collide and pucker. Rain patters on the roof.
Damini reaches the corner of her dupatta through the window,
wetting it to wipe her cheeks and forehead. Then her cupped hand
for a little rain to drink.

The cooling shower is a blessing from the gods.

The bus fills up with people and belongings, then takes on more.
Two hours later, a singer who perfectly imitates Lata Mangeshkar
strikes up a song on the bus speakers. "Which movie, which movie?"
Damini asks, igniting energetic debate among the passengers.

Phir Teri Kahani Yaad Aayee. Again I remember your story. The
driver settles it. The bus lumbers forward with its aluminium sides
vibrating and begins to wind its way uphill.

En route to Shimla
August 1994

ANU

THE WOMAN WITH THE HENNA-ORANGE HAIR AND LONELY
look in her eyes seemed familiar, but Anu, sitting in the back seat of
the convent jeep beside Sister Imaculata, can't place her. She breathes
a prayer for the woman to find her way safely to Gurkot.

The jeep heads north as if aligned with Anu's inner compass. Pure
cool mountain air spreads like a benediction in her lungs. Healing is
in these mountains, waiting to be found in contemplation, meditation, silence and service to others. She shouldn't read as the jeep loops
its way through the hills, but the letter is from Rano. Dot-matrix text
jumps and blurs on preprinted flowered paper.

*I've enrolled Chetna in a summer camp for children of landed immigrants,
and the local Sikh school in September. Not that Jatin and his family are
very observant Sikhs—remember he married Hindu me—but following
Sikh tenets, this school doesn't allow smoking. I can swallow a little religion
so that our little girl remains drug-free.*

*Most of our friends are Sikhs so they mostly have the last name Singh.
She keeps asking Singh what? She wants their caste names. Some have them,
most don't. I explained that Sikhs don't have castes. Or are not supposed to.*

*She actually cried when I explained she must flush the toilet after using it,
since we always have enough water for each flush. And when I explained she*

has to clean the shower after using it since we don't have sweepers, she said, "Rano Aunty, you should get a sweeper!" And then our clever puss says, "If Jatin Papa doesn't mind, let him clean it!"

Were we as young when we began to worry about getting polluted or falling to the level of sweepers? I didn't know how privileged I was by my religion, caste and class until I came to Canada.

Chetna is going through the same status shock. She came home from camp asking, "Rano mummy, is India older or younger than Canada?" In India, people get respect for being one or two months older than each other, so why not countries. I said, "Older in some ways, younger in others." She shot me her explain-how-the-world-got-this-way look.

I told her that if you believe a country is born on the date of its flag— India is older because its flag first flew in 1947, almost twenty years before the Canadian flag. And if a country is as old as its constitution, then India had one thirty years before Canada. But if a country is as old as its earliest inhabitants, India might be only five thousand years old and Canada ten thousand. And if a country is born from the wishes of its people, then India is only forty-seven and Canada is about three hundred years old. So, I said, "It's hard to say if India is older or younger than Canada." She didn't find this satisfactory—forgive me if she's scarred for life!

When Chetna questions me, I wonder if Mahatma Gandhi had agreed to dominion status for India in 1942, would there still be a statue of a queen at India Gate and would Indians be as Anglophilic as Canadians? Would we still be a dominion as Canada is? We'd all be Christianized by now.

Chetna has been taught about Laura Secord at her camp, and today we're taking her to the chocolate factory of that name. She's been making new friends by telling them that her Jatin Papa works there.

Yesterday she gave us quite a scare—we couldn't find her for three whole hours! I was beside myself till we found her hiding in a closet. She heard Jatin shouting while watching a game and thought he was angry. I can only imagine what she must have gone through with you. She misses you. I remind her that you and Bobby lived with us while you were growing up. I tell her she's lucky to have so many people who love her. Even my in-laws are *delighted with her. It helps that she speaks Punjabi, of course. My father-in-law has promised her a prize if she learns the Japji prayer by heart. I think he would like to offer me the same, but you know me—I had trouble memorizing the few words of the Gayatri Mantra.*

I feel you did the hard work of birthing this child, and we are enjoying her. I can't thank you enough, though I know how difficult it must be for you. Don't write to her too often. I'm worried it will only confuse her and delay her adjustment to us and Canada. Okay?

The letter is signed *Second Mother.*

It is difficult. Very difficult. Repeat the mantra, *It's for Chetna's sake.*

The jeep passes through the foothill town of Barog and begins the climb to Shimla. A truck crammed with bundled goods looms, spewing black smoke. The driver swears under his breath as he swings the steering wheel. He leans out, yells in Urdu, "The car going uphill has right of way!" The trucker keeps coming. A horn-blast fills the jeep like Vikas's shouting. Imaculata holds her cross to her lips, but seems otherwise quite prepared to die.

Has Anu suffered and come all this way only to be killed on the road before beginning god's work?

The jeep skids to the verge and stops. The truck thunders by. Imaculata kisses her cross again.

"If we had crashed," Anu says carefully, "would that be god's will?"

"I certainly hope not," says Imaculata. "Ask him when you get to the pearly gates, dear. And thank your guardian angel. I say give the devil credit for mishaps and let the bishops worry their heads cogitating such things." She soon nods off, missing several more near-accidents.

She must have made this journey many times.

Anu has only made it once, with Dadu and Mumma, and was too filled with the horror of Bobby's injury, coma and untimely death at the time, to feel the power of these precipices and waterfalls, these soaring blue pines.

Back to the letter, her only connection to Chetna right now—

You can't believe what a feminist icon Madam G. is here, Anu. Canadians think Indians are so enlightened because India had a woman PM years before they elected Kim Campbell. They have no idea that Madam G. let her unelected son become maharaja of India, or that she had a streak of violence in her like the grey streak in her hair. They don't know she locked away opposition leaders if they disagreed with her, or that she ordered the Indian army to enter the Golden Temple with tanks. But Sikhs in Canada certainly do. In the eighties, some Canadian Sikh guys blew up an Air India plane mostly full of Hindus as if all of us Hindus were responsible for Madam G.'s megalomania. What Indians call communalism should be called groupthink! That investigation continues, but no Sikh I know condones either Madam G.'s assassination or the bombing of 329 innocents.

But much as I enjoy the Sikh community here, I swear I'm turning into a closet Hindu. Jatin says I should ignore his sisters when they talk about "idol-worshippers" even as they wake up the Guru Granth Sahib, *put it to bed at night, circumambulate it in worship. Where do they think their rituals came from but from Hindus and Muslims? And if they really believe their book is a person, the eleventh guru, isn't that idol worship?*

Rano has predicted that Anu will be bored within days of trying to be a nun, but Rano doesn't know her anymore. Doesn't know Anu still dreams of killing her husband. That Anu could end up in prison or hanged if she . . . Who is the real Anu? How can she know when she is herself?

Several more hours of switchback driving through rain showers and flooded areas bring the jeep to the capital of Himachal State as purple shadows are gathering in the folds of the hills. Shimla—formerly Simla in the days of the British Raj.

The British viceroy moved the administration of India to this hill station every summer to escape the heat of the plains. From their

Tudor manors and offices on the central Mall Road, a few thousand Europeans bent three hundred million Indians to their will. British officers and soldiers took leave here, Victorian women promenaded on the Mall and acted at the Gaiety Theatre. And after they tore the country in three and went home, Indian refugees fled here to escape the civil war that raged across the plains. Waves of Tibetan refugees came in the fifties, to get away from the Chinese. And by the seventies, Shimla was the summer resort of the Indian elite—government officials, army officers and the landed gentry.

"The Mall Road is now called the Mehl Road," says Sister Imaculata with gentle mockery. "The Cart Road is the Caht Road." Sitting in a clamour of traffic at the main bus depot, she points uphill to a green and white Tudor building that looks on the verge of collapse over the mass of humanity and buses below. "Lord Ripon's hospital," she says. "Whenever I pass it, I think of the women doctors who were excluded from practising in England in colonial days. What courage it must have taken to book a passage to India and set up practice at that hospital."

"Lord Ripon," says Anu. "Like a god's name."

"Yes—I never remember its new Indian name. But look how it's falling apart! Most people go to Lord Snowdon's hospital on the other side of Shimla. Politicians renamed that one Indira Gandhi Memorial. But if you're a poor patient who can't bribe an official to get an appointment or a bed, or can't read the signs, it's a nightmare to navigate, whatever its name."

The coma ward at Snowdon . . . a white shirt . . . brown blood . . .

The Mall Road is for pedestrians. Only VIPs and VVIPs are allowed to drive through the state capital, so the jeep takes the lower cart road. Past the central roundabout of Chhota Shimla, Little Shimla, where two rows of shops scissor up and downhill, the jeep rumbles uphill for another half hour before it comes to the convent gates.

Here Imaculata asks the driver to stop so they can stretch their legs. She walks down the long level driveway, leading Anu past the shield emblazoned with the coat of arms of the Order and the motto of the convent. *Non nobis solum*—not for ourselves alone.

Past the basketball and tennis courts, Sister Imaculata points out St. Anne's grey stone mother house, almost a hundred years old. Then a girl's dormitory and the grey stone library, closed for the evening. Says Imaculata, pride shining in her voice, "Its holdings are on par with many private libraries in New Delhi. I pray the Good Lord doesn't take me before I see more libraries like this all across India. Not only in schools and colleges, but can you imagine if they were open to everyone?"

"Everyone who speaks English, you mean?" says Anu.

"No, I mean everyone who can read. We have Hindi books and magazines too, now. In Ireland, public libraries have books in Gaelic as well as English; we should do the same here."

"With eighteen official languages, we will need a larger library immediately," says Anu, smiling.

It is the first time she has said *we.*

Imaculata flashes a smile. "You cannot believe how I persuaded— implored—parents and alumni to donate money for this building." She gives a wry laugh. "I'm as good as a professional beggar on the streets of Delhi. I'm just more subtle and ask for larger amounts."

She leads Anu around a rickshaw circle. The driver has continued past the nave of a grey stone chapel and the jeep is parked before a statue on a red sandstone pedestal, a white figure in flowing robes. Facing the statue, several two-storey red-roofed buildings painted lemon-cream with green trim snake across the flattened knoll.

Lord Jesus's hands are raised in welcome.

"Please take the suitcases to the nuns' quarters, Shafiq Sheikh," Sister Imaculata says. She turns to Anu. "Would you like to say a prayer of thanks?"

Prayers seem appropriate after the hair-raising journey. Anu covers her head with her dupatta, dips her middle finger in the holy water font by the chapel door, crosses herself and enters. She follows Imaculata up the central aisle, which gives way to flagstones as the pews give way to dhurries.

A group of women in salwar-kameezes are sitting cross-legged on the dhurries, rocking and praying, as if in a temple. The candles are like diyas, and the fragrance of sandalwood incense accompanies her genuflection at the altar. The saints stand in their niches with offerings of incense and flowers before them, just like intercessor gods. The Order of Everlasting Hope has Indianized a bit since her schooldays.

Anu kneels in a pew and bows her head beside Sister Imaculata. She gives thanks to all the gods and to Lord Jesus, whose suffering body hangs before her.

In the refectory, Sister Imaculata shows Anu to a seat at the nun's dining table. Steel serving bowls are arrayed on a long buffet table against the wall, along with a stack of compartmented steel plates. Forks and knives are provided so Anu knows not to eat Indian-style, with her fingers.

Sister Imaculata introduces Sister Clare. Very black eyes peer from a deeply lined brown face, framed by a black wimple. Sister Clare's habit is white, the skirt of mid-calf length. Anu's cheeks warm as Sister Clare's gaze flicks to and away from her face. Sometimes she forgets the damn scar herself.

Oh dear, don't even think damn.

More nuns file in. Middle-aged Sister Roshni and Sister Lorena are wearing white saris with black sweaters, and three younger nuns are dressed in grey salwar-kameezes. They greet Sister Clare with namastes and in Hindi. Sister Clare's pidgin Hindi response sounds worse than Sister Imaculata's, and marks her as an Indian Christian.

A tall thin woman in a white salwar-kameez approaches. "Bethany," announces Sister Imaculata, "our second novice." Bethany's smile sparkles against the red-brown of her face. A fall of straight bangs over Keralan features makes her look as if she just graduated from school, but up close, she seems older—probably just graduated from college. Anu raises her hands in namaste, but Bethany offers a handshake. Her compassionate onyx-black eyes contrast with her purposeful look. The handshake is quick, as soft as the brush of a birdwing. And when it's past, Anu senses a new warmth from her.

An unnecessary test of touchability between Christian women, surely?

"This arrived for you," Bethany says, handing Anu a brown envelope festooned with Gandhi stamps and bearing Mrs. Nadkarni's return address. Anu thanks her and puts the envelope in her handbag.

"I just arrived two days ago and already I'm feeling at home," Bethany confides as they queue for red lentils and rice. She nods at two very dark nuns wearing white dresses and stockings, with nurse's caps. "Sister Rose and Sister Sarah have been so welcoming."

Anu holds her steel plate close to her chest, and nods. Sister Roshni and Sister Lorena are talking about a school play. Sisters Rose and Sarah are greeting Sisters Clare and Imaculata with utmost respect.

"I felt my calling as a little girl, in the second or third standard." Bethany's merry eyes light the dining room. "So long ago, I knew I wanted to help the poor."

"I remember you at your First Communion in Delhi, Bethany," says Sister Imaculata from the middle of the queue. "So small in the large cathedral, and filled with the love of god even at that age. I always thought you would join us after school. How is it you waited till after college?"

"I played basketball, no, Sister?"

"So?"

"So I loved wearing shorts. I thought I'd have to give them up if I became a nun."

"Silly Billy! If you play or teach basketball here, you can wear shorts. Just as if I were to go swimming, I would wear a swimsuit."

Bethany exchanges an amused glance with Anu.

"Don't be giggling, now, you two!" says Sister Imaculata. "I don't look so bad in a swimsuit. Really, we should give our students a few lectures to explain that nuns are not in the dark ages."

Sister Clare sets her plate down at the head of the table. "Hindu politicians would send protesters immediately. They'd accuse us of trying to convert Hindu girls."

"You're right, Sister." Sister Imaculata sighs as she spoons rajma beans over her rice. "As it is, our young ladies are under so much pressure to study the National Council curriculum, get good marks, get a corporate job, marry an engineer, doctor or accountant. I tell my relatives in Ireland they should come and see our classes—fifty and sixty students to a teacher. If they saw how much competition there is even to enter this school, their children might stop all their whinging and whining about too much homework."

"You young nuns are all so busy with your ministries, with teaching and healing," says Sister Clare. "You all say no time, no time. Not even time for introspection."

"Oh, no Sister," says Sister Imaculata, taking her seat at the middle of the table. "We have constant introspection. I'm forever worrying."

Anu takes her seat and unfolds her serviette on her lap as Bethany approaches the chair beside her.

"Anu, with your background, I'm sure you will really help the poor," says Sister Clare.

Is Sister Clare too old to know everyone now realizes that the word *background* is code for caste? Her compliment implies that caste decides your competence. Anu addresses her plate so as not to respond.

"Bethany, what is your full name?" Sister Clare, again.

Bethany sits down. After a pause, she says, "Valmiki."

Sister Clare nods. "You often can't tell these days, but I thought so."

Anu reddens with indignation for Bethany, and shame for Sister Clare. What would Jesus say? Sister Imaculata distracts them by leading grace. Sister Clare begins eating as soon as the prayer is over, dabbing her lips with her serviette from time to time. Bethany stares at her plate as if worms have sprouted from the rice.

"Don't you be heeding her," Imaculata whispers to Bethany. "Bit of a superiority complex." She picks up her spoon. Rajma beans add their red-brown colour to the brown rice grains.

The saucy fragrance of cumin and garam masala informs Anu she is hungry; she follows Sister Imaculata's lead. Sister Clare tips a jar of mango pickle in Anu's direction. Anu shakes her head.

"When I arrived here," Imaculata says to them all, "I thought only Hindus had caste. And I thought intermarriage meant a Christian marrying a Jewish person, or a Catholic marrying a Protestant in Belfast. Here it can mean a caste Hindu marrying a Valmiki, anywhere in the country! Now eat up, my dear—god's work is waiting."

Bethany looks up, manages a smile.

After a while, Imaculata rises. Anu isn't finished, but jumps up to help an elder.

But Imaculata says, "It's my turn," and takes Bethany's plate, Sister Clare's and her own to the kitchen, plainly demonstrating how the refectory operates without servants or the tyranny of the old over the young.

Sister Clare goes to the corner of the room and washes her hands at a small sink Anu hadn't noticed before. Anu sits down and turns to Bethany. If they were two women meeting for the first time at a party, the first question Anu would ask is, "Are you married?" and then, "How many children?" But here?

"Were you ever married?" she asks.

"No" says Bethany. "And I don't think I will ever feel married to Lord Jesus, even when I take my final vows."

"I don't remember any nun really believing she was married to Jesus," says Anu.

"I never wanted to be married," says Bethany. "I told my parents, please don't plan a wedding for me, I will join a convent."

"Were they sad when you left?"

"No, relieved. My number one sister just got married, and in a few years they'll have to marry off number three sister then number four."

The black Bake-lite phone in the nun's common room makes choking sounds as Anu dials Purnima-aunty's number after dinner. She gets through on the seventh try. "Hello, Aunty. We arrived safely. How are you?"

Purnima-aunty gives a sigh. "I'm well, I'm well. I should be editing my speech for the Cairo Conference on Population. Instead, I'm sitting here worrying about you. You know, in the old days, people would renounce everything and go live in an ashram. But only after raising a family, after all expectations were met—it's too early for you to go into sanyas."

"I could live to be a hundred and never meet everyone's expectations, Aunty."

"Want to give me a phone number?"

"No—it's best if you don't know how to reach me. Just call Mrs. Nadkarni if you need to get in touch. I don't want to cause any more trouble. I have put you through too much."

"No trouble, darling. Please, call your mother?"

"I'm about to."

And she does, listening at arm's length to Mumma's telling her how immature, short-sighted, irrational and unrealistic she is. Ungrateful for the best match any girl in Delhi ever dreamed possible. And selfish, always selfish. And how dare she create more drama by telling everyone, even her parents, to contact her through that meddling woman, that lawyer. "You're the most stubborn girl in the universe," says Mumma, making the first statement Anu can readily agree with. "I don't know how you think you're ever going to become a nun. Well, at least no one can blame me for this one."

"No one would dare blame you for anything, Mumma." A bubble of giddy laughter is rising in Anu.

"Don't give me any backchat or I'll tell your father. You have no consideration for your parents whatsoever."

After evening prayers in the chapel, Bethany shows Anu to her room on the second storey of the mother house. "I'm next door. Knock if you need anything."

Anu switches on the bedside lamp. Light coagulates, viscous and yellow under the shade, barely reaching her suitcase in the corner. She lifts it onto the bed.

But wait. First, the envelope from the lawyer. Anu pulls the straight-back wooden chair in the corner over to the bedside table and opens it.

Newspaper cuttings. Some in Hindi, some in English:

Paper Trail Points to Hindu Nationalists in Congress for Killings of Sikhs in 1984.
Bajrang Dal Hindu Patriots Take Credit for Muslim Killings in Ahmedabad in 1990.

And one of those new colour newspaper photos, with a note clipped to it. A crowd of men brandish iron trishuls, the trident of Shiva. The caption: *Swami Rudransh followers march to the Babri Masjid.*

Call me, says Mrs. Nadkarni's note.

Anu tiptoes downstairs, back to the black phone. Like most people with home offices, she probably won't mind a call at this hour. Besides, it sounded urgent. Anu gets through on the fourth try.

"Some things cannot be written down," says Mrs. Nadkarni. "When I asked about organizations to which Vikas donates, you said the Bajrang Dal."

"I did," says Anu, and waits.

"The Bajrang Dal," says Mrs. Nadkarni, "is the youth arm of the Vishwa Hindu Parishad. Both Hindutva organizations, you know. Affiliated with the Rashtriya Swayamsevak Sangh."

Anu knows of the VHP and the RSS, hardline Hindu organizations founded by the upper-caste ideologues who spawned the assassins of Mahatma Gandhi in the 1940s. Radical nationalists, they run colleges and ashrams to promote the worship of Aryan Hindu gods, Aryan history, Aryan superiority. They admire what Hitler did to the Jews and Gypsies in Europe and would like to sweep away democracy and pluralism in the same way to create a Hindu-only India.

"And?" she says.

"You could accuse Vikas of participation in the crimes of the Bajrang Dal. Standard procedure to accuse the other side of something," the lawyer says, "i.e., to fast-en up the process."

"Just a minute," says Anu.

She scans the clippings again. Could the charges be true?

Were she to accuse Vikas of participation in the crimes of Hindu jihadis it would hurt Vikas's parents. And her daughter too.

She must begin from Christian forgiveness, no matter what her lawyer counsels. This is her first challenge. The events in these cuttings are past—the people who were killed cannot be brought back. "Let it be," she tells Mrs. Nadkarni. "Membership in a group doesn't mean Vikas is personally responsible. He may not know what the swami is doing with his money."

"Up to you, Miss Lal."

To Anu's ears "Miss Lal" sounds strange—as if she is an unmarried girl again.

Back in her room, Anu stuffs the clippings back into the envelope and the envelope back in her suitcase. She unpacks a kaftan, takes off her clothes, and stands on the dhurrie beside her bed, clad only in her white bra and panties.

On her wedding night she had wanted her husband to see her like this, just as she was, and hold her close. Wanted him to feel her shakti, know it could create and nurture more than children.

Stupid, stupid Anu. Expecting the impossible.

Outside the casement window, the mountains shrug their shoulders and allow pashmina-soft snow to sift into their valleys. A plaster statue of the Madonna in a blue sari gazes from an alcove as Anu slips on her kaftan. The Blessed Virgin looks so compassionate. She too was a wife only under the law. She too knew what it is to be a mother. Was her choosing to bear Jesus a true choice? Especially if she had no alternatives? "Magnificat anima mea, Dominum . . ." says her song in the Bible. Whether pregnant by miracle or rape, she must have been terrified of what people would say. Did she ever consider an abortion? There were ways, even in her day.

Anu unpacks a small photo album, touches Chetna's cheek with her finger and lets her mind leap overseas. Does Chetna feel abandoned and alone, or as grateful as Anu was to live with Purnima-aunty rather than Mumma?

Anu places her few saris and salwar-kameezes in the dresser drawer. Then her sheet music, a book of Liszt études, and *Contemporary Solo Piano Hymns for Praise and Worship.*

She will play the piano again, and hear chant. Repetition, quiet repetition of prayer will open the connection between her heart and the bright warm light.

But how can she sing without Bobby playing his guitar?

Little brother who tried so hard to be a man. Bobby would be twenty-six if he were alive now. And if he were, Mumma might not be as wounded and Dadu wouldn't be buried in his work. Anu would be tying a rakhi-bracelet on Bobby tomorrow, and feeding him milk-sweets and he'd be renewing his promise to protect her.

Think Christian: he's not coming back. He's with Lord Jesus. Wherever that is.

Anu lies down on the thin mattress, and draws a blanket over her, turns to face the rosary on her nightstand. Her spine shifts and lengthens to match the rope-weave of the bed.

Strange not to hear Vikas stomping, raging or shouting on the phone. He can't chastise her for cutting his sandwiches lengthwise instead of obliquely, or for stacking his books horizontally instead of standing up, or for not smiling warmly enough at one of his clients. He and his mirror world are left behind.

It's strange not to feel faintly fear-sick and ready to run to the bathroom to lock herself in. She hears herself exhale in the darkness. And then truly hears the silence. She listens to her heartbeat, a half-remembered language. Her skin feels as exposed as if she were sleeping nude. For the first time since her menses began, her body doesn't belong to her family, Vikas, or Chetna. It belongs to her, and she sleeps.

In the morning, Bethany enters with new clothes for Anu, a solid white salwar and kameez, white dupatta to drape over her shoulders, and a white sweater. White for the purity and virginity of Catholic novitiates, rather than white for the mourning of Hindu widows. And a second salwar and kameez—steel grey with a white dupatta, and black sweater.

When you become Christian, you are no longer supposed to practice caste. Which means that when there's no water from the municipality, you have to fill a bucket of water yourself, and pour it down the flush. No sweeper will come and do that. Bethany also shows Anu how to clean the toilet.

If Bethany can, Anu can. Even if it makes her feel as if a film of dirt has settled over her.

"Mass in twenty minutes," Bethany says. "Then breakfast, then an hour of Delectio Divina."

It's Lectio Divina, but Delectio sounds delightful.

Anu watches from the window as her companion sister exits the nun's quarters downstairs and walks across the flagstones to the chapel. Does Bethany miss anyone as deeply as Anu misses Chetna?

Her daughter is safe, a mother cannot ask for more. Even if Anu were with Chetna, she still could not protect Chetna from every hardship and all pain, just as she couldn't protect Bobby.

When you're Christian, you die and it's over forever and no one like Vikas can find you again in a future life. When you're Christian, there's a day of judgement when Vikas will have to answer for his sins: hurting her, hurting Chetna. When you're Christian, you don't have to be his judge. Or executioner.

Ungainly flat sandals. Anu slips them on. She glances around, instinctively searching for a mirror.

No mirror. Here she will never glimpse her scar, except by accident.

Away from the mad scramble of Delhi, all that is relevant is the abiding silence, the wind piercing her body to find her soul.

Anu buttons up her sweater, runs a comb through her long black hair and braids it. She will work with the poor, help others. She will be impelled by her own spirit, her own intelligence—and guided by the Lord. She has warmth, food, safety, a spectacular vista around each corner, and Vikas is left far behind.

Her stomach growls. *Off to mass, and pray you don't faint in church.*

On the road to Gurkot village

DAMINI

DAMINI TAKES A WINDOW SEAT ON THE EARLY BUS TO Jalawaaz.

Five hours jolting through the hills yesterday. The bus had lurched left, then right on hairpin bends as it crested one mountain and circled down into a valley. It turned and turned along the low rock walls edging the road, until its motion and the body-smell of every passenger crept within Damini, and her head was spinning in fumes. Once the monsoon downpour had passed, the bus driver halted several times for swollen streams and waterfalls spilling across the road. In some sections, he slowed where avalanches pinched the road to one lane. By dusk when the bus had climbed out of the heat, it was vomit-streaked and caked with dust and exhaust and Damini had learned the words to all the film songs endlessly repeating. She spent the night recovering at Choba Shimla gurdwara just past the cool breezes and red roofs of Shimla. Another five hours today, but at least the morning breeze flowing through the bus is cool, almost chilly.

The thunder thighs of a Punjabi woman in a parrot-green and purple salwar-kameez settle into place beside her. Damini quells an urge to pull the slender ringlets dangling by the woman's pinked cheeks.

The bus comes to a halt before two massive iron gates set in concrete pillars. A man with a cloth bag of books at his hip alights and sets off on a level paved road. That driveway is built for people with cars and drivers—Vee-Eye-Pees and saab-log. Indistinct sounds of children playing rise from a cluster of English-style peaked roofs. A bell peals from the Christians' temple, Damini counts nine.

"My two cousin-brothers are in the army, and their daughters study in this convent," her seatmate points with a maroon-nailed finger. She's bursting to tell anyone, everyone—almost bursting her kameez as well.

This must be where the Jesus-sisters were going. Suresh's swami-ji says British people tried to make all the Hindus into Christians, so brave Hindus fought them and drove them from the country. Which is not the story of non-violent struggle she heard from her father, who actually lived through 1947, but maybe Suresh's swami-ji knows better. She must ask her father next time he appears.

"Did your cousin-nieces have to become Christians?" she asks.

"No!" says the Punjabi woman. "Both girls are absolutely BRILLiant." She stares ahead in pouty silence as if Damini had maligned her bloodline.

The bus waits for a bleating herd of gaddi goats to wander across the road, then starts up again. Last time Damini made this trip, she sat with Mem-saab in the back seat of a well-sprung car. They had stopped for a picnic by a waterfall.

Damini has saved the orange the Indian nun gave her, and peels it with renewed gratitude. Its texture satisfies, even if sweetness eludes her.

She still has her bundle of parathas and the mutton curry for Leela and her family—thanks to eating in the dining hall of the gurdwara. She would become a Sikh again, just for the comfort of knowing a gurdwara will never turn her away from food or shelter. Last night, she sat cross-legged before a steel tray and glass while a beardless boy in a black turban, wearing a bomber jacket over his kurta and pyjama served her from the same bucket as everyone else. He offered her rotis from the same stack as other Sikhs. She reached out her glass, Mem-saab's steel kara gleaming on her wrist alongside her own, and he poured her water from the same jug with which he served every devotee sitting in line.

She has two rotis from the gurdwara kitchen wrapped in a handkerchief and would like to share, but her seatmate is lighter-skinned, wearing clothes and shoes that would soil if she did a moment of manual labour. The Punjabi woman has her own tiffin, anyway; when she opens it, the scent of garlic pickle rises into the morning breeze.

Was it only yesterday that she left Mem-saab's house in New Delhi? Khansama, Zahir Sheikh, Aman, Kiran, Loveleen, Timcu and his wife already seem to belong to another woman's life. But they don't, really. Going to Leela makes it inevitable that she will encounter Aman and Kiran again, whenever they come to their summer home, Sardar-saab and Mem-saab's Big House in Gurkot.

Don't think of that.

Steeper now, the road narrows to half its width and a single lane. Vehicles travelling downhill pull onto the gravel shoulder, squeezing close to the grey stone embankments as the bus climbs past. Traffic signs at crossroads become fewer—few hill-people need or read signs.

The bus cannot travel too fast downhill, nor too slow as it climbs. Yet, four hours later, when Damini arrives in the river-valley town of Jalawaaz, the minibus to Gurkot has departed—whoever scheduled it didn't care if anyone on the only bus from Shimla might need a ride beyond. No one is at its wooden ticket counter. And when she marches off and finds the ticket seller sipping chai on the veranda of his home, she is informed that she can try again tomorrow in case the gods of the state bus service decide there will be a minibus. But unless more powerful gods intervene, no minibuses are scheduled till tomorrow.

Jalawaaz town nestles on the banks of the Meethi Darya, river of sweetness, surrounded by the shadow-shapes of mountains, too low for her to catch a glimpse of the dazzling snow peaks. At the entrance to the village, where the bus has stopped, a staircase rises to the carved stone gateway of a temple to Lord Ram and his consort, Sita Mata. Past this temple, a single paved road runs between two lines of shops, long narrow cells with proprietor's living quarters on second storeys, looking grimier and more fragile than five years ago. At the far end is a truck stop where Kateru peaches, Red June and Ras-pippin apples, and logs of deodar set off on journeys to the plains. Beyond the truck stop, Damini can just see the silver-green shine of rice terraces along the riverbank.

She lifts her bedroll onto her head, and swings her bag over her shoulder. She walks past the movie hall—Piara Singh took her to that wooden shed for her first movie, *Mughal-e-Azam*, and sang the songs for her all the way home. She remembers the Muslim actress, Madhubala—her hair was so black, her face was so pale. Piara Singh loved watching Damini imitate Madhubala's graceful gestures.

Here's the post office, where she came to sign a ledger every month after Piara Singh died, proving she was still alive and eligible for a widow's pension from the government electricity department. She will return without baggage in a few days and fill out forms to request the government to redirect her pension to Jalawaaz again.

She passes the general store, owned by the head of the village council, elected just as his father was before him, and as his son will be after him. Here you show your ration card to buy flour, rice and sugar at government prices; she must return in a few days to have her ration card address changed as well. She remembers Piara Singh putting a ten paise coin on the pine counter in the general store, so many years ago, to give her a taste of her first Orange Bar from the Kwality ice cream freezer.

Several men are hunkered down watching a tele-serial outside the electrical shop. She passes the TVs and video players, hotplates and hot water heaters—villagers must now want hot baths just like

Vee-Eye-Pees in the cities. But the shop also sells bukharis, the wide steel bowls you fill with hot coals, because old-style things, like people, never truly die.

The fruit seller calls from behind his small pyramids of guavas, lychees, mangoes and chickoo from the plains. He points out Elberta and Floridasun varieties in his peach basket and offers her crimson apples from the higher ranges. Damini greets him but only samples a lychee-nut.

She passes the sub-district magistrate's office and then the low grey perimeter wall of the police station. A few sweeper-women squat before the police station veranda—probably asking for news of their men.

In Jalawaaz, the shopkeepers, policemen, teachers and students filing into the cement-grey secondary school building, the chance arrivals at the post office, the sweeperwomen, are all connected to each other by blood, marriage or loans. But Damini doesn't have family members here, and doesn't want to spend the night at Jalawaaz ashram when she is only fifty kilometres from Gurkot.

Fifty kilometres can be a long distance in the hills. Maybe her henna-orange hair will win enough respect for her age for her to thumb a ride in a passing jeep. Maybe someone will know Chunilal at the Jalawaaz diesel station, maybe he'll be there and can arrange a motorcycle ride . . . Her neck is straining beneath her bedroll—only a few metres more to the diesel station. She picks her way around a pool of black oil to the nearest Tata truck—gold-nosed with a bed of pale blue. A pile of stones substitutes for a missing wheel.

"Ay, hero . . . !" she yells at a long-bearded flabby trucker sporting sunglasses and a reflector-yellow turban, over his idling engine and the clunk and thunk of logs loading. Then she yells her question, and the trucker points to a purple-cabbed green truck parked at the end of the row. That's Ustaad Chunilal's truck, he says, calling him teacher. But he hasn't seen Chunilal.

"How long, ji?" she asks. Chunilal used to say it felt as if his heart had stopped whenever his truck was idle. Yet he shudders at suggestions that he should become a company-man, saying he'd lose his side income. He takes passengers like young Nepali women and their so-called aunts south to Bombay, and carries monks on their way north to higher and higher planes.

The flabby man removes his sunglasses to consider. "Three, four, maybe six months—who knows? His Second Driver and helper have found themselves a new Ustaad from whom they can learn."

"Gone to his village, ji," says a tempo-driver with face as pinched as the nose of his three-wheeler truck. He wipes the windshield with an oily rag. "Manager-saab was asking for him."

He means Aman-ji's manager, a pitiless prune of a man, who lives far better than he should on a caretaker's income. Damini can't imagine him asking about Chunilal's health.

"Chunilal sent his son to get his pay—the son said Chunilal is sick."

"Sick—all this time?" she says. "Is he in Gurkot?"

"That I don't know."

"Where are you going?"

"Taking this load to the sawmill," the tempo-driver gestures at the back where two stringy-looking men are loading logs onto the flatbed. "In an hour or two," he says, looking up at the gathering clouds.

"I'll come with you?" She hopes she doesn't sound too desperate.

She can tell he doesn't want to say no, maybe out of respect for her age. He should remember his grandmother, mother and sisters. Maybe he'll take her for free?

But the tempo-man is rubbing finger and thumb together, looking reproachful.

She can't claim a discount for being almost-family. She doesn't have anything he would want as barter. "But you'll take the new road around the mountain to the sawmill," she says. "Then I'll have to cross the river again and walk up the north face to Gurkot. It's too steep with my luggage . . ."

"I'll take you on the old road as far as the bhoot-sarak." He means the ghost-trail that crosses the river. "Then you can climb to Gurkot," he suggests, going back to wiping.

"I don't know the spirits on that path anymore," says Damini, "What if they are disagreeable?"

"Sometimes it happens," he says.

"And if it gets late, I may have to stop and sleep along the way. Can you please arrange a porter? Someone you know—not just anyone. An older man who will know the spirits."

"My cousin-uncle is there, ji," says the tempo-man. "He will carry your luggage, no problem."

He names a price, and Damini offers half. They compromise at three-quarters.

A drop plops to her shoulder, then another and soon the mountain road acquires the silken polish of rain. In a few minutes, a bead veil sweeps across the diesel station, obscuring the bright colours of the trucks. The trip will have to wait.

Damini dines on a leaf-plate of chaat in the fume-filled air of a chai-stall. Afterwards, she takes a shawl from her shoulder bag and wraps it around her. She curls her fingers around a steaming glass of chai. Sitting on her bedroll, she listens to Lata singing on the radio and watches white mist shift and swirl between ridges and descend upon the valley town.

Thunder rolls as if a gigantic game of marbles were in progress above her—that's Lord Indra trying to overcome Vrita, the asura of drought. That demon hoards the waters for himself each year. *Damini is here*, she breathes to Lord Indra—*Lightning is here; use me.*

A serrated flash follows as if invoked by her name. Maybe her prayer brought a moment of good karma.

Two hours later, the rain has abated. The tempo lurches forward on its single front wheel, grinding Damini's bones. She's squeezed into the cab beside the pointy-nosed driver, her bedroll taking up half her seat. She leans against it and rests her feet on her shoulder bag, like the woman on the pink poster.

She tries to smile that woman's carefree smile, but anxiety will not allow it—possibly because she's hanging on while the tempo careens down the half-disintegrated road.

She will have to face Chunilal as well as Leela and the whole village.

This is how she felt after her wedding, when she came to live in Gurkot. "When you leave home," her mother said, "you believe everything is coming to an end. But really, it is only the beginning of your life's battles." Piara Singh was beside her, then.

And again now. Boyish, diamond-eyed—and now half her age. His favourite Kullu hat upon his head, the one with the rainbow band. The wiry body she came to love so dearly, covered with a pale blue muslin kurta and pyjama. His cheeks look smooth as if he's had a shave at the barber. Those two black fringes above his lips—she can almost feel them whisking her cheeks.

I heard your name among all the others my parents proposed and said, She is the one. I said, She will be like lightning, travelling between earth and sky, plains and hills, fearing nothing. And I said lightning brings the blessing of rain. And then I met you and found you were such a fearful little thing! And remember I told you, you had nothing to fear?

Though he's less substantial than air, his youthful energy and hope envelops her.

He was right, for his parents made her welcome, not only when she was fourteen, but for all six years she was married. In those days people said a woman from Rajasthan wouldn't have the stamina to live in the hills, but they didn't know Damini. At first she thought it impossible to love a place that wasn't her own, just as she could not love her birth village. But since no one *said* she could not love her husband's village, she did—to her own surprise.

She had returned to her birth village in Rajasthan only twice during her marriage. The last time was when she found her mother— she stops herself before the memory overcomes her.

Anyway, she was the luckiest of her sisters. Her mother-in-law would never refuse permission if Damini wanted to visit her parents;

she said Damini's father knew his duty, which meant he sent gifts with Damini on her return. But there was never enough money, or there was too much work to be done or no one to escort her since she didn't have a brother who could come and get her. And in those days young women did not travel alone. The question of visiting her sisters in their new homes didn't arise—her sisters couldn't afford to send gifts for all Damini's in-laws.

If Damini forgot important things like who was older than whom as she served family, her mother-in-law, Ramkali Bai, would forbid Damini to enter the kitchen even for a drop of water, as if she had suddenly become unclean or outcaste like a sweeper. But she never ever beat Damini. And once her new daughter-in-law was trained, Ramkali developed mysterious ailments that kept her from chopping vegetables, washing clothes, cleaning out the cowshed, milking the cows, and kneading dough for rotis. Ramkali became "house manager" and house managers do not hand-water timorous shoots or weed cauliflower beds.

Everything, everyone was full of shanti till you died, she tells Piara Singh's spirit.

She doesn't mention the three times she threatened to leave and take Leela and Suresh home to her own parents, when the jooa cards stuck to his fingers and the hopsy smell of hooch stank in his clothing. But he hears her now as he never did alive.

I gambled, I drank—of course. But when Nehru-ji said big landlords had to reduce their land holdings, did I wait an instant? No—I borrowed money from every relative and went to Sardar-saab and bought our land.

You did, you did. I tell Suresh this story often. But you didn't borrow all the money—quite a bit of it came from my dowry. A little far uphill from Jalawaaz, it's true, and not as fertile as your parents would have liked, but *land.*

Old Sardar-saab! He sold it, thinking it useless. And I cleared the jungle and built our house. With my own hands, and with the help of my brothers and my jooa-playing friends.

And when the house was built, and before we moved in, we held a special ceremony for Lord Golunath, so he'd always bring us justice. And then your mother became angry because we hadn't honoured Anamika Devi.

She would say, Anamika wishes to speak: and her body would shake and tremble and a deeper voice would come.

Damini smiles inside. The last time the goddess spoke through Ramkali Bai she informed Ramkali's astounded husband and remaining sons that widowed Damini would be going to the plains to work for Mem-saab. And that Ramkali would no longer be house manager, but would raise Leela and baby Suresh. This decision was, the goddess said via Ramkali, premade by the universe, stemming from their family's ancestral loyalty to Sardar-saab's. And if Ramkali Bai's husband didn't agree, Anamika Devi's curses would ruin him.

Of course Damini's father-in-law agreed—though he did say he would miss Damini's cooking. That man's decisions usually stemmed from his fears. Whereas his son, her dear Piara Singh sitting beside her in spirit form, could have been kind enough to have *more* fear, especially of heights.

Piara Singh's grasping brothers didn't dare object. Not then, or when they learned Ramkali Bai had reregistered Piara Singh's house and land in Leela's name. "If owning this land is not in Suresh's stars," Ramkali told Damini, who was visiting Gurkot with Mem-saab for the summer, "then neither is it in theirs." Her gift was for Leela's dowry, and Piara Singh's brothers were too afraid of a dead mother's curses to give Leela trouble.

Suresh both appreciated and resented his grandmother's bequest— by putting the farm in Leela's name, Ramkali Bai had gifted away her grandson's patrimony, but relieved him of responsibility to provide a dowry for his sister. Suresh could have challenged the registration, but it would have taken years in court and more money than he'd ever seen in this life.

I didn't live in your house long, Damini says to Piara Singh's spirit. Your family was supposed to be my protection, my anchor. But only your mother understood that your brothers could kill me. When my life was in danger only she knew what needed to be done, what needed saying . . . All those years, she looked after our children in that house.

Return there, now. Live there now.

So many relatives' feelings to consider, not just our children: what about Chunilal's family—Leela's in-laws. His parents, his brothers and their wives will say we took from a daughter.

Don't be afraid.

Don't go far from me.

I am with you.

The tempo arrives where the ghost-trail begins. Two bamboo poles prop up a dingy canvas that marks a one-chair cubbyhole of a barber-shop, a phone stall, and a chai-stall nestled in a cleft in the mountain.

The tempo driver alights and a burly Tibetan man leaves his pipe to set the chai kettle on the clay stove. A messenger boy is dispatched to the porter's hut. The tempo driver sits down at one of the tea-stained tables and orders a plate of potato pakoras. A saab on the radio says not to panic but plague has broken out again in India. Another saab says England beat South Africa by eight wickets, which seems unfair—Englishmen are always winning. A third is saying it's possible India may not sign a Comprehensive Nuclear-Test-Ban Treaty when it comes up for renewal next year, citing national security concerns. Damini only listens in hope that film music will follow.

She surveys the single-use shampoo packets hanging from the ceiling. Her gaze moves to the Liril and Lifebuoy soaps, Vicco Turmeric vanishing cream, bottles of Fair & Lovely lotion, and trial packs of Rin stacked on the counter. Large jars on the counter keep rusks and vegetable patties safe from mosquitoes. She points at the Hajmola sweets and hands over a rupee. The four sweets will taste of the churan and betel mix her mother administered to quell hunger. The Tibetan man inquires where she's going and doesn't seem to remember her—years ago, men remembered Damini if they saw her even once.

The Hajmola settles her stomach. She relieves herself behind a bush, climbs back into the tempo cab and waits some more.

The ponderous energy of the rain-soaked mountain towers above her. This knoll didn't exist when she first came to Gurkot—an avalanche formed it after the state government used dynamite to make the road cut. The Tibetan man and his wife were children of road workers back then—they've certainly climbed higher than their refugee parents. The wife, she recalls, wore rainbow blouses with her full-length bakus and gave teenage Suresh an extra pakora on his way home from selling vegetables in Jalawaaz market. Suresh hated taking vegetables to market. It wasn't warrior-like, he said. Not what a kshatriya should do.

When the tempo-man's cousin-brother arrives, Damini alights. The porter greets her with "namaskar" instead of namaste, which tells her he too is a kshatriya, just poorer. He has a longer beard and whiter hair than the sage Vyasa. The wicker basket on his back is supported by a band around his forehead and pulls his bushy eyebrows into a look of constant surprise. The grey rinds of his feet are at least two centimetres thick; Damini's trust surges.

He manages to stuff her bedroll into his basket and tie her shoulder bag on top. He squats beside the tempo and shares a beedi with his cousin-brother. Damini would like one, but she doesn't want to buy a whole cone. When finished, he hoists his basket and sets off on the ghost-trail without a glance in her direction. Damini hastens to follow, hitching up her salwar as she picks her way between the puddled ruts and the rain-filled gutter. Radio chatter fades behind her.

When the ruts vanish, the porter finds cart tracks, then hoof marks to guide them down a bridle path to the river. In May and June this was a mountain stream that wound its way downhill to feed the silver-grey rush of the River Sutlej, but today it could smash a body to pieces against its boulders and rocks. One year its wood-slat footbridge washed away, and her husband and all the villagers came together to rebuild it.

Damini puts one rubber-sandalled foot gingerly before the other on the footbridge. The rope-railing is slick and rough in her palms. The bridge sways as she grips one side then the other. In the middle of the foamy roar, boulders and timber toss up spray.

The railing is Lord Hanuman's tail. She's walking across just as Lord Ram walked the monkey bridge from India to Sri Lanka to rescue abducted Sita Mata—she murmurs the Hanuman chalisa to give herself the bounce and surefootedness of the monkey-god.

Today Hanuman is listening—Damini crosses the bridge safely.

Beyond the riverbed, the porter enters the forest, with Damini following. At this pace, it will take only four hours instead of five to climb the scraggly track that traces the mountain slopes like a balcony grafted to a crumbling tower. But she can't keep up.

"Slow down!" she yells. "What are you trying to do, kill an old woman?"

The porter settles into a more bearable rhythm.

Up and up goes the steep footpath where the dead survive. In this dwindling jungle, the spirits of those who died a violent death linger like poems in Pahari, the ancient language of mountain tribes. Sad spirits are sustained by fear-thoughts, and many simply tethered by love.

As she breathes and paces upward, she's taking in the shape and cry of birds, the shadows of things seen and unseen, beings revealed and hidden, the burn in her thighs, the churn of her own digestion.

The mountain seems to grow and grow as she climbs. Rock fragments skitter as she scrambles for footing.

The porter seems to make his way by unseen footholds. She can feel every stone and twig beneath the thin soles of her rubber sandals. She slithers and skids in muddy patches. The heavy scent of wet bark, rain-soaked earth and undergrowth fills the air.

Deep breath and a step up, deep breath and another step.

Piara Singh isn't a sad ghost—at least she doesn't think so. Once when he appeared, he said he had been reborn abroad in a place where people take birth but once. A place with no brahmins, no kshatriyas—he has fallen a little. She felt his happiness, along with her own sadness at his distance.

Muscles contract and release in her thighs and buttocks. Shadows expand and collide on the sun-dappled footpath. Every day her Leela uses this footpath to carry a headload or backload of firewood.

She can bear a lot, Damini thinks. *She gets that from me.*

Tiny purple and pink flowers sprinkle the underbrush like the laughter of the gods. Lantana is everywhere, since the British saab-log imported it, grown beyond control.

A precipice falls to a chasm beside her.

Don't look down, don't look back. Small steps, smaller steps.

Cinnamon sparrows chirp and shift through leaves as she passes. A tiger moth dances uphill. A white-eyed buzzard cocks its head at her, like the blind man in the train. For a long stretch, there's only gloom beneath the shushing oaks. A goat bleats behind her on the muddy trail. Then another, a baby goat.

If she thinks how far the village is, she might stop. If she thinks of mountain cats or women who have died in childbirth and become churails, she might stop. She takes a swig from her bottle—the water retains the heat of the plains—and keeps going.

A griffin with a worm wriggling in his beak swoops clear of the mountain, glides into the valley below and floats free of time. Flesh and blood seem so fragile here—she had forgotten.

Trees darken and glow. Birdchat and twitter signals nightfall.

Damini keeps her gaze on the basket bobbing with the porter's loping gait. She matches her footfall to the rhythm of his bare heels.

The mountains loom larger, as if bursting and birthing through ground. Through gaps between the trees, whole lower peaks come into view, half flesh-toned brown, half hirsute with pine. On the horizon, snowcaps are colouring with the last rays of the sun.

Damini is beginning to shiver with worry about walking the rest of the trail in the dark. Her gaze sweeps the looping trail, looking for a familiar red flag, a vermilion-smeared stone and a trident. The very trident with which Anamika Devi, guardian goddess of Gurkot village, called forth the water. Water that draws strength from the mountain soil, and tumbles and sprints as if inspired, all the way to the Meethi Darya. The flag and trident mark a cave—and now it opens like a nostril in the mountain.

The porter stops, leans his basket against the mountainside, and removes the band from his forehead. Damini follows him inside. He strikes a match, illuminating Anamika Devi in her niche, her shakti contained in the bulbous belly of a pot.

The clay pot is robust, despite its fragility. Straightforward, practical, modest, perfectly ordinary. It reveals no great thought, likely turned roughly on an irregular wheel. Sand sticks to the pot's surface; its firing was careless. There's no meekness in the goddess's painted snow-leopard eyes and arching eyebrows. Only that smile at our follies in Kaliyug, this age of greed.

She who named each god when the gods had no name, who now names every being and thing, goes unnamed—she is Anamika Devi, the goddess without name. And though she is not outwardly beautiful, her foreknowledge is trusted. You can say anything to Anamika Devi and she doesn't answer, but her eyes say she is as empty or full as you. Some say her husband was Lord Shiva, but then who named Lord Shiva? The writers of the vedas and shastras do not say. Childless, though she could have been a mother, she offers her power to women who wish to be mothers. She requires no elaborate rituals, no animal sacrifices—though people will sometimes slaughter a goat in her honour anyway. She does not require regularity, but most people say Thursdays are most effective for propitiation.

Damini folds her hands and bows before the graceful black eyes, nose-jewel and slightly upturned lips painted on the terracotta surface. She places a rupee before Anamika and her match illuminates cave paintings from pre-Vedic times. She lights a cone of camphor and one of the clay diyas before the goddess.

"All she needs is a little respect, then she showers her blessings," she says to the porter.

The first time she worshipped Anamika Devi in this cave, the rupee was but a chauvani and the cone of camphor was lit by Ramkali Bai in celebration of her son's wedding. Daughters-in-law are gold, Ramkali Bai said. Her dowry had been sufficient for the expectations of hill people, provided her labour made up the difference. And sufficient to marry off Piara Singh's three sisters—Damini has a silver toe ring, a silver nose ring and a pair of gold-wash earrings commemorating the weddings. And her father-in-law could then divide his property between Piara Singh and his elder brothers.

Quickly, before the day dies and night cold sets in, Damini directs the porter to clear a space for sleep. "Don't get me stung by a viper, or a scorpion," she tells him. "And make sure there's no goat dung."

She returns to the footpath to wait till the porter has laid out the bedrolls.

The sky turns sapphire and burns the far razor-sharp ridges. Very soon, the hazy glow of a new moon catches between branches. Damini turns back into the shadows leaping in the womb of the cave.

The porter has spread his jute bags and is fast asleep.

Damini lies down on her side, knees drawn up, so her rupee-wad crushes into her waist.

Why did I waste that rupee? What is Anamika Devi anyway but a terracotta pot?

Sleep comes, troubled by a half-waking dream.

A naked young woman with flowing river-black curls drifts across her inner eye. Her perfect body sits in lotus position, eyes half-open, in blissful trance. A tree rooted in her yoni rises to merge with her torso. Where does the woman end and the tree begin? Her veins and arteries fork and net beneath her skin, her breasts, and within her arms and these are also branches, branches of the tree. The life-tree's face is serene as a goddess. Her hair is a halo of coiled springs and for the tree becomes a canopy.

Swaddled newborns surround her, swimming in the air like fish in a sea. This is the goddess whom Damini called just a terracotta pot. Anamika Devi, the source of all being, origin of the world. Damini tries, but cannot call to her familiar spirits for protection.

The goddess says in a low voice, as if imparting a secret, "What comes through you changes you, what comes through you creates you."

The words resonate in Damini as if her heart were a pounding gong.

She wakes with a bitter taste of foreboding in her mouth.

She washes her hands and feet in the nearby spring, brushes her teeth with a neem twig. If she could taste sweetness, this living water would be sweeter than ever before. The tree woman is still vivid, still with her.

To one who doesn't believe, a pot is just a pot. But to one who believes, a pot becomes the goddess.

Returning to the cave, Damini gazes at Anamika.

You too are daughter, sister, mother, grandmother.

I placed so many offerings before Lord Golunath for the long life of my husband. But did that god of justice listen? No. Only a goddess like you would come to a widow in dream.

O mother of sound, mother of language, you who name each newborn being. O goddess of flowing, who washes away sorrow in her streams and rivers. May I always hear your music, may you ever protect my son.

She places a second rupee before Anamika Devi.

Outside the cave, mud and meltwater soak her sandals and the legs of her salwar. The porter shoulders his way into a muslin curtain of dawn, and Damini follows.

Two hours later, Damini crests the ridge, and straightens to her full height in the brisk mountain air. She takes in the blue of the sky as Mem-saab used to, drinking it in with her eyes. The tarred smoothness of the new Gurkot road feels warm beneath her sandals. A paint-dripped sign set in the grey stone embankment reads "Meeni-bus" in Devanagari script. A dog is barking, a goat bleating.

From here, she should see the back lawns of Sardar-saab's massive bungalow, the tennis courts, a bit of the cricket pitch, and a stone fountain or two, and the stately columns supporting the back veranda. But all she can see is a very long green fence and the flare of red slate roofs and skylights. On the next peak the white cone of Lord Golunath's temple is unmoved; Sardar-saab's house is exactly where it is supposed to be. The fence is new.

"Don't go too close," says the porter. "Big-big dogs. Aman-saab ordered his manager to buy them."

"You're making me walk all the way around the house?" says Damini. "Remember I'm old."

"Sorry, mata-ji." He's trying to be as respectful as if she were his mother. "There's no other way. Aman-saab says 'yeh priy-vate hai' and doesn't allow us on his property anymore."

A yowling and barking chorus strikes up behind the fence.

"Then maybe farmers shouldn't allow him to cross their farms when he goes to fish in the river."

The porter permits himself a wry smile. "Aman-saab crosses where he wants to cross," he says, and sets off around the fence to the front of the house.

"It's a good road," Damini says grudgingly, stepping on the tarred surface.

"Yes, it helps farmers take their fruits and vegetables to market before they spoil. But motorcycles, trucks and buses also use it. Very bad for us porters."

"How come the village council allowed a double lane?"

"*Huh!* The village council voted for single lane, but Aman-saab paid the sub-district magistrate under-the-table to authorize a double. He said the government should make a double lane now— why tear up the hillside again later?"

The white glistening crests of the distant snow peaks soar above cloud patches floating in their valleys. Mountains so high, no bird can fly above them. With a sudden rush of feeling for these hills, Damini stops. How each struggles up to its ordained height in the face of lashing winds and rain. If she were standing on any one of those peaks, she could barely linger a few minutes.

A flock of chattering cranes rises on a column of warm air and arrows toward her, then over. They have skimmed through the high passes into India, like so many migrants, traders and raiders. Eagles will claim a few of their exhausted young, but most will survive and multiply.

It was for this northward view that an Englishman built the Big House, the Bara Ghar. It had an English name too, but no one re-members it. How durable are those peaks compared to that builder's short spark of life. For these mountains, even a greedy eon of Kaliyug is but the blink of an eye.

The porter says, "With this road, trucks go back and forth from the sawmill to Jalawaaz. And supplies can come all the way from Shimla to build new cottages."

"Where?"

"There." He points to the next forested peak, where the conical dome of Lord Golunath's temple shines white against verdant green. It too has a tall curved fence, but that's to keep out monkeys. Beyond the temple fence lies jungle so thick only tribals and sweepers would be desperate enough to crawl through the tangles of branches and thorns.

"People from the plains will travel many miles to enjoy our cool summers and this view of the hills. And they'll be like Sardar-saab's family, going back to the plains in winter."

"One-two more homes don't matter."

"He's building twenty-five."

"Twenty-five! That will disturb the ener-jee of Gurkot."

Before Damini saw Delhi, she compared all things to Gurkot, the centre of her world. Now . . .

What you see depends on what you expect to see, and what you've seen before.

Below Sardar-saab's Big House, houses and terraced fields dot the hill—some no bigger than Mem-saab's drawing-room. All depend on the mountain stream that begins near Anamika Devi's cave.

Jade and tan terraces follow the contour lines of the hill, each curving swath representing hours of carving and shoring that belies their permanent look. There must be thirty or forty farms if she counts the hand-built white houses that stud the two hills from peak to valley, kilometres apart. Resembling railway carriages at this distance, each has one or two cantilevered levels of rooms, with bright blue or green shutters. Doors from each room open onto cement terraces with filigreed balconies, where you can hang washing to dry.

Leela's home is a short walk down the north-facing slope. The porter lopes away before Damini.

Damini's sandals tug between her toes as the road dips. She passes the overgrown British cemetery, and the run-down chapel with its white bell tower. An outdoor display box still stands by its wrought-iron gate. In British times, the priest used to keep a large Bible in the glass case, for all who could read in Hindi. The road levels for several meters, now, and Damini trudges past the weedy grounds of a school for Britishers' children, then a compound with an adjacent row of administrative buildings. All built on land confiscated by the British from Gurkha kings, hill rajas, or tribals, and assigned to Sardar-saab after Independence as compensation for the lands he lost in Pakistan. The only areas that have seen use since British days are the stables and cowsheds, and the unpainted tin-roofed cement block where Amanjit Singh's manager lives.

The porter falls behind, wheezing a little, letting her show the way. She approaches two roadside storage sheds around the next bend, then leaves the road to descend a stone stairway.

Two tiers of rippling red corrugated tin form the roof of Chunilal's home on the mountainside. She and Piara Singh built only the first, upper tier.

Damini breathes in the fragrance of oakwood fires. Women are bending and straightening on terrace fields. Damini's sandals stir up dirt, flame-coloured hair strands flick her cheeks. Leela must be in the lower tier of rooms, in the cookroom, or the cow's room. "Leela!"

Hens peck and scratch between the bricks of the lower level, and two night-black cows turn their heads to low softly as she clambers down the steep stairs. A breeze teases the leaves of peach trees clustered at the far end of the cement terrace. From here she can see terrace fields, fields Piara Singh cleared so many years ago, glowing green with vegetables.

"Leela! *Arey-o*, Leela!"

There's her baby daughter—a woman now. Joy surges like a wave within.

Yes, Leela is the tall, very pregnant woman in a mustard-yellow sari who's standing in the half-open door.

Gurkot village

DAMINI

A whirl of exclamations and laughter mixes with the smell of woodsmoke and dung. Leela directs the porter to unload Damini's bedroll and shoulder bag in the upper level sitting room, the one with benches and chairs for visitors.

Damini attempts to pay the porter as he leaves, but Leela has already done so. A moment later, his spindly legs are climbing up, then disappearing over the slate embankment to the road.

Damini pats a seat beside her on the low wall surrounding the terrace. Leela sits down, half-facing the peaks draped in their shawls of snow. Damini strokes her daughter's arm, her cheek, her hand.

Those eyelashes fringing Leela's large black eyes. That small mouth, puckered as if she has never outgrown babyhood at Damini's breast. That shiny black tangle of hair, now oiled with coconut and rolled into a dung-cake-shape behind her daughter's head.

"*Hai,*" Damini places her palms on Leela's belly. "Let it be another boy."

Leela's eyes brim suddenly. "Voh . . ." she uses the respectful pronoun instead of her husband's name. She looks away, swallows. "He used to put his hands on my stomach like that when Kamna and Mohan were coming, but for this one—no."

"No? But you are making a child—that is good. Your mother-in-law is happy with you, na?"

193

"He hasn't told his mother," Leela says.

"Then who does he think will come to help you?"

"It's for him to send word, if he wants his mother or sister to come. The gods heard my prayers and sent you instead."

Damini opens her cloth-wrapped bundle to postpone any discussion of why she is here and how long she is staying. "From Delhi," she says, displaying the stack of parathas and the tiffin-box of mutton curry. Then the presents for Kamna and Mohan.

Both are in school. Leela says Kamna lives in her own world, hearing tunes no one else can hear, seeing dances no one else can see. "I tell her, 'Get married and if your bhagya is good, your in-laws might allow you to dance.' What else to say? I don't remember being so immature at her age."

"You used to sing and dance."

"Too many cares—I don't feel like singing now."

"Does she dance well?"

"Oh, we all enjoy it, but I don't want unrelated men to see her dancing. You know, now she's fourteen."

"And Mohan?"

"Mohan!" Leela's face glows. "He can't write the *ah—aa—i—ee* in Devanagari, but he has learned to write his name in English! He seems to understand everything at the cinema. We recognize the film songs he tries to sing, though others can't. He can carry things and remembers messages word for word. He can change a truck tire and make easy repairs. And he splits logs for me." She points to a woodpile in the corner.

"Does he eat anything but allu-mattar, now?"

"He likes mint parathas from the chai-stall. But otherwise, yes, just my potato-and-pea curry."

"Name-writing is good. Remembering messages is very good. And changing tires is very very good." She returns to Chunilal. "But Leela, tell me, how is he?"

Leela's eyes cloud. "He says he's so tired he can't get up—for five months! Typhoid would be over by now. His eyeballs are white—it's not the yellow sickness."

"Did he have an accident?"

"He says he doesn't remember. Would you forget an accident? When I was only Kamna's age and he was driving along and I threw a rotten apple at his truck and ran away, and he saw me for the first time and nearly plunged down the hillside. To this day, he laughs about that.

"And the time he was driving fast with a load of apples and one sack fell off and down the hill on to our roof, and he found me again—he doesn't forget that. That's how he learned my father had died and you were working in Delhi and my grandmother told him this farm was my dowry . . . He says that was the best accident.

"He tells Mohan about accidents in which his friends died—which truck plunged down which precipice. He can tell you what the truck was carrying, and whether it was night or day, and whether its driver was drunk or sober. He remembers the loads they were carrying, whether they were trucking or smuggling."

Damini nods.

"But," says Leela, "he can't say this sickness is from an accident. Maybe he cursed someone important—he does that sometimes, when he's driving."

Damini pats Leela's arm. "Maybe evil eye?"

Leela shakes her head. "Always he flies a black flag from his truck, against the evil eye." She pulls her ankles into cross-legged position on the parapet. "But he eats in chai-stalls every day on his routes, and maybe one or two have sweeper-caste cooks, who knows?"

"Everyone eats there, not only him," says Damini.

"I said he should do a special puja at the temple, but he says Lord Golunath is for justice, not health. And he said it's too expensive to have the kind of ceremony a bigger god might appreciate." Her voice drops to a whisper. "I asked, 'Have you been sleeping with prostitutes?' and he said, 'No, of course not.' But if he hasn't been using those-those types of dirty women, he wouldn't be sick. But what can I say, now? To a sick man?"

"Men are like that only," says Damini. "They don't think with their heads."

Leela leads Damini back up the stone staircase to the upper level. The sitting room is now painted turquoise and functions as a puja room when no relatives are visiting, but the ceiling is black with soot from its previous incarnation as a cookroom. A magenta and orange cotton dhurrie covers its earthen floor, and plastic lace doillies cover the tables that flank two straight-backed double-seat chairs. Carved low stools are stacked in a corner for children and lower-ranking guests. Leela flips a switch inside the wall cupboard to show off how the long nose of Lord Ganesh, the slightly flat features of Lord Golunath and the other idols inside light up.

She helps Damini unroll her bedroll on a rope-bed in the corner, then takes her back to the terrace. Damini follows the lucky footprints of Lakshmi Devi stencilled in red, removes her sandals and enters through the double doors of the central room as she did as a bride, right foot first over the threshold. The large room is dark and cool, and the blue-grey flicker of a TV screen in the corner throws shadows like the paintings in Anamika Devi's cave. When Piara Singh and his father used to sleep here there was no TV, only a radio. Damini would bring their copper platters from the kitchen, and her father-in-law would sometimes gesture to her to squat beside him, allowing her a few moments of rest.

Chunilal is hunched under a blanket on a rope-bed near the window. If he looked between the window-bars, he would see the white-capped peaks, but his gaze is riveted to an ad for Bata shoes.

He turns to Leela, then notices Damini. "Mata-ji! Kaise aey!" He calls her mother as Leela does, perfectly mixing delight and surprise. He brings his palms together in greeting; his right hand and arm are sun-blackened from leaning from his truck window. An intense man of about thirty-five, his brown pate shines above a jet-black fringe of hair. Chunilal's eyes glitter. He flashes a gap-toothed grin.

"Arrey!" says Damini, squatting beside his blanket cocoon. "What has happened to you?"

Chunilal says, "Buss aise." No reason. He tries to rise. His skin is tinged grey, like eucalyptus bark. "A little weakness—something I ate." His normally vigorous voice sounds as hunched and pallid as his body. He looks away and says, "Did Leela ask you to come?"

"No," she hastens to say, "Leela would never ask me to visit without your knowledge."

For the first time Damini has to tell someone her Mem-saab is gone to a new life, and that she herself has been let go. "I couldn't go to Suresh, na. He doesn't have any place . . . and you are also a son to me."

Chunilal strokes the black line of his moustache where it dips like the handlebars of a Hero bicycle. Damini waits for her statement to sink in—a man who comes to live in his wife's village is an almost-son. His shortcut around the normal way of inheriting land disallows him the right to criticize.

But—men do things they say women shouldn't. They can be shameless, even if we can't.

And Chunilal wouldn't disrespect an elder. Unless he's base as Aman.

"It's your home," he says, though both black eyebrows wag like left and right indicators on his truck.

"How long will you stay?" says Leela.

"I don't know."

Chunilal is silent a moment, considering. "So that is how it is."

"Yes."

"Some say a house full of your wife's relations is like a field full of birds."

"Yes," says Damini, careful to agree before she disagrees. "But the tree cries for its fruit, even if the fruit doesn't cry for its tree."

"Life in New Delhi is not like our life in the hills, mata-ji. We cannot provide you with halwa puri as you ate while living with Mem-saab."

"I have learned many useful things in the city. My pension is two hundred rupees a month—it is yours."

She doesn't mention her bonus—she has seen what happens when an old woman gives away too much money too soon.

A wry grin passes across his face. "Mata-ji, you probably spent your pension for the month just taking the train from Delhi. What does two hundred rupees buy?"

Something falls in Damini's stomach. Receiving her pension is like receiving a letter from Piara Singh every month. She says, "I don't need much—just a place to sleep, a little food. To this day, I can carry heavy loads and walk up and down mountains."

She is a guest here, though he may politely call it her home. It's no different from being a guest in her father's home, then living with least respect as a bride in her husband's home, then sleeping beside Mem-saab all these years. Guests should try to be helpful, useful.

"You do look strong, mata-ji, younger than fifty."

"I have maybe five-six years left to live, not more." Less, if she has to sell her body to survive.

"What work can you do here?"

"More than you can, I think," Leela says to her husband.

The Chunilal Damini knew would have had retorted with raised voice to so cheeky a comment. But this one appears to be carrying an oversized load of troubles. He watches TV reporter Barkha Dutt for a while. "I send Mohan to the chai-stall every week," he says. "To buy me a Himachal State lottery ticket. But I haven't won a single rupee yet."

"I hear you haven't been driving for months," Damini says gently. She gestures at the TV. "Which farmer lies in bed all day watching TV people's stories?"

"It is not months, just a few weeks. I will be all right tomorrow

—you wait and see. And if I can't go, I'll send Mohan." With that, he doubles over coughing.

Could it be TB? And how can he dream of sending twelve-year-old Mohan to drive a truck? Mohan, who can only mimic and repeat without understanding?

Leela peels back Chunilal's blanket to show Damini the red splotches on his leg, "These haven't healed for—I can't remember how long."

Damini would know which antibiotic cream to try from Memsaab's blue sweet tin with its picture of Durga, the eight-armed, many-weaponed goddess astride a tiger. But there is no tin full of English-people's medicines here. "Have you applied turmeric?"

"Of course, but it still didn't heal. What else is good?"

"Honey or Kharda moss should draw out the poison," says Damini, remembering her mother-in-law's remedies. "I can show you the right kind."

The frown lines on Leela's forehead are relaxing. Her step springs, despite the weight of the baby, as she leaves Damini with Chunilal and goes downstairs to the cookroom to make chai.

Damini asks Chunilal about the health of his parents, his two older brothers and their wives, growers of apricots and plums a few villages away. She names each member of his family in turn, hoping she does not miss anyone. All are well—except him. "Have you been to a doctor?" she asks, half-knowing the answer.

"No—who can take me to Shimla?"

"Have you seen a vaid?"

"The vaid moved to Shimla to give lectures at one of the new hotels."

"What about the government nurse?"

"She came from Jalawaaz a few days ago—some busybody must have told her Leela was pregnant. She took Leela's blood, gave her a tetanus injection, left her some iron pills, filled her own quota."

"Did she see you?"

"Me? No. But the ojha came yesterday and gave me this tonic." He pulls a brown glass vial from beneath his pillow, opens it and takes a gulp. "Made from cow *and* elephant dung; very powerful."

A scuffing sound outside says Leela is removing her sandals. She pushes through the double doors with a tray bearing three glasses of unsweetened tea, and a small bowl of jaggery. Damini takes a lump of brown sugar and holds it between her teeth. She hasn't sipped tea through jaggery in five years. The texture is pleasurable. It would be perfect if she could taste sweetness.

"Have you asked your mother to come for the birth?" says Damini to Chunilal.

"No. I thought by now we would be finished with that problem."

"I can help Leela when the time comes, but . . . last time, the dai came when Leela was born, and she was here along with your mother and sisters when Kamna and Mohan were born. All of us were here, but only Vijayanthi knew how to save both Leela and Mohan when the cord was wrapped around his neck. We have to ask her to attend." Both Leela and Chunilal are looking at her, saying nothing. "No?" she says. "Is there another healer in Gurkot?"

Still they say nothing.

Damini puts her tea glass down carefully. "Oh no, no, no," she says. "I have had two children. I can do massage. I have seen a child delivered in a hospital—but cutting the cord or taking away the Lotus? That's unclean. Vijayanthi always did it for us—for families of her own caste."

"Should we pay Vijayanthi, if you are here?" says Chunilal.

Damini purses her lips, but cannot hold back her retort. "Next you'll ask me to clean the latrine? I could do that, and just wash afterwards, but cutting a cord is like cutting a power line. I don't know where to bury the Lotus so that the spirits of women who died in childbirth cannot covet it. I can't do someone else's dharma!

"If Vijayanthi can't cut it for us, send Mohan down the hill to the Christians and tell the sweeper-woman to come. Goldina—she worked in Sardar-saab's home every summer. She used to clean the ash from the fireplaces, empty the thunderboxes, and carry the manure from the stables. Women like her are used to waste and decay—they've been cleaning it away all their lives. And they are fearless enough to separate a dead Lotus from my Leela."

"We don't need to talk about delivering," Leela says quickly. "Mata-ji, this is my third child—fifth, if you include the two I could not heat to birth. I would try for another son for our old age, but with him—" she lifts her chin in Chunilal's direction—"in this condition . . ." She swallows, carries on. "I already have one daughter for whom we must provide a dowry and one son who needs—and will need—care all his life."

She dashes at her eyes with the corner of her sari. "Every day I've been telling myself I'll go to Shimla and get it cleaned out. I thought I could be back in a week. But every day, there was wood to be fetched, rows to be hoed, seeds to be sown, clothes to be washed, vegetables to be curried, and cows to be milked and watered. Every day I thought, who will look after him and the children while I am gone? Kamna will be off in her own world, dancing, and Mohan will sit at the chai-stall eating mint parathas all day."

"Very good mint parathas," says Chunilal, in his son's defence. "It makes me ill to think of them right now, but they are the best."

"Why didn't you go to Vijayanthi?" says Damini.

"He said not to," says Leela, with a nod in Chunilal's direction. "He said Vijayanthi is too old and blind. He was afraid for me."

"She could have told you what to do."

"He was afraid of that as well. Every day he said, 'Wait. Tomorrow I will feel better, and I'll take you myself.'" She adjusts her marriage collar, then her sari pallu and turns to her husband, "Anamika Devi herself has sent my mother. Now I will get it done."

"Get what done?" says a high perky voice at the door.

It's Damini's granddaughter Kamna, with Mohan close behind.

"Nothing, nothing. Come and see who is here."

"Nani!" The little girl Damini remembers has grown into a jaunty fourteen-year-old with two long sleek braids and sun-whipped cheeks. She's graduated from a frock and thong sandals to a daisy-print salwar-kameez and canvas sneakers. In Kamna's embrace, Damini gazes into brown eyes flecked with green.

Too disturbingly direct—at her age, thinks Damini, Kamna should behave a little more shyly, even around family.

The young girl smells of coriander from the fluffy bunch clasped in one bangled fist. "From the roadside," she says, dropping it in her mother's lap. Leela begins separating the coriander from the wild cannabis that grows with it in the ditch.

Kamna has too much purush ener-jee. Cooling foods, that's what she needs.

Mohan comes forward, with his usual round-eyed open-mouthed look of surprise, unpretentious as uncarved wood. Leela reminds him to touch Damini's feet in greeting. He stoops to receive Damini's hand on his head in blessing, then steps back and stares at his dusty feet splayed in a pair of rubber thongs. A soft down is beginning on his chin. His Fanta-orange kurta further brightens his bronzed cheeks. It flaps about his thin frame, and so do his pants. His black hair ripples almost to his shoulders; he must still be frightened by barbers.

Poor boy—such bad bhagya from his past lives.

Mohan perches at the end of Chunilal's rope-bed. Kamna places a cushion on the floor for Damini, and flounces into a crouch beside her. "I'll show you all the bangles I have collected since you came last time." She jingles the rainbows on her wrists. "Papa buys me a dozen from every city."

"So now you're in secondary school," says Damini. "You take the new road—it's far?"

"Only twelve kilometres. A jeep stopped for us this morning so we didn't have to walk."

If Chunilal were still driving his truck, the children wouldn't be walking to school—they could pay to take the new minibus.

Kamna probably throws rotten apples at trucks just as her mother did. She's lost the baby softness Damini remembers, and looks lithe and willowy even when seated, holding herself tall.

Damini fetches her gifts. The bangles tinkle and spark. "They look nicer on your wrists than in the shop," she says.

Mohan blows into his new flute; everyone applauds his honking. Chunilal says proudly, "He whistles all the time."

"Especially at girls," says Kamna. "Papa wants him to be a policeman—then he'll whistle more!"

"Not a policeman," says Damini. "Everyone would just hate and fear him."

"You know how often I drive from here to Shimla, to Amritsar, past the Border Security Force at the Wagha Border," says Chunilal. "Every time, my truck is stopped, but they never tell me to unload and reload all my goods. They never search my cab. You know why?"

Mohan honks through the flute. Kamna moves neck and eyes in sundari movements, left and right like a dancer.

"Because I know how much grease is needed to grease whose palms so my goods find their way into Pakistan. But I've often thought, as I was bumping across the Line of Control, that it is better to be receiving rather than giving." He tousles Mohan's hair with rough tenderness. Mohan grins as if he understands, and blows another blast. "Who will dare to question the father of a police officer? Who will dare peek at his contraband, whether tea or hashish or heroin? Police officers will finally know who I am, and refrain from even hinting at bribes."

Chunilal is so sure, it would be cruel to object. Or to mention that if Mohan became a policeman, Chunilal would have to pay a labourer to split wood.

"Stop now, Mohan!" Leela stays the boy from blowing.

Mohan leaves off, and says, "Dance, Kamna!"

Kamna rises. She hums a tune as her arms arc above her head, her hands twirl. Her hips slide left and right, like a Bollywood filmi dancer. She slaps her bare feet on the floor and gives form to each note, as if an invisible thread stretched between her and the humming. Then her dance changes. Even Mohan watches.

She sways and folds as if all around her have disappeared. Slight and deliberate, she connects with the ground, with the air, claiming space boldly as if it is her birthright. She steps on her shadow, around it, into it, slanting forward and back like a spring coiling and uncoiling, her face to the window, her eyes shining bright.

Damini's breath catches, then soars. Kamna's dance is unlike anything she has ever seen, even on TV. It doesn't imitate Bollywood or the wriggly dancing of saab-log in clubs.

Kamna twirls and lunges, dips and rocks, humming to herself.

Movies don't capture this kind of joy, the animal glint in Kamna's eye, the delight of childhood. Her energy shimmers and amplifies itself in the small room. Chunilal is smiling and clapping along with Mohan.

Leela isn't watching Kamna. She is sitting on a low stool, hands clasping the weight of her belly, gazing at the ground.

At last, the girl collapses, laughing and panting. After a moment, she snuggles close to Damini.

"Who taught you such steps?" says Damini.

"No one." says Kamna. "I saw them in my head." She becomes serious, telling her grandmother earnestly, "I want a dance guru. I want to be trained, become a real dancer."

A dance guru won't help her shape this dancing to the visions Kamna sees in her mind. He'll teach Kamna to perform to his bol, his verbal command. Will require obeisance and obedience. Will demand gestures, expressions and poses men wish to watch, will teach Kamna to dance stories that have been danced and choreographed through centuries. But it would be cruel to say so. "That kind of guru. I don't think you'll find him here."

"And Papa says no," Kamna says, mock-tattling.

"We're not some low-caste people," Chunilal says as if speaking for an unseen tribe. "Our girls don't need to become dancing girls. I'll get you married, then you work in the house." To Damini he says, "Kamna says she can learn enough to teach dancing someday. I said we all have to eat today. If she becomes a dance guru, she'll only spend any money she gets on clothes, bangles, and nail polish. She shouldn't be taking a job away from a man and his family. I say, do your dharma in this life, and maybe in your next life . . ."

Kamna shrugs, but the corners of her mouth tremble. Leela is gazing through the barred window at the ridges of the hills. Kriya—creation—is like dancing. It needs Leela's whole body, it feeds from her body, it happens through her body. Both times Leela gave birth she was back in the fields without more than two days of rest. But this time . . .

Leela can make an ordinary bowl of lentils into a fragrant wonder, or fill a simple brinjal with the taste of remembered dreams. Once Leela transformed an old sari border into a quilt, another time, she transformed an old quilt to a bag, a bag to a pillowcase, a pillowcase into a shawl for Lord Golunath. All without much thought. But how can a woman create, transform seed, transform anything without joy?

"Are you a good cook?" Damini asks Kamna.

Kamna wobbles her head and smiles; she is not boastful.

"Can you cook as well as your mother?"

Kamna laughs—"I'll make dinner tomorrow, and you tell me." She rises and skips out, mercifully taking Mohan and his honking flute.

"Leela," says Damini, "how long till the baby is due? Two months?"

"I think so."

"No government or private doctor in Shimla will do a cleaning now. And if you find a bad doctor who will do it so late, you could die! And you know how much it costs? The later you get, the more expensive. In Delhi they take a thousand rupees per month of pregnancy. Must be less in Shimla but not that much less. Do you have five or six or seven thousand rupees?"

Chunilal and Leela exchange a glance. Both shake their heads.

"A thousand rupees per month . . ." Chunilal marvels weakly. "And a dai takes only twenty, maybe fifty for a live birth—even for the birth of a son. That means you can get more money for cleaning a child out of a woman than helping to birth a live child."

His breath sounds shallow and laboured. "Did you see the new latrine?" he says. "When I had a little money, I built it for Leela and Kamna. With a bathing-stall, because I heard women lose their heat and have trouble with their wombs if they bathe in open air. But no—nowadays I don't have seven thousand."

Damini turns to Leela. "Is the hair on your legs growing faster, now?"

"I—I don't know."

"Have your nails been growing?"

Leela examines her fingertips. "They break," she says. "Especially when I pull out weeds."

"Was your sickness mild or all the time?"

"I don't know—there was too much work to be sick."

Damini gazes hard at Leela's distended stomach. It looks like any other pregnant woman's stomach. "Like a watermelon," she decides. "Larger than a green melon. It *could* be a boy . . . you need another boy."

Leela breathes the question that entered the room with Kamna and has not departed, "Yes, but what if it's a girl?"

A weighty silence follows.

Chunilal says to Damini, "We truckers know one thing. Always, there is a shortcut."

"I'll talk to Vijayanthi," Damini says, eventually. "Let's see what she says."

A newborn sun warms Damini's right cheek as she sets out the next morning, her head covered by a dupatta, and wearing a shawl over her salwar and kameez. The footpath descends from Chunilal's farm, and wends its way down the cascade of terraced fields past homes and farms clinging to the flank of the mountain. Along the way it turns into ladders, and any shortcuts are treacherous and snake-ridden.

This hard soil grudges its bounty, but for those who work cleverly and long, it eventually yields. Meltwater flows from the mountain beside Anamika Devi's cave and the two-inch-diameter aluminium pipeline joins home to home, angling down the bulge of the hill to the sweeping Meethi Darya. It, and the women who are already tending the fields this morning, make everything possible. *Khata-khat-khat!* Buckets clank as they fill beneath its flow. *Tha! Tha!* A woman bangs a cricket bat, softening her wash beneath its cold stream.

A farmer leading a goat uphill greets her and she scrambles off the footpath and about a metre up the hillside, so he can pass. Another farmer follows, carrying a milk canister uphill to the road—Damini clings to the pipe as he goes by.

A brown cow blinks with somnolent eyes as Damini clambers down a ladder between terraces. Her rubber sandals squelch and sink in newly watered fields, some no larger than Mem-saab's dining room. She ducks under laundry on clotheslines, and detours to scrape Kharda moss from a fallen oak, and pick a few shocking pink flowers.

She has a sick feeling in the pit of her stomach just thinking about what people will say, could say, might say about her taking from a daughter. What will be insinuated, what will be assumed about her, and the shame for Suresh. Even so, duty requires that she stop to pay her respects to elders and chat at each home. She asks how many children each woman has left unmarried, and how many sons survive for secure old age. Women wearing their gold-studded marriage collars ply her with tea, as they once did each summer when Damini visited Gurkot with Mem-saab. This time it's offered with sympathy, and not only for her collarless state. They don't ask what happened in Delhi—they know. They've also heard about the orders Amanjit Singh has given his manager to open the Big House, have it dusted and cleaned so he can come and inspect it. The Toothless One still remembers when Sardar-saab was alive and Mem-saab could hear and was more beautiful than any maharani; she joins a little in Damini's grief.

Damini is all praise for her erstwhile family, and doesn't tell them how Mem-saab's educated son behaved. But she can't help the little sarcastic note that creeps into her voice when she refers to them.

In each home, she hears again that Amanjit is planning to build twenty-five cottages on the forested hill below the Golunath temple. He has a permit to cut down several hundred trees, and money from the government, they say. In return, Aman has promised to build a school and a clinic for the people of Gurkot.

Damini hugs herself in secret glee: the government is requiring Amanjit to carry out Mem-saab's wishes. Karma always catches up. That's its beauty, that's its terror.

At the home of one of her husband's relatives, who can recite his lineage back to a Hill Raja, Damini holds a cup of head-clearing ginger tea with the corner of her sari. His wife Chimta—so grasping of gossipy details, she's nicknamed for a pair of tongs—crochets a shoulder bag. "Amanjit-saab said there will be many jobs."

"When?" says Damini.

"Now, as he redesigns his father's home. My husband says the sawmill manager is increasing production, the trucking company manager is calling in more trucks. And later, there will be even more jobs when Vee-Eye-Pees from Delhi and En-Are-Eyes from abroad buy his cottages."

Damini doesn't think people like Timcu, the only non-resident Indian she knows, would buy cottages so far from Shimla airport. But they all drive imported cars now, like rajas and ranis, and those cars are smoother over potholes than Mem-saab's old Ambassador... "What kind of jobs?" she says.

"Construction," says Chimta. Her needle dips and flashes; the net widens.

"Those won't last," says Damini. "Then there will only be sweeper jobs."

"Our family doesn't do sweeper jobs," says Chimta, not missing a stitch. "If that's what he has, let him offer them to low-castes. Get some Sikhs, Christians and Muslims, or bring in workmen from Nepal and Bihar."

Damini takes her leave and goes on to the next home.

To those who ask, and many do, Damini says she is only visiting to help Leela through her delivery, and doesn't mention she only learned Leela was pregnant when she arrived.

"But you should tell her to go to her in-laws for the delivery," says Matki. Her older children used to play with Suresh and Leela and she earned her nickname—earthen pot—because she looks just like one when pregnant. "She's lost two children because she lives separate-separate from her husband's family." Loyalty restrains Damini from saying that Chunilal is estranged from his father and brothers. *And everyone knows it—I shouldn't remind them.*

Halfway down the hill, sipping tea in an inner room with a relative nicknamed Tubelight, Damini can feel the woman's assumption that she will leave soon after Leela's delivery.

"Is your son all right?" Tubelight asks in snide tones. From the shadows, Tubelight's mother-in-law and three sisters-in-law watch Damini intently.

"Oh, yes," says Damini and delivers her prepared speech: "Suresh is looking for a better job and a flat where he will have room for me and a daughter-in-law who will look after me—but it's very difficult to find a girl from a good family." Meanwhile, she stresses, she will look after Chunilal so Leela can work.

"Leela doesn't have enough children to help her," Tubelight says. "But that's why she still looks so young. You too look young, because only two." Why does Tubelight have to emphasize Damini's widowhood, and resulting inability to bear more children?

She was nicknamed Tubelight because she was never very bright.

Kamna's name comes up; Tubelight arches an eyebrow.

Damini says, "Kamna is too young," and does not say Chunilal cannot pay for a wedding at present.

But Tubelight, who also has a fourteen-year-old daughter says, "You'll keep young girls safe, making two families responsible if you go by reeti." She doesn't have to say, Forget custom and follow law, and she'll be with you longer. One more mouth to feed and clothe. She doesn't have to say, And don't forget, later marriage means higher dowry.

"She must be eighteen," says Damini.

"Ha!" says Tubelight. "Maybe in Delhi. Our police don't notice the bride's age as long as you invite them to the wedding."

Further downhill, old women tell her who has married whom, how many children they have, how old they are, whose son has left for which city, whose land is in dispute, and most important of all: which girls and boys are eligible for marriage. Good breeding, as every woman here knows, requires the best information about blood-lines and caste genealogies. They are required to breed out dark skin, cross-eyes; near-sightedness, tendencies toward deafness, weak di-gestion; tendencies toward laziness, hairiness, susceptibility to ma-nipulation, mental instability, gambling, poor business sense, low ambition, over-ambition; too much influence of Mangal in the stars, selfishness, obstinacy and the like.

"Selection," says Supari, nicknamed for the betel nut that always stains her tongue and lips, "is our work. I too have a daughter who's almost Kamna's age. I must plan her seeding. And we must arrange marriages for the boys in the family. But if there is one problem, ji, just one—will I ever hear the end of it from my husband or his family?"

By the time Damini arrives at Vijayanthi's home, it is mid-afternoon and monsoon thunder is rolling across the sky. The old midwife

squats beneath a thatched awning, her purple sari matching the
shutters of her home. Her marriage collar has but two studs of gold,
instead of the usual six. The terraces of her home are edged with
pipe-railings instead of latticed cement walls, but she is respected for
achieving more years than seventy. A little girl of about eighteen
months rolls bare-bottomed on a mat beside her.

Damini folds her hands in greeting and identifies herself, beginning with her in-laws, then Piara Singh. She mentions Suresh with
some trepidation, remembering Vijayanthi once twisted his ears for
disrespecting a boy only a few months his senior.

Vijayanthi calls to a granddaughter to bring tea. She takes a turquoise and rose-pink fertilizer sack from a pile, and spreads it before
her. She shakes out the urea-smelling plastic sack and separates the
warp from the weft, raising a thread to close view, then laying it
either to left or right. The toddler wanders perilously close to the
edge of the cement terrace; Damini grabs her, saving the girl from
plunging through the pipe railings and over the precipice. Vijayanthi
doesn't notice.

Placing the little girl safely back on the mat, Damini squats beside
Vijayanthi and begins to help.

"I can still tell if the threads are blue or pink," Vijayanthi says,
smoothing a sheaf of blue threads. "There'll be one pink rope, and
three blue ones."

Vijayanthi says her seven sons now have nineteen grandsons
among them, and only a few granddaughters. This one, she says of
the little girl beside her, is her first great-grandchild. "Came instead
of your brother, *hein*, Madhu?" she says, chucking the smiley little
girl beneath the chin. "So, you have come all the way downhill to an
old blind woman. Someone must be having a baby."

"My daughter, Leela."

"Naughty one, *han!* I remember. Married the trucker and *he* came
to live here. Ttt-ttt."

"Yes."

"She already has a boy. *Chalo!*—maybe she will have a smarter one this time."

Vijayanthi's granddaughter brings Damini what must be her fifteenth steel tumbler of tea that day, and softly pads away.

"And you, have you attended a birthing before? I hear that son of yours is still looking for a girl to marry, so probably not."

"I helped a cow once," says Damini, taking a sip. "And once I saw a dog give birth. And I went to a hospital with Mem-saab's daughter in law—"

"Hospitals—ha! Then you have seen what can happen."

"Yes."

"Never, ever let a woman go to the hospital," says Vijayanthi. "We don't believe in cutting."

"Which cutting?"

"They cut the woman to let the baby out."

"Oh, that cutting—yes."

"They take more money for that. Then they put stitches. Then they take money to remove the stitches. And the woman is useless for many weeks. Now I—I do massage."

"Massage is better," Damini says agreeably, confident that she knows how to massage. And she knows the proper way to use Dettol, and about the ghosts called germs. Which is more than many women in Gurkot know, but it might seem like boasting to say so.

Madhu reaches up and tugs at Damini's dangling dupatta. Damini sets her tumbler down and helps the child stand and fall, stand and fall again.

Vijayanthi crosses the terrace to the railing, counting her steps under her breath. A bottlebrush plant arches over her head. "You won't be much help to your daughter during childbirth," she says, after some thought. "I try to teach my grandson's wife, but she says she can't learn, even though her children are no longer at her breast. She just doesn't want to be woken up in the middle of the night to deliver a baby. Says she works hard enough already. When I first came here as a bride, no one heard me complain, but young women these days—no dumm in them at all. They're like this," She reaches up, snaps a twig to demonstrate. "Still young women like your Leela—they need help. Babies—they need help." She opens her arms wide as if taking in the immense bowl of tarnished silver sky. "Who else can help here? Doctors and nurses? Dais, ojhas, vaids, compounders—we are the only ones who help. I can tell you what to do, but I can't do it anymore. Learn from me before I go to my next life. If Leela has any problems, you just pray to Anamika Devi."

Standing beside Vijayanthi, Damini gazes down. The hill, verdant with monsoon splendour, slopes from the last ploughed terrace below the house to the river. Waterfalls and feeder streams glint in the folds of the ranges, as if following the bones of a giant fish skeleton.

Her eyes trace the river path as it enters a patch of trees and leads to a thin line of beach. Damini and Piara Singh used to meet there, out of sight of his parents. It was where they made Leela just the way Lord Brahma created the world—for no reason, just for play, just for delight. *Hai*, she must help Leela find delight again.

In this season, the river, fed by monsoon water will be flowing wide and fast, drawing its clay colour from its bed. The silver flicker of the river below dances with the flicker in her stomach. She has to broach the subject.

"Vijayanthi-ji," says Damini. "You know my son-in-law Chunilal? He is unwell."

Vijayanthi is looking past her, but Damini can feel her listening.

"He has been unwell for months. Leela is doing all the work. She has one daughter already, one son. Now is not the right time for Leela to have a third child. Yet she is already at seven months."

"She should have come to me or gone to Shimla before now."

"Yes, she should have. But she kept thinking Chunilal would get well. And then she thought maybe she would have it because she wants another son. But now . . . what if it's a girl?"

Madhu crawls over. Vijayanthi lifts her great-granddaughter and settles her on her hip.

"If it's a girl, Chunilal can't send Leela away and marry another wife," says Vijayanthi. "Leela is the mother of his son. It's true, that son will be cheated by every buyer in the bazaar, but she gave him a son. What kind of son is Chunilal's bhagya. Besides," Vijayanthi gives a hearty cackle, "where would he send Leela—this is her village, she's already home. So you're thinking—what are you thinking?"

Damini pulls her cloth bag forward and takes a pink flower from its depths. She takes Vijayanthi's calloused hand and places the flower in her palm.

Vijayanthi lets the little girl slip to the quilt and turns her face to Damini. She's listening.

Damini says, "After Suresh was born, I told my mother, I have two children and one is a son. I don't want more. She said if I became pregnant again, I should scrape and grind the root of a lal chita, apply it deep in my yoni, then wait for the bleeding to come. I did, and the bleeding came. Later that year my husband died, and there were no more children. Now I don't know if I had no more children because I had no husband to plant them, or because the fire plant stopped them forever. I thought: Vijayanthi will know."

Vijayanthi rubs the pink flower between thumb and forefinger and breathes in its scent.

"Lal chita. So long since I've seen one. I can't climb to where they grow now. I used to make a liniment from it with a bit of mustard oil for stiffness in the joints. And I used it one time when we had a plague, and another time when a scorpion stung a child. Your mother told you to dry and grind the root?"

"Yes. But she never said how much to use."

"No one knows how much is too much, or how much is too little. Are you certain Leela wants to drop this child? And in her seventh month ..."

"Yes. She would have come to you herself, but she had to water the large terrace today."

"Apply very very little, then. Not more than the thumbnail of your right hand. And feed her carrot seeds ground with jaggery—that heats the womb. Then prepare to birth a lifeless child very soon."

Vijayanthi's hand, gripping the railing beside Damini's, is large and rough. Her thumbnail, well trimmed and filed as if ready for work in a birthing chamber, is double the size of Damini's. Damini is about to ask whose thumbnail she should use, but the old woman is musing . . .

"Lord Golunath knows what an ideal world might be, but one thing is certain: this is not it," she says. "Until he brings balance, we must find many different kinds of courage to do what is necessary for our families. Sometimes we do what men want done, but don't have the courage to do." Vijayanthi's fingertips graze Damini's cheek.

Damini's eyes have brimmed and spilled.

Foolish woman, to mourn an unborn grandchild.

Vijayanthi turns and enters the house. Madhu has crawled back to the ledge. Damini grabs the errant toddler, lifts her to her hip, and follows.

Vijayanthi leads Damini into a storeroom. She opens a trunk with an air of reverence. "I'm giving away things," she says. Not to just anyone who needs, but to people within her clan and caste. She rummages beneath a chenille quilt, pulls, then heaves. Out comes a black boot with a bulbous rubber toe and laces, then its mate. Army combat boots.

"My father's," she says. "He was a miltry man: a subedar-major in the British Army, then the Indian Army. If they fit you, you can have them. You're a kshatriya—you must fight for women's wishes. Remember, no miltry in this world fights for women's wishes."

Damini sits the child down on the packed earth floor, removes a rubber sandal, folds the leg of her salwar tight and wedges her foot into a boot. It accommodates her broad instep. It clasps her heels, her toes. In Delhi, such boots would make her feet sweat, but here . . .

She puts on the second boot and stands. The boots grip the ground, adding an inch to her stature. With these boots, she can march from here to Shimla.

Vijayanthi cocks her head, listening to the patter and gurgle beginning on the roof. She glances over her shoulder as if sensing the white glow outside. Rain is swirling into the valley.

She pulls a large blue and white striped umbrella from the trunk. "All of Gurkot knew me by this," she says, leading Damini back to the terrace. "People looking downhill or up will know you too. Come back every day, and I will teach you."

All the way home, with rain dancing *tupa-tup-tup* on the large blue and white umbrella, and her combat boots repelling mud and water, Damini feels like Narada on the path of the devotee: she is a pair of ears again, listening to women. Helping women do as they want. Beginning with her own dear Leela.

Shimla
September 1994

ANU

SISTER ANU'S FINGERS FLY OVER BLACK AND IVORY keys, as she accompanies the choir, rendering the minor arpeggios of "Ay Malik Tere Bande Hum." The hymn does as it says in Hindi, surrendering her being to god. Today she even experiences a flash of all she's been reaching for when she plays it. But what truly transports her is the postcard in the packet from Mrs. Nadkarni. The photo is of a long needle tower, bulging at the top. Overleaf, it said:

> *Hello Mama.*
> *Are you okay?*
> *Love,*
> *Chetna*

Should she reply? Would it hurt Chetna or help her?

After choir practice, in the nuns' recreation room she opens the letter from Rano.

I told Chetna about your divorce. She was actually relieved to hear it. She's worried about you without anyone to look after you. I told her Mummy and Pop are looking after you.

Chetna's ahead in Math, behind in Science, but that's all right. I have begun working from home so that I can enjoy more time with her, help her with homework. It's an adjustment for all of us, but we're loving it.

After just a few weeks of working from home, I have been thinking of our nani's mother. This is how our great-grandmother must have felt. I find myself shopping by catalog now, instead of going to stores, just as she had home-visiting vendors. No one says I have to, but there's some ancestral memory of seclusion that makes me avoid malls and other public spaces if I can. People may imagine me beautiful as she was behind her veil, but I'm usually sitting in front of the computer in yoga pants and a T-shirt. If it wasn't for Chetna's activities and my weekly visit to Loblaws for groceries, I might never leave the house. Maybe you and I are in purdah and have taken the modern veil just like her. And so many Muslim women must experience the same in modern times. I imagine you in similar seclusion and silence in your nunnery.

Anu looks up at the sunshine pouring through the window of the recreation room. Birds debate loudly in the trees outside. Girls are yelling on the basketball field, and a chorus of children is rote reciting in the distance. Her nunnery isn't all silence.

You have to get on the net, Anu. It's like the first time we watched TV in colour in the eighties. The circumference of my mind has expanded. I'm alone, yet connected to a huge network. And that there is no pinnacle, no single point of reference.

On the net you see the world isn't only binary in that phallic on/off way, but connected. That's why they need women to make technology work in the real world.

I bridge the technical and non-technical worlds, come between human and machine, the seen and the unseen. Like a pandit, I tend the new gods and explain to users how to pray to them, how to propitiate them, how to make them offer their power for our use. We demand the high salaries and consulting fees, like brahmins demanded donations throughout the centuries, and when systems break down, we charge the high prices to fix them. We set up the credentials, we exclude to ensure our system's security, we operate in silos that protect information, we have the secret mantras and expertise to control the power of these gods. And where once there were only a few mainframe gods, now the gods have multiplied onto each desk.

When a client reports a problem, my boss says "RTFM"(Read the Fucking Manual). He's like my fertility doc, who believes that if fertilization doesn't occur it's my fault, whereas I begin by assuming it's the fault of the designer, the machine or the system. Today he called me negative because I pointed out his pro forma profit-and-loss statements were as fictional as Surfacing, *the Atwood novel I'm reading right now.*

I can't progress based on seniority here as Pop did at the bank. I need to find a guru, enter his fiefdom and learn. Just like our old gurukul system. All that's missing is the Code of Manu spelling out that women have to do the shitwork.

My engineer brothers all say their new technologies are changing the world. Lord Shiv is always at work, destroying to create. We in technology sell the illusion of coolness, "You must have this new gadget to stay alive!" Chetna already wants a beta (test) version of PlayStation that isn't even out yet. But we can't refuse her anything. Still I need to teach her how to choose. Because as long as she's here, she will always have choices . . .

It takes Sister Anu a few days of agonizing before she makes her choice. Then a postcard with a photo of Christ Church, Shimla's Anglican landmark on the Mall, goes overseas to Chetna.

Hello my sweetie,
I love you always.
Your Anu Mama.

Gurkot village
October 1994

DAMINI

LEELA IS MOVING LIKE A GIANT SNAIL, SLOWLY DOUBLING into an extra body that with first breath could light an extra atman. She says she can feel the child twitching, punching, even turning as she gathers firewood, milks the cows or pulls weeds.

"You are mistaken," says Damini. "The child is still."

"I could fall or hit myself," Leela suggests.

"If you get sick, you will only make everything worse," says Damini.

She must prepare herself to leave after the birth or face hurtful remarks. But where can she go?

A few days after she arrived, she returned to the booth with the black and yellow sign adjoining the chai-stall. She used the battered telephone resting on a wobbly table to call the factory number for Suresh. "Tell him to phone his mother," she said, and gave the woman with the air-conditioned voice the number, six digits Suresh would recognize immediately. She waited two hours till Suresh called.

"It's my bad bhagya," he said, "that you cannot live with me. But tell Chunilal it is not for long. These days, sweepers are getting all the good opportunities, but I'm still looking for a better job." He didn't say that better jobs are difficult to find in the capital when you can only speak one language, and it isn't English. Most sweepers have that problem, too. "And as soon as I do," he said, "I'll marry a girl from a

good family to look after you. Can you send me any money at all?"
Damini promised to send him a little as soon as she could predict her
own future beyond a month or two. "Forget marriage right now," she
told him. "Only a very poor family would give you a bride."

My son—always trying to do his dharma.

Chunilal too has been trying to do his dharma. Every day, he says
he will walk down to Jalawaaz and climb in the cabin of his truck.
He rises, washes, brushes his teeth with a datun-twig, puts on his
kurta, pyjama and weskit. He drags himself outside and squats on
the terrace. Whenever he attempts to climb the staircase to the road,
he begins gasping, then coughing. On a good day, the *tunk-tunk-tunk*
of his hammer echoes periodically off the flanks of the mountains.
Between coughing jags, he's stacking and trimming slate, building
a half-metre-high square feeding trough outside the cow's room.
And when Leela passes him, he shakes his head and says, "She still
has a passenger."

"All she has to do is pass it," Damini tells him.

Damini shoos the hens out of the upstairs storeroom and drags in a
rickety old rope-bed. During the day, sunlight will slant between the
window bars. At night—if it goes on that long—there is the swinging cord and bulb Piara Singh installed years ago.

A day later, Leela falls on the straw beside the milk bucket—her
water has broken. Kamna helps her mother upstairs.

Damini spreads an old quilt on the packed-earth floor. If Leela
dies this brisk October night as women do—*but please Lord Ram,
please not Leela*—her body must be touching ground, or she will haunt
the world forever. And whether Leela lives or dies, her mother must
be guardian and witness in one.

Damini tells Mohan, "Call Goldina to cut the cord." The boy
hears it once and can repeat it like an actor's line.

Just like his grandmother.

Except that Mohan repeats it and repeats it and repeats it as he runs downhill to the sweeper-colony.

Kamna helps Damini boil and carry a large pan of water from the smoky cookroom to the storeroom. Damini examines her fingernails—all short, all clean. Vijayanthi and Mem-saab would approve. She pours two capfuls of Dettol from a bottle she purchased in Jalawaaz into the pan. Then she plunges her hands in the water. *O Anamika Devi, O flowing one. Keep away all unclean things, keep away ghosts, keep away germs.* She lifts her hands, wipes them with a towel.

Damini settles Leela cross-legged on the old rope-bed and encourages her to groan and growl like a tiger, to moan as she must have in lovemaking, to push down and grunt as if passing stool. She opens the windows and doors. She gives Kamna keys to open every lock in the house. She unbinds Leela's hair to suggest to Leela's body that the baby should come.

"Curse and scream," she tells Leela. "This is your time to sob to the wilderness. I will pretend to be deaf. All you have to do is be brave."

Leela squats, then crawls on all fours. She pulls on a rope Damini has attached to the window. She grabs Damini's hands and screams. Her head lolls back till the whites of her eyes are all Damini can see. Damini massages her, kisses her, strokes her to release all Leela's fears.

"The right time will come, my beti," Damini soothes Leela. "Your body will know."

Far from being as flighty and careless as Leela predicted, Kamna fills buckets of water from the pipe and carries them upstairs to the birthing room, one arm outstretched for balance.

Since Damini is doing unclean work, Kamna must do the cooking. Kamna brings sweet halwa and roti for her mother, and crouches beneath the smoke layer in the cookroom making Chunilal's favourite Kachalu vegetables and Mohan's potato and pea curry. For Damini, she double-boils a continuous stream of chai. Damini watches for signs of daydreaming, but Kamna milks the cows early the next morning without even being asked, so that Mohan is able to deliver milk to the co-op on his way to school.

When she sends Kamna to gather firewood, the girl doesn't complain and takes the ghost-trail down the south face all by herself.

"Be respectful of the spirits," says Damini.

"I don't fear them," says Kamna.

She will learn, she must learn. In time she will learn to fear.

Leela has been in labour for eighteen hours. Holding Leela to her chest, the pulse of Damini's breath and heart merge with Leela's. She feels the flow of her daughter's blood and intestines. "Leela," she whispers, "anything important happens slowly." Leaving Leela under Kamna's watchful eye, she sweeps a heavy shawl about her shoulders and emerges from the armpit-smell of the birth chamber.

Beyond the terrace railing, wavy lines of hills separate the realms of earth and sky. Sheaves of maize, brinjal, carrots, red beans and gourds lie on gunny sacks in a corner of the terrace, drying in preparation for winter. The peach tree on the lower terrace has lost almost all its leaves. Fireflies glow and fade, glow and fade, on the cascading terrace fields.

The sweeper-woman Goldina squats by the door, looking up at the cold burn of the distant moon. Her honey-brown face is a perfect oval, with deep-set fierce eyes. Her forearms rest on salwar-clad knees, as if she's ready to rise at any moment and get to work. She seems to be listening to the TV sounds coming from the men's quarters.

Goldina wears a kerchief knotted behind her head, instead of a dupatta over head and shoulders. In the parting that burrows beneath that kerchief, she wears no vermilion powder—yet Damini remembers a daughter or two helping Goldina in the Big House; Goldina is married. Her salwar and kameez are worn thin, but look clean enough. A large flower-shaped jewel sparkles on her nose. Several silver toe rings and silver anklets adorn her bare feet—probably the sum total of her husband's savings.

Goldina has cleaned the latrine and washed the bedclothes. She says she has cut many a cord. Her patient watchfulness has been reassuring over the past day and a half. Damini has not told Goldina a stillbirth is possible—cord cutters don't get paid unless a live child is born.

Yesterday, Goldina brought her own rotis and daal in a tiffin carrier, assuming Damini wouldn't want to defile a platter from Chunilal's cookroom. But Damini is also a Sikh and has eaten from the same daal bucket as others whose castes she never knew, and Chunilal is a trucker and has eaten in chai-stalls, so today Damini told Goldina, "This family doesn't believe in differences. Everyone is equal-equal." And gave Goldina four or five rotis in a bundle.

Which doesn't mean Damini would touch an afterbirth, or allow Goldina into the family's cookroom without her son-in-law's permission. Only that she has nothing against giving food to sweepers.

Or a shawl—she fetches an old one for Goldina. Goldina wraps herself in it. Damini notices the cloth bundle beside her—she must be taking the rotis home to share.

Damini leans against the outer wall and gazes at the sequined indigo sky. Unbidden, an image of her mother comes—her mother's body, black and burned. Just a bundle on a rooftop terrace. Tiny embroidered sprigs on the remnants of an indigo sari.

And she's very small again, walking behind her four big sisters, all following the sway of that indigo sari. Two miles each way to the pond, in the days when distance was still measured in miles. Two miles to fetch water once the well in Khetolai ran dry. Twice a day, sometimes three. The six of them, walking, walking.

"Something happened?" Goldina sounds warmer.

"No, just—I remembered my mother," says Damini.

Damini pulls a low wicker stool beneath her bottom before sinking to a squat, to keep herself a few inches above Goldina. She keeps her misted gaze on the blurry spines of the hills, till her vision sharpens again.

"Birthing is the time to remember mothers," says Goldina. "I was remembering my own."

"Is yours alive?"

"Yes," says Goldina. "And I'm a Christian and married in Gurkot because of her."

Goldina's mother was from Punjab, like Damini's. When Multan became part of Pakistan in 1947, Goldina's mother slung her youngest on her back, took Goldina's three eldest sisters and walked hundreds of miles to what remained of India.

"I too had four older sisters," says Damini, letting the solidness of the wall draw the tension from her back. "Three are alive, living in their husbands' villages, near Khetolai. Only I was sent so far away. I used to call them often from Mem-saab's home, but now a phone is so far . . . And your father?"

"My first father's ancestors were like my husband's, from the first-born tribes of India. But during the Partition . . . we don't know if he was killed by a Muslim or a Hindu, just that he was knifed."

"*Hai,* your poor mother!"

"Yes. She was hungry and weak like everyone else who fled when Muslims rose up against their Hindu landlords. She followed the landlord, because he was her only hope for a job—in those days Hindus began to call outcastes like us Hindu, you know, because they needed our votes. But when they reached Delhi, the landlord had no land for his servants to till. My mother said, 'My children will die if I remain in a tent city and wait for the British-saabs or the new brown-saabs to help.' And she went to the nearest church and promised to be a Christian if they would feed her family."

"I would have done the same," says Damini, remembering how she became a Sikh to accommodate living with Mem-saab.

"But she said my sisters should always remember to be Hindu as well, in case the Hindu landlord ever wanted us to return to work."

Damini touches her kara, the steel bangle that still circles her right wrist. "Yes, I'm a Sikh, and I'm also Hindu."

"Two-in-one," Goldina wobbles her head in agreement.

"And that's how you became Christian," says Damini. She rises to go look in on her daughter, who is so fatigued she has managed to fall asleep.

"Yes, for a while. But when my two older sisters turned fourteen and fifteen my mother wanted to arrange their marriages. The Catholic priest refused. He said they were too young. Imagine, he said girls that age are still children!"

"I got married at fourteen," says Damini.

"Right! My mother got hot as a pataka. She was afraid for my sisters' reputations, and needed to share the responsibility of looking after them with other families as soon as possible. But that padri just wouldn't understand. So my mother said, 'I'll marry them off to Hindus—Hindus will understand.'"

"So you all became Hindu again?"

"Oh no. My mother liked being Christian—pretty music—so only my sisters became Hindu and she remained Christian. But then my third sister became pregnant. She was seventeen, and unmarried. The eldest son of the house where she worked saw a pretty girl and suddenly forgot all his own rules about who is clean and unclean."

"This is what happens," Damini says. "This is why early marriage is best. So did your third sister have a cleaning?"

"My mother wanted her to. It was a child of rape—she wasn't doing anything against the law. But the padri said my third sister would fry in hell if the baby was cleaned out."

"Hell is—what?"

"It's where Christians go after death. If we have done bad things."

"Cleaning out a child is a bad thing?"

"Oh yes—if you do it you go to hell."

"What happens in hell?"

"You fry like a pakora in ghee. For-ev-er." Goldina rocks on her ankles.

"No coming back? No repairing this world?" Damini glances over her shoulder into the birthing room, to check on Leela. "But we often don't know if we're doing good or bad until we die. But no matter. Then what happened?"

"Then my mother went to a pandit and paid for a penance ceremony. That way he made her a Hindu again. Then she got my third sister cleaned out, and married her off to a Christian to make her a Christian again. After that, my mother returned to the priest and confessed."

"Confessed is—what?"

"Told the padri all what she did—"

"Why did she tell him about the cleaning out? Why not just let the man think she did what she was told?"

"Because when you sit in his forgiveness chair, you get shanti by telling when you've done wrong things."

"I have sat in many chairs. Never one like that," says Damini. "Did the padri make her fry in hell?"

"No, hell is only after death. But since she was still alive, he just told her to say many prayers."

"When a man threatens something, he usually does it."

"No, the padri said god would do it for him."

Damini considers this for a moment. "Very powerful man. I pray, but the big gods don't listen. Was he praying to Lord Shiv or did he mean karma . . . ?" Lord Shiv could have burned Goldina's mother immediately, while karma takes centuries.

Goldina looks blank.

"Did he send your mother on a pilgrimage?" asks Damini.

"No—but he said she would feel her guilt inside. An inner voice would speak."

"That happened to my mother-in-law," says Damini. "A goddess came inside her and made her tremble and tremble. So then you were all Christian again."

"Yes, for a while."

Goldina's fourth sister had, by this time, married. She had a nine-month-old boy. The child caught dengue fever and died. Goldina's mother helped her daughter lay out the tiny corpse, sewed its shroud and waited for the priest and congregation to come and mourn with her, as they had so often done for others. But by nightfall, no one had come and they realized no one would be coming.

Goldina's mother went to the priest's home to find out why. The priest explained he could not bury a baby who had not been baptized.

"Baptized is—what?"

"When the padri pours holy water on you and says you accept Christ."

"I became a Sikh that way," recalls Damini. "Mem-saab took me to her gurdwara and the granthi stirred water with a sword, poured some on my forehead and gave me some to drink. It was sweet."

"Yes, like that," says Goldina. "The priest said my nephew was unbaptized. My mother was furious—she said the priest could pour his holy water or Ganga-water or any water he liked on the dead baby if he wanted, but he said no."

So Goldina's mother went to her Hindu relatives by marriage. That baby was young enough that they would have buried him, but they didn't want anyone to think they had performed Christian or Muslim rituals, so they collected firewood. And that night, they cremated the tiny body by the banks of the Yamuna River. Goldina's mother seeing her son-in-law, the little boy's father, too overcome to do it, lit the pyre.

My mother had no son. My father would have lit her pyre for her, if she hadn't self-cremated. But he would never have allowed my sisters or me to do it.

"So you became Hindu again," says Damini, inner tension abating.

"For a while," says Goldina. "Then my mother went to work for a Hindu woman. But when she wasn't allowed to enter the kitchen, and was beaten for touching a cup of water intended for her mistress, she found a Christian padri who would baptize her again."

"And then you all became Christian?" says Damini, warming to the swing of the tale.

"Yes, and we still are. My mother arranged my marriage to a Christian."

And that is how Goldina came to live in Gurkot, downhill, downstream from Damini.

"But explain me this," says Damini. "Your mother must be very old if she was twenty or so during the Partition. My Mem-saab was in her twenties during Partition. And you—you're so young. How is this?"

"My mother remarried. I came from her second marriage, that's how I have two fathers."

"Your padri performed the marriage of a widow, but he wouldn't bury a baby who hadn't been bapt—bapt—"

"Yes. My mother worried that she was Hindu when her husband died, so she must not be allowed to remarry. But the padri told her even Hindu women can remarry. You could, too."

"I?" says Damini, "Who would arrange such a marriage for me? My mother-in-law? If I had remarried, any chance that my children might inherit these three terrace fields would have gone—*pffft*, just like that."

Damini rises and peeks into the birthing room. Kamna looks up, puts her palms together and rests her cheek against them, miming: Leela is resting. Damini takes a feather from the peacock fan she brought Leela, and lights it. When the flame settles to a glow, she props it in an incense holder and returns to her stool.

"Who was with your mother when you were born?" asks Goldina, after a few minutes of gazing at the far peaks against the blue-black sky.

Damini shrugs. "We weren't saabs who sing Happi Burday each year and tell stories about the day they were born. One of my grandmothers must have been with her. In Punjab the custom was for women to return to their parents' home for birthing—but we did not speak of such things. I know only there was great sorrow. I was born after four girls, you see. Where is your mother now?"

Goldina says her mother lives in New Delhi. She is seventy and works as a sweeper in the archbishop's residence. "Is your mother still here or gone?" asks Goldina.

Damini shakes her head. "Khetolai, my birth village, was only two day's journey from Delhi where I was working for my Mem-saab, so I went to visit my sisters in nearby villages, and then my parents—this was only a few years ago. When I arrived, my mother told me my father had found a second bride to bear him sons. And just a few days later, she went up to the roof—houses there have terraces on the roofs, you know. And she poured kerosene on herself and lit her own funeral pyre. When I found her, her face was black as if with shame—I couldn't recognize her."

Every bone and muscle hurts to say it. She should say no more.

"*Hai!* What a terrible way to die," says Goldina.

"Mem-saab needed my ears, but I wrote to say there had been an accident and I could not return on time. I tended my mother for a month, till her body released all the ener-jee of her atman. And I knew then, that I killed my mother by taking shape, entering the world when I did. Couldn't I have waited? Why didn't I listen to her wishes and die in her womb? Couldn't I have gone to some other woman and not added to the burdens of a woman who already had four daughters?"

Damini's eyes feel like hot wet marbles. She can feel her heart pulsing and skipping.

"You didn't kill her," says Goldina. "She did it because your father took a second wife."

Damini should say no more, but she cannot seem to stop. "He would never have needed a second wife if I had come as a boy."

After a while, Goldina says softly, "She didn't have you cleaned out of her. Was she a Christian?"

"No," says Damini. "She was a Hindu."

"Then she must have wanted you to come."

Damini doesn't remember receiving such a feeling from her mother. "She could have had me cleaned out, it is true. She knew the ways, yes." Another knowing that always travelled inside her as a little girl, was that her mother could have been poisoned or turned out of the house for giving birth to her, and that all of them were grateful for what had not been done to her. And she remembers that helpless feeling that she and her sisters just could not stop needing. They kept growing, eating, taking, learning. Knowing, yet unable to stop needing. Saris, sandals, bangles, nose rings—five schoolings, five dowries, five weddings. Later, after her eldest sister died, only four.

"Tell about your family?" she says.

"My husband, his brothers, cousins, father are stonecutters," says Goldina. "And Samuel carved the idols for the Ram-Sita temple in Jalawaaz, even though he's Christian." She says her husband's name straight out, with no fear of hurting him or meaning any disrespect. Damini is fascinated and repelled. "But he comes whenever called— you know, wherever dirty work needs to be done. When someone dies, people come and ask him and his brothers to burn or bury the dead, just as their forefathers did. And last night he and his brothers went to clean the cesspit at the Big House. They had to get drunk to stand the stench, but they did it. If you need help here, you tell me— he'll come."

"Do you eat beef?" asks Damini.

"Never," says Goldina. "We have many Hindus in my family and they wouldn't like it. Now some have become Sikhs and a few of them do eat beef, but my husband and I can't stomach it. We eat pork from our own pigs. Especially," a note of virtue strengthens her voice, "on Easter, so no one thinks we're Muslims. Our pork is so tasty, Hindu men from brahmin families come to eat it."

"No! Samanya men? Aren't they vegetarians?"

"Oh, respected men come. At night, of course. They take it to Jalawaaz, to some single man's home where elders won't see them eating it. Sometimes I take it to them."

The Christians of her community have many babies, she says, and Goldina has plenty of work. "Our padri, Father Pashan tells us not to use the topi or any medicines," she explains, referring to condoms and pills, "but I tell women, after two-three, make your husband wear a topi. Too many children wear out your body."

"Not before three, surely." These days, Damini sometimes wishes she had one more son to share the burden of her old age with Suresh.

"We have so many Christians now, Father Pashan is opening up the old chapel at the top of the hill, near the Big House. You've seen it—the one that was empty since British-times. He's paying my husband and his brothers to weed the cemetery. A few gravestones are so old, Samuel will have to recarve them."

"But still, your padri needs money for the materials."

"Amanjit Singh-saab has donated money. And given more for a school."

Ha! Aman's buying good karma for his next life. He's afraid he will be reborn as an ant for the way he treated Mem-saab.

"Hindus always came to the top of the Christians' hill to pray to Golunath-ji for justice," Goldina says. "Now we Christians will come to the top of the Hindu hill and ask Yeshu if he can find any justice for us?" She raises her head and laughs—a bit too loudly.

"Huh!" says Damini.

Goldina must be watching TV somewhere. Getting ideas, thinking she can joke with her betters, do chitty-chat, answer-back. It's okay-okay when no one is here to see, but . . .

"Father is also reopening the school building for children, and he will have classes so that even women like me can learn to read and write." Goldina adds, "I only have one book I want to read, maybe his teachers can teach me."

"The Bible?" says Damini.

"No, I know my Bible by heart. This one." She pulls a book from the cloth shoulder bag beside her. The title, in Devanagari script, is *The Buddha and His Dhamma* by Dr. Bhimrao Ambedkar. "I bought it in Nagpur—Samuel and I went for Ambedkar-ji's birthday celebration after my second daughter was born. So that was fifteen years ago."

The name Ambedkar is unfamiliar, but the photo on the cover shows a man with spectacles; he must be learned. Goldina kisses the book, puts it back in her bag.

"How many children do you have?"

Goldina looks past Damini at the long arc of icy ridges in the distance. "Seven," she says eventually. "Five are left. Three girls to marry off. The padri says his teachers can teach them English."

"English. *Vah!*" says Damini. Maybe Suresh is right—the good opportunities are going to sweepers, giving them airs. "The church school is closer than the government school. Maybe Mohan can go." But then he may have to sit beside Goldina's daughters.

"Your mother will be rewarded for her suffering in her next life," she assures Goldina as she rises.

"Why should she wait till after death?" says Goldina. "Her reward should come in this life."

"Be grateful your mother is alive," says Damini, "and her spirit is not wandering and wandering, like my mother's."

Damini pops her head into the men's quarters. Chunilal's blanket is over his head, the TV is on and wasting electricity. Scent of rum; Chunilal must have sent Mohan to buy him some this afternoon.

On TV, her son's spiritual guide Swami Rudransh, is sitting on an ornately carved high-back chair, a saffron shawl drawn under his double chin. He's on a platform, his rupee-size red bindi moving like a searchlight over a gathering of a Cow Protection Society. Hindus, he is saying very gently and calmly, must protect the cow from slaughter. Muslims, he says, are slaughtering cows and getting rich tanning leather, selling it abroad. He is saying Muck-dun-alds company has been granted permission by the government to come to India. But they will slaughter cows and make their customers eat beef. Shameful, he says, and quotes Mahatma Gandhi, "Because the cow is my mother. The cow is everyone's mother. They should ask its blessing, never slaughter it."

Cows should do the kind of labour Leela does every day before any man calls it mother. What can that swami know about mothers? Or cows. If the mahatma or Swami Rudransh don't want cows slaughtered, will they look after old cows?

The swami sits in lotus, hands in dhyana-mudra position and says about a crore of people—one hundred hundred thousand!—have been helped in his ashrams and centres for Vedic creationism, and another fifty crore more "via media." His tummy constricts, demonstrating kapalbhati-breathing, which, he says, cures diseases known and unknown, "including wrinkles, knots in the uterus, fibroids, cysts, fistulas, philaria, nicoderma, cholesterol, uric acid, weakness in the gonads, heart blockages, chest pains, diabetes, bronchitis, asthma, cancer, epilepsy, deafness . . ." If tummy-tucks could cure deafness, wouldn't Mem-saab have done kapalbhati for a few months and been cured?

This man is now her son's second father, when no man but Piara Singh should be called Suresh's father. Maybe the swami connects him to Piara Singh's ghost and Suresh visits his father as frequently as Damini—an ojha can open himself to the spirit world as easily as any woman. But demons can enter through a medium who cannot set himself aside—she must tell Suresh to be careful.

Mohan is sitting at the foot of his father's rope-bed, playing with the red-brown stuffed monkey Suresh played with, and Leela before Suresh. The white patch on Lord Hanuman's tail waves like a bandage, and his black and white button eyes look amazed by this world.

Chunilal's blanket flips down. Glittering eyes hold Damini's gaze.

"Mata-ji, if that child is still rolling downhill, it's your fault."

"This is now in the hands of the gods," says Damini. "You should be praying, not watching TV."

"I am watching a holy man," says Chunilal. He rises on one elbow with an effort. "And I'm thinking: if it's a girl, I don't want to see her."

"Then what should I do?"

"Whatever is necessary," he says. He lies down and flips the blanket back over his face.

The swami's nasal voice fades, letters scroll too fast to read.

Young boys and girls prance across the TV screen and an announcer cries out *Jo Chahe Ho Jaye.*

"If drinking one bottle of Coke can make you young people think you can make a wish and it will happen," says Damini, "then drinking a whole bottle of rum will make you believe all your wishes will happen."

She continues on her way before Chunilal can retort.

The dancing people on TV, Chunilal, Suresh—all same-same.

Inside the birthing chamber, her exhausted daughter is doing her dharma, still groaning.

It's three in the morning when Leela's baby emerges. She's standing, using earth-pull, as the baby uses her as its gateway to the world. The child competed with its mother for twenty hours before Leela gave in and let it slip into the basin of water Damini held between her legs. Any longer, and the baby might have killed her.

Damini is breathing as hard as if she too had given birth. She directs Kamna to tear up an old sari for rags.

Kamna must have noticed Damini's surprise when she saw the baby responding to larger space, stepping on air as if beginning a new dance. Kamna must have noted the sadness in Damini's eyes when the child gave its first cry. Still Kamna is quietly efficient, helping Leela sit up, move over, lie down.

Leela covers her face, but Damini can see the glint of tears through the fabric of her sari. Did this child dream, in its soft cocoon, that it would enter the world to such a chorus of sighs, tears and recriminations? Does it see, as it opens its eyes for the first time, that condemned look on Leela's face?

The baby is slick with blood, sticky with birth-fluid, its head and dark hair so soft against her shoulder. Damini wipes it clean gently, so gently.

No tail.

She wipes and wipes again between its legs, looking for a penis.

None at all.

What terrible deeds must this soul have done in a past life, to now be punished by taking form as a girl. What will she face but suffering that leads to more suffering.

Did this baby girl know, as she grew according to some intricate plan of the gods, that her incredibly complex form is yet inadequate?

Does this girl feel that she has become the node of sorrow, that she is born disabled by her womanhood? Does she know yet, from the sad melody of speech heard in her mother's belly, just how unwanted she is?

Give her a few days, and she will know.

Damini rubs Leela's trembling back and shoulders in sympathy. She wipes her daughter's eyes with her sari.

Damini waits—all wait—in the fluid quiet for the creeper-like cord to stop pulsing and the afterbirth to emerge. When it does, Damini directs Goldina to grasp the cord. Goldina binds it in two places, and cuts between, turning the Lotus almost harmless.

Damini cannot find it in herself to berate old Vijayanthi, who had cautioned against applying more than a thumbnail of the fire plant. She can only berate herself in Punjabi and Hindi, and even in English: *Are you or are you not a moron?*

Goldina croons as her large dark hands slide over the baby in the basin. She lifts the baby and gives her to Damini. Damini rubs the baby's butter-soft skin with turmeric paste.

With a kajal pencil, she makes a black dot bindi just above the bridge of the baby's nose to ward off evil eye and bring her any luck she's been granted in this life. She swaddles the baby in an old sari and lets Kamna hold her sister for a few minutes, while she and

Goldina bind Leela's stomach tight to keep out bad air and demons lurking to use Leela's emptiness.

Damini places the child beside Leela, but the exhausted mother has drifted off to sleep. She directs Goldina to clean up, and wrap the afterbirth in a paper bag. Goldina retreats outside and the door creaks closed.

"Watch the baby," Damini says to Kamna.

Goldina hasn't gone far—now she'll want to be paid.

Standing on the cement terrace, Damini fills her lungs with the cool night air. She hunkers down, her back to the wall, and gazes at the moonlit mountains. The gleaming snow on those peaks will melt before any girl crosses the many ranges between here and that far ring of mountains.

Goldina, sitting cross-legged on the ground a few feet away, proffers the shawl Damini lent her earlier.

Every time she wears that shawl it will remind her that Goldina has worn it.

This is not a city. Here someone is lower so that someone else can be higher.

"Keep it," she says, sounding magnanimous. In memory of their mother's stories, told and untold, she bestows a ten rupee note on Goldina. Goldina touches the money to her forehead, but still looks expectant.

Damini rises, enters the storeroom and fetches a sack of potatoes.

"This is all?" says Goldina.

"Be grateful you got something for delivering a girl."

"This is my fault?" says Goldina. "Plant a radish, expect a cauliflower?"

"Be more respectful, *churi!*"

Goldina mutters under her breath, "*Hein!* Do I get anything from being respectful . . . ?" but heaves the sack of potatoes over her shoulder. She reaches for the paper bag with the afterbirth and cord.

"Bury it deep," says Damini. "Don't let stray dogs dig it up."

Goldina cocks her head in assent, and melts into the shadows past the terrace.

Back in the birthing chamber, milk is beginning in Leela's breasts. Damini massages to rid Leela of it, then binds Leela's breasts temporarily because her mother-in-law, Ramkali Bai, always cautioned first milk is impure.

"Go Kamna," says Damini. "Tell your father he has another daughter."

Leela turns her face away and sobs and wails.

DAMINI

"Stupid women," Chunilal yells. "Can't do anything right."

I should have faced him myself, but I was tired. Poor Kamna.

"Even if I win the lottery, where will I find money for two dowries? Even if I find enough for one wedding, even if I find enough for one dowry—these days a son-in-law's family keeps asking and asking for more every year. I don't need the ojha to come and foretell our future—I see moneylenders gathering like vultures. I'll have to sell my truck. Soon Mohan will have nothing left to his name—my name. What use are girls?"

Damini parts the wooden doors between the two rooms and yells, "Chot lagi pahard se, torde ghar ki sil!" Your hurt was caused by the mountain, don't take it out on the grindstone!

"I'm only telling the truth," he says. And coughs and coughs—he's going to cough out his lungs.

Kamna is standing there, a look of shock on her face.

Kamna must learn what women learn.

Kamna strokes her father's back as he spasms. "Don't worry, baba," she says. "I won't get married."

"What? You want to stay a girl forever?" her father spits out.

"I'll just look after you," says Kamna.

"You will get married and go to your real home," says Damini.

"This is not my real home?"

"It is, it is," says Damini, unable to face the hurt in Kamna's eyes, "till you get married."

"Why do I have to get married?"

"Dharma."

"Whose dharma?"

"Your father's." That's Chunilal's role in the movie of his life.

"I will have to find you a lesser family. We will have to sell the farm. Or Mohan will have to look after you." Chunilal is almost weeping, as if all these calamities are arriving tomorrow.

"I will look after Mohan," says Kamna, setting her chin as Leela used to.

Damini hides a smile. Truly, Leela has taught her daughter little. Even if she does look after her brother, Kamna should know by now to pretend her brother looks after her.

"I can be a dancer *and* drive your truck."

"You? Drive my truck? Ha! The first time you break a bangle you'll come running home, crying."

Kamna is undaunted. "*And* I can look after the farm as well."

She shouldn't tell any man she can do so many things—he'll only sit back and let her do all of them. The girl looks as if she's going to challenge her father again.

"*Chal!*" Damini takes Kamna by the shoulders and shoos her toward the door.

With her back to Chunilal, she hears him say, "Who ever heard of a woman farming?"

"Leela is," Damini objects before she can stop herself. "When you are playing filum songs in your truck, who do you think farms these three terraces? Leela hacks and carries loads of wood from the forest every day on her head. Leela cooks the cows' feed, Leela milks them. Leela stacks the bricks to repair each terrace retaining wall. Till two days ago she was bending in the field, giving each onion shoot a handful of water at a time."

From just outside the doorway, Kamna says, "Ma-ji cooks for us—two meals a day." Her indignation is tinted with mischief. "She wields the hoe, she weeds, she knits, she sews our clothes and washes them."

"You women," Chunilal shouts. "Always complaining, complaining . . . never finish complaining. See if any of you can stand the heat of the plains, do battle with death hour after hour on the road, go sleepless, alone-alone, day after day, breathing kerosene and diesel. See if you can judge where to pay a fee and where to pay a fine, where there's a speedbump and where there's a cow, which fuel is diesel and which is kerosene . . . all of you just sitting here, eating and waiting till I come back."

Damini should not say more. Anything more will only set a bad example and encourage wrong tendencies and rebelliousness in Kamna. She sinks to her haunches and rests her head on her knees for a moment. Guests should be like rice grains that take on the flavour of a curry. Chunilal may be sick, but he is still a man and master of the house. She is a guest. But she is also Leela's mother.

She lifts her head. "Leela does puja every day to the gods for your health. She sows seed potatoes, harvests them. And the brinjal, cabbage, peas and cauliflower . . . And she has children. While you're watching TV, she never sits down from morning to night."

Leela calls weakly, from the next room. "See what lies in store for this girl too."

A protracted silence follows, waxes, and approaches the threshold of discomfort.

"See?" Chunilal sticks his feet out from his blanket and wiggles his toes. "She agrees."

"If you didn't want more children, you should have left her alone," says Damini. "Even children know about wearing the topi . . . Or you should have allowed her to go to Shimla several months ago."

"Did I apply the brakes? I said she should go. She's the one who kept saying, Then who will look after you? And I didn't want her to go alone—I said, I should be with her so the doctor-saabs can't ignore her."

Damini stops herself from saying more. The impact of her bitter words should be softened by sweet, even if she isn't feeling sweet. "*Chalo!*" she says. "We're all tired, we don't know what we're saying. It's five in the morning and we haven't slept in two days. Kamna, you sleep beside your mother. I'll take the girl in a minute, and feed her some sugar water." She raises her voice to be heard in the next room. "Leela, rest now, and I'll give you the baby in a few hours. Chunilal, don't worry. You make preparations for this child's gauntrila ceremony. Think, what will you name her?"

"Let the gods find her a name," Chunilal turns to the snow peaks. "I refuse her mine."

Three days later, Damini crosses the upper terrace to the latticed parapet. She stands beneath the unpitying stars. She gazes at the dark glimmer of the snow peaks. She has placed a sickle beneath Leela's pillow to ward off the evil eye and prevent nightmares, but Leela has cried out a few times tonight and Damini cannot sleep.

She strikes a match and lights a beedi from the cone Vijayanthi gave her. She inhales; tobacco hits her lungs.

A live child. Clearly a girl was in this family's bhagya and Leela should say: "Brahman, the power beyond all power, sent her." And persuade Chunilal to give thanks. Sometimes a moment of great joy contains great sorrow.

She was not in Gurkot while Leela was growing up. Other women might have felt banished, other women might have felt more pain than she in leaving her children behind, but Damini was only twenty and full of the excitement of seeing New Delhi, navel of the world, where Jawaharlal Nehru ruled as first prime minister. The place where Mahatma Gandhi was shot by a Hindu, Nathuram

Godse, for being too friendly to Muslims and Pakistan. At twenty, she took in with matchless delight the cries of vendors, the Mughal monuments centred in roundabouts, the Republic Day parade, India Gate, Rashtrapati Bhavan, the sounds of constant construction and the whizz of tubby Ambassador cars. And the shame of her widowhood faded as she tried to help Mem-saab overcome the shame of deafness.

But her shame is always there, waiting for a harsh word to wake it.

Could she raise the girl-baby as her own—feeding and loving her until Leela and Chunilal recover from the shock of her birth?

"What if people thought this child is not Leela's, but yours, mata-ji?" Chunilal said today. So casually, as if asking her opinion. "What do you think would happen?"

If a widow were accused of bearing a child, she could be stoned, she could be banished. The child could be killed. Other women would do it—Chunilal wouldn't have to raise a finger. All he'd have to do is pretend. How loudly could Leela defend Damini and the baby without endangering herself?

"Understand me," Chunilal said. "I never intended to make this child. She happened. A terrible mistake. Look how ugly she is. That too is my doing—I'm an ugly man. Kamna is ugly too, that's why I named her so. Desire. Cause of my troubles, from the time I was a boy."

Two of Leela's babies died before birth—perhaps the spirits took them. In a city, Leela could have walked into a government clinic in her first three months and said, "I can't afford another child," and any doctor could have performed a cleaning out—legally, easily. But events conspired to deny Leela's wishes at every point. Not being able to leave the family to go to Shimla, not being able to cleanse the child from her body. All wrong timing, as if not one god or goddess has been listening to Leela's wishes.

Damini fists the cinder of the beedi, containing its heat in her palm.

Lila's breasts are now swollen and painful, but she will not feed her baby. Today all persuasion failed again, so Damini sent Kamna to

Vijayanthi's house to ask if there is another woman in the village who can feed it.

One sweeper-woman, came the answer.

Damini threatened to bring that sweeper-woman to feed Leela's child if Leela wouldn't. But all Leela said was, "Let the sweeper-woman feed the child and keep her—we won't take her back."

What use is it to feed this girl for a few days if Chunilal and Leela refuse her love and caring thereafter? All girls need is a little love and caring, but . . . so many die of falling down hillsides or into wells, so many catch fevers or starve. *Petal-like eyelids beneath her fingertips— closing, closing.*

Damini inhales as if the smoke will fumigate fear. She holds it, exhales; smoke curls and dissolves in the crisp air.

Chunilal is coughing so hard, he could have TB. But TB is not as common as when she was young. And his sores . . . the white coating on his tongue . . .

Her gaze falls to a smear of hardened white paste and a broken pink plastic shell on the ground.

Ten rupees. The price of one of Chunilal's lottery tickets. That's all Kamna spent two days ago. Ten rupees for a sample bottle of Fair & Lovely. Chunilal snatched the skin-lightening cream, and smashed it on the parapet because she bought it without his permission. Until his anger is spent, Kamna must sleep on the lower level with the cows each night.

Chunilal's voice is in her inner ear . . . *If it's a girl, I don't want to see her* . . . "Let the gods find her a name, I refuse to name her." Vijayanthi's voice . . . *"Sometimes we have to do what is necessary for the good of a family."*

Damini was the one who said to apply the fire plant. Damini should have known how to help her daughter. But even when teachers teach girls up to class eight, they don't tell you what you really need to know in life. Maybe they tell boys.

An answer may present itself if she gives it her whole undivided attention, if she really listens. Damini, who was a pair of ears for thirty years, often hears things people do not intend to be heard. "Tell me your wish," she said to Leela a few hours ago. "And remember you will have to live with your decision forever."

Leela wept. "You know what I wish. I wish the girl had never been born."

Threads of pink, threads of blue shuttle across the pale gold loom of the morning sky.

In whitewashed houses scattered across the wavy lines of the hills, women are stirring, lighting fires in cookrooms or walking into the forest with their scythes, to gather firewood for the day. Their life is the only life this girl will know. Not as bad as the life of a sweeper, but so difficult.

A red strand of hair falls across Damini's face. She turns to face the cool breeze. Mist and rain clouds obscure the far snow peaks. Birdsong sounds all around her, but the gods are silent.

Damini returns to the birth chamber. She lifts the newborn from Leela's side and takes the baby to her bed. She lies down, nuzzling close to the sleeping child, a taut ache in her chest.

Four days later, Damini sits cross-legged on her rope-bed, her granddaughter wailing in her lap. A bukhari glows in the corner; the shallow basin of orange-grey coals warms the room. Chunilal and Mohan are asleep in the men's quarters next door. Kamna sleeps on the floor below in the cow's room. *Hé Ram!* How can any of them sleep through this child's crying?

Damini shelters the infant beneath her sari-pallu and opens the child's swaddling.

She is so beautiful.

A N U

Dearest Rano,

Sitting in a cane armchair on the grey stone terrace of what will be the nuns' residence in Gurkot, looking out on a panoramic view of the snow peaks. Father Pashan, Sister Bethany and I arrived yesterday to check on the renovation of the Anglican chapel, the red-roofed schoolroom and cement buildings that will become our clinic.

Anu chews the end of her pen. Past Father Pashan's cassocked figure seated beside her, sunlight flavours the early morning air, washing the treetops, reaching fingers of shadow down the mountains—lighting but not warming. A bird calls *kewkew*. A slight breeze stirs clusters of pine cones.

"Did you notice the rainwater harvesting tank?"

"Where, Father? My city eyes are missing half the landscape."

Father Pashan points to one end of the terrace. He's quite old—at least fifty-five—but has been untiring since the moment the expedition left the Shimla convent, taking turns driving the jeep on the looping roads, lighting the coals of a bukhari to warm the small house, arranging that the driver will replenish their petrol jerry cans in Jalawaaz and bring them to Gurkot, spreading sheets and quilts in the bedroom, and opening his own bedding roll in the main room, making chapatis on the gas hotplate in the little kitchen, right along with Sister Anu and Sister Bethany. Then he sat cross-legged with them on a dhurrie, eating daal bhaat, and only stopped talking about plans for the ministry when All India Radio said Bishop Tutu and the newly appointed government of South Africa were holding seminars and workshops to help people understand a draft National Unity and Reconciliation Bill. "I wish we could have such trials in India too," Pashan said, "to face the results of caste."

"What made you choose this area for our mission?" Anu asks.

"The good Lord led me here," the priest says. "I needed a flock, and Mr. Amanjit Singh wants the cemetery maintained by a Christian." His eyes glow as if there is nowhere he would rather be.

Anu says, "Do you feel there's something special about Gurkot? I do."

"Jesus first spoke," Father Pashan says, his blue eye reflecting the sky, "to the outcastes. They heard his message, they responded first. It will be so here as well. Our Catholic congregation as far as I have been able to count is about two hundred families. Two hundred dalit and tribal families thirsty for the Word. About the same number are Sikhs—some have caste, some converted from outcastes. And it may be necessary to feed the belly before we feed the soul."

His concern for social justice is contagious. And his warmth. The way he talks to her! As if he thinks she's intelligent. Anu has never before had a friendship with an unrelated man. Growing up, she learned to flirt, admire a man's achievements, exclaim over him, but a *friendship*? Men in her life were either gods, bosses, husbands or servants. In school and college if she so much as spoke to a "boy" older than herself, Sharad Uncle or Mumma would have made sure she was married off to him to preserve her reputation. When friendships with men were becoming commonplace for other women in New Delhi, Anu'd been afraid Vikas would find out if she said more than a few words to an unrelated man, or met a man as she was now—alone and unchaperoned.

Maybe it takes a vow of celibacy to be friends with a man.

Pashan takes a final gulp of tea and gives the dregs to a flower bed. He goes indoors to dress. Sister Bethany has gone to meet the village headmaster, and see how the mission can supplement his efforts. She'll return with list upon list of tasks and equipment.

Anu savours the vista for a moment, flexes cold-numbed fingers and writes:

We're converting the chapel to Catholic—all that is needed is a crucifix and holy water for consecration. I thought holy water came from some fount in the Holy See, but it comes from a tap. Still, once blessed, it has the healing powers of Ganges-water.

It's strange to be out of the convent routine—prayers at five became prayers at six this morning. I don't think we will be stopping for noon prayers . . .

Oh, scratch that! Prayer focuses her, allows her to peer into herself. Through it, she attempts to link herself to the bright warm light once more. She's never succeeded even for an instant, but each attempt leaves her feeling effortlessly attentive, boundless and spacious. Rano probably wouldn't understand.

Remember I told you Father Pashan was the priest at the Vatican Embassy in New Delhi? Well, this morning my companion Sister Bethany told me his Provincial actually banished him to the hills for giving a sermon in which he said the story of the loaves and fishes in the Bible shouldn't be interpreted literally. He said Christ may or may not have fed five thousand people. Instead, he said Jesus was rebelling against the dietary laws of his day about unclean food. He was demonstrating sharing and justice.

The clinic he has founded here is called The Bread of Healing. From Ecclesiastes—you remember it too, from school, I'm sure.

She won't. Rano went to Moral Science classes while Anu volunteered for Catechism.

"Cast your bread upon the waters . . . Give portions to seven, yes to eight, for you do not know what disaster may come upon the land."

The lines I always liked come next—

"As you do not know the path of the wind, or how the body is formed in a mother's womb, so you cannot understand the work of god, the Maker of all things. Sow your seed in the morning, and at evening let not your hands be idle, for you do not know which will succeed, whether this or that, or whether both will do equally well."

I doubt if we'll be idle at any time of day. Our chapel is simple and elegant, with a whitewashed bell tower. The adjoining clinic is basic—very basic. My nurses' station has a desk—we need another chair. I have the luxury of a double burner, a saucepan and a tin of Brooke Bond tea. There's a small doctor's office and examination room, a three-bed women's ward, a three-bed men's ward, an x-ray shed, two storage rooms where I will set up the lab for blood, stool and urine tests.

Dr. Gupta, our hairy, happy, roly-poly bear of a Punjabi doctor, is already holding court (oops, office hours). I've been making day visits to assist him two days a week when the convent jeep and driver bring him from the nearby valley town of Jalawaaz. He's retired and either too old or too lofty to take the minibus. He has a huge heart, but is the kind of chap to whom that organ is just a pump. We argue occasionally about matters at the cellular level. Like, what force could it be that activates a chromosome? He calls it chance. He says, In the beginning was the word, and the word was Algorithm, generator of patterns. I say, In the beginning was the Word, and maybe it was A, C, G, T, the nucleic acids that make up our DNA. I feel as you did, when you tried explaining a Faiz ghazal to a systems analyst.

The chapel, school and clinic are on the estate of an old Sikh family, and we feel very blessed to be running it. Oh, you'll like this: our chapel stands on the same knoll as an older Sikh gurdwara. So both faiths will share space, and Christians are invited to dine in the Sikh community dining hall after worship. Father Pashan says sitting side by side and eating "langar" breaks caste and he approves of that, but cautions he doesn't want us becoming Sikhs!

A power line skims the treetops and darts downhill to meet orange-painted giants carrying it to Shimla. A path down the mountain passes terraces planted with rosebushes and apple trees. She can see women on the path in salwar-kameez, sweaters and kerchiefs, some are just specks beneath cone-shaped baskets on their backs. Older women wear the full-length rejta skirt and dhattu headcovering. Young women wear the salwar-kameez and dupatta like Anu, but in many colours. Most wear sandals or sneakers—the high heels she misses would be treacherous on these slopes.

The Church also has its caste system. Father Pashan says Indian priests are still second class in the Vatican heirarchy, and nuns are definitely below priests. In many parishes, we are required to do menial work for the priests, but Imaculata says,"My nuns don't."

   When I finish my nursing course, I'll be the Parish Nurse here in Gurkot. Bethany and I will share this two-room Tudor cottage built by a British colonist, tucked beneath the chapel and clinic, across the road. You'd think it spare, with its jute dhurries, chic-bamboo blinds and navar-beds, but it's quite comfortable. We've applied for a phone, but of course that will take several years. Still, we'll have electricity, a kitchen with a refrigerator, a tiled bathroom and a flush toilet. And a breathtaking north-facing view of the ranges. Beyond them may lie legendary Mt. Meru. And Tibet (oops, China).

   She pulls Rano's last letter from her hip pocket. Rano says she and Jatin's family and now Chetna too go to the Dixie-Derry gurdwara every Sunday, as if they keep a Sabbath and as if the gurdwara is a church. Rano asks for a sooji-halwa recipe—she's taking it to a Punjabi poetry gathering. Anu writes that one from memory. What are the names of the rasas—Anu can only remember seven of the nine aesthetic emotions, and writes those. And the debut dance of a bharatanatyam dancer—jatiswaram or arangetram? Arangetram.

   Rano sounds afraid India will slip away from her. Yet she says

Canada has a policy of multiculturalism that allows you to be yourself, and Indian, and Canadian in Canada. Which means Chetna won't be asked to sacrifice being Indian. Sacrifice—blood—

Rano, we've begun daylong education camps in this area. We leave very early from Shimla, and Bethany holds a legal clinic and a letter-writing camp, and I teach teenage girls about menstruation, reproduction, babies—subjects the nuns never taught us. I began thinking I won't be with Chetna when her time comes. Could you explain menstruation? I don't want her to pick up ideas about being polluted and untouchable during your menses. Sikhs aren't supposed to have these Hindu customs but a couple of my Sikh students say their grandmothers still don't allow them in the kitchen during their periods, just like our grandmother. So anyway, please can you make sure?

There is a hole in my heart where she was, and I'm trying to do without her. It's been six months since I saw her. In a few days, she will see snow for the first time and so will I. I'll send her another postcard. Hope that's okay.
Love,
Anu

She folds the letter, inserts it in an envelope. She takes her billfold from her shoulder bag and from it removes three stamps.

Only the most interesting for Rano and Chetna. She found these at Combermere Post Office in Shimla, undemanded, slightly battered since British times. She remembers these same stamps from Dadu's collection, and the way he held them so gently with a pair of tweezers when he showed them to her.

p.s. The one with the Indian flag is the first issued after Independence in 1947. And the one with the emblem of the Ashoka lions was the second. The ten-rupee stamp was issued on the first anniversary of Independence, to commemorate Mahatma Gandhi after he was killed by that RSS man, Nathuram Godse. Dadu told me,"Finding all three is like finding the trinity:

Lords Brahma, Vishnu and Shiv. If you are ever compelled to sell or trade them," he said, *"be sure it is for something vital."*

She tucks them in, licks the envelope closed, and sticks a modern international stamp on the outside. On the back flap, she writes her new name: Sister Anupam.

DAMINI

"WHAT MORE DO YOU WANT?" SAYS VIJAYANTHI. "I GAVE
you advice, boots, beedis for tobacco . . ."

Icy mountains loom all around. Snow patches are appearing on
nearer mountains, too. Today it feels as if it will take longer for
Damini to balance her karma as for wind and rain to lay the mountains low.

She follows Vijayanthi beneath the overhang. As Vijayanthi hunches
to enter her cookroom, Damini too doubles over to duck under the
smoke layer, crouch-walking till she can drop her bottom and sit
before the four-legged bowl of the stove. Vijayanthi pushes a jute sack
cushion at Damini and she takes it, gratefully—Vijayanthi is according Damini some respect, trying to make up for her harsh words.

Heat from the twig and coal fire singes her face. Her eyes smart—
must be the smoke. "I didn't think it would be so difficult," Damini
says.

Since she brought the tiny body home from Anamika Devi's cave
two weeks ago, she has been feeling weak. Ever since that small body,
too young to cremate, was buried under the peach tree on the lower
terrace, her heart has been jumping as if missing beats, as if she has
taken too large a hit of tobacco. And she has been heavy with longing
to lie down.

Lying down is impossible since Leela is still in her unclean stage, unable to cook, and too depleted to work in the field. Today Damini was washing clothes beneath the waterspout by five, collecting firewood in the forest by six, and then working with Kamna to milk the cows for Mohan to carry milk to the roadside storehouse. Muscles she never felt are informing her of their presence.

You can be thrown in a rat-infested cell for what you did. You can hang for this if someone tells.

"Did I say it is easy, fighting for women's wishes?"

"No." Damini's throat feels knotted and dry.

"You saw my Madhu—when she was born, I couldn't do it. I told my grandson I have become too old and soft. But you are strong, still. Tell me, is Leela glad?"

"She's . . . no, not glad. She is doing what needs doing."

"But?"

"She does not speak."

"Does she blame you? Sometimes they do."

"She said when I left her and went to New Delhi, she began to learn never to want what she cannot have. And she says the girl's bhagya took her early. But no, she's not grateful."

"Huh—what gratitude can you expect from children these days?"

"She says if Chunilal had not withheld his name, she would have fed the girl."

"It's too late now. Who came to mourn?"

"If I had told Chimta, Tubelight, Supari or Matki, they would have sent the men in their families. But I didn't. As it was, the sweeper-woman, Goldina, and her husband, Samuel, came. Samuel dug the grave."

"What did you tell them?"

"That a ghost came into the child and gave her a fever, and she died."

"Did you pay the sweeper well, to believe you?"

"Yes—twenty rupees." And because the thought of jail sent her into mindless panic.

"Is Leela's husband glad?"

"He has stopped blaming Leela."

"And how is he treating you?"

"He doesn't refuse my care. Maybe he is trying to please me by accepting it. I had to feed him tea with a spoon today, he was so ill, and I'm tending him only because it's my dharma. I can't be angry at a sick man."

"*Arey!* If you still have a roof over your head, what more do you want?"

Vijayanthi reaches around till her hand meets a brass bowl of wheat flour. She pulls it toward her and says, "People think a dai has to do something like this every time. It's only sometimes that such acts become necessary."

Damini draws an uneasy breath. She wants to forget the feel of that tiny body nestling close, the smile that bloomed on those tiny lips when she massaged the baby's face. That the baby's eyes opened, and that the child looked directly into her eyes as if she could see. What she has done is—say it, name it!—killing. The horror of that fact encases her in ice.

And though her *Gita* tells how Lord Krishna urged Lord Arjun to do his duty as a warrior without regard to outcome, even if those outcomes included the killing of his relatives, it does not say if Arjun felt as heavy-hearted, as full of remorse as Damini when he returned from battle.

"If it had been someone I didn't know, if it had not been my granddaughter . . ."

And there's the matter of her remaining granddaughter. Kamna is not speaking to her father since he smashed her bottle of Fair & Lovely. Kamna is afraid of him, though he grows sicker by the day. Damini has told her a bottle of face cream isn't important, but today Mohan asked Kamna to dance, and she wouldn't.

Mohan is oblivious, blowing his flute tunelessly till the cows low and roll their eyes in agony. Damini shouldn't have bought it for him.

Vijayanthi cups her hand in the bowl. Damini follows the prompt, taking up a nearby jug. She pours water into Vijayanthi's hand. Vijayanthi lets the water run into the flour for a few seconds, and then gestures with her other hand to stop.

"At least it was you, not some stranger, who returned this atman to brahman," Vijyanthi says. "At least it was done with love. Tell Leela, next time the gods will send a boy. And if you can't do what women want"— contempt rings in Vijayanthi's voice—"don't come anymore. I have too little time left in this life, I'll teach someone else."

"No, no, don't say that." says Damini, misery eating at her insides. "You see, my pension . . . *aye-hai*! The gourmint has stopped my pension. I went to the post office in Jalawaaz—a letter from the pension office was waiting. The guormint says now my son has a job, he should now look after me."

"Then? Did you tell Suresh?"

"I can't." says Damini. "When I lost my job and couldn't give him money every month, Suresh couldn't afford to live in Delhi anymore. So his swami found him a job in Jalawaaz as a teacher in the RSS school beside the temple. He came to see us yesterday in his new khaki shorts, white shirt and saffron scarf with Lord Ram printed on it. He's now wearing a tail of hair from here," she touches the crown of her head, "longer than the rest. 'Jai Shri Ram!' was his greeting, full of pride. But they don't pay him a salary, only living expenses, and travel expenses when he goes to teach the sweepers and jungle people in surrounding villages. Sometimes they give him a share of the temple donations."

"That's more than many other men get."

"But he needs money to find a bride from a good family, with a bit of land maybe—so how can I say, Oh please give me money?"

"You don't need money till you go to a city. Till then, just exchange this for that."

Vijayanthi gropes around till her fingers meet a hollow iron pipe lying beside her. She hands it to Damini. Damini blows into it, enlivening the coal-flame beneath the stove. "I had promised Chunilal my pension. Two hundred a month," she says. She will give it to him from her bonus money until she begins earning.

"Two hundred rupees: that's four babies a month," says Vijayanthi. She finishes working the dough, twirls the bowl. The flour paste turns sticky as it changes to roti dough. "In a city you'd find four babies a month. But here—only ten or fifteen a year. You can charge more if they come out boys. If they are girls, ask if the father wants to greet a marriage party or not . . . if he says no, you know what he is asking you to do . . ."

Damini blows into the pipe a few more times and the coals burn brightly. "If the baby comes out a girl," she says, "would I be blamed just as they blame the mother?"

"Sometimes." Vijayanthi taps her breastbone. "I tell young men, if you want sons, plant sons, then only can you reap sons and carry on your family name. Plant a daughter, reap a daughter. But they! They think a woman's koke can turn a daughter into son or a son into a daughter."

"I will only take fees for children I deliver live," says Damini.

"Then you will get half the pay you could get," says Vijayanthi. "But it's your bijness. I can tell you what to do, the rest is up to you."

"It's not a bijness," says Damini. "In our family, men do bijness, not women. I'll take donations. People can pay what they feel my skill is worth."

"If that's how you want it, then you'll need to learn to heal all sicknesses. I will teach you." Vijayanthi pats the dough into a large ball, scrapes her fingers and adds every last morsel to the whole. "Most people only want to tell me the old ways are wrong. When I heard the padri is going to open a full-time clinic beside the church, I immediately went to ask him if I could help—a year ago I could still see quite well. But he said I'd have to learn many new things." She reaches into the dough and scoops out a small ball.

"Learn about new medicines or new plants?"

"Neither. Medicines come from Delhi and abroad. The plants—
what can he teach me that my mother-in-law didn't? See, the padri
isn't like our ojha—the padri only prays, he doesn't heal. And he only
becomes possessed by his Lord Jesus on Sundays, no other day. And
he and his followers pray only to Lord Jesus for healing, not all the
gods. He needs a doctor-saab to come and do healing.

"Then what did he say you had to learn?"

"To touch strangers and clean away shit like any sweeper. He said
he himself is a sweeper and all of us are just like sweepers. But I
thought, *I'm not so desperate*, and came away."

Vijayanthi rolls the dough ball between her palms, and then
dredges it in flour.

"Will the new doctor have medicines to stop girl babies from
coming?" says Damini.

Vijayanthi laughs with no amusement. "Ask Lord Golunath. He's
Lord Brahma's incarnation, and only Lord Brahma can stop girls
from coming," She holds out the ball of dough. Damini takes it, looks
around, finds the rolling pin and stone flat by the stove and rolls out
the roti. "Medicines stop boys as well as girls from coming. But you
can find out if an atman has by mistake entered a girl's body, so you
can clean it out. You must find out early, mind you. Not so late as
Leela—that's why I didn't tell you before."

Slap-slap. Damini flips the floppy dough from palm to palm and
places the roti gently on the tava, heating it in the concave bowl of hot
iron. "Then you don't need to . . ."

Vijayanthi nods. "And more live children will be born." She pauses
for effect, and rubs her thumb over her forefinger. "The padri said his
clinic won't have an ultra-soon."

"Ultra-soon?"

"What," says Vijayanthi, "is the use of opening a clinic if village
women still have to walk all the way to Jalawaaz for ultra-soon?"

"What is ultra-soon?"

"A machine that looks inside a woman," says Vijayanthi. "With it, there is nothing the doctor can't see. He sees the flower of her womb, the stems that hold it, the passage, the gateway the baby will use. He takes a photo, *click!*—right through the woman's skin—to see if a tail is growing in front of the child."

"Can the machine see her past?"

"No. And though it foretells if a girl or boy is coming, it can't—" Vijayanthi's voice drops to a whisper and she shifts a squat-step closer, "it can't foretell what the woman will do if she knows a girl is coming. Of course, doctors know what she will do, but they pretend they don't."

Vijanthi gropes around again, comes up with a pair of tongs, which she hands to Damini. The roti is rising slightly. Damini pokes at it with the tongs.

"And if she is told a girl is coming?"

Damini lifts the roti from the tava and places it upon the flame.

"She can have it cleaned out right there, at the Jalawaaz clinic— but first the woman needs to know."

"Does a husband or father or brother have to go with the woman to get it cleaned out?"

"No, the woman doesn't have to tell anyone. But it's difficult if she doesn't, because its so far to either Jalawaaz or Shimla. And sometimes doctors ask the woman to bring her husband with her, to prove her husband says yes. And if the woman can't bring her husband, some doctors charge more money. If she takes you with her, you can say you're her mother-in-law."

The roti has begun to blister and smoke. Damini removes it from the fire and drops it onto a steel platter. Vijayanthi scoops into the glistening wheatish skin of the roti-dough, and begins another.

Damini watches, thinking. A child in the womb is unnamed flesh, and the vedas say all destruction is disappearance. Not every seed takes root, not every one that falls becomes an oak or pine. Everything is important—soil, water, wind, incline. A seed is only potential seeking the heat of a womb.

If the form is destroyed before breath, the girl's life cannot happen. The decision to return being to non-being, return a child to brahman, should belong only to the woman who harbours a child in her womb. No government, doctor, nurse, midwife or grandmother should be a selector of souls.

Vijayanthi is saying she's sure the new ultrasoon clinic in Jalawaaz will give Damini a commission for each woman referred. A commission that will help her pay Chunilal two hundred rupees a month so no one can say she took from her daughter's home.

On her way home, the mountains look less forbidding to Damini. The sky has turned as turquoise as yearning; the trees are tensely green and waiting. Inside her, a nub of feeling rises to a prayer of gratitude: she will never need to do what she did again.

The ultra-soon is the answer.

Shimla
December 1994

ANU

Sᴜꜱᴛᴇʀ Aɴᴜ ꜰᴏʟʟᴏᴡꜱ ᴛʜᴇ ʟᴏɴɢ ꜱᴛʀɪᴅᴇ ᴏꜰ ᴀ ʀᴀɢɢᴇᴅ man with a large knife tied to his walking stick like a bayonet. It's the tenth anniversary of Bobby's death and she needs to see the spot where he died. Her guide is the man who carried her wounded brother on his back uphill to the car and accompanied Bobby all the way to Snowdon Hospital. He leads her downhill from the Cart Road on a pocked byway that ends where a footpath begins, swivelling at intervals to assure her in lilting Himachali Hindi that the spot she seeks is just ahead. Sister Anu keeps her eyes on the footpath, determinedly ignoring the ravine beside her that plunges through December sunshine into darkness.

One more curve and the footpath opens onto a long grassy clearing flanked by ancient pines. A canopy of branches floats above Sister Anu like lances ready to thrust or parry. Monkeys chatter and screech at their approach. The guide bows to them as incarnations of Lord Hanuman, then raises his stick and feints. They scamper away.

Details—telegrams from memory.

We sent Bobby here. All of us—Dadu, Mumma, Sharad Uncle, Purnima-aunty and I. It was a month after Madam G.'s assassination and her party's anti-Sikh killing spree and Dadu had came to Delhi to help the Home Minister shoo away questions from Sikh widows asking why the army wasn't called in to stop the carnage. Bobby was fifteen. We all thought a hiking trip in the hills with four other boys in the winter would knock the sissy out of him. His friends would do what we couldn't, make him a man.

What friends! One boy invited Bobby to his home for a party and forgot to send his car for him, so after two hours of watching Bobby wait by the gate, I flagged a scootie and escorted him there. But he was so mortified to be late, he couldn't go in. So I brought him home. The other three had been invited to Bobby's fourteenth birthday party—they wouldn't have forgotten to attend if Dadu was a raja or an industrialist. Yet Bobby wanted to go to Shimla with these boys.

Beyond the clearing, the ground falls away sharply again. The guide leads her to a group of huge boulders. "Isko Angrez log kehlate theh Council Rock," he says. The English called this Council Rock.

Wasp-waisted women with ruffled parasols must have come here, and ordered their uniformed khidmatgars to spread blankets and Irish linen for a picnic. Those white-gloved manservants would have laid gilt-edged china and sterling place settings under these looming pines, and darted around pouring whisky from cut-glass decanters for portly men with handlebar moustaches.

Instead, Bobby and his friends went hunting chukar partridge. Friends with guns.

One friend's gun went off on this very day in 1984—how did it just go off, she asks the guide.

"No, Miss-saab. I didn't lead them here. They themselves came here. But I helped them take the wounded boy to hospital. That's how I came to know there were guns."

Did a gun threaten the one boy in the group who wasn't man enough?

Where was Bobby standing, where was the friend standing? What might Bobby have said, what did that friend make him say? The police didn't ask any such questions.

Because after wounding Bobby, his "friend" didn't call an ambulance. Bobby's friend called his father, who paid off the Himachal

State police and made arrangements for Bobby to be taken to Snowdon Hospital. Only then did anyone call Dadu.

Bobby's friend's father said his son didn't mean any harm—remember, he was Bobby's *friend*. Dadu and Mumma should not press charges, he told Dadu—there was nothing to be gained. Besides, if they did, he would fight them in court for the next twenty-five years before he would let his son pay for a careless mistake. Bobby, he told them, couldn't have felt anything. Just one minute he was here, the next minute he was in a coma, and a week after that in the next life. "So why ruin a young boy's life? Can you imagine a young boy of fifteen, a boy from a good background sentenced to jail along with darkie low caste criminals—just for an *accident*? What good would that do?"

Eventually, Dadu and Mumma were persuaded to go along. Dadu told the world Bobby and his friends went hiking in Shimla. That Bobby fell down the hillside and was killed. No mention of a shot, no mention of a gun.

It wouldn't have done Dadu's career any good if he'd reported his son's murder. And since a murdered brother would have been a liability for Anu's prospects of marriage, Mumma told Anu she too must say it was an 'accident.' For so many years, Anu has not been able to speak of it, even think of it. Yet Bobby is why she has asked to study nursing, Bobby is why she is doing her nurse's training on the coma ward at Snowdon. But his death is also the lie that comes between her and Mumma.

Now a similar lie must be told to the world about Dadu so Mumma can save face. They all must say that his death, too, was an accident, which happened during an inspection tour of his district. Because if it wasn't an accident, than what was Deepak Lal doing eating onion pakoras and egg karhi on the veranda of a widow's home? Just the two of them (and her servants). Mumma said, "Everyone knows how loose and immoral widows are."

Notified of her father's death by her lawyer ten days ago, Anu returned to the plains for a week. Mumma said everyone in that small town must have seen Dadu on the veranda with the widow. "Accident is a better word," she said. "More heroic."

Her sparrow face was suddenly worn and large-eyed. The corners of her mouth drooped. Grey gleamed at the roots of her hair, and two creases were beginning in her neck. "How could he be unfaithful to *me?*" she kept saying, as if Dadu could have been unfaithful to any other woman.

Anu dealt with the details because Mumma, who maintained English ways and spoke and taught only English in every city and town of India, could no longer speak enough Hindi to deal with them. And Anu insisted on performing Dadu's last rites.

She must have called every pandit within a radius of a hundred kilometres—none would agree to allow a daughter to be present. But then she found one who said it was just for a daughter to perform last rites. He said the gods would countenance a woman's performance of last rites, even if society will not—provided every man and woman in the family swore never to tell a soul his name. Thanks to that pandit, Anu sent her father to his next life as her brother would have, going to the crematorium, pressing a switch to reduce Dadu's body to ashes.

As she had when Bobby died, Mumma took her handkerchief and swollen eyes to the darkened drawing-room to sit beside Dadu's garlanded photograph. And just as when Bobby died, a legion of mourners entered the room, and each communed with her in silent grief. Old friends, former students, even acquaintances entered Mumma's silence in a way Anu could not—some without exchanging more than a deep namaste and murmured greetings.

"Selling off half that plot way outside New Delhi, the plot we bought for retirement. No consideration for his wife. And what's left? One little acre. In a market town on the way to Jaipur, nothing but the old Maruti car plant in sight. Gurgaon! Of all places, Gurgaon!" Mumma raged to Anu. Had she forgotten Dadu sold off land to pay for Anu's surgery, or did she need Anu to feel guilty? "He could have built a house before he died, at least. Only thinking of himself. That was your father."

Mumma was left a son-less widow, and once bereavement befell her, no one else's bereavement could compare. Beside her mother's suffering, Anu's need to mourn her father had seemed selfish. But that need has led her here on Bobby's death anniversary.

Sister Anu pays the guide. He stomps back up the trail; his long staff is soon out of sight.

Christ, where were you? Lamb of god who taketh away the sins of the world, why didn't you take away Dadu and Mumma's paaps, as well? Why only Christian sins?

Could you not find it in you to love Mumma as well as me? She's not easy to love, I know, but does she deserve her suffering? Did Dadu?

Sister Anu allows herself ten minutes of tears—any more and she'll unravel.

Mumma's elder brother did not come, nor did his wife. Anu told herself Mumma's brother and his wife would come as soon as they learned of Dadu's passing. Surely they would come. But punishing Indu Lal for marrying 'out' was more important than brotherly love. Purnima-aunty said, "He didn't come when Bobby died and your mumma didn't invite him for your wedding. Why do you expect him to be here?"

Sharad Uncle explained, "Your uncle is a fine man, completely unattached to the outcome of his actions. He's just doing his dharma."

Anu said, "He doesn't care what effect his actions have on Mumma? What a cruel brother, what an unfeeling uncle."

Purnima consoled, "Your Sharad Uncle is here, I'm here. We represent your uncle and all of Mumma's family by our presence."

Anu said, "No, you can't. You only represent yourself. But you are the epitome of kindness."

Sitting on Council Rock, she draws her knees to her chest. Red monkeys chatter and swing through the branches above her. The moon rises, plump and white-faced as the goras who once ruled India.

The sun slips away between the pines. Moon-shadows grow large and dense.

The government will allow her mother six months before she must leave the bungalow allotted to her late husband. After that, she says she plans to build an English language school on what remains of the plot of land. "No more moving every few years, no more private tuitions," she vows. "You wait, I'll give your convent schools some competition. I'll open an English Academy. I'll offer training in manners, personality development and life coaching."

Mumma would refuse a single rupee from Anu, even if Anu had crores to offer, because Anu is a daughter. Dadu's life was one long apology to his wife for his lower birth, but he never took one paisa from Mumma's family or let them tell him how to live. And he wanted Bobby and Anu to define themselves, too. Bobby never stood a chance. Is Anu moving toward self-definition? Perhaps only by learning who or what she doesn't want to be.

The stars are ancient silver rupees strewn across the sky. Take one away, does the universe implode? No, it goes on, oblivious.

People we lose are still in our neural networks. I still want to talk to Bobby and Dadu, smell them, laugh and chat with them.

Where did their life force go? Can it return?

How long will it be till Jesus returns? Jesus resurrected Lazarus . . . Why was that resurrection, and not reincarnation? Oh, because Lazarus got back his same body, fixed up.

Sister Anu prays for forgiveness for the dreams that still trouble her in which Vikas is wounded by her hand. For fantasies in which he is publicly shamed or stoned.

Blood courses through her ears in the silence. She crosses her arms and rubs, becoming aware of cold limbs. Alive, while Bobby and Dadu are not.

All that survives is the love they gave me.

The cold drives her to her feet, and follows her as she climbs to the Cart Road and the waiting convent jeep. Because of Bobby and Dadu, she cannot—will not—relinquish faith in reincarnation. No god would be so unkind as to make her wait till Judgement Day to see her brother and father again. Though she might suffer the burning flames of hell, and it may mean that she will encounter Vikas again in another life, she will have faith in reincarnation. No matter what Church doctrine says.

Gurkot

ANU

PEOPLE FROM JALAWAAZ, GURKOT AND HAMLETS AROUND
are gathered beneath the red-gold fabric of a shamiana. It's
Inauguration Day for the chapel, St. Anne's School, and Bread of
Healing Clinic. Some sit cross-legged, wrapped in shawls and blankets, on the dhurries Sister Anu and Sister Bethany have spread
before a platform. On the platform, a table draped in white stands
before five white plastic chairs. A chrome microphone, rented from
the electrical shop in Jalawaaz, inclines its oval head beside the
table. The snow peaks, blue-white in December splendour, embrace
the festivities.

Sister Anu leads the guests of honour, along with Sister Imaculata
and Father Pashan, on a tour of the clinic, past the doctor's office,
the nurses' station, the lab room and tiny dispensary. Mr. Amanjit
Singh zips up his North Face ski jacket, warms his hands before the
bukhari in the women's ward and declares, "Women's health, children's education—there can be no development without it." At this,
the sub-district magistrate of Jalawaaz, a South Indian brahmin of
about thirty-five who is new to the hills but well-equipped by his
training in the Indian Administrative Service, smiles a Chiclet smile.
"My last posting was Kerala," he says, "Verrry dev-lupped. Women's
literacy there: almost ninety percent."

Mrs. Kiran Singh says, "Very nice, Sister," when they tour the women's ward. Large sunglasses ride the bridge of her diamond-studded nose and mask her eyes. Sister Anu can't see much of her face, but hasn't seen a woman wearing so much makeup or such ornate gold and diamond earrings since she left New Delhi. Kiran-ji seems so supremely confident and detached, or maybe so studiously bored, that to her own ears Sister Anu's enthusiasm and hope seem positively gushing.

In the men's ward, the weary-looking superintendent of police looks with longing at the red-blanketed beds. At least Father Pashan and Sister Imaculata seem impressed by Sister Anu's attention to detail and her explanations.

Sister Anu leads the dignitaries outside, down a path to the chapel. Everyone stops to remove shoes at the door. The superintendent of police takes a scarf from the bin outside to cover his head in respect, and so does the SDM. Kiran draws her dupatta up over her head. Turbaned Amanjit Singh doesn't need a scarf. Father Pashan points out the marble confessional and introduces Samuel, the loving re-storer of its carved surface. Samuel gazes at the ground as Father Pashan complements him for recarving cemetery headstones and clearing the colonial-era graves. The priest offers to show Amanjit Singh Samuel's handiwork in the graveyard, but Amanjit shudders. "Let's not spoil such an auspicious day."

Exiting the chapel, the dignitaries climb the platform, and sit down. The lambardar of the village and the head of the village council come forward to greet the chief guest and benefactor, Mr. Amanjit Singh, then everyone else. Milk from Gurkot cows is served in alu-minium tumblers.

Sister Anu helps Sister Bethany sling a long red ribbon between the pillars on the clinic veranda, then takes a chair behind the chil-dren's area, to survey the platform and the now-milling crowd. Glancing over her shoulder, she can see that better dressed men and women have claimed all the seats on benches on the clinic veranda.

A few dalit and tribal men and women squat at Dr. Gupta's office door. Inside, the doctor is already stalking disease by palpating spleens, bellies, livers and kidneys, and listening to lungs. The new x-ray machine is installed, but no one has yet broken a bone, twisted or sprained an ankle, or dislocated a shoulder. They will—Dr. Gupta says ortho is the most important speciality in a hill practice.

After the SDM and the superintendent of police have made their speeches, Father Pashan comes to the podium. He says in Anglo-accented Hindi, "I see the Holy Spirit shining in your eyes." His voice booms across the clearing. "You are probably wondering, 'Why are these city people here, why have we begun this clinic?' Because we feel the body is god's way of being in the world. And shareer," he says of the body, "is how we manifest ourselves in the world, how we express our souls. And just as Christ used his body to bring god's message to everyone, we too can use our bodies in the same way. Your body is the centre of your choices, decisions, actions. It becomes conscious by the Word, just as Jesus incarnated the Word. So we honour our bodies."

Sister Anu crosses her ankles and sits with her hands clasped in her lap. People are listening with rapt attention, no one more so than Imaculata. The SDM's little son has fallen asleep in Bethany's arms. Surveying the crowd, it strikes her that an old woman with henna-red hair looks familiar. She's sitting with a striped umbrella resting across her knees, her feet encased in boots beneath her sari—ah, Anu recalls, she met her at the railway station.

"And today as we consecrate this clinic to god, let us ask what is sickness? Is it a shameful thing or a calamity? No. It is a precious experience. Those who are sick have so much to teach those of us who are well." His blue-black gaze sweeps across his audience. "Illness is a symptom of larger problems, and it may be our one way to ask for help from others."

Sister Anu had driven to the chai-stall earlier in the day to call her mother. She mentioned her nursing course and the clinic opening, but Mumma did not want to know what Anu is learning about healing, or the miraculous complexity of muscle, skin, rib and bone. Mumma can only think of her daughter working with filth, fluids and decay. "I could understand your trying to be a doctor," she said. "I was academically inclined enough, but my father didn't want me to live unchaperoned at a medical school. Bobby was going to be a doctor. But a nurse? Your father's blood has eventually shown through. He's left me a widow and my daughter is choosing to do sweepers' work. For this we educated you?"

For once, her mother's reproaches inspired no guilt, because at least here in Gurkot, and in Jalawaaz and Shimla, Sister Anu is no longer invisible. People accord her an almost embarrassing level of respect, attention and solicitude, not only for being a nurse in train-ing, but because she embodies the Church. Most don't know the difference between a novice and a nun. Sister Bethany says there is none, but Sister Anu still feels an outsider to the Order.

Father Pashan's voice booms, "Your body expresses you. Do not scorn, hate, reject or renounce your body. Or the bodies of your children and grandchildren. Instead, care for your body with love and hope. And we must care for our children, the sick and disabled with love and hope. Some sicknesses are accidents, some are signs. Sometimes we contribute to the happening of what is happening. Always, how you treat your body, as gift or burden, will be how you experience it."

A little girl a bit taller than Chetna, dressed in a sunshine-yellow frock has taken a seat beside the woman with the henna-red hair and leans against her as if she has known her for years. At first the old woman sits stiff and straight, but after a few minutes, she puts her arm around the girl and draws her close.

"Your body's dignity is your dignity," Father Pashan is saying. "Your body is what makes you unique, what makes you and me different. Your body obliges your soul to reveal itself. It will not allow me to pass for another, even my twin. Your attitude towards your body reflects your attitude toward the bodies of others. Why?

Because through the body, we witness the world, we make our stories."

After he sits down, Mrs. Kiran Singh speaks on behalf of the patron family, and reads her speech in Hindi, spattered with Punjabi. She says in a monotone, "The clinic and school are the legacy of my beloved and respected mother-in-law, whom everyone knows as Mem-saab. Mem-saab attended one of the first Sikh girls' schools in Firozepur. And it was at another Sikh girl's school in Chandigarh, Punjab," says Mrs. Kiran Singh, "that I learned what the gurus taught about equality—barabari—of girls and boys. Mem-saab would be proud to see this school inaugurated today and know that girls and boys will be taught here. She would be proud to see the gurdwara where people of all castes will eat together, proud to see that people no longer need to travel all the way to Jalawaaz or Shimla to consult a doctor. This school and clinic may be our donation," says Mrs. Kiran Singh, "but they are Mem-saab and Sardar-saab's legacy."

Amanjit Singh starts the clapping and cheering then leads the dignitaries from the tents to the clinic door. The SDM flashes a smile. Mrs. Kiran Singh comes forward and cuts the red ribbon. Then Sister Anu leads them to the red ribbon before the school door. Mrs. Kiran Singh cuts that ribbon and returns to her seat on the platform, looking fatigued.

Musicians take their places with nagara drums, a harmonium and an ektara. Women come forward to dance and sing old Pahari folk songs. Five young men, all dressed like Bollywood's Govinda, perform a breakdance from the movie *Aankhen*. The red-haired woman sings along or lip-syncs all the songs, with the girl in the yellow frock attached to her arm. An elder with a flowing white beard takes the mike for twenty minutes to notify everyone that Kaliyug, the eon of greed is here.

After the event, Sisters Anu and Bethany escort Imaculata to the convent jeep. "I've given Mr. Amanjit Singh's daughter Loveleen admission to boarding school in Shimla—she's riding back with me," Imaculata tells them.

The little girl in the yellow frock is sulking in the back seat. Amanjit Singh supervises Shafiq Sheikh and his own driver as they move a trunk and bedding roll from his car and lash it to the roof of the jeep. Imaculata raises her voice as she speaks to Amanjit and his wife, so their little girl will hear her clearly too. "Loveleen knows how lucky she is to get admission to an English-medium school, doesn't she? And she's looking forward to making friends at St. Anne's."

But Loveleen glowers and wipes her eyes. Amanjit Singh leans in, chucks her chin, and gives her a peck on her cheek. Kiran pats Loveleen's shoulder and says, "Be a good girl, Lovey."

Loveleen begins to wail. Amanjit says, "Kiran—explain to your daughter."

Kiran looks helpless. The wailing rises to screeching. Sister Imaculata tries to intervene, but no one can hear what she's saying.

The red-haired woman comes forward to lean in the jeep window. "Loveleen-ji!" The screeching falters, drops to a wail. "Your grand-mother isn't here to tell you why you should go to boarding school, so I will. Don't go just to please your father or mother. Go so that you can learn more than them. And if you don't want to learn English and become a saab like them, just come home with me. We'll speak Hindi together, and you can stay as ignorant as me. You can become Bore every day, all day, because I won't have enough movies to show you. Say what is your decision?"

Loveleen's tears stop as if a tap were turned off. She wipes her eyes, rolls up her window and waves everyone goodbye. The red-haired woman melts into the crowd before Sister Anu can ask her name.

Before she climbs into the back seat beside the girl, Imaculata says to Sisters Anu and Bethany, "I won't see you both together again till Christmas. Be sure to practice my favourite carol—'Chestnuts Roasting on an Open Fire.'"

Sister Anu has no idea what chestnuts might look like or why or how they should be roasted, but smiles and promises to oblige.

Imaculata rolls down the window and adds, "Now mind, Sisters, I'm relying on you to keep this institution Catholic."

The jeep rolls away across the clearing, then dips downhill to the road.

Anu takes her place for the first time at the nurses' station, volunteering though she still has months to go before she's qualified. She begins to triage the haphazard queue, asking each person his or her story. It takes time, because some have never been asked who they are, few have addresses, many cannot read, a few need others to help translate from Pahari to Hindi, and some are here because they felt curious. But she knows this will be the best part of her work, learning about and from the people to whom she will be ministering, offering that generous listening for which doctors no longer have time. She cleans and dresses cuts and wounds on three ragged but sturdy little boys. Two men have symptoms of malaria, one presents with influenza. The only prediction she can make is that each will have a different experience and tell a different story.

At the end of a very long day that includes lab time and taking three x-rays, Sister Anu writes in the registration ledger under *Patient:* Chunilal. She records his age and sex, remembering a gaunt man with bushy black eyebrows and a valiant gap-toothed smile. He leaned on the arm of a willowy hazel-eyed girl with apple-cheeks. *Occupation:* Truck Driver. Usually visits home once a month. Then *Marital Status:* Married. *Address:* Gurkot near storage sheds and minibus stand.

In his file she records his blood pressure and physical status: Poorly built and nourished. She records his respiratory rate, that he has no pallor, icterus, edema, but that there's clubbing in his fingers. There's no box on the form for it, but she writes *Smoking history:* Beedis, 10/ day x 20 years.

Complains of: "Saans nahin aata." Chunilal had said he couldn't catch his breath even when lying down, and Dr. Gupta's stethoscope picked up a sound like dry leaves rustling in his lungs, below the clavicle. Chunilal's x-ray will probably say pneumonia or pleurisy. She writes: Cough, fever, fatigue. By roundabout and repeated questions she has the answer to *Itching in genital area*: Yes. No history of broken bones but *Stitches*: Yes.

History of Presenting Complaint: Feverish feeling in the evenings, non-productive cough, night sweats, weight loss, decreased appetite for past six months. Unable to work since April or May.

Chest examination: crepts right infra clavicular area.

Investigations: Complete blood count—ESR raised.

And here's his chest x-ray, which was the first on Bread of Healing's x-ray machine. Right anterior segment lesion in PA and lateral films.

Plan: Investigate for TB; sputum for AFB, TB and fungal culture. No history of contact with TB patient. Although, misunderstanding her question, he did volunteer he has a Binami brand TV.

Under *Family* she writes: Wife, Leela. If he does have TB, the family should be tested. *Children*: One girl—Kamna. One boy—Mohan.

But what Chunilal had said was: "One mistake, then one son."

PART IV

Pay 5,000 now or 50,000 later.

Advertisement for sex selection

Toronto
January 1995

Dear Anu Mama,

How are you? I am fine. Rano Mummy is teaching me email.

I collected fifteen Canadian Tire dollars.

Jatin Papa cooks rotis in the kitchen at our gurdwara. He doesn't mind.

Last Sunday, we went to a kirtan. Everyone was singing in Punjabi. But I don't yet know the words. Rano Mummy doesn't know them either. But I can sing "The Woman in Me" like Shania.

I made up a song in French. I wish you could hear it.

I wrote to Vikas Papa. He doesn't answer. I don't care.

Love,

Chetna.

p.s. Please send me 5 Star chocolate bars, an Indian Barbie, and a light pink dupatta with spangles. Little India shops on Gerrard Street don't have these. When you come, I'll take you there.

Beijing, September 1995

My dear Anu,

Writing this email from the Indian Embassy in Beijing and the Conference on the Status of Women. The first few days were interesting. Mrs. Clinton said we need to take bold steps, and that women's rights are human rights, even as thousands of Chinese women could not gain access to the sessions. My speech wasn't blacked out like hers, I didn't stumble at all. The conference declaration is actually going to say we will "take all necessary measures to eliminate all forms of discrimination against women and the girl child."

Your Sharad Uncle says he's already tired of managing servants, deciding the menu for each meal, purchasing food, staying within a budget, making sure clothes are washed, and servants fed and paid. And he says, "Next day it begins all over again!" (I wanted Rano to come and look after him, but she doesn't have enough vacation time left this year, and my daughters-in-law are all in Canada. Maybe I should have asked you.)

BBC TV in my hotel room showed milk being poured on Lord Ganesh and other statues and just vanishing! They showed temples mobbed by worshippers in Delhi. They reported that shops selling milk near Indian communities in England ran out. A scientist on BBC explained it as capillary action, and a saffron organization chap said it's a miracle. I think it's mass hysteria. How to explain to delegates from other countries why in the world we are giving our gods milk and letting children go without? Even I am having trouble swallowing this one.

Will write again from Delhi.

Much love,

Purnima

Gurkot
February 1996

ANU

AT THE SINGLE WINDOW OF THE POST OFFICE IN
Jalawaaz, Sister Anu signs a registration card for an order of pills
from Delhi, another for a parcel of donated medicines, and the last
for a letter from Rano.

She opens the parcel of donated medicines immediately—everything from Disprin pills to eye drops to antibiotic samples is more
than a year past expiration. Yet donating companies receive tax
write-offs for their dumping. She must decide what is and is not
usable—another issue. Along with power failure issues, water
shortage issues, drinking water issues, latrine and sewage issues,
waste incineration issues, patients-with-no-toilet issues, no living
quarters suitable for paid nurses issues, dangerous unlit road issues,
no-ambulance issues, last week's oxygen-cylinder factory strike
issues, villagers' distrust of her city-accented Hindi issues, villagers-
who-speak-incomprehensible-Hindi-mixed-with-Pahari issues, and
the issues of patients who trust the ojha's alternative medications
over Dr. Gupta's prescribed medications, and all the case-reporting
to the Department of Health . . . sometimes she can't stand Gurkot
for another minute.

Most of the time, though, she is having the time of her life.

People here may padlock their doors just as they do in Delhi, but she finds them more sharing, caring and courteous. They keep their word, so promises are not made lightly.

Working in the clinic, she no longer needs to stop to think but is all movement and doing. The training and reading for the nursing certificate she was granted in Shimla makes sense now. With limited resources, she and Dr. Gupta must be creative generalists, diagnosing with the most rudimentary of tests, sometimes doing surgery and minor ortho work—setting bones that would require specialists in city hospitals. Just listening and praying can bring comfort, maybe even healing.

This dev-luppment work, as the sub-district magistrate calls it, feels more patriotic than standing for "Bande Mataram" in a movie hall. Better than faking admiration for the ideas of Swami Rudransh, or feeding the pampered glitterati of New Delhi, or teaching spoiled children of VIPs. And though a second transcendent experience of god has not yet happened and distance makes her feel an outsider to the community of nuns in Shimla, she's on the Path, doing the Work.

Still her heart writhes in guilt for having the time of her life without Chetna. For answering no to the question, the friendly inquiry directed at every woman, "Have you any issue?" She confessed to Father Pashan that she finds it possible to love the children who attend Sister Bethany's one-room school in Gurkot as much and as easily as Chetna, but he merely said he wished more people could love children equally for who they are, and gave her no penance. She still hasn't confessed that her divorce is still wending its way through the courts—but she will, she will, as soon as Mrs. Nadkarni says it's final, and before she takes her vows.

The convent jeep is parked before the sub-district magistrate's office compound. At Sister Anu's approach, Shafiq Sheikh quickly flips his boat-shaped karakuli cap over his head, and jumps out to hold the back door open. "No, no—you rest," says Sister Anu. She hands him the parcels and takes the driver's seat.

"I don't need rest, Sister," the driver says. But he puts her parcels in the back seat, and gets in beside them.

In the rear view mirror, Sister Anu sees him stroking his beard, as well sculpted as a Mughal garden. He's needlessly worried that she will decide she doesn't need him.

As Sister Anu fires up the jeep, a few shawl-wrapped men sitting on their haunches, warming their hands over the coals of a bukhari, give her only a passing glance. The jeep, her nurse's cap, maybe even her leaf-shaped scar have become a familiar sight. She drives slowly down the street, avoiding yipping stray dogs, wandering children and trash-collecting cows. Past the fruit seller, the dry goods store, the chemist, the astrologer, and the Jalawaaz Fertility Clinic with the signs "Pay Rs. 5000 now or Rs. 50,000 later" and "Only Son will be Born."

Outrageous! She met with the SDM six months ago to tell him the clinic just down the street from his office is flouting the 1994 Prenatal Diagnostic Techniques Act, the anti-gender-selection law and laws against advertising gender selection. The SDM said he understood that the Jalawaaz Fertility Clinic was competition for Bread of Healing Clinic. Which it is not. How can a private clinic run for profit be competition for a free clinic? Still he promised to "look into the matter." He's been looking into it ever since.

A woman in a sari that may once have been green is standing at the minibus stop, a blue and white umbrella shading henna-orange hair. Well-worn bulbous boots peep from below her sari border. Sister Anu slows. The extended arm requesting her to stop has no bangles at all—she must be a widow. Sister Anu steps on the clutch and brakes. She leans from the jeep. "Going to Gurkot?"

The umbrella folds. The woman approaches, her boots crunching. She narrows her large curious eyes, appraising Anu. "Main aapko jaanti hoon." I know you. Said with certainty, directness and assurance. Most women would say main aapko pehchanti hoon—I recognize you.

"I saw you first time in Delhi at a lady-lawyer's office," says the old woman. "Then at the train station in Kalka. You gave me an orange."

It's the red-haired woman who persuaded Loveleen to go to St. Anne's. In the rear view mirror, Shafiq Sheikh's ears are twitching, but having transport is such a privilege. She leans over and opens the passenger door. The woman sits down and swivels her legs in like a city woman. She doesn't cover her henna-red head as most local women would when riding with an unrelated man. Well, she's old.

"You had a scar," the woman says. "It looked like the skin that forms on cold tea. But now I had to come this close to see it."

Sister Anu's hand rises to her cheek—her facial nerves are less sensitive on that side. Thank god for the Vitamin E oil and concealer Rano sends. These and toilet paper cannot be renounced. "Yes," she says. "Some of us have scars on the inside, some on the outside."

"I am Damini," the old woman says.

DAMINI

THE JESUS-SISTER IS THINNER THAN SHE REMEMBERS, with a marked resemblance to Rekha in the movies. "I have to go to the last minibus stop."

"My home is near the stop " the sister says.

Damini clings to the armrest as the jeep turns on the switchbacks. She's hitching a ride so she can to avoid a lonely uphill walk on the ghost-trail, and memories of brown eyes shining like twin fireflies. The spirits of the last two girls she stopped tormented her this morning as she led another worried pregnant woman down the hill to Jalawaaz and the ultrasound clinic. *When will it be safe for us to come again?* The spirits asked.

What do they think she is—an astrologer?

She asked them, Is it better for you now you have released your woman-bodies and become spirits? They laughed—what could that mean? She called on her Piara Singh to help her, but he remained in the shadows. Maybe he's forgotten her. No—he's angry. He too never expected that Damini could kill.

She tells herself all actions are ordained, that no one but the gods are to blame, just as Krishna told Arjun in the *Gita*. But whenever she does, her own forefinger comes before her. Again it pushes the wad of chewed tobacco between those tiny lips.

Jalawaaz Fertility Clinic paid her a commission today when she brought the young woman to their general physician. And today the nurse let Damini watch as she applied jelly to the probe and rubbed it on the young woman's body.

Damini, who was a pair of ears for so many years, has learned that goonj—echo—can turn into pictures. The ultrasound looked into the dark box of the young woman's womb and the wavy black and white pictures answered all the young woman's unspoken questions. *Will I be safe in my home after this child? Will I be respected, will I get enough to eat, and will my old age be comfortable or will I go begging? Will my husband send me home and take another wife? Will we be paupers and have to begin again from scratch?*

When the doctor told her she could prepare to distribute sweets in celebration, the young woman understood her child was a son. She took the minibus home to protect the baby rather than strain herself walking uphill on the ghost-trail. But after shopping in Jalawaaz, Damini couldn't bring herself to spend an additional ten rupees for the minibus fare—every morning, Chunilal swallows the pills provided by Dr. Gupta, and the cow-and-elephant dung potion provided by the ojha with equal faith, but neither appears to be working. He no longer has energy to finish the feeding trough.

Riding in a jeep is such luxury, but it does feel strange to be driven by a woman. Sister Anu is speaking of Bread of Healing.

"Aman-ji should have named the clinic after my Mem-saab," says Damini. "Sardarni Roop Kaur."

"The lady I saw you with at the lawyer's office?"

"Yes, Aman-ji's mother. I stayed with her thirty years, till she—died. She was deaf, and I was her ears." After a moment she adds, "Mem-saab wanted the Church land and buildings to be used for a clinic and a school."

"And we are grateful to Amanjit-ji *and* your Mem-saab," says the Jesus-sister.

Damini looks out the window at the peaks vanishing into immense emptiness. "Sometimes Kiran-ji asks me to come to the Big House when they have parties. I don't sweep; I serve at table and help in the kitchen." Call it her duty, to check on the welfare of Mem-saab's family. It's good for her own as well, not only because of the money, but because sometimes Potato-face gives her some meat curry for Chunilal, and Kiran gave her an old salwar-kameez that she adjusted to fit Kamna. So far, Kiran has not asked her to iron. She treats Damini as a temporary worker, not even a wage-earning labourer like the other house servants. "I give Kiran-ji massages because . . ." Damini clasps her hands before her stomach. She glances at Anu meaningfully, so as not to mention pregnancy before a man. "Kiran has decided to spend the next seven months in the hills," she says. She mimics Kiran's flat voice, "'Delhi is so-oo crowded and smoggy.'"

The Jesus-sister suppresses a smile.

Amanjit Singh prefers the hills these days, too. Khansama told her that Timcu refused to return to Canada and is still living on the ground floor in the Embassy-man's old residence. He says Timcu wants market price for Mem-saab's house, but the house price rises weekly, far more quickly than in Canada, as more and more people want to live in the posh area of the capital. The two brothers now communicate only via lawyers.

Anu nods. "I saw Aman-ji's car go by early this morning. He must be checking on the cottage buildings."

"I heard he sold one to a retired general," says Damini. "And another to an En-Ar-Eye." She means a non-resident Indian. "The buyer lives abroad and didn't even come to see it before buying."

Shafiq Sheikh says, "Amanjit-ji will arrange a three-day prayer ceremony in the new cottage." He seems impressed by such piety.

Aman may try escaping the cycle of rebirth with pious deeds, but he'll return as a toad for his treatment of Mem-saab. "All Sikhs do that ceremony, not only Amanjit-ji," says Damini. "We take turns reading the *Guru Granth Sahib* from beginning to end."

"Aren't you a Hindu?" says Shafiq Sheikh.

"Yes, but I am also a Sikh, because of my Mem-saab."

"So you can believe in one god and many at the same time?" says Sister Anu.

"Yes, why not?" Damini fishes in her bag and holds up the bottle of Dettol she just bought. "See, brahman—all of god—is like this. Very strong, like Christ-god or Allah or Vaheguru. Kills many germs but it can hurt you, too. So you take a small amount, add water to make it less powerful—like making smaller gods. Smaller gods kill fewer germs, but they still kill them, and they don't have enough power to hurt you."

"I never thought of it that way though I've been studying god and germs for a long time," Sister Anu says, smiling. "What other medicines did you buy?"

"Black pepper and tulsi leaves for cough; gram flour—I make a paste with yogurt, for my granddaughter's complexion. Better than Fair & Lovely. Honey to prevent allergies; kumari leaves for skin problems; coriander seeds for headaches; tamarind, pomegranate and gooseberries to improve appetite. And I gathered some madhupatra to sweeten tea so you don't have to buy sugar or jaggery. It also makes you speak more kindly . . ."

ANU

DAMINI IS JUST THE WOMAN SISTER ANU HAS BEEN LOOKING for—a traditional healer who also knows about germs and cleanliness.

When Dr. Gupta comes to Bread of Healing, the queue snakes off the veranda with people sitting on the steps, hunkering down waiting on the path and the clearing. But when Sister Anu checks if women are taking prescribed medicines, she finds they don't yet trust the doctor's advice. Women come to the clinic once problems become so bad they cannot work, often accompanied by husbands, fathers or brothers who speak for them and describe their symptoms. Seeing Damini working at Bread of Healing might give them confidence.

"Can you speak Pahari?" says Sister Anu.

"Oh yes."

"Can you help us register pregnant women?" says Sister Anu.

"For cleanings?" says Damini.

"No," says Anu. "Not abortions."

"No license?"

"We are Catholic," says Sister Anu.

Shafiq Sheikh chimes in behind her, "They believe it's bad karma." He's putting it in terms Damini can understand. Anu should have thought of that.

Damini says, "You mean you'll fry in hell for it?"

"Yes," says Sister Anu, a little surprised. She would rather Damini knew about Lord Jesus and his love of life, but hell and damnation are just as effective starting points.

"But it's like weeding—not all seeds can take root," says Damini.

"No," says Sister Anu, rising in her seat as she steps on the clutch. "Human life is more precious than potatoes and cauliflowers."

"Achcha," says Damini.

Sister Anu takes her eyes off the snaking road to glance at Damini. *Achcha* can mean anything. She decides this funny old woman agrees. "We need to make sure every pregnancy and birth in the area is registered," she says. "And every child needs a birth certificate right away."

"What use is a cirtifitak?" says Damini.

"It's needed for school, now. It's required for life."

"*Right* away? Immi-jately?"

"Yes."

"Surely not before thirteen days. Better still, forty. Child may not survive."

"Nowadays, children survive," says Sister Anu. "Our clinic doctor has been counting how many babies die in the first year of life in Gurkot and five other villages. The number is much lower than last year."

"How many of *your* children are alive?"

Shafiq Sheikh says, "Nuns can't have children."

"Nuns don't have children, so that they can do social work," says Sister Anu gently, spinning the steering wheel counter-clockwise to round a bend.

"Very sad that you have no children. I have a son. He does social work too—he's a teacher in Jalawaaz—but I hope he will have many sons."

Damini's son sounds commendable to Sister Anu. But Shafiq Sheikh asks with a note of suspicion in his voice, "He teaches in a government or private school?"

"Private," says Damini. "The one near the temple. He teaches tribals and sweeper-caste people to be Hindus."

"He wants them to vote for the BJP?" says Shafiq Sheikh, referring to the nationalist Hindu party. Sister Anu shifts into first gear for the climb.

Damini nods. "I say, Doesn't matter if they vote BJP or Congress. All politicians do is make big promises during elections. Afterwards, they only care about saab-log. Anyway, my son will take me to live with him as soon as he gets married. I have to find him a girl—it's very difficult these days. Girls the right age, from good families, all seem to be taken. You know a good girl?"

"Good Muslim girls," says the driver.

Damini turns to Sister Anu. "Maybe you know a good woman from a kshatriya family?"

"But you're also a Sikh," Sister Anu says, "Sikhs don't have high and low castes. Everyone is the same level—no?"

"I don't make differences. Everyone is equal-equal," says Damini. "But everyone *else* does, so what can be done?"

"I don't know any girls for your son," says Sister Anu. "But since you don't make differences, would you like to work with me in the clinic? I need a community health worker."

"What is the pay?"

"Seventy rupees a month. You would explain medications, make sure they take their medicines, help me make patients comfortable . . ."

"You won't make me clean toilets, na?"

"No, our helper comes every day after cleaning at the Big House."

"Goldina?"

Sister Anu nods and steps on the clutch and brake together.

"I don't know . . . I look after my son-in-law. He's very sick—many months now."

"Has he seen Dr. Gupta?"

"Several times."

"His name?"

"Chunilal."

"I know him. Dr. Gupta enrolled him in a special test programme for new medicines. How is it I have never met you?"

"His daughter, my granddaughter Kamna, takes him to the clinic."

"Kamna! Such a sweet girl. I'm teaching her to drive." The jeep's wheels squeal faintly as she veers around a bend.

"That girl!" Damini says. "Wants to do everything, learn everything. One day she's dancing, next day driving. No one is going to give her a car. Instead, please find a boy before she's left unmarried. A kshatriya—that's what we want."

Sister Anu says, "Have you asked what *she* wants?"

Damini hesitates. "She's a girl yet. What can she know about wanting?"

"Ask her, at least," says Sister Anu in coaxing tones, as the jeep arrives at the storehouse.

Damini gets out, shuts the door and then leans through the passenger window. "You said a right thing. Even a girl should be asked what she wants. I have thought this, but I never heard anyone say it. And you are saying I can get money for doing what I do every day for my son-in-law for free." She tents her hands and bobs her head. "I'll come to the clinic tomorrow." Using her umbrella as a hiking cane, she disappears over the verge of the hill.

As the jeep climbs the short drive from the road to the whitewashed chapel and adjoining buildings, Shafiq Sheikh says, "That woman. Her husband died of electric shock—be careful."

"Why?" says Sister Anu, not wanting to play the usual blame-the-widow game. "Did *she* give her husband an electric shock?"

"No, Sister. I'm just saying . . ." Shafiq Sheikh's arms flail, as he searches for a remark that will please. The best he can come up with is, "I heard her lecturing a drunkard once."

Well, he's Muslim; he'd approve. He once gave Sister Imaculata a fatherly lecture when she bought a bottle of Baileys Irish Cream.

"Do women in the village like her?" asks Sister Anu.

"She's the only healer in Gurkot," he says. "Though everyone feels sorry for Chunilal that all these months he is still looking after his mother-in-law."

Local women will talk to a local woman like Damini, they will trust her.

Sister Anu brings the jeep to a stop beside the clinic. Above, the chapel bell tings gently in its belfry.

Tomorrow is Sunday. This little knoll will be crowded and colourful with Sikh men and women attending the small domed gurdwara at one end of the quadrangle and Christians coming to Father Pashan's mass in the chapel at the other. Sister Anu dips her head to the crucifix over the door before entering the clinic.

She unpacks the medicines and locks them in the steel cupboard in the nurses' station and only then allows herself a few minutes to read Rano's letter.

Wish you had an email address. Email is like fax, but quicker. I reread The Optimist's Daughter *when I started using an email programme called Eudora, for Eudora Welty, but the programme doesn't live up to her name. We use punctuation to make smiley faces :-).*

Having a child in the house is the best form of birth control—did you know? I do miss my multiple orgasms, but I love having her.

Multiple orgasms? What does it feel like to have even one?

Your baby is growing into a beautiful young woman. Yesterday she bought her first lipstick—yes, I know we weren't allowed to wear any till senior year in college, but this is Canada . . .

Remember how everyone in India told me Jatin was such a catch. A Canadian! In truth, he's just a worker on the line, swirling dark chocolate into white. But I cheer him on. He calls me on his lunch hour every day, and then he calls Chetna. On Valentine's Day last week, he sent me a dozen roses.

And a little further down . . .

I use Hindi words and god names as passwords—LordRam, LordGanesh, LakshmiDevi, LordHanuman—uncrackable! I excel at DOS commands and Lotus 1-2-3 spreadsheets, and train others in the branch. Three nights a week at Basics of Computers is paying for my IVF.

So Rano is continuing IVF though she has Chetna. Why does she need to bear a child to be happy? Can't she just adopt another? Anu can't fathom it.

Yesterday a trainee asked, "I see the A and the C-drives. Where is the B?" I explained there used to be a B-drive, when computers had two floppy drives and no hard drives. "No hard drives?" he said, amazed. I felt ancient—just because I remember a time before hard drives! Have you felt old yet, Anu?

At work, praise has come my way, but I was passed over for promotion today. I am too good at what I do, and management wants me to keep doing it. Mr. Xhu, from Hong Kong, was promoted instead. He could tell I was upset especially since I do exactly the same work. We started the same day, but I know his starting salary was about ten thousand more. Over dim sum, he explained: male programmers won't take direction from a woman. Didn't I see that? I didn't. I said, "Most computers used to be women, women computed for corporations and universities and calculated for the Manhattan Project at Los Alamos to create the first nuclear device. Now we try to be like computers and give them Turing tests to see if they can pass for women." He said did I know it has only been about fifty years since Canadian judges declared women are people? What's fifty years? In his opinion it may take fifty more before men don't mind being managed by women. Men, he said, are just naturally domineering. "There will come a time," he said, "but this is not it." "When will it be time?" I asked. "I don't know," he said. "But till then, women must endure." Then he pointed out that both of us may have been members of a majority in the old country, but are now minorities in Canada. "Minorities should not create disharmony," he said in pleading tones. "Mr. Xhu," I said, "If I wanted to be treated like this, I could have stayed in India."

Yet India is the song that's always playing at the back of my mind. In this vast land, I miss India's millions of unnecessary people. Miss the dust, the hubbub, even diesel fumes.

Jatin stands on guard for "Canada O Canada"—but then he was only a few years older than Chetna when he came here.

Still, the India I imagine is no longer there, just as you are no longer in Delhi. I haven't seen you in Shimla, so I can't imagine you there. There's always some elsewhere, a place where I am not. Like the past and future, it is not necessarily better. I am not in all the places on Earth that I could be at this moment—I'm here. Me. But in my head, I'm back in Delhi with you. Yet, you're no longer there.

When I read Pop's letters I can't believe the same man who carried us on his shoulders, and taught us to drive can make such snarky remarks about *people who aren't Hindu. Have I become so Canadian and multicultural, or is his attitude part of aging?*

Multiculturalism must be successful indeed if Rano now finds her father's prejudices remarkable. Sister Anu folds the letter, lifts it to her nose. *Canada smells like this; Chetna smells like this.*

New Delhi
March 1996

VIKAS

A BUGLE SOUNDS THE END OF THE FIRST CHUKKER. IN the final match of the last Sunday tournament of the season Vikas's team, the National Polo Club, is down 0–1. He straightens in his saddle, leaning back slightly to check his bay. He raises his mallet, rests it across her black-maned crest, and turns toward the sideline.

Both open-air and covered stands are full today—army, navy and air force brass; ex-maharajas; corporate sponsors. Men who control New Delhi and the country, or will someday. Many probably wearing Ralph Lauren shirts with polo players—as if they play! The kind who used to rag him unmercifully when he was a fresher at Delhi University. The über-educated, with their foreign degrees, for whom the motherland is never enough. He could have been one of them—his marks were always high, till that second division in his final college year . . .

Vikas posts at the canter back to the lineup, in case video cameras are rolling. His two teammates' horses snort as they follow him.

Freeloaders, both of them. Handicaps lower than zero. His number 4 man isn't bad—a lieutenant colonel with a bit of a belly—weekend player. Not too smart. The opposition, Calcutta Polo Club, is more evenly handicapped. In fact, the four army officers play as if they're brothers. Have to beat them in four chukkers, no overtime, because unlike a military officer with a stable at his command, Vikas doesn't own a fifth horse to ride for another seven-and-a-half-minute chukker.

"Vikas! Vikas!" An older man is standing by the ponies, waving. Three-button grey suit, white shirt and diagonally striped tie. *Brown* pointed-toe shoes. So retro—can't be someone who matters. Maybe a client.

Then he realizes it's Anupam's uncle, Mr. Talwar. What does he want? He's walking too close to the lineup. Serve him right if a horse bites or rears.

A khaki-uniformed syce runs onto the field, grasps the bay's bridle, then Vikas's mallet and whip. Vikas slips from his stirrups and vaults off at the chalk line. He needs to change horses smoothly, quickly, and be back on the field in minutes. He's playing pivot, position three, and victory depends on him. "Move it, *oy!*" he yells at the syce.

The syce pats the bay's neck, then her heaving flanks. He loosens the saddle, crosses the stirrup leathers over it and leads her away.

Sharad Talwar says, "Left you three messages yesterday. Give your lazy servant a talking-to." He thrusts an oblong of peppered white into Vikas's hand.

A clipping from an obscure newspaper, judging from the paper quality. Vikas sees a woman in a salwar-kameez and nurse's cap standing beside a priest. Vikas doesn't know any priests. "Who's the Florence Nightingale?"

Mr. Talwar points triumphantly to the scar. "Anu!"

Vikas looks closer, having trouble distinguishing shades of grey. But that face is hers—slightly asymmetrical. He skims the Hindi article. Where is she? Where?

Past Jalawaaz. Gurkot village. Bread of Healing Clinic.

What a name—mixing food and illness. Bread is roti. Not to be polluted. And medicine is for illness. Illness is polluting—all those horrible body parts, blood, discharges, skin blemishes, deformations, imperfections . . . not to mention menstruation and childbirth.

Scanning quickly, now. The clinic, says the article, is an example of religious cooperation—apparently the church stands beside a gurdwara. Religious cooperation! Between Christians and Sikhs?

The rest is about the priest. Father Pashan. Pashan's mother died of post-partum haemorrhage and his father brought him to a Christian orphanage run by the Sisters of Everlasting Hope because he couldn't look after a child and work. Probably sweeper-caste. Reads as if the priest wrote it: attended seminary in Old Delhi. First social work—rescuing burned and maimed Sikh men and women after the 1984 riots in Delhi, counting and identifying the dead, trying to find people's relatives, resettle orphans. Working for human rights and social justice issues ever since.

Fuck social justice—inciting unrest in the lower castes is what that means.

Father Pashan's favourite song: "Imagine" by the Beatles. Favourite hymn: "If You've Courage to Give, Give It Now." What an ass.

Mr. Talwar is holding out his hand. "I read in the *Pioneer* that you're attending a car rally in Shimla," he says. "Take a ride, beta. Patch things up with Anu."

Vikas ignores the outstretched hand and it falls back to Mr. Talwar's side. "Patch things up, Mr. Talwar?" He takes a stride forward. Mr. Talwar backs away. "Find out make, model, year, and where to find a good mechanic, and you can patch up a car." Vikas lowers his voice so the syces can't hear him arguing with an elder. "Show a horse who's boss, it does what I want. But your niece . . . she's untrainable. And you're responsible. You arranged this—this marriage."

He strides over to his dappled grey, raises his left leg to place his boot-heel on the outstretched palm of its syce. The syce staggers back as he mounts.

Vikas tightens his chinstrap and yells for a 54-inch mallet. Another syce jogs over with it immediately. Vikas slips his right hand through its tape loop and lets the cloth-bound handle roll against his palm. He stands in the stirrups. Bamboo whips and cuts through air as he tests the stick. Offside forehand, backhand shot, under-the-neck, under-the-tail strokes. Now the near side—forehand, backhand, under-the-neck, under-the-tail. Nice whippy mallet.

Mr. Talwar has sidled up to his horse's side again. The grey swishes her tail. He buttons his suit coat, then unbuttons it. "Well, up to you, beta. I just thought . . ."

"You *thought?* That must have been a new experience."

Mr. Talwar blinks, "Anu's father passed away," he says.

"What does that do for me?" says Vikas. "He hardly owned anything."

Mr. Talwar nods sadly. "Hardly a few square metres. But now Anu has no one to look after her."

The older man seems to have forgotten that Anu is the one who filed for divorce. Vikas shrugs. "You can do the needful."

"Chetna sends you her love," Mr. Talwar says, in doggedly friendly tones. "I spoke with her yesterday."

His daughter's name conjures up her soft arms around his neck, her wide serious eyes with their worshipping gaze. But he won't give Mr. Talwar the satisfaction of hearing Vikas Kohli ask about his daughter. One of these days, though, he'll just take her from the Lal family and send her to boarding school. Not a convent school, but a place that will toughen her up, so she won't whine like her mother if someone smacks her precious face. But right now, he merely says, "Thank you—ji."

Vikas's leather-padded knees lock onto the saddle. He tightens the double reins, shifting the grey's weight to her haunches. Then he digs his brass spurs into her sides, galvanizing her from standstill to a half-rear, then a canter.

The ground is baking. After tournament season its well-watered green will bald, and dust will churn beneath flying hooves. He should be enjoying the smell of horse sweat and leather, the starting bugle, the cloud archipelagos scattered across a cobalt sky. Instead he's responding from habit, letting his mare seek the ball in the melee of mallets and hooves after the umpire's throw-in.

Damn it—Calcutta 3 has the ball. Vikas gallops after him, marking the Calcutta pivot along the line of the ball. His left knee edges closer to the player's right, then slightly ahead.

All this time Vikas has assumed Anupam was living with her parents while the divorce was in progress. Insult to injury, a whole lot of insult to injury.

Swami-ji teaches that when you like something too much, you must have self-control, enough self-control to give it up. Control your thoughts, he says. But Vikas loses all control as soon as he feels his blood surge up into the madness of anger.

Whumph! As horses and riders collide.

Got him.

With his knee locked over the other player's, Vikas can ride him right off the field if he wants.

Why didn't he just ride Anupam off his turf years ago? He should have.

Because women have the plumbing. Without women's shakti, even Lord Shiv would have remained forever in corpse pose. And you need a woman to convert purush energy, your masculine heat to matter, just as this mare is converting her feed into motion, speed, pulls and turns.

Unstable particle, that Anu. Disappeared from Delhi only to re-appear in the photo, without having been anywhere in between. Not instantly of course, but incomprehensibly. Unpredictable. All outcomes are possible, not only desired ones. Mad woman—doesn't appreciate her advantages.

Sister Anupam! Why not Nurse Anupam? Makes her sound like a nun.

Surely she can't have converted?

The priest. He's brainwashed her.

His grip loosens. The Calcutta player slips from his control. Damn!

The priest is her paramour, of course. A Christian Ravan. She's easily influenced, weak-willed.

Vikas extends the grey's gallop, comes up on the man's near side.

Idiot, trying to lock his knee in front of Vikas's.

Vikas easily evades. Paired players chase down the field on the line of the ball. A quick turn of his helmet. The two umpires' black and white striped shirts recede in the distance.

Now he's riding neck and neck in a thunder of hooves.

Like the night he raced down Rajpath, raced with that fuckwit on his motorcycle. Oh, Anupam and her whole family blamed him. As if he didn't lose his beloved Cord Roadster. Shit happens, as his dumb American clients say. And when she got out of hospital, there she was again, Mrs. Mournful Eyes, with a face no magazine editor would love. Made him feel like thrashing her—he did, once. Maybe twice—he can't remember. Let himself go. Made the mournful eyes more mournful.

Vikas arcs his stick above his head as the ball lines up right below his offside stirrup. His forehand smashes down with tilted mallet, and swings through, right past the forelegs of the Calcutta pivot's gelding.

The gelding checks, almost stumbles. The Calcutta pivot reins back with a shout. "Foul!"

But the umpires are too far away. There's no whistle.

Turf flies as Vikas wheels the grey onto the new line of the ball. He's at least sixty yards from the goalmouth with no one to mark him.

Where are his forwards? Way behind. Probably never learned simple vector theory to predict the line of the ball. Playing cricket instead of polo. Bloody girls, both of them.

Girls are always playing a different game—you just can't tell what it is. Your family provides you with one around age twenty-five—twenty-nine in his case—to satisfy your biological needs. At which point you attain householderhood, and all you get after that is responsibility and more responsibility. And blame for not being sentimental or charitable enough.

He'd only liked one—loved one? Met her riding. A jumper. Ample breasts. Wore skin-tight jodhpurs that showed off hips like a Khajuraho sculpture. Would have made her a Hindu and married her if her family hadn't rejected the proposal and married her to some Sikh bugger. She disappeared forever. Not even a surreptitious goodbye call.

Then came Anupam. Who could have predicted that behind the facade of a sweet, kind, gentle, accommodating, unambitious little travel agent lay an obstinate woman intent on a complicated dance of deception and eventual betrayal?

Vikas shortens the reins in his left fist. He's up on the bouncing, darting ball again. The bit digs into the mare's mouth. She slows.

Because—it's still bothering him. What if sweet little Chetna isn't Vikas's at all? AskJeeves.com said one in ten children isn't sired by the chap told he's the father. Of course, the study was about Americans—most studies are about Americans—but should he be required to pay for Chetna's upbringing and education and her wedding? What is he, just a chequebook?

The ball is just sitting there. Size of an ostrich egg. With no one but him to hit it.

Tha! Vikas's mallet connects.

Anupam could take a lot of thrashing without waterworks—he'll give her that. As if she knew something, understood something about him, something he couldn't understand about himself.

"Lovely lofted shot . . ." shouts the commentator.

People in the stands are clapping. Anyone who is anyone in New Delhi is clapping. Mr. Talwar is clapping, the syces are clapping.

Maybe also laughing.

Families abroad break up with divorces. Not the family of a high-caste, high-class man about town. He's been explaining Anupam's absence at corporate product launches, fashion shows, embassy parties, cocktails and dinners hosted by his parents' friends by saying she is in Canada visiting her cousin. Bachelorhood is a demotion to boyhood. Makes him want to challenge other men to stupid stunts. The press is speculating—might have been less embarrassing to advertise his divorce in the *Times of India*.

He thought Anupam was living in some small town with her stamp-collecting bore of a father and her social-climbing Anglo-aping snob of a mother. Who could have imagined this? For almost two years!

If he were shooting this movie, there would be a burst of welcome, tears. And he would raise her up and tell her she must never leave him again. He would stroke her beautiful long black hair, enjoy her touch on his skin. How long has it been since anyone touched him? The thrill would be unbearable, the mysterious tension of it would ignite, explode . . .

Ravan the demon can't have her. Even if he's converted her, even if he's slept with her. She's Vikas's. Like this horse, like his new saffron-orange Mercedes with its black interior and soft-top.

Vikas leans back, jerking the reins. The mare tosses her black mane and halts. Stirrup buckles bite Vikas's inner thighs, as he urges her into a tightly curving canter. Red spittle appears at the corner of the grey's mouth. He touches his whip to her withers, his spurs to her belly. She rolls one gelid black eye at him. Hooves drum; she extends her gait to the lineup.

Vikas pulls the grey back on her haunches just inches short of Mr. Talwar's pointy brown shoes—"You're quite right, Sharad-saab." He bites off his words in the man's alarmed face, "I'll go. I'll patch things up."

A clang of the scoreboard; thanks to Vikas, National is now even with Calcutta 1–1.

Two days from now, Vikas' black and saffron capsule will speed from the cacophony of the car rally in Shimla. Fearing gossip, he'll drive alone, without chauffeur or batman to serve him. Alone, he will climb the terrible stillness of the blue-misted ranges, looking into the depths of lowland valleys. The stimulant and anaesthetic of speed will replace image with image in dreamlike rapidity. Milestones will flash past, and despite sealed windows and air conditioner, dust will settle on his hair and moustache. With the article in hand, and the authority of the twice-born in his voice, he will inquire in Jalawaaz about the Catholic clinic, and by lunch time, will be helpfully guided to the Jesus-sister's house.

Gurkot

ANU

FOUR O'CLOCK MIST CONGEALS TO A MILKY FOG OVER Gurkot and Sister Anu looks forward to a mug of hot tea. She stops at the decline of the driveway to the nuns' residence and shifts *The 5 Minute Clinical Consult* book from one arm to the other. A saffron-orange car is parked at the cottage door.

The peace sign proclaims it a Mercedes, and the HIM license plate says the car was registered in Himachal state. Perhaps one of Sister Imaculata's donors has come from Shimla to tour the Work?

The screen door creaks as she steps in. "Koi hai?" Then in English, in case the stranger doesn't speak Hindi, "Who is there?" She lowers the heavy volume to the dining-room table, and drops her shoulder bag to a chair. Her eyes adjust to dimness. She flicks the light switch. Nothing—another power outage. More frequent and lengthy than in Delhi. And why people from Gurkot don't allow themselves to become accustomed to electrical appliances. "Koi hai?"

Travel Health in India crowns a stack of *Economic and Political Weekly* magazines on the coffee table. *Ten Twentieth-Century Indian Poets* is angled above the atlas. All these were on the bookshelf this morning. On the stone terrace, the reading chair isn't facing the peaks. "Bethany?" she calls in the direction of the bedroom.

Dark trousers and black leather shoes swing off the bed. "Hello, darling."

Sister Anu gasps, steps back. That scent.

The room seems to whirl, her heart races. *Don't be silly.*

He's standing in the bedroom doorway, hands in his pockets, smiling. Emerging from the fog-shape of her fears, walking into the room as if he owns it. "Just had to come and see the panoramic view from your bed. Took a shower while I was waiting. What *are* you doing here?"

"I live here." Her voice comes out crisp and professional, though she'd like to spring from her skin. "And I'm not your darling."

"Habit of speech, darling, habit of speech. You're supposed to have the habit of listening. What? You're not going to give your husband a kiss? Speaking of habits—don't you nuns have to wear the superwoman cape . . ." His fingers stroke the air by his ears.

"Each religious order is different." She shouldn't sound so defensive—he likes her to be defensive.

"So I've found a modernized nun in Gurkot?"

"How did you . . ."

Vikas takes a long slip of paper from his pocket and holds it up. "Someone gave this to me."

"Who?"

"I won't tell you, just because you want to know."

Sister Anu stares at the photo of herself with Father Pashan. "I didn't think you read the Hindi newspapers."

"I didn't think you spoke Hindi well enough to be interviewed."

"I speak Hindi most of the day."

"But you still think in English, na? I hate that I think in English, don't you?" He makes a show of consulting the article. "Says here you're some kind of nurse? What are you trying to do?"

"You wouldn't understand." If she can find a knife or . . . something. She could drag his body across the dhurries. She could settle him in the driver's seat, put the car in neutral and simply send him over a cliff. That would be justice. Or would it save him from god's justice?

"I'm listening." He wears a look of exaggerated patience.

"I—I'm putting myself in the place of others. Trying to help."

His laugh whip-cracks across the space between them. "Couldn't you have just donated your saris or even some jewellery?"

"People here need ongoing help." Her tongue feels like shoe leather.

He strolls across the drawing-room with loose-limbed grace, and inspects a few pages of *The 5 Minute Clinical Consult* on the table before her. So close now, too close. Scent of horses, leather, power.

"I've been alone here for a whole hour—going out of my mind with boredom. I called for a servant to make tea but no one came."

"We don't have servants. You could have made it yourself."

"Your home is mine, *Mrs.* Kohli. Why should I have to make my own tea? Besides, there's no power—your kettle doesn't work." He flops into the cane reading chair, and puts his feet up on her footstool. He looks up at her expectantly.

Anu mutters, "Ever heard of a saucepan?"

"Already with your burd-burd!" he shouts. And after a second's pause he says so gently, "Aren't you going to offer me some tea? I've driven hours from Shimla to see you."

"I'll make you tea, and then please leave." Was it her convent-school manners or the imperative of hospitality or playing for time that made her say that? She must placate him—or kill him.

"What? Not even a night in the sack for old time's sake . . . ?"

"No," she says evenly.

A grin slides across his face. "Why? Is someone else sharing your bed these days?"

"My companion sister will be here very soon."

"*She* shares your bed?" His lip curls in disgust.

"As you see we have two beds."

"Is she the prettier one?"

Distract him. She walks into the kitchen and fills a saucepan with water. *Keep him talking. Please, god, make Bethany return.* She turns on the gas burner.

"I can't believe you left me and Chetna, and life in Delhi, for this hole in the wall."

"My definition of family is larger than yours." She pulls opens a drawer as if reaching for a spoon.

"What're you talking about?" A dragon-breath roar blasts into the kitchen, "My family is *much* larger than yours. Much! You hardly have a family. Why would you say your family is larger, when you *know* mine is?" She hears him pacing the drawing-room.

Sister Anu covers her ears with trembling palms. Another shout and she'll be right back where she started . . .

She hears him take a huge breath. "But do I leave my duties? I don't run away to hick towns in the Himalayas."

"No, you just beat up anyone you can," she mutters.

Shut up! Don't remind him. Don't plant the seed in his mind.

"Burd-burd, again. Don't think I can't hear, Anupam."

Anu lowers her palms, she makes no response.

Vikas sits down on the divan and stretches, arching his back. His left arm thumps across the roll pillows. He drops his head, presses the forefinger and thumb of his right hand to his forehead. "Oh, Anu. I don't know what made me say that. I get angry when I'm tired and hungry, you know that. I let off steam! But don't worry—it's past. I have forgotten it."

He seems to think she has erased it from her memory, too. Now he'll mimic vulnerability.

"I really apologize if I have been insufferable—that's just how I am."

Sister Anu takes a spoon from a drawer, and leaves the drawer open. She opens the tea tin and puts a teabag in a small teapot. She waits for the water to boil, willing the crunch of footsteps on the driveway, but all she hears is the tinkle of wind chimes and the hiss of the wind. *Please god, be with me now.*

The pan rocks a little. *Pick it up, throw boiling water over him.*

Don't anger him. You could have an "accident" off the cantilevered terrace, like Bobby. You could end up in the rain-harvest tank.

Should she add milk? If she does, it will either be too much or too little. She takes the lid from a steel pan of milk, pours it into a milk jug. He doesn't take sugar. But if she doesn't serve it, he'll want some. She finds a tray. Her hands tremble only slightly as she arranges the milk jug beside a teapot.

Vikas leans against the door jamb, blocking her exit. "You've put on weight." In fact, Anu has lost four kilos from walking up and downhill. "I haven't." He boxes himself manfully in the solar plexus. "Polo on Sundays. Handicap still plus two."

Sister Anu clenches her fingers around a knife handle. "Good for you," she says.

"Come, I don't hold a grudge, unlike you. You hoard every incident and bring it up months later."

"You would too if you had been hurt and shouted at."

"You get hurt too easily."

"Yes, I do." She turns slightly to block his view of the drawer, and reaches for the sugar bowl at the same time.

"What's the matter with you? You know I don't take sugar. My tastes haven't changed in just a year or two."

Sister Anu gives a shrug, "People do change. People do learn."

"I don't. I don't need to. You're the one who *changes*." He spits out the word like an epithet. "You've been serving tea and god-knows-what to unrelated men all this time, haven't you?"

"I'm a nurse. I look after ordinary people." The knife has made it from the drawer and now lurks on the countertop beneath the short legs of the hotplate.

"And for that you had to convert to Christianity and become a nun as well?"

"No, I could have converted to any religion that says you should help the poor."

"So you rejected Hinduism because we have *no* requirement to pay the poor?"

"I don't reject it. I'm still a Hindu."

He cocks his dark gelled head. Knitted eyebrows rise. "Strange Hindu. Not a Ganesh at the door, not even a Lakshmi calendar in this house. I should have brought you our latest on coated paper." He gestures at the crucifix over the fireplace. "Jesus, Jesus everywhere."

"Most Hindus find everything is god and god is in everything whether Ganesh or Lakshmi or Christ. But you're right, that's beyond your understanding." She spreads a table mat on a tray, and arranges the tea pot, milk jug and sugar pot on top. She walks toward him as if utterly confident he will let her pass, as if she hadn't just slipped the knife beneath the table mat.

He steps aside with exaggerated chivalry. "What can you do that will last here? There isn't even enough power to run a bloody kettle."

Sister Anu places the tray on the dining table. "I am a nurse, now. I know a bit about the human body." She knows all the points where a knife should enter his flesh to do the most harm. She can see the artery pulsing in his neck, knows the soft area below his ribs where she could thrust it upwards.

"I know your body better than you know it, Mrs. Kohli. I've seen areas of it you've never seen. You don't know anything about your body—let alone the bodies of others." Chair legs screech on cement as he sits down. He takes a sip; his face scrunches. "This is tea-dust, not tea. And this mug—why are you giving me a servant's dishes?"

"I told you we have no servants. Bethany and I have one mug each. Both are alike."

"What a way to live. Okay, do you have jam-toast? Pakoras? Jalebis? I'm so hungry. I drove four hours to get here."

"I'm afraid not."

He grimaces again, but sips the tea. "Why not do something more necessary?"

"What's more necessary?"

"I don't know. Charity fashion shows in New Delhi—all my friends' wives are organizing them. But you're so selfish, Anu. You abandoned your child and think you're going to help strangers?"

Lead me not into temptation, Lord. Deliver me from evil . . .

Aloud, she says, "You seem to have abandoned Chetna too."

He shrugs. "I was invited to five Holi parties this year and at each one, people were asking, 'Where is Anu?' Told them you were away in Canada. Couldn't say I was single! Lord Ram has Sita Mata, Lord Vishnu has Lakshmi Devi, Lord Shiv has Parvati Devi, Krishna has Radha, salt has pepper—didn't you miss the Holi parties?"

"No. The hosts were your friends, not mine."

"You've always been so judgmental, so critical and harsh. Man, your superiority is so insulting." He pauses for breath. "Most of us just want to get the most out of life for ourselves and be cool, and the hell with the rest."

"I believe in Christ's ideas, Gandhian ideas." The fog seems to have crept indoors and she's shivering. She should have made a second mug of tea, but it didn't occur to her. Vikas doesn't notice that he is drinking while she is not.

"Gandhi! Ah, that little brahmin—the Congress Party's mascot. No one tells me what to do with my money."

"No one can. But I don't have to contribute my labour to your lifestyle, either."

He laughs as if he will fall off his chair. "As if you did any."

"I worked!"

"Hardly! If you quit or were fired, you could just say, 'Oh it was my hobby,' and no one would call you a bloody failure, as they would a man." He takes a gulp of tea. "And what's so terrible about my lifestyle? Every man in my Old Boys Association strives for it. All the comforts of Europe—plus servants. India is no longer backward." He stops. "Except here. What can anyone sell to these people? Hmm, let's see—family planning? But you're a nun." He slaps his knee as he laughs.

When he stops, she says, "I don't have to sell them anything. They just need health, education and clean water. Which could be supplied by the government, but isn't."

He gestures around the cottage. "So you call this living? I mean, great view, but you can't eat it. Can't fuck it either. And live here? It would drive me crazy."

"We're closer to god, here," says Sister Anu. "I pray for you to be so, too."

And I pray I don't have to use the knife.

"Oh, how she cares—she prays for me! What happens to you women? There's my mother, stuck on Swami Rudransh and here's you, a Jesus-lover." He drums his fingers on the table and looks at his watch.

If she kills Vikas, it will undo all the prayer and healing she has accomplished over the last year and a half. "Isn't that a photo of Swami Rudransh that you're wearing around your neck?"

"You like it? We've sold thousands, lakhs—maybe crores by now! And not only to our friends in RSS but every saffron organization. Swami Rudransh doesn't have to name Muslims, Christians or Sikhs, you just know who he means is the enemy of all Hindus. He gives the same discourse in every city but you feel as if you're hearing him for the first time . . . This is the Übermensch, Anu! A ruddy marketing phenomenon, yar—a godman brand like Shirdi or Sai Baba. We'll use his photo on incense boxes and khat-meeth bags. He'll have his own brand of tea, *Rudransh-Tips*, his own airline, *Rudransh Viman*, his own product line of Ayurvedic diet foods. With his account, I no longer have to sell print ads or make commercials for government and international agencies. Anu, we're no longer overpainting movie billboards by hand, we're doing desktop publishing! Now all I need is a few artists to rejig ads from abroad, hacks to write worshipful ad copy, and translators to translate it into eighteen or twenty languages. Give the swami credit for a few Jesus-type miracles, like producing ashes as his blessings—although I don't know why these godmen can't conjure up something more useful..."

If she kills Vikas, Jesus will return from his past lives on Judgement Day and judge her to be just like her ex-husband. And then she'll burn in hell with Vikas. Then what use will be all her prayers or this Work? Any hope of linking to the warm bright light ever again will be gone.

He is cradling his teacup in both hands, leaning back, legs apart, as if he owns the place. He's talking about working very hard, too. "The only mystical force I acknowledge is the market. So if it leaves the world littered with unsuccessful chumps, is it my fault? I didn't cause other people's poverty or the castes they were born into. I'm sorry for them, but they have their karma to begin with and their bhagya to continue."

"Vikas, do you even know what you feel?"

"Who cares how I feel? Image, yar, image is everything. Look like you're having fun, and everyone will think you are. Act like a media mogul's wife and . . . but you know. That role is your dharma, and dharma the role. I never wanted to run Dad's business, but I do. And you are no help to me here, no help at all."

Can Anu be beginning to feel sorry for Vikas?

Everyone has his suffering.

He straightens in his chair, and she braces for a mood shift.

"Look, you people in the religion business are all alike." His tone has turned fatherly, explaining. "Zero investment required, zero risk taken, zero experience required, zero inventory to carry, no taxes to pay. And if the client isn't satisfied, it's not your problem, but the client's own fault. You can make any claim you want—all are unverifiable. All of you believe your own ad copy."

Sister Anu glances out of the window, but Bethany does not take shape from the fog. "Everything in the world is not ad copy and money, Vikas."

"Ah, there you're wrong. Ads are a universal language, darling, un-i-ver-sal! All about fear and desire. Without desire, nothing fucking happens—don't you see? We create maya. Illusion for any brand. Hinduism, Christianity and Coke are strong brands, and we make them stronger. You religious types can try to stamp out desire, but people like me make new ones every day."

He stands, strolls over to *The 5 Minute Clinical Consult* and opens it. "And money is also a universal language—most women understand money for sex. Why don't you?"

She smooths the table mat, feeling the long hard shape beneath it. She keeps her voice calm. "I wasn't your mistress, Vikas, I was your wife."

"Same thing." He rifles through the pages of the tome. "Room and board and a secure old age in exchange for exclusive access."

"That is not the same thing!"

"Well, it's close." He flips the cover, the book thuds shut. "I'd often like to run away to the Himalayas, too. So why don't I? Because I'm like a horse in the traces, just doing my dharma. I've never even taken a vacation. As for the fuckwits here—they're not my blood! I don't owe them a goddamn rupee. I have enough relatives and employees and employees' families to look after."

"Vikas, it's not right to give people in the villages leftovers after the needs of people in the cities are satisfied . . . we each need to give, and soon."

He returns to the dining table, places his chair next to hers and leans toward her. She won't let herself back away. He whispers in her ear, "Next you'll start talking about their rights, like the pinkos on CNN."

"Well, yes. We all have fundamental rights, not only you. Check the constitution. All you want is for people to have duties, preferably to you."

"That's because democracy isn't half as much fun as feudalism, darling. Feudalism works for me. The British left us our institutions, all set up to rape the common man. Don't you see? All we have to do is use them." She goes stiff as he puts his arm around her shoulders. "Come with me, and I'll make it all work for you. Don't you feel *my* need? My parents and your daughter are suffering, and you're just heartless."

Amusement at last bubbles up in Sister Anu, penetrating her fear. "I doubt you or your parents are suffering, Vikas." She shifts beneath the weight of his arm. "And *our* daughter Chetna is better off with Rano than with either of us." She rises, as if it's the most natural act in the world to leave the circle of his mallet arm. "Let me show you the wonderful things we've done here. You'll feel how these hick town people are connected to you, to the larger world."

"Still a tour guide, aren't you? No thanks."

She faces him. He's sitting. This is better. "Then why did you come?"

"I came to find out how could you leave me? Why do you hate me so? I gave you so much. I gave you anything you asked for. An air-conditioned house, gold and diamond jewellery, saris, priceless shawls. Without me, would you have met people in the top families in Delhi? We are invited to three events a night, sometimes four . . ."

He is wearing a little-boy look, a piteous look that once pulled at her heartstrings.

Beware.

"Vikas, tour Gurkot with me. You'll see that the bigger your roti gets, the less there is for people in these villages. The injustice is ongoing."

He looks as pleased as if she had presented him a polo trophy. "*Ongoing.* You're beginning to get it. That's how the world is, baby!" He jumps up, crosses the room, steps over the door jamb to stand on the flagstone terrace. He declaims to the snow peaks, "We're in the top two percent of the world! We own half the world's wealth." He bounds back inside and he's beside her at the table, too close for comfort but not close enough for the knife to do lasting damage. She sits down, preparing to thrust upwards. "We make ourselves rich, but as your Jesus said, 'You always have the poor with you . . .' He's so comforting, na? That's just the way it is."

"Oh stop your self-justifications, Vikas! You're just a professional consumer—"

"People like me make the world go round, baby." His forefinger makes a circular motion. "Why judge me so harshly when every guy in America consumes twenty-five times as much? Aren't *they* professional consumers?" He sits down again.

Keep him talking.

"Because you're here. In India. You proclaim you love India, yet you see the poverty and pain of poor Indians every day. What use is it to love India if you hate Indians?"

"Hate them? Your heart is bleeding all over me. Without me, hundreds of hacks, artists and musicians would go hungry. But you? You're making them dependent. Very bad idea."

"Since when did other Indians become 'them,' Vikas?" Sister Anu says though she shouldn't, she mustn't.

"Oh, my Anupam. You'd want me to give everything I have to the poor. Even Swami Rudransh doesn't ask that." He reaches down, grasps his ankle and rests it on his opposite knee.

"Yes, I know. He tells you you deserve your good fortune, instead of how blessed and lucky you are."

"He understands that if I gave away every paisa to the poor, I couldn't generate more wealth. But," he scratches his head, in exaggerated perplexity, "I don't understand why you expect the people you should be serving, your own family members, to stand in line behind strangers."

"Well, that's the question, isn't it—what you think I ought to be doing, and what I think I ought to do."

"So you gave up—me! And you've neglected your child to come to this godforsaken little town and eat dirt with the backward castes."

"Chetna is well taken care of. If you're so worried about her, why don't you look after her?"

The heat of his anger swirls in the narrow room.

"I'm the ogre? I'm the one you love to hate. But I'm a very caring person—I gave blood once! I can't say what sappy Americans say, 'It makes me feel good to help others.' I say what any decent Hindu would say, 'It's my dharma.' Either way, it's bloody self-interest. So, right now it's not in my interests, okay? Got that?" He bangs his mug to the table and rises. "But what I don't understand is *you*. Look at you, without even a nose ring or a single bangle, as if your husband can't afford to clothe you."

"There's no audience to please here, Vikas. I don't live in Delhi's mirror world."

"But are you really a woman who acts against her own self-interest in this deliberate, planned way? You must have a secret reason."

"No secret reason, Vikas."

Oh please Bethany, come home.

He comes around the table, blocking her exit. She jumps up, her chair crashes behind her.

"Oh, Anu, come with me. No one will notice you ever left."

"No, thank you." She backs away.

"It's the priest. Admit it, you're sleeping with him."

"No, I'm not! I have taken a vow of celibacy—do you understand?" He will hear her spiking terror, taste it, smell it.

"What celibacy? We're not divorced yet, darling. I'm your husband."

"You have no authority over me," she says evenly, then lunges for the tray.

A sweep of his arm; the tray slides just out of her reach, the knife clatters to the floor, spins away into a corner. For a moment, both look at the gleaming knife in disbelief.

Vikas hisses, "You little viper. You've mistaken all my kindness for weakness."

He moves toward her. Anu begins to scream.

DAMINI

DAMINI'S HEAD BOBS TO THE THUNK-THUNK OF HER umbrella, as she walks the road to Bread of Healing Clinic, her gaze on her boots. Her heart feels like a live coal in her breast. By day, she locks up her demons and attempts to restore herself while helping Leela, nursing Chunilal, working with Sister Anu in the clinic, and serving at table in the Big House. But by night, asuras emerge, spewing self-hatred as soon as she lies down to sleep, filling her dreams.

Kuri-mar, say the demons. Girl-killer.

She must think of the task at hand, so as not to think of her paap, or how angry she is at Chunilal. She must think of what she will say to Sister Anu instead of seeing those brown eyes, twinkling like fireflies.

She will say, Sister-ji, my grandson is almost fourteen. He doesn't look very smart, but he listens to everything. We call him a pair of ears—he gets that from me. He can repeat what we tell him. Which is very good if you want to send him downhill to summon me or Goldina. She will say, Sister-ji, Mohan can't write anything but his name, but he can whistle if there is danger. And when you hear him play the flute you will say Lord Krishna has taken birth again.

No, not that last one.

She'll say, He can lift heavy weights for you, but we don't want him to do women's work—no cooking, no washing clothes or dishes. He likes to guard his mother, his sister—we will tell him you are another sister to him. You see, when other children see he can never be like them, they laugh at him. He doesn't want to go to school anymore.

A truck passes, going downhill, then the minibus, grinding uphill. May Kamna be in that minibus, coming home. The girl's run away again. She's afraid of Chunilal, afraid of all of them, because she knows what happened to her sister. But if anyone finds out that this girl's family can't account for her, sometimes for two or three days at a time, she'll be unmarriageable. If Damini had ever done such a thing her father would have beaten her till blood ran, but Leela says she can't beat Kamna, she isn't a man. And Chunilal is too weak.

Leaves obscure Damini's view of the peaks but with just a few metres of walking and around another bend, there they are, merging into a clear blue sky. Stopping a moment at the stone parapet that edges the road, Damini sees women on terraces far below—some planting and others carrying bricks. Three more cottages are taking shape, clinging to the hillsides where farmer's homes once stood.

Should she ask for fifty rupees a month for Mohan? If so, the sister-ji will say twenty-five. Then maybe Mohan will get thirty-five or forty.

Bargaining for pay is bijness; I am not good at bijness.

But someone must do it—Chunilal's appetite has not responded to triphala or chavanprash, his muscles remain weak despite Damini's mustard-oil massage and pomegranate tea. From dawn to midnight, Leela is in the jungle picking up firewood, milking the cows, heating water, and working the terrace fields. Damini does the cooking and manages the house. "A woman also needs a wife," she told Leela, and was rewarded with a tiny smile.

It will be all right. Kamna will be home by the time Damini returns. She'll be reclining on a gunny sack with Mohan as usual, a map spread between them, her bangles tinkling as she points out cities and towns. Damini will tell her, A good daughter needs to forget much more than she remembers.

Now Damini has passed the minibus stop. The driveway and wrought-iron gate set in the perimeter wall of the church compound are in sight. Further uphill, the green fence of Sardar-ji's old home begins.

Aaaaaaaaaaaaaaaaaeeeeeeeeeeeeeeeee.

Was that a scream that floated downhill? Damini stops.

There's another. Spiralling this time, like a cheel taking wing and soaring. It comes from the cottage tucked against the hillside. The nuns' cottage.

A third scream sends Damini scrambling down the driveway to the cottage.

The screen door is open. Clothes, books, papers strewn everywhere.

A young man has Sister Anu pinned against a wall by her throat. A saab, from his pants and shirt. Sister Anu's hands are scrabbling at his knuckles, her black curls unbound, whipping left and right. She's trying to kick and keep her balance at once.

At the sight of Damini, he shouts, "Ja, buddi!"

Damini is not old enough to be called a buddi.

"Ghar ki baat hai."

Choking a woman is not a family matter. Damini advances. "Enough!" she says, bringing her umbrella down across the man's shoulders.

He grunts, lashes out. She hardly feels the blow across her chest. She hits again, and again, though her heart is banging like a nagara drum. "Enough! Stop!"

The man's hands drop, and Sister Anu falls like a washerman's bundle. The Jesus-sister clasps her throat, coughs and gasps for air. Her attacker rounds on Damini. "Didn't I say, 'Ghar ki baat hai'?"

Damini backs away, holding her umbrella before her like a sword. "And I said, 'Enough.' Even if it is your family matter."

The man swears at her in English, then Punjabi, just like Aman. He grabs her umbrella right out of her hand and tosses it aside. Now he's so close she can hear the thud of his heart, smell his saab-perfume.

Sister Anu struggles up. "Vikas, don't you touch her," she rasps from swollen lips.

"Sir, I warn you, ji . . . this house, this place . . . it belongs to very powerful people," Damini gasps out. "You better not . . ." His hands are pincers on Damini's shoulders and he's shaking her, shaking her. Her brain spins in her skull. Vision blurs. Red strands of hair whip about her face. Her kicking feet are rising off the floor. The man's eyes bore into Damini's.

"Don't you tell me what to do, monkey-breath! I'll kill you and fling you down the hillside."

She would knee the saab in the groin, but that would enrage him further, and one cannot know all consequences.

Sister Anu hisses through her teeth in English, "Vikas, kill me or her and you'll pay—you're no VIP here."

"So?" he says in English. "It'll just take more money."

His thumbs dig into Damini's bones. Sister Anu is tugging at him, screaming, "Vikas, you'll go to prison. Leave her!"

Vikas flicks the Jesus-sister away like a mosquito. "It'll look like an accident." His thumbs are boring through Damini's shoulders.

"No!" Sister Anu stoops, picks up Damini's umbrella.

And then she runs away! Runs right through the open screen door—leaving Damini still in the man's grasp.

Anger floods in and Damini kicks harder. Her boot makes a satisfying crack against Vikas's shins, but his vice grip doesn't budge. A huge hand punches her stomach, smacks her against a very hard wall. She slides down and feels herself crumple to the floor. "Beta, don't do this," she gasps, calling him son. But he's still grabbing at her. She rolls away, scrabbling hands reaching, searching. She touches, then grasps something long. A knife flashes into view, scaring her even more.

Vikas rears away. "Kuthi! Pagal aurat!"

Damini hates being called names like that. She slashes the air with the knife, keeping him at bay.

"Vikas! Your car!" Sister Anu shouts from outside.

Any second, Vikas will knock the knife from her hand. He glances at it, glances at the open door. Then he plunges through it.

Damini scrambles up and runs after him, knife in hand.

Outside on the gravelled drive, Sister Anu stands beside the orange car, her hair a halo of coiled springs. She's wielding Damini's blue and white umbrella like a cricket bat. It's poised over the windshield. "I'll smash it, Vikas," she shouts.

Smashing car windows will stop this man?

"Achcha, achcha, Anu." The young man is slowly raising his hands, like a villain at the end of a Hindi movie. "No need to get hysterical."

"Get in the car," says Sister Anu in English, her voice like steel.

The young man wipes his mouth with the back of his hand. "I'm getting in, see, I'm getting in. Have your romance with this bloody village."

Before Damini's astonished eyes, he meekly opens the orange door and gets in. Sister Anu comes around to the driver's side, umbrella grasped at shoulder level.

"Wait'll I tell my lawyer," he growls at her. "Your conversion is no longer secret. Grounds for speedy divorce, baby. All it will take is one petition to the courts."

Sister Anu feints, as if to bring the umbrella down. The man laughs. High-pitched, like a hungry hyena. "Thanks for the tea, darling. I'll be back. You never know when."

"Come again and I'll not only smash your windows but slash your tires as well."

The tinted-black pane rises. The orange car backs up the dirt driveway to the road, and turns at the top. It fades into the fog, but Damini's head is still spinning and her heart racing. She hands Sister Anu the knife and stands beside her, gulping air.

Sister Anu returns the umbrella; a rib is hanging loose, but it's otherwise intact.

"Are you all right?" says Sister Anu.

Damini nods, still breathless. Her arms tingle, losing their numbness. The sister leads her into the house. She points to a chair, but Damini drops to a low stool. Sister Anu brings a shawl and puts it around her shoulders. She rubs them, until Damini pulls away in embarrassment.

"Is he a movie star?" says Damini. "I have seen him, or maybe his photo."

"That was my husband," says Sister Anu. "I left him."

"You have courage!" Damini says. "I would have been too afraid to try, even if he beat me sometimes. A saab with a car like that is a very big man. He probably has cooks and drivers and ammas. How could you leave him and come here?" She massages her own shoulders.

"Staying with a man like him for my own comfort or my child's well-being would have been nothing but atm-bandhan," says Sister Anu stoutly.

Damini's brow puckers. Everyone has some form of voluntary servitude. She does, looking after Chunilal, afraid that if he tells her to leave his home . . .

"But Sister-ji, you're from a saab family, a rich woman like my Mem-saab."

Sister Anu shakes her head, and her hair spills over her shoulders like a canopy. "I had many things," she says. "I just couldn't *do* anything without permission or criticism."

"But you had a home, food, money, clothes . . ."

Sister Anu pulls another low stool forward and sits beside Damini. "Those are nothing, Damini, if you can no longer respect yourself."

Damini's demons screech agreement; she cracks her knuckles to master them.

"A few beatings were so bad, I thought he'd kill me. I was afraid every day, all time for nine years. I lay awake so many nights, afraid. That is no way to live."

"You said we should ask each woman her story, before treating her," Damini says. "But you are so healthy, I never asked yours."

"Everyone has a story, Damini. I have one, and yours began the moment you were born. Even Vikas has one."

Damini tilts her head. "Achcha? Are you all right now?"

"I don't know," says Sister Anu. "I don't know anything. I'm such a fool." She sinks down on the divan and covers her face with her hands.

"See: women cannot live alone."

"I am not alone. Sister Bethany is here."

"I mean, with no men."

"I know what you mean." Sister Anu squares her shoulders.

"Must be that your father gave you too-too much independence, too-too much freedom. That's why you never adjusted to marriage. It is his fault—you should go back to your parents."

"How much should I have to adjust?" Sister Anu doesn't sound serene or patient right now. "My father has passed away, and I can't go back to my mother like a schoolgirl. I'm here, and I need to do my job."

"Tell Aman-ji what happened here today," suggests Damini, in consoling tones. Then, "No—he's not like his father. Sardar-saab would have hunted your husband down and recited what the Sikh Gurus said, that kings are born from women, and without woman, there would be no one at all. Then he would have dragged your husband back here to touch your feet. But Aman won't do anything. Tell your padri." She rises, moves behind the younger woman, gathers the curls spread across Anu's back and begins rebraiding.

"I can't." Sister Anu swallows. "I—I haven't told Father Pashan or Sister Imaculata that my divorce is still not final. My lawyer is still working on it."

"Hello-ji! Will becoming unmarried again make your life better? A widow's life is not easy, and a divorced woman's life must be as difficult."

"Yes it will. I'll tell Father as soon as Mrs. Nadkarni says it's final. But meanwhile, I can't tell him Vikas came here. He'll worry.

"Achcha, then I won't tell the padri either."

"I have to tell Bethany, of course, in case Vikas comes again. But . . ."

"You both need a sekurti guard." Damini comes before Sister Anu, sweeps her own hair back, knots it into a bun.

Sister Anu laughs shakily. "I think I should have you for a security guard," she says. "Thank god you came."

"Often I hear even what the gods don't," says Damini. "I will send my grandson. Mohan's almost a police officer—he will be very good. He has a Diana airgun; he can shoot. He can at least shoot those tires. He doesn't need much—please pay him forty rupees a month—achcha?"

Sister Anu nods and rubs her neck.

VIKAS

WILDFLOWERS. TREES VIKAS CANNOT NAME. ROWS OF blue-misted ranges alternating with lowland valleys. Every layer of forest has living beings in it, beings who don't know whose son he is, his name, the name of his school or college, or that his home in the Lutyens area of New Delhi is worth crores and crores of rupees. Wilderness outside, a jungle of confusion within. He's driving too fast.

The silly bitch thought she was going to kill him! Bluffing—she'd never dare. Still, it's good thing no one saw him beat that retreat. No one of any consequence. Made him feel five years old again.

That Anu! Still an atom bomb of a woman, even with no makeup or jewellery. Fire in her eyes. Always challenging him. But how can he desire a Christian? He can't. He won't.

He hasn't eaten since early morning and it's evening now. Anupam wouldn't give him even a pakora with that horrid soapy tea. Still he must not eat too much before taking the winding road back to Shimla and the lemon-grass-scented comfort of Cecil Hotel. He pulls over at a row of shops near Jalawaaz, enters the only chai-stall there is, and plunks down on a wood-slat bench.

He asks and ignores the chai-wallah's recommendation of mint parathas and kali-daal, curtly requesting mooli parathas instead. This will take longer—the chai-wallah has to send a boy to pull some radishes from his field. Vikas nurses a Lion lager and a growing hunger, as he waits in dwindling light.

The chai-wallah's eyes are too slanted—must be a spy for the Chinese. No moustache or beard; girlie-faced as an American. Shopkeepers always remain shopkeepers. And their sons become shopkeepers too. Whereas Vikas . . .

Where is the priest profiled in the article? Maybe he should stop at the sub-district magistrate's office in Jalawaaz. He can say he's on vacation, looking for land to buy. No, he's too angry for that, and they'll be closed by now.

The scent of mint draws his attention to a round-faced man with a beard like a close-trimmed hedge sitting at the next table. The medallion around the man's neck flashes a photo of a man with a rupee-sized red bindi, then settles. Vikas's hand rises involuntarily to his own.

A Kohlisons Media product has made it all the way here—well, of course.

"Bahut sundar car, sir," says the round-faced man, as the parathas are served. "Very beautiful car." The translation informs Vikas the man can speak English. Very little, judging from his accent.

"Yes," says Vikas. His radish-paratha arrives and he tears off a wedge and dips it in daal. Almost as good as his cook's—but not quite. The mint parathas might have been better.

"HIM9236—a Himachal state license—you are coming from Shimla, is it?"

"No, from Delhi." The license plate was for the car rally.

"New Delhi? I lived many years in New Delhi," says his interviewer, obviously delighted by the coincidence. He touches his medallion. "And I am devotee, like you."

"Haan—yes." Vikas wouldn't call himself a devotee, exactly. Not like his mother.

"I used to listen to Swami-ji's lectures every day, every day in Delhi." The round-faced man abandons the formality of English for Hindi.

"Buy his CDs," says Vikas, unable to resist an opportunity to sell. "VVIPs are listening to Swami-ji now. BJP politicians, RSS and VHP members, Bajrang Dal."

"Ah—BJP, RSS, VHP, Bajrang Dal." The man raises his chai-glass to the Hindutva family of nationalist organizations.

Vikas follows suit. The saffron organizations are his bread and butter.

"Jai Bharat-Mata!" says the man, hailing the goddess of the motherland, invented by nationalists during the freedom struggle. Vikas gives himself a mental pat on the back for effective advertising, flashes a raffish grin, and introduces himself. The man follows suit. His name is Suresh Singh Chauhan, a fellow kshatriya.

Suresh points to the newspaper cutting beside Vikas. "You are reading?"

"About the Christian church." Vikas points vaguely uphill. "Came here to see it with my own eyes."

"It's for sweepers. Though they call themselves Christians." He winks a long-lashed eye.

Turns out Suresh is a teacher in Jalawaaz. With connections. By the time Vikas has finished two orders of parathas and availed himself of a fingerbowl, he and Suresh are the best of friends. Suresh is, Vikas tells him, the hope of all Hindus everywhere. He assures Suresh he will recommend him for a job as local campaign manager for the BJP. And maybe he will pull strings in New Delhi so Suresh can return there eventually. But meanwhile, there is a side job—no qualifications required, only love of the motherland.

"Of course, ji—just say what I can do."

"My company, Kohlisons Media needs a reporter," says Vikas looking down at his spotless hands. "To report about this Father Pashan and his school and clinic. You know what these Christians do, don't you?" A pause for effect. "They hoodwink villagers. They mix Aspirin in water and call it holy water. Then they give it to sick Hindus and these poor Hindus feel better and convert."

"Achcha?" says the younger man.

"They give jobs to dalits, fill their stomachs and the dalits become rice-Christians. An unmarried girl gave birth to their Jesus, so they have no shame if one of their girls gives birth without marriage—if you don't believe me, watch *Baywatch*—it happens all the time. And no one is stopping them from stealing Hindu babies and converting them."

"No one?" says the younger man.

Vikas wags his head slowly, wisely. "You can do your part—tell us whatever you learn." He offers leaflets, money for whatever permission clearances and no-objection certificates may be required. He points to the photo again, "Oh, and about this Sister Anu. The padri is sleeping with her, you know." He shakes his head sorrowfully, "Such bad bad things going on."

"All because of Gandhi and Nehru. What they did for Muslims and Christians!"

"Good that they aren't here to protect them anymore," says Vikas. He glances around the chai-stall. The chai-wallah looks on impassively from behind the counter.

A kerchiefed woman with honey-brown skin enters and asks for a single-use packet of washing powder. Vikas notes the brand—Rin. And that Suresh's gaze doesn't follow the packet, but the contours and sway of the woman. It takes a woman's curves to sell anything. This one is too low on the totem pole for Vikas, but her oval face and those fierce eyes would certainly feed a city-dweller's nostalgia for rural authenticity. The woman can feel their gaze. She turns, and at the sight of Suresh, her eyes flash and then dull. She turns back to the counter, snatches her change and the washing powder and almost scuttles out, keeping her gaze averted.

So the man can inspire fear. Very useful.

Now it's time for earnest money to change hands, with promises of more to come. Then Suresh makes several namastes to his new friend and employer and descends the chai-stall stairs to the road.

He's probably wondering at his unbelievable bhagya in meeting a man like me.

Just then, Vikas sees someone he never expected to see again in this life.

Kiran removes her sunglasses, tosses her hair back, smooths her dupatta over the rim of her bosom. She surveys the jars of rusks, biscuits and Hajmola sweets. "No film?"

"I will order it, ji," says the chai-wallah. "It will arrive next week, no problem."

Anu and his recent humiliation are wiped from Vikas's mind. Time rolls back eleven years.

Those breasts. He still remembers those breasts.

Kiran turns. What a bombshell of a woman!

Not as young, hasn't aged well.

Vikas says her name as a question. Kiran glances at him, stops, and stares.

"Vikas Kohli," he says, in a drawing-room voice, as he gets up. Why does the sight of her make him feel guilty? She should feel guilty, or at least embarrassed for her parents, who had not wanted their daughter to marry "out."

Kiran's gaze darts around the chai-stall as if someone could be watching.

He points. "You're still using the camera I gave you." He laughs as if it is funny that her Nikon FA single lens has lasted longer than their relationship.

Fuckwit! You're acting like that callow kid you used to be.

Trying to impress her, boastfully promising marriage and more. More things than he could ever deliver.

Kiran seems poised to flee. "It's a good camera," she says. "I've become quite expert with it."

The gift once brought down her guard. That she kept it all these years shows she's been yearning for him. "Bring tea!" Vikas orders the chai-wallah. "Please sit," he says to Kiran and draws up a chair, facing the few stairs to the road.

"My husband—" Kiran begins. But she does sit down, coal-black hair falling past her hips like a veil. She tucks her hair behind her ear on the side nearest him, so he can see her profile along with a side view of the breasts.

"That Mercedes outside—yours, I assume?"

He nods, speechless from the breasts.

"Very smart."

Now she's telling him about her husband, Amanjit Singh, his factories, his money. Bugger even drives a BMW. Pride in her voice, as if his accomplishments are her own. She mentions a daughter, a little older than Chetna.

He finds his voice, orders more parathas, though he doesn't need any.

She's really bragging now, telling him how kind her husband is. So charitable, he's renovated an old chapel, opened a Hindi-medium school and a free clinic for the people in Gurkot.

"Who's running it?" says Vikas.

"Catholics. They sent in their priest and two nuns."

"Letting Christians use his land is stupid. They'll squat. Never let it go."

"One policeman who didn't stand by or disarm Sikh men or lead the mobs to kill during the '84 riots was a Christian, Maxwell Pereira. He saved our main gurdwara from the mob; Aman wanted to do something for Christians in return." She stops. "Sorry. But you did ask. Now tell-tell about you?"

Vikas opens his mouth to tell her all about himself, but a round face pops up at his elbow. Suresh again—would Vikas like to make a donation to the Jalawaaz School for Tribals, where he teaches?

Vikas rises, takes Suresh aside and stuffs a pair of blue rupee notes into his hand. "You never met me," he says.

Suresh wags his head, "Yes, sir!"

Vikas turns back to Kiran, who is shrinking back into the shadows. "That's our old amma's son," she says.

"Don't worry. I gave him a thousand—he can take it as a donation."

"That was a bribe." She starts to rise from her seat.

"Wha-at? Don't break a bangle, yar. Bribes are just like value-added tax. Besides, for what? We're just having tea. Not even holding hands."

"I shouldn't, Vikas."

"These days, married women sleep with former boyfriends after they've produced a few kids."

"Women in Delhi maybe," says Kiran, "In Gurkot, people talk."

He reaches to take her hand, and she backs away. "At least have a bite with me," he says. "For old times sake. I just ordered . . ."

She sits down at the edge of her seat. "I'm pregnant," she says, as if that makes her impregnable.

"What a pity," says Vikas. He would find it repugnant to sleep with a pregnant woman.

"No, it's not a pity—I'm having a boy."

"A little Sikh boy with a bun on his head, then a turban," says Vikas in mocking tones.

"Eventually, I hope so," says Kiran.

They are silent. Too many wounds to hope for honesty.

Another order of parathas and daal arrives.

"So is the Mercedes new?"

"Yes. The top goes down. Want to come for a spin?"

She shakes her head. After a moment she says, "Vikkoo, it would never have worked."

"Yes it could have," he replies ever so reasonably. "What's so bad about reverting to Hinduism?"

"What do you mean, 'reverting'? I wouldn't know how to be a Hindu, any more than a Christian would know how to 'revert' to Judaism. And you wouldn't have let me remain a Sikh."

"Well, of course not." Vikas reaches for a paratha and some daal.

"And would you have become a Sikh to marry me?"

"Can you imagine me with long hair?" he stuffs a piece of paratha in his mouth to stop giggling.

"Many Sikh men are not orthodox and have short hair," says Kiran. "Anyway, are you happy? I have often wondered."

"Of course," says Vikas. How do you say, My wife is divorcing me for mental and physical cruelty, has converted to Christianity, become a nun, and tried to knife me about an hour ago? He would like to relax into Kiran's body, but that was another man's dream. That other man is dreamed away, and Vikas now lives the life he has created.

Soon—too soon—Kiran rises, takes up her handbag. He escorts her the few feet to the stairs of the chai-stall, watches her climb into a top-of-the-line BMW 740iL sedan and drive away.

Kiran knew him when he didn't feel every man was competition, and every pair of ears or eyeballs was an audience. She knew him before each blow he struck made him feel larger. If Kiran had married him, he might still like himself.

Evidence of parallel and alternative universes.

Look for the void at the edge of your own, that's where you'll find it.

Back in the bubble of comfort that is the Benz.

How could he have even considered marrying her? Too tall, hasn't produced a son all these years. Every Sikh woman is told she's a princess, every one of them takes the last name Kaur, meaning princess—no wonder they're spoiled. Nothing but trouble.

And Anu was going to stick him with a knife? She has no idea, no idea what he can do to her and her bloody priest.

And Kiran . . . She used to look so cute when she told him she was his equal, because her Guru Nanak wrote that women are equal to men. But as a wife? She would have tried to put her name on his property—in fact, put all his possessions in her name.

Say what you will about Anu, she was a Hindu and never asked for much.

But Kiran—Sikh women are insatiable.

Up close, both seemed to decay into the familiar. Next time, the parents better find him a young Hindu woman with Kiran's looks and the warmth, kindness and gentleness that once attracted him to Anu.

The Merc fills with Kumar Sanu's voice singing "Chura ke Dil Mera," moaning for his stolen heart. Vikas sings along, tearing up. He drives between the two rows of shops that are Jalawaaz, windows rolled up, air conditioner on.

Stares caress him as they caress his car. These poor buggers can't see through his tinted windows, but they get that he's a VIP even if Anu doesn't. Unlike Anu, these ragged villagers get what's cool and what's not. She needs a lesson.

All he has to do is play his new fixer, Suresh. Suresh can do a lot of damage, all untraceable.

Kill European-style, from a distance. Make it easy, amusing. Blame it on the system.

And Anu's conversion is grounds for divorce. Vikas'll have *her* served with divorce papers. Let her spend the next few years defending herself. See how she likes that. He can speed it up by noting he never signed a marriage registration, and when it's final, his entanglement with her will be broken.

He pulls the newspaper clipping from his pocket—evidence, now.

April 1996

ANU

Vikas's eyes seem to follow Sister Anu for days.
His face disturbs her dreams, waking her, chilled and sweating. She
hides kitchen knives between the cushions on the divan, behind the
plants, beneath books on the coffee table, rising at the slightest
rattle to confirm they are still there. Fear sidles in, even as she wills
it away. With Samuel's help, Sister Anu has the front door to the
nun's residence reinforced.

Her lawyer writes to inform her that Vikas has filed a writ petition for divorce on the basis of conversion to another religion. She'll
defend Anu, but a divorce for conversion can come through sooner
than for mental and physical cruelty. Activists, Mrs. Nadkarni says,
are working very hard to change this state of affairs.

But, three weeks later, when Damini ushers Goldina into her examination room as the first patient of the day and asks if "that man"
has been back, Sister Anu says no. And realizes she isn't starting at
every passing car and shadow anymore.

Damini nods sagely, "Mohan is a very good sekurti guard."

Her grandson has been proudly keeping watch on the veranda
every day, as careful of Sister Anu and Sister Bethany as if they were
his elder sisters. Morning and evening, Sister Anu and her flute-
blowing bodyguard walk the winding roads. Mohan runs ahead,

334

nimbly climbing clefts and crevices for berries, making her laugh by scooting uphill for a few seconds and returning with red bottlebrush flowers sticking out of his ears. Yesterday he brought an injured fox along with a stuffed toy monkey to the clinic; Dr. Gupta set the fox's leg and kindly bandaged the red monkey's tail. Last Sunday, Mohan recited the Our Father and sang "Make me a Channel of Your Peace" . . . though it was obvious he understood neither.

After her day's work, Sister Anu has begun teaching Mohan to cook so he can help his grandmother and sister. He made a daal so lava-hot, it made them forswear chilies for Lent. And a slushy rice whose uncooked grains gave Anu a stomach ache. This new project has helped Anu persuade herself Vikas won't be back. The belief, even if misplaced, is better than living in fear. If she can't be free of danger, she can at least be free of fear.

Other women have greater fears—for instance, right now, in the examination room, Goldina is telling her she's worried that because Aman-ji is installing toilets in place of thunderboxes in the Big House, it will mean less work for her.

"God always finds work for us to do," says Sister Anu.

"Yes, but I can't work for free, like you—na, ji, na! I won't do that."

"The clinic is free for you all," says Sister Anu, "but Dr. Gupta and I do get paid."

Not much. But more than a community worker like Damini, now changing bed linen in the women's ward next door. Anu thinks of her savings for Chetna's wedding. Not much at all. She rubs her hands together, then places her palms very gently on Goldina's stomach. Her touch calms and reassures; and she does feel slight movements.

"If a baby is coming," says Goldina, "it's all because of Dr. Gupta and you. I asked, but he wouldn't give me a single pill, though I have five children already."

"Everyone's life is important, even the unborn."

"Ha, what do the unborn feel?"

"We're Catholic," Sister Anu murmurs. And Catholic nuns must believe life begins at conception, even if her nursing school textbooks say the fetus emits brain waves at eight weeks. She still feels guilty for mentioning to Goldina that most chemist shops carry Ovral pills. But even if Goldina bought them, she would need someone to read and translate the instructions from English.

"Dr. Gupta isn't," says Goldina. "He's Hindu—brahmin—vegetarian. Doesn't eat onions or garlic. I told him, 'I'm on my way to a cricket eleven if you don't stop me having children,' but . . ." she wags her head ruefully and pats her stomach.

Sister Anu inserts the eartips of her stethoscope in her ears. Like Dr. Gupta, she can advocate abstinence when advising men, but not to a woman like Goldina who seems to have little say in her sex life. And having used contraception herself, Anu prefers silence. "There's always the rhythm method," Father Pashan has said. But Vatican roulette requires a husband's cooperation; she can't recommend it.

Sister Anu doesn't stock condoms or Pills in the dispensary but answers "No" whenever women ask if they will become too weak to work if they take the Pill, relying on her own experience. And when women ask if they must believe in the power of the Pill for it to work, she tells them no, as well. But there she stops so as to keep the clinic Catholic.

She listens, palpating Goldina's stomach gently. Without an ultrasound machine, her hands must "see" into Goldina's womb and divine the baby's position. She guesses Goldina is about four months along. "Good news," she says, and is unprepared for the liquid shimmer that wells in Goldina's eyes, the tremble in her lips. Goldina raises herself on her elbows, wipes her cheeks.

Sister Anu waits. "What's the matter?" she says gently.

"Nothing, nothing. I'm happy."

"Goldina—such a pretty name," she says.

Goldina relaxes a little. She lies down again, wipes her eyes with the corner of her sari.

More composed after a while, she says, "I named myself. When I was a little girl, I met a Christian woman, Goldina. She gave me leftovers to take home for my family. I promised myself, if ever I have leftovers, I want to be generous like her. I call myself Goldina so it will always remind me."

The weight scale shows Goldina is too thin. Malnourished, probably anemic. She says her eyes hurt.

"Is there a window in your cookroom?" says Sister Anu. "Or a chimney?"

"No window, no chimney. The government is offering free chimneys for low-caste people, but now they tell us, oh, you've become Christian and Christians don't have high and low castes, so you can't have a free chimney. I said I'm also Hindu, but the government says you can't be both."

So Goldina's eyes are smoke-damaged.

"Close one eye and tell me which way the bars point on this chart."

"My eyes are different," says Goldina. "I see patterns, movements, the outlines of things."

Seeing patterns and outlines doesn't help Goldina discern any directional bars past the third line. Sister Anu writes the results in her ledger and asks, "So you believe in the gods *and* in Christ?" She hasn't met many who believe as she does.

"Goddesses," says Goldina. "Mary Devi, mother of god, is an avatar of Anamika. She only named Yeshu; Anamika named all the other gods. Amanjit-saab, the SDM—all of us give Anamika respect. She protects our village."

"And Lord Golunath?" asks Sister Anu.

"Sometimes," says Goldina. "But when I talk to Anamika, she brings justice if Golunath-ji's power has failed."

Sister Anu fastens a blood pressure sleeve on Goldina's bared upper arm. She closes the valve on the rubber bulb, feels for a pulse in front of Goldina's elbow joint and places the diaphragm of her stethoscope over it. She squeezes the rubber bulb. With the cuff pumped up, she releases the valve on the rubber bulb and begins listening for a beat.

Goldina is watching the needle fall. "I told Samuel, we should become Sikhs. They also make offerings to only one god and say all castes are welcome."

"That seems much like being Christian."

"Only inside their gurdwara," says Goldina. "Outside, dalit Sikhs and dalit Hindus get the same treatment from the respected castes. I said, at least we could get a free chimney—but Samuel's too proud."

"You have excellent blood pressure," Sister Anu reports, noting it on Goldina's record.

Goldina glows. "It's better to be Christian," she says, as if reassuring Sister Anu. "We only spend on offerings to one Jesus-god, and only on Sundays." After a moment, she says, "Don't give me any medicine that might make me sleepy or unable to work, or Samuel might slap me."

"Does he?"

"If I complain too much."

How much complaining is too much? Sister Anu's experience of violence pales by comparison with women in Gurkot. They seem accustomed to being slapped, pushed, and punched, not only by men but by older women—but who can become accustomed to humiliation? Yesterday she helped Dr. Gupta wash the stomach of a woman who "mistakenly" took insecticide. To protect her children from retaliation or loss of inheritance, she would not charge her husband or in-laws with emotional cruelty. The day before, she helped Dr. Gupta put a cast on a woman whose father-in-law smashed her patella because she served him cool tea. Men of Gurkot beat the women in their families hardest when women are most vulnerable—often when pregnant. Yet the women here don't divorce their husbands or leave their children as Anu did; they laugh and joke and carry on working.

"If I had a daughter old enough," says Goldina, "I could make her deliver and cut the cord for this baby, but Samuel and I just married off our eldest two. Now we have to take loans and start again."

"We can do it here. Did you ask Damini to come and cut the cord for you?"

"A slow child can do it." She purses her lips. "But Damini won't. She's respected, she's too much high-up."

If I learned to overcome disgust, to clean my own toilet and deal with bodily fluids during my nursing courses, Damini can too.

"And if she did it, we Christians would have even less work." Goldina says, "Besides, I don't want her to—she makes me afraid."

"Why?" says Sister Anu, placing her stethoscope bell against Goldina's back ribs.

Goldina tilts her chin. "Buss aise hee," she says. Just because— which is no answer. Sister Anu folds away her stethoscope, and says. "Come to Bread of Healing as soon as you feel contractions. You mustn't walk uphill after your water breaks."

After a tetanus injection and some iron pills, Sister Anu ushers Goldina outside, back to Damini and a longer line of patients.

"Damini," says Sister Anu. "I will attend Goldina when it's her time, but you must help and learn."

"Of course, Sister-ji," Damini's servile tone is a Delhi-sound in the pine-scented air of Gurkot.

After Goldina, Sister Anu has so many patients she has no time for lunch. At teatime she crosses the clearing to the school. Father Pashan is sitting cross-legged on a dhurrie spread on the veranda. His diary lies open on one knee and he's reviewing a list of Catholic girls and boys of marriageable age. Beside each, he has written their caste name or tribal origin, to help him arrange marriages.

Bethany brings three glass tumblers of milky tea on a tray, along with some artificial sweetener for Father Pashan. "Mix them up,

Father!" she says, as she offers the tray. "Intermarriage will rid us of caste."

"Slowly-slowly, Bethany," says Father Pashan, taking his tea. "It will happen as people begin to follow Jesus's example. He was the rebel of his day, you know."

Bethany says, "Do you ever wonder if he thought he was god and then, in Gethsemane, learned he was merely a man?"

"Even if he was only a man, his story would be inspiring," says Father Pashan. "Now then, give me some ideas. How do we explain that illness is not caused by spirits and angry deities? I want us to discourage people in Gurkot and Jalawaaz from attending ceremonies with the ojha."

"Oh, the ojha!" says Sister Bethany. "I don't know what I was expecting but he doesn't look very different from anyone else."

"Except for his tattoos," says Sister Anu. "All over his arms and neck."

"He had a jacket on, so I only saw a wiry man with greying hair. He seemed like a bottle of Pepsi—full of compressed energy."

"Why did he come to Bread of Healing?" says Pashan. "Everyone in Gurkot says he can heal every ailment."

"He said he can't heal those in his immediate family," says Sister Anu. "He said that's why he was unable to heal his wife and granddaughter. The wife wasn't sick, just argumentative. I was more worried about his granddaughter."

"I didn't meet his wife or granddaughter," says Bethany.

"Because they weren't with him. I told him Dr. Gupta would want to examine them and talk to them, but he said they had too much work to come. He was annoyed too because he let me know he would give them 'takat pills' instead, by which I think he meant vitamin supplements. He said his cousin-brother sells them in Vancouver."

"Dr. Gupta, Damini and I drove to his village the next day, but he wouldn't let me talk to either woman. Finally, he opened his door to us because Damini offered some madhupatra for his wife, and told him the sweet leaves would make her kinder."

"And the granddaughter?"

"Dysentery. Dr. Gupta prescribed oral rehydration solution and an antibiotic. I'll return to check on her soon."

"So very pagan—" says Father Pashan, "these beliefs in plants and spirits and spirit possession."

"People do things because there is some benefit," says Sister Bethany, taking her glass from the tray.

Father Pashan says, "You're right, Bethany. Other people's beliefs are real to them. We mustn't mock or judge. Our strength comes from reliance on Jesus, theirs from reliance on spirits. But our god is theirs, there can be no doubt—and their gods are all facets of Jesus."

Sister Anu crosses her ankles and drops into lotus on the edge of the dhurrie. "We should pray to the Holy Spirit to help us stop the villagers from believing in spirits," she says with a smile.

"Good idea," says Father Pashan, with ever-ready optimism. Bethany hides a grin.

"There's another matter. We now know we have a case of AIDS."

Father Pashan says, "In India?"

"There must be thousands of cases of AIDS in India," says Sister Anu. "This one is a trucker."

"AIDS doesn't happen to married men," says Father Pashan.

Sister Anu says, "This man is married and a father, but it's definitely AIDS. He needs antibiotics by IV and different blood tests. We need to order antiretrovirals, and I can't find any companies that are donating such medicines . . ."

"He must be a married homosexual," Father Pashan is speculating out loud. "Families arrange marriages believing it will cure such men, but they go on sinning. We can't treat AIDS—tell Dr. Gupta."

The coma ward at Snowdon . . . a white shirt . . . brown blood . . . Snowdon Hospital doctors didn't ask how much of a man Bobby was before they treated him, but then, Snowdon isn't a Catholic institution. "Dr. Gupta enrolled him in an experimental trial of zidovudine," says Sister Anu. "Which is better than doing nothing."

"All right, continue the trial, then. But we can't condone homo-sexuality." Father Pashan adjusts his collar.

"I don't think Chunilal is homosexual," says Sister Anu. "But even if he were, we can't turn him away!"

She had not thought Pashan capable of withholding treatment from a poor man like Chunilal, no matter what Church doctrine says.

The priest runs his fingers through his hair. "If anyone in Delhi comes to know we are treating AIDS, we could lose funding."

She can't argue with Father Pashan, but is she an obedient daughter of the Church first, or is she a nurse? Sister Anu rises and busies herself with saucepans, tea leaves and tea glasses.

When the priest is gone, Sister Bethany opens a packet of mail from Shimla. "For you," she crows holding an envelope out of reach. "Guess who it's from?"

"Give it here! It must be from Rano."

But it's from Mumma, forwarded by Mrs. Nadkarni. Sister Anu talks to Mumma on the phone every week, but Mumma doesn't usually write. Anu slits the envelope, unfolds several newspaper cuttings within.

Roman Catholic church attacked by RSS workers.
Hindu movement pays dowry to prevent woman's conversion to Christianity.
Christian preacher attacked in Jaipur.
Mass reconversions of Christian dalits to Hinduism.

There is no note. "Nice of Mumma to be worried for her daughter," says Anu.

"Now, Sister, no sarcasm," says Bethany. "She's a mother; she's concerned. She just has . . . strange ways of showing it."

September 1996

ANU

SUNSET BURNISHES THE CHURCH BELL FRAMED IN THE
window above Sister Anu's desk.

Dr. Gupta has left for the day and she is about to finish her paperwork and go home as well. But here's Damini, pushing open the gates of Bread of Healing. She leads in a doubled-over Goldina.

Sister Anu helps the young woman to a bed in the women's ward, then draws the curtains. When she returns to Goldina's side, Goldina's strong hands grip hers as contractions come. No need for Pitocin. Damini unbinds the woman's hair, loosens her sari.

Anu wipes Goldina's brow with a wet towel. She'd feel more comfortable if Dr. Gupta were here to advise, but reminds herself she's usually the one delivering the babies because women prefer being attended by a woman. It won't be long now—Goldina's pelvic muscles are stretched from earlier births, her body supple from squatting. Sadly, only the mother of god can give birth without dilating her cervix.

Damini begins massaging Goldina's stomach to move the child downwards, but Sister Anu stops her. "Massaging can cause the womb to fall forward later on," she explains. Damini looks unconvinced, but steps back.

With a last howling contraction from Goldina, the baby comes through, into the world.

343

Damini sniffs as if she expected a sewer smell, but there's only the usual. She checks that the infant is breathing, then pats Goldina's shoulder.

"*Shabash!*" she says, in congratulations.

Sister Anu holds the child up to confirm—sometimes genitalia can be swollen—but it is a boy.

She holds the baby up before Goldina, "*Kya hai yeh bachcha?*" she says, asking the mother to identify the sex of the child.

"A boy," says Goldina. No joy in her voice—well, she must be tired.

Damini holds the child still for the cutting. Sister Anu works quickly, clamping the cord with a toothed artery forceps and cutting it with surgical scissors.

Please notice, Damini. Women of our caste can and do perform polluting acts.

Sister Anu drops the afterbirth in a receptacle for incineration. Damini stands beside the waste bin as if guarding it.

"Come here and help, Damini," says Sister Anu.

Anu clears the mucus from the baby's nostrils with a suction tube. She adjusts the pads beneath Goldina to soak up the blood. Damini doesn't come forward to help.

After Sister Anu takes the baby's footprint, then wraps him in a sterile swaddling cloth, Damini leaves her corner and takes him from Sister Anu. She places the child on his mother's breast. His skin is wavy and puckered from swimming for nine months. He looks like a sheaf of pale wheat lying across his mother's honey-brown belly. He will turn darker as he gets older and works in the sun.

He's sleek, strong and demanding, already moving to suckle. Sister Anu lets him—ignoring Damini's silent disapproval. "Have you decided on a name?" she asks Goldina.

"Moses," says Goldina, caressing the baby's cheek with her finger.

"*Hein?*" says Damini. "Already you're naming?"

"Yes, he'll live. Daughters don't."

"Actually, more girls survive than boys," says Sister Anu. "But you don't have to name the child today. You can name him officially when you apply for a birth certificate—you have a few weeks' time. And Father Pashan will be here in a few days—he'll baptize your baby."

"No, not in a few days," says Goldina. "I'll baptize him myself." She takes a water bottle from her cloth bag and pours a little water on the baby's head. "I baptize you in the name of the Father, the Son and the Holy Ghost," she says. The baby stirs slightly, yawns. "Now," she says, "Father Pashan can't refuse to bury him if he dies." She glances at Damini.

"He won't die, Goldina. And Moses is a very nice name." Sister Anu takes a seat beside Goldina. She has to weigh the child, fill in the birth record, write in the nurses' log, record birth weight . . . she passes the back of her hand across her brow.

Goldina must be even more exhausted. She's taking in the presence of the baby, gazing down at the boy with half-closed eyes. But after a few minutes, Goldina rises up, supporting herself on her elbows, black hair unbound and silver nose rings jingling. "Now I will go home, sister."

"Now? Doesn't Samuel know you're here?"

"Yes, he knows."

"Are you worried about him or your children?"

"Oh, no—his mother, his sister are there to look after him and the children."

"Then rest."

"No—" Goldina's eyes redden and fill. Her tears are falling on Sister Anu's hands.

"What are you afraid of?" Sister Anu asks.

"Nothing," Goldina swallows, then makes a wide arm-gesture that includes the baby. "The worst has already happened."

"What—what do you mean?"

But Goldina won't say.

"It's gabrahat," says Damini.

That word describes everything from anxiety to worry to madness. Maybe it's postpartum shock. Goldina isn't usually weepy. "You can't walk downhill in the dark with a newborn," says Sister Anu.

Damini says, "I'll sleep beside her."

Goldina says, "No need." Nevertheless, Damini lies down on the foot carpet beside the bed.

It takes all Sister Anu's gentle coaxing to draw Moses from Goldina's arms. She places the baby in a crib in the corner of the ward then brings Goldina a glass of warm milk with honey. "Rest now." Authority colours Sister Anu's voice. She leaves a Petromax lamp burning and turns off the lights to conserve electricity.

In the adjoining room, she turns the coals in the bukhari and takes her seat at her desk. She hopes Bethany ate dinner without her, and hasn't fallen asleep waiting in the reading chair. Oh, for the warmth of her cotton quilt and her own bed.

"Kholo, Kholo!" Someone is banging on the door.

Sister Anu's nurse cap has come unpinned—she must have dozed off.

A car is honking right outside the clinic.

She gropes beneath the table. The cap has rolled almost under the bukhari and is streaked with ash. She glances through the door into the women's ward—Damini is on her feet, startled awake too. Goldina sits up, sweeps her hair back into a bun.

"I'll see—you sleep," says Sister Anu.

Mr. Amanjit Singh's driver is at the door with Mr. Amanjit Singh beside him. When she opens up, Amanjit almost drags her down the path to his car. A moaning body wrapped in a cotton quilt lies on the back seat, illuminated by the dome light in the roof. At her approach, the quilt opens to reveal a pink nightie and large furry pink slippers and Mrs. Kiran Singh, crying, panting, almost unrecognizable without sunglasses.

Mr. Amanjit Singh helps his wife from the car. Kiran leans on Sister Anu.

"She's not due yet, not for a whole month," Amanjit says as they stagger back down the path like a six-legged animal. "I can't get her to Shimla. Not in this condition." He is wide-eyed with worry, the pleats on his forehead rising into his turban. He helps Kiran up the stairs to the veranda and deposits her on a chair. He strokes his rolled beard as if he doesn't know what to do with his hands. "Dr. Gupta said she needs a Caesarean."

"Dr. Gupta has left, ji," says Sister Anu. Panic rises in her. "I can't perform a C-section."

"Driver!" Amanjit Singh shouts over his shoulder. "Go to Jalawaaz and fetch Dr. Gupta."

"Then how will you go home, sir?"

"I'll walk, you ass," says Amanjit. "Now, go!"

"Sir, how will I find the doctor's home?"

"You don't know where he lives?"

"No, sir."

"Ask in the village—oh, never mind. I'll come with you."

He mutters under his breath about a shortage of Muslim brainpower, reaches for his wife again and half-carries her into the clinic. He looks relieved at the sight of Damini.

"Damini-amma!" Kiran groans with another contraction. "Come sit with me." But when she sees Goldina occupying one of the three beds in the women's ward, she says, "Is the men's ward empty?"

Sister Anu says, "Right now it is, but Dr. Gupta will come tomorrow, and . . ." If there are complications, please god, let there be answers in *The 5 Minute Clinical Consult.*

"Put Kiran-ji in the men's ward and tell Dr. Gupta the men's ward is occupied," says Amanjit Singh. "Amma, you look after Kiran-ji. Make sure she is not shaved. And here, look after her handbag and this kit bag. Careful now, here's her gutka." He hands Damini a prayer book wrapped in silk. "I'll be back with the doctor soon."

A typhoon withdraws with Aman's departure.

Sister Anu and Damini help Kiran to a bed. Damini brings black tea laced with cardamom and jaiphal. She kisses Kiran's prayer book, touches it to her forehead, and places it on the nightstand. Kiran reaches her right hand to touch the book, then her forehead. Sister Anu has the urge to touch the talisman as well.

But she barely has time to prep Kiran with an enema. The baby refuses to wait for Dr. Gupta. The baby doesn't know it should arrive by C-section, and surprises everyone by arriving through the normal gateway.

"It's a girl!" Sister Anu says joyfully, relieved and proud of a smooth delivery.

Kiran gives a low moan. Her face sinks behind her upheld hands.

Kiran has been asked the same question as Goldina, "Yeh baccha kya hai," and was too tired to answer. The girl has been cleaned and swaddled. Damini and Sister Anu are standing side by side with the infants on an examination table before them.

Sister Anu circles the boy's ankle with a strip of white Johnsonplast.

"Did your husband ever return?" asks Damini.

"No," says Anu. She can't find a pen so she adds a blue thread.

"He won't come here again," says Damini, taping the girl's ankle. Sister Anu ties a pink thread. "Men can't take pain. Not like us." Damini surveys her handiwork, then takes a reel of black thread from between her breasts, and adds a black thread on the boy's arm to prevent the evil eye. Should Sister Anu object? It's a harmless superstition. But if Damini is going to do it, she should do it for the girl as well.

"I'm still nervous," says Sister Anu, holding the girl's arm out. "But right now, I'm wondering where is Dr. Gupta? The car should have been back from Jalawaaz by now."

"Aman-ji won't find him in Jalawaaz," says Damini, tying a black thread on the baby girl's wrist. "Dr. Gupta went to his cousin-uncle's wedding in Shimla."

"Oh," says Sister Anu. "Poor Aman-ji. You should have said something."

"Aman-ji would have called me a moron, or told me it was my fault—let him go to Shimla."

"But it's dark and the roads are dangerous."

Damini looks unmoved. Sister Anu clenches her jaw in frustration. Damini can be so kind, then suddenly so harsh. "Well what to do now? I wish we could reach him to tell him Kiran is all right."

"I am here, you are here. Of course she is all right. What would he do if he were here? When Loveleen was born, he came the next day."

"But you will look after Kiran-ji?"

Damini cocks her head in assent. "Yes, I have to look after Mem-saab's family." This from the woman who has just sent Mem-saab's son on a wild goose chase on winding hill roads in the dark.

"By the time Dr. Gupta comes tomorrow or day after," Damini says, "we women will have finished all the work. He can just check Kiran-ji and get his fee and tip from Aman-ji. He can check Goldina, too."

Moses's hair is so soft beneath Sister Anu's fingertips, and his face so adorably delicate, she could *almost* want another baby. But no—not really. She lays him back in his crib, then Damini helps her move a crib into the men's ward for Kiran's baby girl. So much has happened already tonight, but there are still several hours before dawn and she must be here when Aman-ji returns with the doctor.

A cup of tea will keep her awake. She enters the nurses' station, and places a pan of water on the burner. A blue flame licks up. Small bubbles begin rising to the surface.

Sister Anu is making her second cup of tea when she hears shrieking. She turns off the burner, and hastens into the men's ward. And there's Kiran sitting up in bed, twisting away from Goldina. A swaddled infant is in Kiran's arms, "*Hut!* Hut-ja, churi!" she shouts.

Damini is trying to restrain Goldina.

"You stole Moses!" screams Goldina. She whirls to face Damini as if demon-possessed. "You gave Moses to her! That's my son!"

Sister Anu takes a huge breath and shouts at all of them to stop.

Damini and Goldina turn. Goldina's face is ugly with hurt and rage.

"Get the sweeper-woman out of here," says Kiran to Sister Anu in English, looking down her nose with half-closed eyes.

Sister Anu unwraps the infant Goldina has laid on the red-blanketed bed beside Kiran's. It's the girl. Sister Anu gives the girl to Damini and reaches for the baby in Kiran's arms. Kiran's expression turns unreadable.

"Mrs. Singh, please would you return Goldina's baby."

Kiran says in English, "You get this filthy woman out of my room."

Thankfully, Goldina doesn't understand the words, but she can't miss the tone. Sister Anu's hands fall to her sides. She can't wrest a baby out of Kiran's arms.

"I told you I shouldn't come here, I told you!" Goldina screams at Damini in Hindi.

"It's a mistake, Goldina," Sister Anu says. "Don't worry. It's easily corrected."

Can Damini be the culprit? No—the kind old woman isn't capable of such a deed. She wouldn't let Sister Anu down. Mrs. Amanjit Singh is just taking advantage. She turns back to Goldina. "Go with Damini, she'll help you back to your bed."

Goldina doesn't budge.

Sister Anu summons all her gentleness and turns back to Kiran. She sits down on the next bed so their eyes are level. "Mrs. Singh, you and your husband have done so much for this clinic. Don't you think it would hurt its reputation in the community if a baby were switched . . ."

She persuades, cajoles, coaxes . . .

Suddenly, Kiran is waving a white envelope before her eyes and cooing, "A small donation for an auspicious day."

It's outrageous! Kiran obviously came prepared in case a bribe was needed. She probably intended her envelope for Dr. Gupta. Customary procedure, just as it was for Vikas.

Goldina knows what is in the envelope. So does Damini. Some things need no translation. Yet Kiran doesn't care if they see her offer a bribe. Who will believe Goldina or Damini if they tell?

Sister Anu musters the remnants of her compassion and looks Kiran in the eye. "Kiran-ji, when a mother feels compelled to give up her child, how can this day be called auspicious?"

DAMINI

CAN A MOTHER MISTAKE ANOTHER WOMAN'S SON FOR her own? Impossible.

Damini has not seen gentle Sister Anu so annoyed since she fought with her husband. She wants to tell Sister Anu that she would never exchange a baby for Kiran—why, she still remembers how Kiran and Aman besieged Mem-saab. And why should she do such paap for Kiran when Kiran shows her no respect? But she can't say this. Leela and the children need the occasional work Kiran gives Damini at the Big House.

At the sight of the envelope, Goldina seems to have lost faith in Sister Anu's ability to persuade Kiran. She squats on the floor between the two beds, looking up from Kiran to Sister Anu, in turn. Her whole lower body must still be stretched and aching.

Kiran-ji shouldn't think Damini agrees with her actions either. Damini moves behind Sister Anu. She can see Kiran's face and Goldina's, but not the sister's.

"You're afraid to have a girl," Goldina accuses Kiran, wiping her eyes and blowing her nose with the end of her sari. "Will you be beaten? After one or two beatings, you get used to it. But," she leans forward, clasping each knee, "don't do this paap. Give my son back. Moses needs me."

She shouldn't talk to Kiran-ji this way—she could lose her job at the Big House—but desperation seems to be carrying her away like poppy-fume.

"You're afraid to bring another girl into the world. I know, I know. It is your bhagya that is the problem. But see me. I am living proof you can improve your bhagya with hard work."

Kiran's brow furrows as if she's having trouble understanding Goldina.

Goldina says, "Is your mother-in-law telling you today, 'Make me happy, give me a grandson'? What will she ask for tomorrow? What will she ask you to do?"

Damini cannot remain silent. "Goldina, Kiran-ji's mother-in-law is no longer in this life. And if she were, she would never ask Kiran to do anything like this. There's some other reason."

Kiran wipes her eyes. "I can't believe even Damini-amma is against me! You all wait till my husband comes. All of you will be sorry . . ."

"I know, I know," says Goldina, "Women like me can't get any rest or food or a single word of praise unless we have a boy. But you? Don't worry, you'll get rest, you'll get food even if you have a girl . . ."

Kiran looks away as if Goldina had not spoken.

"You're a Sikh," Goldina says to Kiran. "Sikhs have the same names for men as for women. Sikhs say men and women are all equal-equal. I know, I know—they only say that, don't they? But you can give your daughter a boy's name and consider her equal to a boy. You know, when your Damini-amma asked if I would get this baby cleaned out because I already have many children, I said no. I said this child is a piece of my body even if it is a girl. I said what the padri says: god will provide. My mother had five girls, and she loved each of us and told us how lucky she was to have us. She told us we were precious, special even if the world said we were just sweepers."

Damini says, "Han, han! But my mother also had five girls. She mourned our births and told us how unlucky she was to have us."

Goldina shoots a look at Damini, then says, "Sister-ji, keep her away from the girl baby. I cut the cord at the birth of her granddaughter. The baby girl was alive when I left but died a few days later."

Damini presses her lips together. Her lungs expand in mixture of guilt and pain. This is not how she should be repaid for befriending a sweeper!

"And she takes women to the Jalawaaz clinic for the machine to tell if they are having a daughter or son. And if they're having daughters, she gets them cleaned out there or gives them her medicines to put inside."

Sister Anu glares over her shoulder at Damini. "Did you take Goldina to the ultrasound clinic?"

Damini avoids the righteous flash of those black eyes. "I offered, but she said she didn't want to know if she was going to have a boy or girl, that it doesn't matter. These sweeper-women are foolish that way, Sister-ji. They don't think: how will I live if I am thrown out? On fresh air?"

"At least Goldina knows what is honourable," the sister says.

"*Hein?*" says Damini. "I'm not like you! Letting women have babies one after another, like cows. You don't even tell them their husbands should wear topis! If Dr. Gupta did cleanings here, I wouldn't have to make poor pregnant women walk five hours down the ghost-trail to Jalawaaz. I listen to women's wishes—that's honourable."

Sister Anu looks as if Damini has slapped her.

"How is it that every woman wants the same thing?" Goldina's voice sounds as if she's calling up a well shaft. "Only wanting sons, like Kiran-ji? If women really are telling you their wishes, then won't some want sons and others want daughters?"

Damini has no answer—she really hasn't thought about it. It's true. How can it be that all the women she has taken for ultra-soons want the same thing? "It's kudrati to want sons," she says, keeping her tone elaborately matter-of-fact while pretending to know what's natural, "and kudrati not to want daughters."

Kiran unfolds Moses's swaddling a little at a time, and begins examining him.

Goldina gives a sardonic laugh. "When someone wants her wealth written in her stars, my poverty becomes natural. When someone wants her intelligence to be ordained, my stupidity and the stupidity of my family becomes natural. You asked what I wanted but you wanted me to want what other woman want. And you wouldn't help me act on my wishes. You must be thinking: Goldina's not 'in-telli-gent' enough to know what she wants, Goldina can't even write her name. You told me I should do what every woman you've taken there does—find out if it's a girl and kill her before she takes birth."

Damini holds the baby girl out to Goldina. "Love girls so much? Take this one—go on. Starve in your old age."

"If she was mine, I would," says Goldina. "And I would sew, knit and clean in my old age just as I do now, and as my mother does. But god didn't send me this girl. I want Moses. Even if I never wanted to make him, now he's here. He's a piece of my body, he came from my koke," she holds her lower belly as if reliving the pain.

Damini gazes down at the baby girl. How very small and light she is. She opens her eyes, lovely sweet brown eyes, and looks right at Damini, as if she sees. Damini lays her down on the bed again but she feels the baby looking at her with those twin firefly eyes.

Goldina appeals again to Kiran, "I can feel the fear you're feeling. I fold my hands before you and ask: try to feel mine. If you don't give me my son, and I tell my husband and his family what happened, they'll say I should never have listened to Damini and Sister Anu. They'll say I should have had this child at home, like all the others."

"Are you stupid enough to prefer having a child at home instead of here?" says Kiran. "Ungrateful creature."

"I'm stupid, yes. But you—all your education and money and you can't face your friends in your high-up society and say I am a woman and a mother and I was once a baby girl? I know, I know. The more you have, the more fearful you are of losing it, but socho . . . socho."

Yes, think, think! What should Damini do? What can she do?

"What rubbish!" Kiran says to Sister Anu. "This woman dares to believe she can feel what I feel! And she thinks *I* should feel as she feels—how can she even think it possible? You wait till my husband comes—I'll fire her, and her family will be thrown out of her little hovel. Then we'll see how she dares to accuse her superiors."

Sister Anu says, "Kiran-ji, even if you refuse to know Goldina's pain, how can you reject your baby daughter?"

Goldina's lips tremble as she struggles to speak, but no words come because tears are in the way. Someone must speak for her. Damini should not take sides but she can't help herself. "Kiran-ji, you took her son," she says.

"You be quiet, Amma. This is my child."

Damini says, "Kiran-ji, open your ears and listen. The gods have some reason why I am acting in the movie of your life. I did not give you that child. You had a girl. I saw it happen, Sister Anu saw it—we can't deny what we saw."

Goldina looks up, gathers her voice. "Didn't you go to the Jalawaaz clinic, Kiran-ji? You don't even have to walk. You can go by car and afford all the tests that would have shown you a girl was coming."

"No one had to take me." Kiran says indignantly. "The doctor brought the machine right to the house, in his Gypsy van."

"Dr. Gupta?" says Sister Anu.

"No, not Dr. Gupta," says Kiran. "He was too afraid he might be the first doctor ever to be sued for prenatal sex diagnosis."

"Even in nursing school I was told to be careful not to get into trouble when using ultrasound."

Kiran rolls her eyes. "The machine is not illegal. Jails would be full if doctors were put behind bars for using one."

"It is, if you learn the child's sex," says Sister Anu. "That's called ling janch."

Kiran shrugs. "It's my body—I have the right to know. If I had been about to have a girl, the doctor would have sounded sad, mentioned pink or a need for 'family balancing.'"

"If you knew you were having a girl," says Damini, "why didn't you have her cleaned out?"

"Because the ultrasound said what you said, that I would have a boy."

Now Kiran is accusing her of being an astrologer! But at least she's still addressing her as *tum* rather than *tu*.

"You mean the ultrasound test was wrong," says Sister Anu.

"Was the power on? Buttons don't work when there's no power," says Goldina.

"Yes, the electricity was on, you fool," Kiran says, addressing Goldina as *tu*.

"Then how did the machine give you a wrong answer?" says Goldina, still careful to address Kiran as *aap*.

"Sometimes the child is too young when the ultrasound is done," says Sister Anu, "and the doctor can't tell. Or the doctor could be inexperienced and make a mistake."

"Or the doctor told Kiran-ji she would have a boy to please her," says Goldina. "People always say what they think will please her. I've heard that the doctors in Jalawaaz always tell women they are having girls, so they can clean the babies out and make more money."

"Hai! Can a woman end up cleaning out a *son*?" says Damini. She has never considered this. Why has she never considered this?

Kiran sits up, smoothing the coverlet over her still-swollen belly. "Goldina—how much money will it take to make you shut up?"

Damini's jaw drops and Sister Anu's hand goes to her mouth.

Goldina looks up from her squat by Kiran's bedside. "How much?" Her weathered hand clutches Kiran's blanket. "How much will you pay for his penis? How much are his strong arms worth? How much is his hungry stomach worth? What will you give me for those little loins? You don't even know if he will be a good man or an intelligent one. You don't know if he will treat his older sister with love or marry her off to merge his bijness with another man's."

Kiran rolls her eyes. She says to Sister Anu in English, "If this is the way you run things here, we'll just close the clinic and tell the whole village you Christians weren't running it properly. You wait till my husband comes. I'll tell him what you're trying to do."

Sister Anu should use her English to explain to Kiran, because Damini can't snatch Moses from Kiran and Goldina must be too afraid of Kiran and of injuring her son.

"Give Moses to you," says Goldina, "and he'll wear silk while your daughter wears cotton. Give him to you and I'll have to call my own son 'Moses-ji' and be ordered to clean his home someday. Give him to you and he'll eat chicken every day while in my home your little daughter will drink the water used to boil rice and sometimes a little daal. Give Moses to you and he'll learn to say 'I want' while your daughter learns to keep silent."

Damini's heart bounds for Goldina, but she braces just in case she has to restrain the distraught mother again.

"I know, I know. In time, I'll pretend to forget who he really is and so will you. We know how to pretend. You're a woman, I'm a woman—we learn it at our mother's knee! As he grows up, I will lower my eyes in his presence, but our secret will bind us to each other, so I can never leave you or your employ. And you—how will you forget your baby daughter? When she comes to learn my trade, will you make her clean your toilet?"

Kiran says, "She's yours. What do I care what you teach her?"

Goldina shrugs. "This baby girl wasn't what you wanted so you'll give her to me the way you give me rubbish to take away from your home.

"But if I give my son to you, he'll learn to be a vee-eye-pee at three, and a vee-vee-eye-pee by ten. His friends will be the sons of your friends, and there'll always be someone below him he can shout at or squeeze or hit. He'll learn to order others, slam doors and cuff anyone in his way. I see such patterns. But I'll teach your daughter sweetness and grovelling and silence to protect her. If she grows up even half as beautiful as you, she'll be raped by some caste Hindu just to 'teach her a lesson' or 'show her her place.' She'll learn to eat from the same plate as Samuel and me, instead of having her own. She'll complain a little when I send her away with her husband, but not very much, because by then she will know how little Samuel and I can do for her."

She takes a deep shuddering breath.

"But when Moses devours whatever he claims, or bribes and fights those who cross him—will you blame my low-caste blood or your high-caste ways? When this boy learns to believe his servants are lazy and steal and have no brains, will that be because of my blood or your saab ways? And when he turns more vicious than a mad dog whenever he doesn't get what he wants, when he changes his whims like the wind just to make others jump, will you blame his blood or your saab ways?"

Kiran turns on her side, shielding Moses from their clutches. Her head covered with the blanket mimics the shape of the swaddled baby.

But Goldina continues, "Only you and I will know he has no right to act like a saab, but by the time Moses grows up, we'll both be too afraid of him to tell anyone. And what if he ever learns who he is? Then will he come to Samuel and me? Will he be shamed to know his mother is a sweeper-woman? Tell me, how will he know himself?

"And what if one day your daughter learns who her parents are, and that she never learned more than her alphabet because she was just a little girl from the sweeper colony. Maybe she will want the kind of toys your daughter has today—just years too late. Do you think she will want what your Loveleen has? Think how one sister will hate the other.

"So you want to pay me for this boy, Kiran-ji? Will that stop your taking? Who will you take from next time?"

"I'm trying to sleep," says Kiran's muffled voice.

"How long will it be before I come to you for more money? How will you keep me from telling Aman-ji and the rest of the world? When you run out of money, will you have me killed?"

Damini says, "Goldina! Don't talk like that to Kiran-ji."

Goldina rounds on her. "And you, where will you stop? Will you keep taking women for the test until every woman produces a son? What kind of world are you making? A world full of men, a world with no kindness, no gentleness—no sweetness?"

No sweetness. Damini already lives in that kind of world.

"Always there are highs and lows, Goldina," Damini whispers. "The gods made the mountains to show us that."

"Which god says that people higher up deserve to be there? Which god says that people higher up are better than us? Which god says she has a right to my child? I clean her shit—it smells as bad as mine."

"*Chi!* Dirty talk!" Kiran rolls back the covers and sits up, still holding Moses close. "All of you go away, just leave me with my son."

No one moves.

Both babies begin to cry.

Kiran opens her nightgown and the ward turns into an echo chamber of Goldina's shrieks. Sister Anu starts forward, then draws back—she can't wrench the boy from Kiran's arms without hurting him. Kiran ignores everyone and begins to feed the boy.

Goldina begins to wail, then to moan.

The baby girl looks up at Damini. She shakes her head from side to side. Her eyes flash, eyes that have seen all this before. Her lips pucker—she's hungry too. Sister Anu whispers to Damini. Damini tears herself away, goes to the next room and mixes some Nestlé powder.

When she brings the formula, Sister Anu sits down in sight of the two mothers and feeds the baby girl.

ANU

THE BABIES HAVE BEEN FED, STROKED AND SOOTHED
but the men's ward resounds with Goldina's moaning. Anu could
snatch the baby. But if Kiran is too mighty to understand Goldina's
pain she might not care if she hurts Moses.

The whole affair has gone beyond Anu's experience or training.
She is here for community support and charity work. If Dr. Gupta
were here, he could order Kiran to return Moses to Goldina, and
Kiran might have some trouble firing him.

Amanjit Singh owns the carpet of land on which this clinic stands
and Kiran can pull it out from under all of them. Without Kiran's
support, all that Father Pashan and Anu and Bethany have worked
for will be gone. Only a few hours ago, Goldina said the worst had
already happened—but she could not have imagined what Kiran
was about to do. But Goldina should be supported, Kiran should be
held accountable—you can't just go around stealing other women's
babies and abandoning your own. If a high-caste woman steals a
village woman's baby at Bread of Healing, women will stop coming,
and again only men will come with reports of their wives' and daughters' symptoms.

"When Dr. Gupta comes," Anu says, "I will send the driver to the
police station in Jalawaaz and ask them to send a constable. Goldina
has a complaint, and she should lodge it."

"No, sister, no!" Goldina scrambles up and lunges forward to
touch Sister Anu's feet. "No puliss, no, no!" Her fingers grip Sister
Anu's ankles tight. "They'll beat me. They'll believe Kiran mem-saab,
not me. Don't let them rape me also. They all know Moses' father—
you probably know him too. He's a respected man, a caste Hindu.
A teacher."

"Ha!" says Kiran.

So that is the source of the boy's light skin.

"You need more explaining?" says Goldina, wiping her cheeks.

Sister Anu almost lifts Goldina to her feet. How thin are Goldina's shoulders in the circle of her arms. "Rape," she tells Goldina, "is not a woman's fault. It's the man who does the harm."

"*Hé Vaheguru!*" says Kiran. "Take all your Bollywood-movie scenes somewhere else, and let me sleep!"

DAMINI

Which teacher in Jalawaaz? There could be two or three—so why does Damini immediately suspect her son?

Because he's unmarried. Unmarried men get the heat.

No, not Suresh. He probably talked to her kindly and she thought he was luring her. These low-caste people begin sitting beside you if you talk to them for a minute. Call her Hindu, harijan, dalit, shudra, valmiki, bhangi, chura, chamar, chandal, pariah or dom. Make her sit on a chair instead of on the ground. Bathe her, clean her. Nothing can change what she is: a sweeper.

Suresh probably mistook Goldina for a loose woman—everyone knows sweeper-women actually enjoy making children.

Making children. Making this child. This boy. This boy who could be Damini's grandson.

"If you were really raped," says Damini, "you could tell the doctor at the government clinic or the private clinic in Jalawaaz that you wanted a cleaning and she would have done it like that." She snaps her fingers. "Why didn't you?"

"I confessed to Father Pashan I didn't know if my husband is the father and he said I'd fry in hell if I had a cleaning. He made me swear to have this baby. He said he would pray that I would have a boy, and that the child would be auspicious for me. His prayers gave me a boy, but see his face—Moses is not dark enough to be auspicious."

Suresh must hardly have touched Goldina, but now she's crying rape, thinks Damini. Maybe he rolled around with her or something—boys do these things. Backward-caste sweeper-women just accuse boys from forward-castes, good boys like Suresh, all the time, all the time.

It's all my fault—I should have married him off years ago.

"I can't believe Father would counsel you not to tell your husband," says Sister Anu.

"He just said I should do what my conscience told me."

"Who is that?" says Damini.

"A voice inside you," says Sister Anu.

"A spirit was talking?" asks Damini.

"The Holy Spirit," says Goldina. "And Anamika Devi."

"Anamika Devi spoke to you?"

Goldina tilts her head in assent. "I lit a candle before her avatar, Mary Devi. Mary Devi said to bring my mind and heart together. So I thought: the padri said not to have a cleaning because he's a man. What does he know about my body, and whether I should have a cleaning or not? I said I will do what I feel is right, not what any man says."

"Then?"

"Mary Devi made a son for me."

"Such bullshit," Kiran says in English. "The Holy Ghost, and now goddesses and Mother Mary. This woman is completely irrational. She's not only stupid but mad as well." She turns to Sister Anu. "Look, it's very simple. Either you get her away from me and my son, or I'll have this place shut down tomorrow."

Though it's said in English, Damini understands the threat.

Sister Anu shakes her head, and doesn't shrink.

ANU

"YOU NUNS DON'T HAVE CHILDREN," GOLDINA SAYS TO Sister Anu. "You don't want children. How can women who don't want children understand anything about having children?"

"But I do have a child," Sister Anu says, shocking herself and the three other women out of their wrangling. She's feeling weak and hungry and at the end of her patience. And now she's being told she doesn't understand and can't understand because how can an upper-caste woman possibly have compassion?

Maybe her story can help this woman, one woman. She cannot know unless she tells it. Hers is a child of rape just like Moses. The story lifts like a sheer dupatta let loose on the wind. As she tells, Sister Anu's scar flushes and twitches with embarrassment for Vikas. Why is she still ashamed for him? Shouldn't he be ashamed of himself, for himself?

"And here I thought you were a saab-woman who can't see bangles she's not wearing," says Damini.

Let even one woman know that she can be optimistic because she still survives. The telling slings a rope-bridge from herself to each woman. She mentions god's role in saving her, though the Christian god means little to two of the three-woman audience, and as she tells them, she learns why she believes in miracles—it is a miracle she had the courage to leave Vikas, a miracle she is here.

At the end, she says to Kiran, "Once Chetna was born, I did love her."

"Oh yes?" says Goldina, "Then where is the girl now? Why is she not with you? Did you get rid of her?"

"When I left my husband to join the convent, I sent her to my cousin-sister in Canada."

"No wonder you seem to think I should give up my son to Kiran mem-saab," says Goldina. "You think Moses will have a better life with her, don't you? But if I take the mem-saab's girl home with me—what kind of life do you think she'll have? My husband and I share everything equally amongst our children, but I tell you this girl will not lead the same life as little Loveleen. Why do you not care for the baby girl's betterment as much as for the boy's?"

DAMINI

IF KIRAN TAKES DAMINI'S GRANDCHILD, HE WILL GROW
up contemptuous of her, and those who struggle. He will have no
obligation to look after Damini in her old age. If Goldina keeps the
child, the boy will at least be near. In a mud hut, not a brick home as
he deserves, but she will see him, know him, guide him.

This boy is surely the avatar of the baby girl Damini returned to
brahman. Damini must not betray this second grandchild, son of her
own son, however he came to be. The gods are giving her a chance to
balance her karma.

"The boy is light-skinned," Damini says to Kiran, "and you're right
that he looks too light-skinned to be Goldina's. But I tell you, he's too
dark to be Mem-saab's grandchild. Even if you rename him, no one
will believe this is your son. Goldina can be thrown out of her home
if you send your girl baby home with her, but you have nothing to
fear. Aman-ji can afford a second daughter. If he beats you up or
throws you out, you can go to a lawyer and complain. You can go to
the police. You can go home to your rich parents. Goldina has only
her old mother, a sweeper in Delhi."

"I can't believe you are taking this woman's side. You, our ancestral
servant, you who have eaten our salt. You, who are wearing my
mother-in-law's kara." Kiran says to Sister Anu in English, "You can't
trust these women. All of them just lie and lie."

Goldina sniffles and hugs her shins, shifting weight on her large
feet. She adjusts her kerchief and glares at Kiran.

Damini says, "Kiran-ji, maybe you lied when you told Aman the
ultra-soon said it's a boy. Maybe the doctor lied. But if you take
Goldina's child, I will tell Aman-ji that a man you liked before you
were married came to see you. Yes, I will tell him he was here, in
Gurkot, that he came in his saffron-orange car. My son told me he
saw you meeting him at the chai-stall. Maybe he came before.
Maybe he came nine months ago? I saw him here once, but I just

remembered where I first saw him. His photo was in Mem-saab's home in Delhi, in your dressing-table drawer. Remember I asked which member of your family had cut his hair besides your father, and you didn't answer. Because he was no relative, na? Because he was a Hindu, na?"

She holds Kiran's gaze.

ANU

SISTER ANU HAS TO SIT DOWN.

How often did Anu wonder what Vikas's first love looked like and what sort of woman was That-girl? Well, now she knows. That-girl is Kiran, a woman who would stoop to steal another woman's son.

Anu could *never* have been like her. But more importantly, nor would she ever *want* to be like Kiran.

It is easy to congratulate herself, since she actually brought a daughter into the world. But did Anu act as gateway to the world from courage, or from fear of damnation?

She must collect her thoughts, set aside this discovery. For the sake of two women and two babies. Her job is to understand the pressure Kiran is under. With no mother-in-law or father-in-law, with a husband who appears to dote on his older daughter Loveleen, why has Kiran felt so much pressure to conform?

Maybe Goldina is right—we learn to want only what we can have in this life, so we tell ourselves to want only boys.

DAMINI

"KIRAN-JI, IF YOU DON'T GIVE ME THE CHILD NOW," SAYS Damini, "I will tell Aman he doesn't resemble Mem-saab or him."

Still holding the baby, Kiran reaches beneath her pillow for a small silver box. "Why should he believe you?" She flips the box open with her thumbnail and pops a pinch of paan masala into her mouth. "Just because of your age?" She closes her fist over the box. She turns to Sister Anu and says in English, "I always thought she looks like a red monkey—don't you?"

Damini understands what Kiran said, even if she cannot answer in English.

It's karma because of her paap, she thinks. The continuous load on her heart is her paap.

"I don't think so," says Sister Anu who should agree with Kiran before she disagrees.

"Amanjit-ji will believe me," Damini says to Kiran. "Because of my years in his family, years in which I protected his family's honour by being Mem-saab's ears. Mem-saab's spirit is in this clinic, and I swear to you on her spirit that I will do it." Kiran opens her fist and stares down at the box. Damini draws close to her bedside. "And because I am faithful to her memory, and because our family has been faithful to Sardar-saab's for so many generations, I ask you . . ."

Damini holds out her arms for the child and waits.

Kiran hesitates, searching Damini's face. Damini's nerves crackle as if in terror of the next moment

After a long long moment, Kiran extends the baby boy to Damini and then begins to weep.

This little one weighs less than Kiran's premature girl—of course, he is Goldina's.

Sister Anu picks up the girl and lays her beside Kiran.

"Damini-amma," says Kiran from behind her handkerchief. "I'm almost thirty-seven now and Aman-ji is fifty-four. He wants his homes, his factories and businesses, the summer cottages he's building to be inherited by his own blood, not a second son-in-law. He needs a son now, to grow up in time to train him into the businesses. He was planning such a celebration—and here I went and had another girl. I just didn't want to disappoint him—I couldn't disappoint him. And you know, Aman-ji is fighting his elder brother for his inheritance—without a son, who will carry on the court case after him?"

"If you and Amanjit-ji really don't want your little girl," Sister Anu says, as if making an effort to be kind, but in Hindi, thereby including Damini and Goldina, "Everlasting Hope has orphanages, and we find parents who want girls. Some baby girls go to America and Canada, some to other countries. Some are even adopted in India." "Some" sounds more optimistic than "very few," but Damini was an amma long enough to know adopted girls can become unpaid maid-servants. Sister Anu continues, "But adoption is usually necessary only if a girl-child is abandoned. And mothers who abandon children are usually terribly poor."

A sudden quiet comes over them. Damini gives Goldina her son.

After all his talk about purity and defilement, Damini wonders, could Suresh lie with a Christian sweeper-woman, even one as beautiful as Goldina?

ANU

GOLDINA IS CROONING AND ROCKING HER INFANT SON in her arms. Sister Anu accompanies her back to the women's ward, and checks her bleeding. After checking her pulse, temperature and blood pressure, she brings Goldina tea and rotis to replenish her calories and fluids. She stokes up the coals in the bukhari, and helps Goldina begin feeding Moses. Within half an hour, Goldina's uterus is already responding to the feeding by contracting—praise the Lord! What complexity and planning it took to create a woman's body and endow it with hormones that activate exactly when required.

When she returns to the men's ward, she finds Kiran holding the swaddled baby girl and wearing the kind of martyred look Mumma wears when thwarted in any way.

"You'll get used to her," Sister Anu says to Kiran. "I was a mother who never wanted her baby, but I got used to her. And now I miss her so much."

Kiran shakes her head. "No one understands. I'm ruined." She looks down at her little girl. A tear glitters on her dark lashes. Is that tear for this daughter or in regret for children she might have had with Vikas?

"You know a Vikas Kohli?" There, the question is out.

Kiran looks up, wariness stirring in her eyes. "There are many men of that name."

"Yes, but only one who came all the way here from New Delhi a few months ago, driving a saffron-orange Mercedes. Do you know him?"

Kiran gives a wry smile. "I thought I knew him. But I didn't."

"When?"

"A long time ago, in college."

"Did he have a Cord Roadster?"

"Yes," Kiran smiles as if watching a fond memory. "He'd take me for a ride, with the top down. How do you know him? I don't think he was ever interested in nuns."

Sister Anu's scar twitches involuntarily. "You were to be married?"

"I thought so."

"If you loved him, why did you agree to marry Amanjit-ji?"

Kiran purses her lips, as if biting back words. After a long silence, she says, "Remember 1984? A Muslim neighbour came to my father's home and warned him to leave. My father thought of taking a train out of New Delhi, but the government radio and TV stations kept repeating that "two Sikhs" had killed Madam G. They didn't say whether they meant Sikh men or women, but the news incited violence in Kanpur, Lucknow, Patna and onward. Sikh men were pulled off a train at Lucknow and massacred. He couldn't decide which place would be safe, so we fled to our local gurdwara, mustered up any weapons we could, and barricaded ourselves within. All the time that Madam G.'s body lay in state, mobs yelling 'Khoon ka badla khoon!' besieged us. They were calling for our blood though none of us killed Madam G. I used a crate of empty Coke bottles to make Molotov cocktails. For three days, Sikh men, women and even children fought side by side, holding the Hindu mobs off with kirpans and swords. Then my father cut his hair. That's how they missed him when other Sikh men were hacked to pieces. When we returned, we found our home had been looted, our cars and Sikh servants set on fire.

"But you don't know about this, right? Because it didn't affect you Hindus. Because the killings weren't mentioned on radio or TV or in print. For my parents, all Hindus had blood on their hands."

"I—I'm sorry, Kiran-ji, but what does this have to do with—"

Kiran says, "My father said if I married Vikas, I should never return. And if I didn't cooperate—by which they meant marry a Sikh man, so I would have Sikh children—they would take me to a psychiatrist. My mother said I would be locked away. They wanted to do their dharma regardless of the effect of their actions on me. I was not Kiran to them, I was their daughter, their duty.

"I cried for Vikas. I called, begging him to elope. He wouldn't." She gives a great sigh. "I don't blame him now. His father told him he would throw him out without a dime if he married a Sikh girl. His father said, 'The Sikhs killed our prime minister,' as if every Sikh was guilty of the assassination of Madam G. Vikas never said his father was wrong. Either he agreed with him, or he loved his creature comforts too much to sacrifice them for love."

"But—aren't Hindus and Sikhs very similar? More similar than Hindus and Christians, certainly. I have a cousin who married a Sikh man . . ."

"Did she marry him after 1984?" says Kiran.

"Before."

"Since the massacre, Sikh men are wearing baseball caps instead of turbans. Many have cut their hair to blend in. Vikas may use Sikh men in government travel ads so Indians look different from Pakistanis or Bangladeshis, but the Sikh men I know try to go unnoticed. Many of us have emigrated. Those who cannot are educating Sikh children to speak Hindi and English—and almost no Punjabi. Sikh families now try to marry their sons to Hindu women to make alliances with Hindu families.

"But when I was a little girl, we Sikhs took pride in never worshipping pictures or calendars or idols—not even idols of our ten gurus. We believed our gurus were teachers, not gods and used to be proud of believing in one god—Vaheguru. But who would dream that Congress Party politicians and the police would lead Hindu mobs to our homes?"

She stops. "Wait—how do you know Vikas drove a Cord? You know him?"

"I was married to him," says Sister Anu. "For almost nine years."

A well-tweezed eyebrow rises. "Oh, truly this is a night of revelations," says Kiran. "First we find out you, a nun, were raped, now that you were married, and to my old boyfriend. A Bollywood scriptwriter could do no better."

"My rapist and your old boyfriend are one and the same."

Genuine confusion and surprise cloud her face. "Vikas? He was such a gentleman."

"He has drawing-room manners when the world is watching." Sister Anu doesn't succeed at keeping bitterness from her tone.

"Well, you left him, obviously. You're a lesbian?"

"No," says Sister Anu. "Nuns are celibate, not lesbians."

Kiran's mouth twists in disbelief.

"I wanted to rule myself."

A short sharp laugh. "As if a woman is a country! Is there a woman in the world who rules herself?"

"You can try raising one," says Sister Anu. "You can begin with believing your daughter is precious, even if everyone around you says she isn't."

Kiran rolls her eyes.

Sister Anu returns to her desk and a night-chilled cup of tea.

Was it because Kiran's parents showed contempt for Kiran's wishes and decisions? No, that's too harsh. All fathers are not as liberal as Dadu, and many parents ignore a daughter's wishes. Yet every woman doesn't try to switch her baby daughter for a son.

Rejecting your baby is like rejecting a limb. How could she?

Mothers can reject daughters in many ways, not only by starving, selling, abandoning or exchanging them for sons. Just look at Mumma.

And what about you and Chetna? Have you rejected her or saved her by sending her to Rano? Did you feel her to be gift or burden? Every time you look at her, don't you feel Vikas's violence again?

With all her anxiety for the baby girl, Sister Anu understands what it will cost Amanjit Singh and Kiran to raise and marry off not one but two girls. She wouldn't wish that on any father, not even Vikas. In hindsight, the solution Anu proposed, adoption of a girl baby just because she is a girl, is as unjust as Kiran's trying to exchange the girl. So Anu too has contributed to the happening of all that is happening.

Lord, give us courage.

How much courage? And why should a woman always have to be brave? Where are fathers like Dadu who are gladly responsible, caring and protective of the girls they create?

Would she be asking such questions if she lived in Canada like Rano? Her neural connections are really not up to thinking this through at this hour of the morning.

It is not only Kiran and Damini and Goldina who need healing. Every man, woman and child in this village needs healing. But if there's one thing Sister Anu has learned while nursing, it is that healing must happen from within.

"He loved his creature comforts too much to sacrifice them for love." Kiran's words rattle around in Sister Anu's head. An image takes centre stage: Vikas, lounging in his most comfortable chair.

Is he dead? There's a terrible look on his face. Her blood freezes as fear grows. Now another fear rises, grows to terror. Has she killed him?

That look, as if he died mid-sneer. *O Lord, help me.*

Sounds, like leaves rustling . . . the image vanishes.

God is merciful.

Sister Anu cracks open the door of the men's ward. An uncanny wind is blowing, carrying Kiran's whispered words to her ears.

Kiran is asking Damini to "look after" the girl. There is no mistaking her meaning. "Tell Aman-ji I had a miscarriage because the doctor didn't arrive on time."

Sister Anu feels herself go rigid with anger and outrage. Even if Kiran owns the clinic, she can't pressure Damini this way! Bread of Healing could be blamed for Kiran's miscarriage. Sister Anu is about to rush in and put a stop to this nonsense.

But wait, this is a test of Damini.

Damini sticks one leg straight out in front of her, then the other. She regards her combat-boots. Finally, she looks up.

"No," she says.

Not "No, Kiran-ji." Just "no."

"See the moon?" says Damini. "I see it, and also my parents' spirits, though they may not be visible to you. My father and mother are saying I am still your family servant. My father says obedience to you is like obedience to a husband. If I agree to do this favour for you, he says, you'll take care of me till I escape from living. But he doesn't know those times are gone. I'm just a labourer you pay for a few hours when you need me, and this is the age of Kaliyug.

"My husband Piara Singh is also here. He is telling me, No. He wants me to do what's good for my karma. He has not come to visit me in many months—he was angry at me because I did a great paap. I will take his advice. This baby has Mem-saab's blood and spirit. I don't have to raise this girl or arrange her marriage, but I know you can."

Tension releases in Sister Anu's neck and shoulders.

Damini holds the baby girl in her arms tenderly and croons to her. Could this kindly, caring old woman have harmed her own grand-daughter? No. Anu cannot believe it.

And would she guide young women to the Jalawaaz Fertility Clinic? Dr. Gupta said the number of infants who died before six months in Gurkot and five villages around is lower than last year. Children are more likely to survive when they're wanted—may the Church forgive that thought. If families abort girls, they end up with wanted children only—sons. Is Damini the cause of the decrease in infant mortality?

It's taken so much work to bring Bread of Healing this far. Its reputation is precious. What is the compassionate thing to do? Sin and salvation seem remote to this situation—injury and healing feel more significant.

In a small town, you believe you know people. But really, you don't. We can't know others, any more than I knew Vikas the night we were married off. We don't know what others are capable of.

There's that image again—Vikas lounging back in his most comfortable chair, a terrible look on his face.

I don't even know what I am capable of.

Outside the clinic, the bell tower shines silver, and the snow peaks are jagged as a hound's teeth. It's 3 a.m. and Sister Anu has left Damini sleeping beside Kiran and the baby girl. Goldina would not return baby Moses to the crib, so Sister Anu has put a towel between Goldina and the boy, so there's less danger of Goldina smothering Moses in her sleep. Unable to sleep herself, she stands at the front gate, looking up at the jewelled parasol of the blue-black sky.

Hard to believe all those far-flung stars were once together, that the events of this night were once compressed to a dot within them. She clasps her elbows above her head and sways, stretching cramped muscles. The universe is fertile—many things replicate and reproduce, not only people, not only stars.

A fricative skidding startles her—a small animal dislodging tiles as it jumps to the clinic roof. A flying squirrel or the ubiquitous monkeys.

She pulls herself together and vows that next time she's in Shimla, she will buy a book with colour photos of mountain plants and animals. And familiar local names, rather than Latin and English ones. If she could name each animal and plant she might feel more kindly toward all of them.

Can she do any more to help Kiran accept her baby daughter? Sister Anu's hand rises to her heart. Like that tiny hand that once groped for her breast—you will love me, said that gesture. She remembers how, incredibly, mother-love came, after fifteen hours of labour, like a life-jolt from heaven. How she connected with a force much stronger than herself. The same force that pulled her to a bright warm light. The god-particle that connects everything in the universe. The force she yearns to reconnect with through daily prayer and her work.

Somehow she must persuade Kiran to love the baby's sweetness, her helplessness, to feel responsible for this little girl's life.

Yet a mother shouldn't be encouraged to believe she owns her daughter or she might act like Mumma. How do you say "son of" or "daughter of" in Hindi, Punjabi or Pahari, or any of seven hundred Indian languages, without suggesting possession? Maybe children should be given temporary names, until they're old enough to give themselves inspiring names the way Goldina did.

A name. Even a temporary one. An inspiring name.

Sister Anu re-enters the clinic and takes up a lighter shawl. Damini is still sitting beside Kiran in the men's ward, the baby girl in her lap.

Sister Anu wraps the shawl about her head, slips off her shoes and approaches Kiran's bed. She reaches for the cloth-wrapped prayer book on Kiran's nightstand.

"Careful!" says Kiran. "That's my gutka."

"I know," says Sister Anu. Book in hand, she crosses her ankles and sinks to the dhurrie beside Kiran's bed, "I'm opening it at random. I'm looking at the top left corner. Let me show you what your Guruji says: it's an Arah—the letter A. The Guru says you must name the baby with the letter A. What will you call her?"

Kiran is quiet. Then she says, "I know what you're up to, Sister. You have no right to do this."

Damini says, "Anyone can read the words of the Guru, men and women, high and low—even Christians."

She strokes the baby girl's forehead, caresses her cheek.

Kiran says, "This is no way to name a child. You dress up in your best clothes and jewellery, you invite guests, you sing kirtan, you distribute food and kara parshaad and sweets to the whole community, you say the Ardaas . . ."

"At least temporarily," says Sister Anu using her most persuading gentle voice. Names flash through her head like lightning. She doesn't know very many Sikhs or Sikh names—just a few names of the Sikh gurus. But she does know that Sikh names can be for girls or boys. "Let's call her Angad, just for now." She pronounces it ung-ud, like the name the first Guru gave his successor.

Another long silence.

"Angad," says Kiran, very low. "Piece of my body."

She takes the girl from Damini's arms.

Sister Anu reads several couplets aloud to let Kiran reacquaint herself with the verses, hesitating a little over the archaic Punjabi. Kiran's makeup is disintegrating, her cheeks are blotchy red.

Sister Anu looks up from the small book as she hears a car. The driver's palm thumps the horn as it pulls to a stop before the gate. She closes the prayer book, bows slightly over it, and gives it back to

Kiran, then hurries to the veranda. "The child is born and the mother is well," she calls calmly to Amanjit Singh as he alights.

He storms past Sister Anu, into the patients' waiting room— "*Ohé*! Where's my boy?"

Sister Anu leads Amanjit to his wife's bed and closes the door to the men's ward. Let Kiran choose what she wants to tell Amanjit Singh, and let Kiran deal with the consequences.

ANU

SO PERTURBED IS ANU BY THE EVENTS OF THE NIGHT, she takes the 5 a.m. minibus and the 8 a.m. bus to Chhota Shimla, loyally accompanied by Bethany. At St. Anne's, they are told Sister Imaculata is in Delhi for an interfaith conference, and Father Pashan and all the nuns are away on a rare outing to Baljees restaurant at the city centre. Two more buses and a ride in a lift up the mountain ensue. Then Sister Anu strides down the Mall from one end of Shimla to the other, closely followed by Bethany. Through the hundreds of tourists thronging the pedestrian-only central promenade, without a glance at Tibetan shawls in lean-to stalls, the antiquarian books at Maria Brothers, the chocolate biscuits displayed at Gainda Mull Hem Raj, or the high-heeled shoes in the Chinese shoemaker's shop. Without a sniff at the fragrance of sizzling ghee and cardamom rising from Lower Bazaar, or a wrinkle of her nose at baboons sunning themselves on rooftops. Her pace slows only when she passes the Raj-era grey stone municipal buildings and nears the hole-in-the-wall Punjabi restaurant at Scandal Point. The nuns have finished lunch and are preparing for a leisurely walk back to the lift.

"I must talk to you," she tells Father Pashan.

"And I'm ravenous," says Bethany.

Father Pashan asks the nuns to continue without him, and orders makhni dal, raita and naan for the two sweating arrivals.

Anu yawns, and covers her mouth with her palm, "Excuse me! I was awake all night—two babies were born." Those two miracles definitely happened. But hearing herself tell him how the two babies were nearly switched at Bread of Healing seems incredible. "Goldina was raped," she adds. "A member of our parish. Should I report it to the authorities?"

Bethany spoons dal onto Anu's plate.

"Does Goldina want to lodge a complaint?" asks Father Pashan.

"Now?" says Sister Bethany, through a mouthful of naan.

"I will support her," says Father Pashan. "She can't read or write, so I myself will go with her to the superintendent of police and help her fill out the charge sheet. I'll go to her house and tell her so."

"That might put her whole family in danger," Bethany says. "From her rapist, his caste-members, and the police."

Sister Anu tells them that Damini was the one who finally persuaded Kiran to give up Moses, but also recounts Goldina's accusations against her. "I can't believe Damini would let a child die—or worse," she says. "But that's what Goldina said."

"Because the child was a girl?" says Father Pashan.

"It was implied, but I have no proof. Just as there's no proof Kiran-ji tried to bribe me."

"There never is," says Bethany, emphasising each word with a flourished fragment of naan.

"And I heard Damini refuse when Kiran-ji asked her to 'look after' the girl."

"Even so," says Bethany. "You can't let her continue working— you'd be afraid to ever leave her alone with a child. Can we find her something else? She can read and write in Hindi. And she wants to help other women—I've seen her reading to Goldina."

"She has a son in Jalawaaz," says Sister Anu. "Maybe he can assist his mother."

"Bethany, maybe she can help you with literacy classes?" says Father Pashan.

"I'll see." Bethany sounds dubious.

"She worked for the Amanjit Singhs in New Delhi for years," says Sister Anu. "She still works for them occasionally in the Big House. But after last night I don't think Kiran-ji will hire her."

"Yes, I'm sure she didn't believe you or Damini would challenge her, much less perform a Sikh naming ceremony for her baby," says Sister Bethany.

"I'm still horrified that she thought she could bribe me. What did I do to make her think I would accept it?"

"Nothing, I'm sure—some people are in the habit," says Father Pashan. "But what made Mrs. Kiran Singh try to steal our poor Goldina's baby?"

Sister Anu hesitates. "She said she didn't want to disappoint Amanjit-ji with a girl. Maybe she thought Goldina could be bought because she's poor and powerless."

"No," says Sister Bethany with tense passion. "It was because Goldina is a dalit. Everyone can be poor—it's much worse to be poor and a dalit. And much worse than that to be poor and a dalit and a woman."

"Well, my child, you managed to return the babies to their right-ful mothers," says Father Pashan. "The Lord was working through you. But as for Goldina—the man should not be allowed to do this to a Christian woman. Goldina didn't name him—just said he is a teacher?"

"Yes. I couldn't tell if she meant he is employed as a teacher, or that he was a private tutor, or a self-styled guru."

"Maybe Samuel did something to anger the rapist, and Goldina took the punishment," says Bethany.

"That shy man? What could he have done?"

"Maybe he unfurled an umbrella while the teacher was walking by," says Bethany. "Maybe he tried to enter the Ram-Sita temple—which other stonecutter is skilled enough to carve those idols? Maybe he squatted on a cushion in the teacher's presence. Maybe he smoked or wore sandals. Maybe he asked for payment on time for his work. Maybe he asked the teacher or principal to give one of his children admission to the school, or the discount the law says they should have. Maybe he just looked the teacher in the eye."

"I have told Samuel often that he's a good enough man to look anyone in the eye," Pashan says, then pauses, adjusting to the implications of those words. "I will put a word in the ear of the SDM. I will tell him, Gandhi-ji's goal of an India without discrimination for untouchability is our goal."

"Gandhi-ji?" Sister Bethany tone drips derision. "He thought caste Hindus could be taught to be tolerant. And they are, now—as long as the opportunity to show it is safely in the past or future. I think more like Dr. Ambedkar. Let's hold evening classes—legal clinics—to inform dalits and tribals of their rights."

"Go slowly," says Father Pashan. "Do it with love, not judgement. Love creates duties. Rights create competition."

"How slow, Father? It's never the right time, never convenient," says Sister Bethany.

Pashan says, "God has a plan; he knows the right time, Bethany."

After lunch, he escorts them as far as Scandal Point. He points to the statue of freedom fighter Lala Lajpat Rai. "That statue stands on the spot where the Maharaja of Patiala once abducted a British viceroy's Christian daughter. The story never tells what happened to the viceroy's daughter. How she felt, whether she had a child or many . . . but I do know the British banished the Maharaja from Shimla for it. Christians don't have such power today, but we can let the Holy Spirit guide us, and pray that our example can change others."

His faith calls to mine, thinks Sister Anu.

And what of Damini? Goldina's accusation is just that—an accusation in the heat of anger. No proof. But why should Goldina lie? Why else would Goldina fear leaving Kiran's baby girl alone with

Damini? And yet . . . she did hear Damini say "No," to Kiran's loathsome request.

Damini kept Sister Anu's secret even when she was telling Kiran; a loyal friend. Anu too would like to be a good friend to Damini. Where in Gurkot can she find another community health worker like her?

And without this job, can Damini's family afford to travel to Shimla for AIDS treatments? And AIDS medicines? Damini will be so afraid that Leela will be left a widow.

Sister Anu will wait a few days before she makes up her mind.

"God takes a longer view of suffering," says Father Pashan. "He sent his son as a man to share our suffering. Because of Christ's life, because of his death and resurrection, he understands that everyone suffers in his or her own way—even caste Hindus. But I can visit Goldina and Samuel, and I can make sure the SDM understands the situation."

Sister Bethany says, wretchedly, "Maybe Our Lord's understanding would be more complete if he planned his second coming as a dalit woman."

"Who are we to say whether the Heavenly Father's understanding is enough?" says Pashan giving them his boat-shaped parting smile.

DAMINI

"Hurry up, Damini!" Sister Anu is standing beside a shack that clings to an outcropping above the throb and rush of the Meethi Darya.

Damini tests the slide of rocks and pine needles, and reaches for the dark grace of tree trunks as she descends the last few yards of the only footpath down the mountain. It's more than an hour since they left Bread of Healing to visit Goldina for a postpartum follow-up and she is thirsty.

Her skin crawls at the idea of entering a sweeper's home, but the nun has gone in and Damini can't stay outside.

A strong smell assaults her in the darkness of the mud and straw shack—pigs, but she can't see any nor hear snuffling. When her eyes adjust, she sees a blue tarp, probably used to cover the roof when it rains, in one corner. A three-sided brick-stack stove warms a blackened pot in another corner. A few platters and tumblers are carefully arranged on a wooden crate. Stonecutting tools are piled in the third corner, and Goldina sits in the last, Moses in her lap, her face in shadow.

Damini looks around for a water pipe, but there is none—Goldina and her daughters must be fetching river water every day. Where are the sleeping quilts? All Damini can spy are blankets which, even in September, are not enough. What do they do when the snow lies thick on the ground? There's not even one bulb wired for electricity, and no latrine. How have Goldina and Samuel raised five children in this tiny space? They must take turns lying down to sleep. She who knows herself poor has never lived in so bare a home.

Goldina rises immediately, though with difficulty. She's wearing the same kameez she wore at the birthing. She offers tea.

Damini hesitates—refusing would look as if she is afraid of contamination, and agreeing imposes work on a new mother. Offering to make it for Goldina would be taking over her cooking area . . . But Sister Anu accepts. She's probably thirsty, too. And if Goldina is making tea for one, she may as well make enough for three.

Moses settles into Damini's arms. "Almost as if he knows you," Sister Anu says.

"Must have met him in a past life," says Damini, looking away from the sparks in those infant eyes. The redness of birth has faded. Moses's soot-black hair is spiderweb-soft, as Suresh's used to be. He has Suresh's round face, his colouring. Damini checks his movements as she would check any other baby, but his cheeks, his bright black eyes and those long lashes are like Suresh's; this really is her grandson.

Sister Anu extends her forefinger, and the baby's tiny fingers grip it, slowly releasing as Moses's eyes flutter closed. "He's strong. Already seems to be putting on weight."

Goldina portions tea into the muddy-looking glasses and considerately places them on the ground before Damini and Sister Anu, so they do not need to touch her hand as they pick them up. She has not made any for herself.

Sister Anu takes Goldina's temperature, pulse, and blood pressure. She checks that Goldina's uterus is contracting well. She examines the whites of Goldina's eyes and asks how many menstrual cloths she has changed since she came home—Damini is surprised to learn Goldina's blood flows no more than a respected woman from her own caste. Sister Anu demonstrates checking for tenderness that might indicate breast abscesses. Goldina takes Moses from Damini and opens her sari-blouse.

Once Sister Anu has verified that Goldina's breast milk is flowing well, and that the child has a good suckling reflex, Damini asks, "How did you meet this teacher?"

"We killed our pig and I went to the school to deliver the pork. He said I should persuade Samuel to make a statue he wanted for the front of the school."

"*Leh*! So he was giving Samuel work," says Damini.

"Samuel didn't want that work."

"Too lazy?" asks Damini.

"No!" says Goldina. "But the teacher wanted Samuel to sculpt a statue of Savarkar. Samuel said he couldn't—and wouldn't—carve a statue of a madman who called for the killing of Gandhi-ji. He offered to carve a statue of Baba Sahib Ambedkar instead. The teacher said Ambedkar-ji was a reformer of Hinduism like Savarkar. Samuel said no, Baba Sahib Ambedkar left Hinduism and became a Buddhist. The teacher said, who did Samuel think he was, correcting his superiors, making up his own history. He said Samuel has had too much good bhagya in this life. He said a stonecutter is given hands for the service of his superiors. A man who refused an opportunity to commemorate a Hindu patriot like Savarkar had no right to those hands."

"No!" says Sister Anu.

Goldina could be lying or she could really be describing Suresh. He threatens when he gets annoyed. He doesn't really mean it.

"But, he said, since he was not a Muslim like the emperor who cut off the hands of Hindu men who carved the Taj Mahal, he would spare Samuel's hands."

"I never heard only Hindus carved the Taj Mahal," says Sister Anu, "Or that Shah Jahan cut off the hands of only Hindu carvers. I thought he cut off the hands of all his stone carvers. And who knows if that story is true? But—what happened then?"

"He showed me his tail, lying along his thigh like a stick."

Damini no longer wants to hear more, but Sister Anu is nodding with a compassion that shames her into listening.

"He said if Samuel didn't want to do it, he would teach me a lesson."

"I told him I would make sure Samuel didn't make his statue," says Goldina, "and I left. But that night, I was walking home from Jalawaaz, and he lay in wait for me on the footpath."

She drops her kerchiefed head, and her shoulders shudder. Sister Anu reaches out and lays a hand on Goldina's bent knees.

"And now?" says Damini, when the heaving slows and Goldina's silence becomes unbearable.

"Now? Now you see, Moses is born, and my husband can't bear the sight of him." says Goldina.

"Why did you tell Samuel what happened?" says Damini.

"He found me the next morning, bleeding and crying on the path. I bled and cried a lot more after that, but I know he only beat me because he could not beat the teacher. Maybe he thought he'd beaten the baby out of me, but a few months later I felt it move and you told me it was alive . . ."

"Did Father Pashan talk to him?" says Sister Anu.

"Yes, he came yesterday afternoon. He said Samuel must remember Joseph, and baby Jesus. He said to remember Lord Joseph too believed in Mary Devi's purity, though he knew the baby was special, and could not have come from him.

"Samuel said, 'Father, I carve statues of the gods. I have carved so many idols I never thought could have come from an outcaste like me. I know my work, even when I can only admire it from afar, even though I was unworthy to receive it. And I tell you, this boy is not mine. I'm not like Lord Joseph—I am only responsible for my own. I won't give my name to another man's son.'"

"But I thought Father Pashan persuaded him . . . ?" Sister Anu's voice trails away.

"Oh yes. By the time Father left us, Samuel was saying yes, yes, yes. But when the priest was gone, he gave me one-two more slaps for 'being unfaithful.' We had a marriage of self-respect, he said, and now everyone was finding out, his self-respect was becoming less and less."

"Women take beatings more courageously than men," says Damini, comfortingly.

"I told him at least the teacher didn't lock us all in some shed and set us on fire. At least he didn't poison our water supply. At least he didn't strip me naked and parade me down the street to shame Samuel. But Samuel said he had to bear what happened, not what could have happened. And today, he was telling: 'leave me, leave my home, go away.' But where should I go?"

"What do you want to do?" says Damini.

"Me?" Goldina seems surprised by the question. "Now I think maybe I should have given the child to Kiran-ji when she wanted him. She could have told Aman-ji she had twins."

"How can you say that!" Sister Anu looks horrified.

"No, you're right." Goldina says. "Damini got him back for me—I am in her debt for that. Sister, you told Kiran-ji she could give up her girl baby for adoption, if she really didn't want her. If you can offer such help to Kiran-ji, you can do the same for me, a Christian like yourself. You understand—you told us your daughter is happy in Canada. Please, find a good woman to be Moses's mother. I am generous as the woman I am named for—but not to any woman who takes what she wants without asking, and feels she deserves it. Give him to anyone except Kiran-ji." She holds Moses out to Sister Anu.

"Oh, no," says Sister Anu. "You're just upset right now. Wait a few days, you'll come to love him."

"I loved him enough to fight Kiran-ji," says Goldina. "I am still fighting for him."

Sister Anu says, "Maybe Damini can persuade Samuel. You are the mother of his five children, and this has happened through no fault of yours."

"And he must be happy to have a son," says Damini.

"Then he will say yes, yes, yes to you as well. But he will still tell me to leave. If I keep him, Moses will become Samuel's daily reminder that the teacher is his superior."

"If you give away this child," says Damini, "you will live with this decision for the rest of this life, and maybe many more."

"You don't have to decide today," says Sister Anu.

"I have decided," says Goldina, using the word *nishchay*, which unlike *faisala* or *iradha*, carries no maybe, wishfulness or longing.

"Dr. Gupta says my son-in-law has to go to Snowdon Hospital— the baby can go to Shimla with me."

"No, not with you," says Goldina. "He has to be with Christians. Sister-ji, you take him. Take him now."

Damini and Sister Anu argue and argue, but Goldina remains as stout-hearted as a worm struggling in the beak of a griffin. "If my husband calls me a loose woman, others will too. And other women will refuse to work with me. But if I send Moses away, Samuel will not send me away—you know what a good worker I am."

"Well," says Sister Anu, when it's almost nightfall, and Damini's stomach is beginning to growl. "I suppose we can take Moses with us. I will keep him three days. In that time you or Samuel can change your minds, and come to the clinic to get him. After that, I will take him to Shimla. He will be at the Shimla convent a few days or weeks. Again if you or Samuel change your minds, he can come back to you . . ."

Goldina's palms caress Moses's cheeks. "Tell my boy his mother never wanted to give him up. And try not to let him go so far he will never see me."

Her hands fall to her sides. There are no tears in her eyes, but her chest is heaving.

On the way home, Sister Anu carries Moses. Trudging behind, Damini keeps her head lowered, her gaze on her combat boots.

She should have told Goldina that teacher is probably her son. But she didn't. Couldn't.

She should tell Sister Anu that Moses has a grandmother and an aunt and cousins. She should tell her that the teacher who raped Goldina can't be anyone other than Suresh.

If she does, Sister Anu might think badly of Damini and her family. Sister might think Moses will turn out like Suresh. It's not right to be silent, but necessary.

The path homewards turns and turns, rising up the moonlit gorge.

October 1996

ANU

Baby bottle, clean diapers, pacifier . . . Sister Anu checks her kit bag one last time before the four-hour ride to Shimla. Moses is fast asleep in a basket on the ground beside the jeep. Sister Imaculata said it will take a few weeks to find him a home in an orphanage, but a fine boy like him will be adopted soon.

Shafiq Sheikh is holding the jeep door open. A few paces away, Mohan is holding an imaginary jeep door open. Damini drops to her haunches beside the basket and rests her hand on Moses's blanketed head, then withdraws. Sister Anu hears a sniff and notices a silver shine in Damini's eyes.

"You want to come with me?" she says to Damini.

Damini shakes her head. "Again Dr. Gupta said we must go to a hospital in Shimla with Chunilal. Tomorrow Suresh will drive us all in the truck."

"I'm very glad to hear this," says Sister Anu, who has offered to take Chunilal herself several times. "I talked to Goldina again today. Did you?"

"Yes. She says Father Pashan grew up in an orphanage, and he's a good man. She feels Moses can do no better."

"Are we sure Moses can do no better?"

Damini seems on the brink of objecting and Sister Anu waits.

But eventually the older woman sighs. "Adoption will be best."

Mohan steps away from his open imaginary door to pick up the baby basket. He swings it gently. "I go? I go?" he smiles, practising his English.

Moses wakes up, begins to squall.

"No, no." Sister Anu responds in English, humouring him. "I'm taking the baby to Shimla. Put him in the car, Mohan."

"Idhar, Idhar!" Damini directs Mohan to the opposite door.

"Taking baby to Shimla. Put him in the car, Mohan," says Mohan, delighted. He places the baby's basket on the seat.

In the nuns' recreation room at the convent, everyone crowds around, voices rising an octave to coo over Moses. These childless women have no trouble dandling him, burping him. "Will he live in India, London or America?" coos Sister Rose.

"Oh, he'll become a movie star in Bombay!" says Sister Sarah.

Sister Anu's spirits soar. At that very moment, Sister Lorena says, "You have a parcel."

It's from Rano. *The Handmaid's Tale* by Margaret Atwood—she will read the novel in private, later. And here's a photo of Chetna in bharatanatyam regalia, dancing her arangetram. How she wishes she could have watched Chetna's debut. Her eyes are ringed with kajal and she looks so much like Mumma. Another photo shows Chetna standing in the woods, dressed like an astronaut, with a pole in each hand. Rano's writing on the back says "cross-country skiing in Penetanguishene last winter," as if Anu knows where that is. A third shows Chetna smiling triumphantly, a jug in one hand and a platter stacked with what look like naans in the other. Rano's caption says Chetna made pancakes with maple syrup.

Canada is too far away. Children should be adopted closer to home, and a mother allowed to watch her child grow up. I have to find a place for

Moses where Goldina can visit him. He needs two mothers, as Bobby and I had.

Rano writes that she is exploring a new IVF technique to make a sibling for Chetna. That Mr. Xhu is leaving the bank because he is making a mint of money selling something called domain names for newborn websites, and she may finally get a promotion into his position. But Sister Anu will read all that after she has mastered her tears. Then she will write,

Dear Rano,

I have found my new calling, finding adoptive parents for unwanted babies.

Two days later, refreshed by prayer and uplifted by mass and discussions with Sister Imaculata and Father Pashan, Sister Anu will return to Gurkot and Goldina. She will carry a Document of Surrender and other adoption papers with her, marked with arrows where Goldina's and Samuel's thumbprints are required.

ANU

SUNLIGHT DRIFTS INTO DARKNESS, BUT MOHAN IS
nowhere to be found. The schoolroom is dark—maybe he walked
home with Bethany.

Sister Anu waits, half-listening to the radio. Prime Minister Deve
Gowda is reiterating that India has no plans to build a nuclear
weapon. He reminds the world that Madam G.'s 1974 nuclear test
was merely for peaceful purposes. Officials have been making such
statements ever since India reversed its long-standing support for a
Comprehensive Test Ban Treaty. But, says the PM, "India reserves
the option to test if our security situation changes."

Anu closes the clinic door, waits a few more minutes—no sign of
her intrepid sekurti-guard. She drapes her shawl about her shoulders, crosses the clearing and walks down the drive to the road.

A conch shell is blowing; either a festival or funeral procession is
coming round the bend. Then she hears a chorus of "*Ram Naam Sat
Hai! Ram Nam Sat Hai!*" Fifteen or twenty men appear, chanting Lord
Ram's name. Each carries a large branch on his shoulder. A shrouded
body floats in the middle of the procession. A young man, since the
shroud is undecorated. He must have died just hours ago and, since
there is no cold storage, his body must be pyred immediately.

"Who is it?" she asks, as the men come within earshot.

She spies a bewildered-looking Mohan at the foot of the bier, and realizes a second before she's told that it is Chunilal. The procession continues past her, and then to her great surprise, she spies Damini, Leela and Kamna following the men at a distance. Damini stops before Sister Anu.

"Suresh drove us from one hospital to the other in Shimla till we worried we wouldn't have enough money for petrol to get home. The hospital-wallahs said no beds were available, but we could tell they didn't want Chunilal to die in their hospital. They told us he was a hopeless case. When we showed Chunilal's pills to one of the doctors he said they were 'like sugar.' He said Chunilal might have survived if he had actually received a testing drug. Instead, he was taking sugar." Anger combats resignation on Damini's face. "Even if I had tried his pills I wouldn't have known because I can't taste sweetness."

"I should have tried one of his pills," says Leela. "But I never thought . . ." Her voice trails into tears.

"A saab would have received proper medicine. Our ojha at least gave Chunilal a tonic made from cow *and* elephant dung," says Damini.

Sister Anu could explain that drug companies don't need to prove a new drug is better than anything currently available. All they need to prove is that a new drug is better than taking a sugar pill, or better than doing nothing. But what would such an explanation do for Chunilal's family now?

Sister Anu joins the funeral procession.

DAMINI

A WOMAN'S DHARMA DOESN'T INCLUDE ACCOMPANYING a dead body to cremation. But Damini remembers how terrible she felt when she couldn't go with Mem-saab and how important it was not to leave the girl baby alone in Anamika Devi's cave. She needs to accompany Chunilal too, though it may not be her given role in the movie of his life.

No one has objected, in deference to her years and henna-orange hair. But her chest feels sore as she walks, and worries chant through her head.

Leela joined the procession to support her mother, afraid someone might say something rude about Damini's being there. Then Kamna joined so as not to leave Leela alone. Sister Anu becomes the fourth woman.

Damini tasted anger as she helped Leela lower Chunilal's body to the floor for death. She bathed and cleaned his stiffening body so Leela wouldn't have to. She added her bitterness to the sweet pind Leela offered to his departing atman, and anger sounded deep in her throat like a prowling snow leopard as she helped remove Leela's marriage collar and all her jewellery, then trekked downhill last evening to tell Supari, Tubelight, Chimta and Matki and other neighbours, related and unrelated, that Chunilal's atman had returned to the formless.

Halfway to the cremation spot, Suresh and Chunilal's caste-brothers place his body on the ground and make another offering of pind. Kamna looks at Leela uncertainly. Leela glances meaningfully at Damini: this would be a good time for them to leave.

Damini shakes her head, determined.

No matter how angry she was at Chunilal, caregiving brought closeness, as it had with Mem-saab. Chunilal gave Damini shelter; thanks to him, she did not need to sell her body: she will not leave him now.

The procession descends to a lonely spot with a full view of the ranges throwing their shadows upon each other, the valleys plunging between. First Suresh, then each man comes forward and places his branch on the ground, over a rectangular pit.

There should be a pandit at this point to chant Sanskrit mantras. But rumours of AIDS have flown on the wind and the nearest pandit at Lord Golunath's temple could not be persuaded to attend. Leela sits cross-legged, with Mohan and Kamna beside her as the pyre is prepared. A pandit should tear at the mouth of the white shroud Damini and Leela placed over Chunilal, and pour ghee in the opening. A pandit should be here to light Chunilal's body from the head, but no pandit is present.

Suresh beckons Mohan to tap his father's skull. Mohan shrinks back and gnaws the back of his fist. *"Na—na—na—na!"* Suresh grips him by the arm and leads him to the body, stick in hand as if he will beat the boy. Eventually Mohan manages to crack his father's skull. Suresh raises his own stick at the boy and Mohan hits the skull again. Suresh raises the stick again, Mohan hits it one last time.

Then he runs back to his mother and sister. He hides his face in Leela's lap, trembling all over. Kamna rubs his back and slips him an orange. He sits quietly after that, peeling it, examining its lobes and flicking them into the void of the valley behind him, as Chunilal's body burns.

Damini wraps her shawl around her shoulders and drapes it over her knees. She saves her remaining bitterness for Samuel, because it is easy to blame Samuel for refusing to prepare Chunilal's body. Samuel may have learned that Chunilal is Suresh's brother-in-law. But even if he had, Samuel's role as an outcaste is to bridge the gap between living and non-living. He shouldn't make others do his dharma; he should be here. But hearing of AIDS, Samuel has refused to touch Chunilal's body.

These sweepers . . . hearts of stone.

Sister Anu covers her head with her shawl, sinks to her knees beside the pyre, joins mind to heart chakra, then touches shoulder to shoulder, and prays silently in her own way. She then joins Damini on a reed mat on the ground, across from Leela and Kamna, and reaches for Damini's hand, just like Mem-saab used to.

After a while, Damini places her hand in Sister Anu's open palm. Together they watch the pyre burn.

Two hours later, maybe three, the flames of Chunilal's pyre still leap and flicker against the serene majesty of the snow peaks. Sitting cross-legged, Kamna and Leela are a large dark egg-shape against the evening sky. Kamna's shawl-clad head rests on Leela's shoulder as she strokes her mother's arm. Suresh paces back and forth.

"You know Leela should be tested," Sister Anu whispers to Damini, chin resting on her knuckles, elbow on one folded knee.

"She knows," says Damini. "She was told in Shimla. But if she had been tested and it came out that she too has ayds, Chunilal might have felt bad, and worried that his children could be left orphans. So she didn't have it done."

"Maybe it would have been a good thing if he felt bad before he died. Father Pashan says telling our sins cleanses us."

Damini shakes her head, "Not when a man is dying." After a while she says, "Some of us do wrong things but don't feel any different. Others feel bad all the time after doing a wrong thing."

Silence gathers grief in its underbelly and spreads around them.

"You feel bad all the time?"

How does Sister Anu know that?

"Most of the time," Damini says. "But I don't stop working or complain or get Dipreyshun. Anamika Devi gives me shakti."

"Damini, *shakti* is woman's power, and that power creates, it doesn't destroy. If you really cared about shakti, you wouldn't lead women to the Jalawaaz Fertility Clinic for ultrasounds and cleanings."

Damini sticks her chin out. "I listen to women, and follow what they want."

Sister Anu folds her legs close, hugs her knees, and shakes her head. "So you think whatever a woman wants should always be done?" She uses the word *murrzi*, which conveys the kind of will and headstrong selfishness Damini expects in a man. But murrzi is the right one. *Ichcha* or *chahut* would convey only yearning.

Damini wobbles her head. "Cleaning a baby out is not illegal—and sometimes it has to be done. People who say never ever don't know what happens to women. And if a woman wants that, she should have it."

Sister Anu says, "If anything a woman wants should be given to her, why didn't we let Kiran-ji take Moses from Goldina?"

"*Huh!* Moses didn't come from Kiran-ji's body. Kiran-ji didn't do the work of carrying him, birthing him."

Sister Anu falls silent, gazing into the flames. Then she says, "How do *you* know if a woman really wants a cleaning? And tell me, was it her own decision or fear when Goldina gave up Moses for adoption?"

Damini says, "She would not have had the child if you had offered her pills or the ring or tied her inside. And she would not have had to give us her child if your padri had not said she would fry in hell for a cleaning."

Sister Anu looks hurt. Damini hastens to explain.

"See, while Goldina was two-in-one and the child was unawakened, she was the head for both. The child's story had not begun. But I don't know how to tell what is women's murrzi, what is fear. Was it murrzi or fear when my mother went to her self-cremation? Maybe both. Was it murrzi when my Mem-saab took pills and died? I think she thought no one was listening or ever would listen to her wishes. Was it Leela's own wish, or fear, when she wanted a cleaning? Now she cries for her baby girl whose soul returned to brahman."

Was it my murrzi or fear the night when I . . .

Sister Anu pulls her handkerchief from her sleeve and blows her nose. "I'm so sorry to hear about your mother, and Mem-saab. Goldina said your grandchild died a few days after she was born. So sad for Leela, too." She wipes her eyes with the end of her shawl. "My brother's and father's funerals are coming to my mind. Tell, where are Chunilal's brothers?" she says. "And his father?"

"Chunilal's family doesn't want Leela or her children to come near them—they are afraid of ayds." Damini sweeps her shawl open like a giant bird as she points to Leela, Kamna and Suresh all sitting cross-legged on the other side of the pyre. "My son is afraid too, but at least he came. He even carried Chunilal here, though it's not his duty."

Sister Anu says, "You can't get AIDS from attending a funeral."

"Ayds is an excuse," says Damini wryly. "I made Suresh send Chunilal's father a telegram the day we took him to Shimla. Then I called his father from the booth at the chai-stall. I said, 'Did you get my telegram?' He said, 'I received one saying *Felicitations on Your Upcoming Wedding.*' The telegraph-man must have printed the wrong message from the code book. I said, 'Your son is dying—come and say farewell.' And he said that Chunilal had disappointed them, shamed them by living in Leela's village after marriage, with his wife's family. He called Chunilal a gharjamai! People like him dishonour the word 'honour.'"

Mohan pulls out his flute and begins to blow. "*Chup!*" Leela shushes him, but he won't stop and his hooting fills the valley, like the wails of a protesting animal.

"When people die," Damini says beneath her breath, "it is a relief not to have to look after them. But how many others are there like him, who are so sick?"

A great rumbling sound approaches on the road above. Mohan's flute fades when the rumbling stops. Lights beam into the dark from two trucks. Four men clamber from the cabs. They kerchief their heads in respect as they descend the hillside and draw close to Chunilal's pyre.

"Chunilal's voice still echoes in my head," Damini confides to Sister Anu. "When we returned from Shimla, he said all my remedies were useless. It was time, he said, to make him a stinging nettle curry."

Chunilal's fellow truckers place stones, leaves and branches beside the flickering pyre in the name of the dead man, make their last na-mastes. Suresh comes forward to speak to them, but Damini cannot hear what they say. They look over their shoulders at the women, though, and must be asking why they are present. Eventually they return uphill to their vehicles. The mountain ranges throw shadows at one another, and their valleys plunge deeper into darkness.

Sister Anu's expectant look prompts Damini. "Chunilal said, 'I have faced death every day on the Grand Trunk Road. I am not afraid to die . . . Make nettle curry tonight, make it with madhupatra,' he said, 'Let it be sweet when I drink it, and then stay with me . . .'"

"I refused him. He said, 'I ask you, have pity. Don't you see, I'm helpless as a woman, I'm as useless as Mohan. I can't even bathe myself. I'm like a newborn girl. I cannot ask Leela to stain her karma, and don't have the courage to do it myself.'

"'No,' I said. 'I am not a selector of souls.'

"'A man who cannot feed his family has no right to live.'

"I said, 'You have love to give, even if you can't work. My mem-saab was like that—old, but she had so much love and dignity, it didn't matter that she couldn't hear, couldn't work.'

"'You could have prevented her suffering too,' Chunilal said. 'Did you?'

"'Of course I didn't!' I said.

"'But why not put useless people out of our misery?' he asked me. 'My death is coming, anyway. Lord Yama is there in my dreams.' I said, 'All of us are dying, day by day, from the very moment of birth. Everyone suffers, not only you. How can I decide that your suffering is sufficient?'

"He said, 'I have decided my suffering is sufficient.'

"I said, 'You're talking as if you have Dipreyshun. Even saab-log like Mem-saab and Sister Anu suffer, though they smile and look rich, healthy, beautiful. They complain, they cry just as you're crying. Maybe Aman-ji suffers. Maybe even Kiran suffers.' I told him, Sister, I told him this. And I said, 'Sister Anu says every person has a story. If I kill you, it'll be like paying for a movie but walking out at intermission.'

"'Are my wishes no longer important?' he said. 'One day every story will end in India and everywhere in the world—think if

Americans or Russians set off another Big Big Bumb, the Atom Bumb. I'm just saying to end mine sooner.'

"'Mohan can't earn, doesn't learn, will never understand money or farming. Should I put him out of his misery, too?' I said. 'Oh no,' he said. 'Mohan's my son. He will carry on my name after I am gone.'

"I said, 'So a useless son is better than no son? Just for a name? What use is a name if a big bumb is going to end all our stories?'

"'Not a name. *My* name. If I die, you make sure he gets married,' he said. He really meant it! He thought I would trick some girl's family into marrying Mohan! But when a man is sick and dying, you have to listen and not argue . . ."

"What did you say then?" says Sister Anu.

"I didn't say anything about arranging a marriage for Mohan. I said, 'I told you when I arrived, Chunilal, you are like a son to me. Even if you are useless and brainless, you have to live for Leela, for Mohan, for Kamna . . .'"

Sister Anu has become a pair of ears for Damini, listening as night blankets the mountains.

When the moon takes shape, Damini says, "Do you know if that is the same moon my sisters see?"

"It's the same," says Sister Anu. "Where are your sisters?"

"Rajasthan. My oldest sister has gone to the next life, the second one became oldest, and she was married into a family in Loharki. My middle sister is now in Bharariya, and the next is married in Mava. The villages are all close to Khetolai, where we grew up. Only I was sent so far away. Sister," she says, struck with a sudden fear, "what if we are dead and this is the next life?"

Sister Anu says, "Then we'd have no experience. We'd feel no change and have no stories."

Damini clasps her head in her hands to think more deeply. Eventually she says, "I feel cold. And the ground is hard; I have experience. The moon is higher than it was a few hours ago. Kamna,

Suresh and Leela were sitting together, but are now sleeping on the ground. And Chunilal's body is burning away, so there is change."

"And we might find ourselves in another place," says Anu. "Christians call it hell or heaven."

"In another place—like Pakistan?" A myriad questions are rising within her. "Which is farther from here, Pakistan or the moon?"

"The moon."

"I can see the moon, but not Pakistan? Still, I know Pakistan is there because Mem-saab escaped it in 1947, and she said that place was born like a bloody twin at midnight with India. Maybe your Christian hell is like Pakistan."

"People in Pakistan who escaped from India during Partition might think hell is like India."

"Has anyone ever escaped hell to tell you such a place is there?"

"No, but—"

"Why don't people in Pakistan believe in gods like Lord Golunath?"

"They believe their Prophet is more powerful."

"Does Muhammad-ji speak to them?"

"No, he's dead, like our Christ—but Shafiq Sheikh tells me how much his life story inspires all Muslims."

"I tell you! Nothing ever finishes," Damini says. "The spirits of the dead are always around, causing trouble, judging the living. Even when we die, it's not over."

"We're all afraid to die."

"Huh! Not I! Next minute I'll be alive again, and again it begins. You Christians and Muslims who only have one life are afraid to die."

"Remember the song, Zindagi aur kuch bhi nahin, teri meri kahani hai?"

Damini nods, "Wait, don't tell me—I'll remember the movie." In a moment she says, "*Shor.*"

"Yes, the song says, Life is nothing more than your story, my story. Muhammad's body, Christ's body, Chunilal's body—all may be gone, but their story remains."

The vigil continues till birdsong stirs at dawn. Sister Anu again takes Damini's hand in her light-skinned one. "Bahut avsos hai," she says.

There is great sympathy. How comforting is her presence; Damini is surprised.

There are worse things than untouchables afraid to touch you, or pandits who refuse to chant at your funeral, or families who do not wish to know you. When Damini, Leela, Suresh, Kamna and Mohan return home at dawn, tired and stiff from their vigil beside Chunilal's pyre all night, Amanjit Singh's manager, that pitiless prune of a man, is waiting with a cheque for Rs. 35,000. For Chunilal's land, he says.

He waves a paper before their astonished faces. "Sale deed," he says.

"What sale deed?" Suresh pushes forward, protectively.

The manager stops waving the paper and brings it under the lantern light. He does not allow them to touch it.

Mohan points proudly to his name—signed large and clear, and in English—at the bottom.

Leela boxes Mohan's ears till Damini stays her hand. Because Mohan couldn't know his land is worth ten times that amount. The boy crouches in a corner and hides his face in the circle of his arms. The manager waits as if he's seen this happen on other farms.

Suresh says, "I'm head of this family, now."

"No, he is not," says Leela to the manager. "I am still alive, still his elder. And Mohan is Chunilal's heir. But Mohan should not have signed this deed."

Suresh's eyes flash, his chest puffs out and he draws himself up as if readying to strike someone.

Damini comes between. She says to the manager, "The land belonged to my husband Piara Singh and was part of Leela's dowry before it ever belonged to Chunilal. You understand? It was her stridhan. Her brother cannot take it, and her son cannot sign it away."

"It was a gift to her husband," says Suresh. "And since he's gone, it comes back to our family."

The manager shrugs. "Amanjit-ji will build a villa here, not a cottage," he says, as if everyone should appreciate the honour bestowed upon the land. Leela and her family, he says, have a month in which to move.

"Move where?" says Leela. "This is my house."

The manager says, "Tell them to take the cheque, old amma. No one else will give you so much. Leela could fall or have an accident tomorrow, or Amanjit-ji can build a latrine over your water supply. Then with what face can you come asking for such a large cheque?"

"Take that cheque back to Aman-ji," Leela says to the manager, "Let him come and till these terraces himself, if he wants. He can build a cottage for us, or around us, because I am not moving."

When the manager has left, Damini says wretchedly, "I have brought you bad luck ever since I came here. A woman spending her old age with a daughter, taking from a daughter's home. I'm sure Kiran-ji made Aman-ji do this, because I refused to do what she wanted."

"Why didn't you do whatever she wanted?" says Suresh. "So what if she wanted you to polish the silver or something?"

"She wanted me to kill a baby."

"Girl?"

Damini nods slowly, her gaze on her son's face.

"Then what?"

"I said no."

"And this is the result."

Men have to be told everything. Should she tell Suresh whose child she saved from Kiran's clutches that night? Damini bites her tongue. *Not now.*

"Aman-ji would have done this whether you were here or not," says Leela. "Kiran-ji may have speeded up his plans. Saab-women are not accustomed to swallowing slowly if they are made to eat thorns." She turns to Suresh. "Tell me brother, what should I do?" she says, in a tone that mollifies and admires.

Suresh folds his arms across his chest with barely contained rage. "These Sikhs and Christians—always up to something against Hindus."

"Aman-ji is a Sikh," says Damini. "But why are you blaming Christians as well?"

"All same. Not-Hindus, that's why."

"Suresh, some Sikhs are good, and so are some Christians."

"Threatening Hindus, all having too many babies, taking away land."

Mohan looks up from his corner. "Babies. Taking baby to Shimla, put baby in car."

Suresh turns, his face lighting up. "What did you say? Say it in Hindi, boy."

"Be quiet, Mohan!" says Damini.

Mohan gets to his feet and shakes his head like a small elephant blundering behind the herd. "Sister said, 'Taking baby to Shimla. Put him in the car, Mohan.'"

ANU

SISTER ANU IS IN THE BACK SEAT OF THE CONVENT
jeep, returning to Gurkot after a weekend in Shimla, swaying as
the road curls and reading a mystifying letter from Chetna about
choosing between costumes for Halloween. Rano and Chetna
always seem to be choosing and deciding. It sounds exhausting.
And Halloween seems dark, pagan and strange in contrast with
Gurkot's blue sky on this crisp clear morning.

Shafiq Sheikh takes a bend in the road, and slows the jeep.

Men have joined hands to form a human garland across the
road at the incline to Bread of Healing. Several men are dressed
in marigold turbans, many sporting vermilion teeka-marks on
their foreheads, as if coming from the temple. "Is it a festival?"
she asks.

"No, Sister," says Shafiq Sheikh. "Dusshera is still two weeks
away. Maybe a wedding?"

"If it were a wedding," says Father Pashan from the front seat,
"people would look more happy and gay."

Shafiq Sheikh stops, rolls down his window and sticks his head
out. "I see some women," he says. Wedding processions are usually
all-male events.

A man in a white singlet and grey pants seems to be the leader.

406 SHAUNA SINGH BALDWIN

Men's fists are pumping behind him as they shout slogans—death to something.

The man in the white singlet carries a large photo frame under one arm, and clasps a megaphone in the other. "My brothers and sisters! Christians are converting Hindus to Christianity," he shouts. "They steal our babies! Sister Anupam was seen taking a baby boy away to Shimla. Ask my nephew, Mohan—he saw her. He saw the baby, he says it was a *boy*. And then the sister returned from Shimla without him. You know, we all know, that someone's baby boy is being sold abroad."

Men wag their heads, shouting *"Han! Han!"* as if certain that people abroad value sons as highly as they do.

The man with the megaphone comes closer, and Sister Anu recognizes Suresh. He yells, "Look at what these Christians want to do to your women."

He lays the megaphone down by the roadside, turns the poster around and holds it overhead. He rotates slowly on the ball of one sneakered foot, allowing everyone to see. A pink poster depicts a woman in a sari, sitting on a European-style chair. One bare foot touches the floor, one rests on a footstool. She's facing a TV, and a couple of pages of a newspaper have fallen on the floor beside her. On a low table beside the woman is a cup, perhaps of tea. The woman's chin is raised. She's smiling as if enjoying herself. A book in her hand is titled in Devanagari script. Her sandals lie beside her on the floor.

Suresh props the pink poster against the hillside. "Christians want all women to become like this," he shouts.

The few women in the crowd gaze at the woman in the poster as if she were a Bollywood starlet. The men are suitably shocked.

Several people in the crowd are former patients, and others must be family members of patients. Enough! Sister Anu opens her door.

"Sister, come back!" says Father Pashan.

"Just a minute," she says. She gets out, faces the crowd. *"Sunno!* All of you, listen! This is a terrible misunderstanding. Please disperse. No one working at the clinic intends to hurt anyone. All of us are trying to help—you who have been our patients know that. Tell him so," she says, pointing to their leader.

Father Pashan comes to stand beside her.

It occurs to Sister Anu that the people think Father Pashan is American or English. It's the one blue eye. But he's Indian as can be! Anu will have to talk to the crowd. Her Hindi doesn't sound Anglo-Indian like Father Pashan's.

Suresh comes forward, a snarl twisting his round face. "You were seen taking a Hindu baby boy to Shimla!" he shouts.

"No," says Sister Anu. She stands her ground. "You are mistaken. That baby was not Hindu, he was born to Christians."

"No! Don't you make excuses. You made that baby a Christian so that Christians get more votes."

He reaches down and picks up a plastic jerry can leaning against the hillside. "See this? It's empty. Where did the petrol go?" He sniffs in exaggerated inquiry. "I smell it—can you? I smell it all around your church."

The crowd shuffles, sways and swarms with its own energy. Sister Anu hears herself begin to plead—two patients are recuperating in the clinic beside the chapel. She doesn't mention that the chapel is a historical monument, that the chapel, clinic and school do not belong to the church, but to Amanjit Singh. A man intent on destruction won't be moved by the hopes, dreams and hard work that created this complex.

"Bhaiya—" she begins, calling him brother. "Let the patients go. They are innocent." For innocent, she chooses the word *nirdosh*, descended from Sanskrit, over the Urdu *bekasoor*, to placate his Hindu pride. She's grovelling, but if it saves one life, it will be worth it.

Father Pashan says, "Don't do this, son."

"Is my name Pashan? No, my name is Suresh Singh Chauhan, descendant of a raja who ruled these hills before there were any

Sikhs, before Muslims invaded, before the British Raj. I'm not your son. We don't want you taking our sons away."

"Your quarrel is with me—let Sister Anu bring the patients out, at least."

"Are the patients Hindu?" says Suresh. "If they are Hindus, I'm not stopping them. They can come out."

All she has to do is think of the women's names, but Sister Anu says, "We don't ask what people believe before we treat them. Hindus, Sikhs, Muslims and Christians all get the same diseases. Whether the women are Hindu, Sikh, Muslim or Christian, they don't have enough shakti to walk without help," she says. "Let me go in with Shafiq Sheikh, we'll help them to the jeep. We'll take them to Jalawaaz or Shimla."

"Oh no no no," says Suresh. "They can't go with any Muslim."

A Hindu patient should die inside rather than accept help from a Muslim driver?

Heads in the crowd are nodding. Voices shout, "No Muslims, no Muslims!" Fists are pumping, "Jai-jai Golunath, jai Ram-ji!" invoking the god of justice, invoking Lord Ram.

Suddenly, a tousled red head fights to the front of the crowd. "Suresh! What are you doing?"

Damini! Suresh looks around, then swats his hand a few times as if she's a buzzing fly.

"Open your ears and listen: I will bring the women out," Damini shouts. "And they will go in the car with Shafiq Sheikh."

"You would let a Muslim . . ."

Damini plants her fists on her hips and glares up at Suresh. "Did you know if you were Hindu or Muslim or Christian or Sikh when you were in my koke? No. You came into this world just a human! You didn't know till your first breath if you were Hindu or Muslim. You didn't know till I named you, till I began your story. Come and help, Shafiq-ji."

The dignified old man doesn't hesitate. He steps out of the jeep, and moves to Damini's side.

Suresh looks as if things are not going as planned. The fists have stopped pumping in the crowd, the sloganeers seem unsure what to yell. "Why should I care for the patients?" he mutters, forgetting the megaphone in his hand. "They're just women." His words ripple through the crowd.

Damini yells, "A woman brought you into the world!" She turns and strides away in her combat boots. "And," she shouts, over her shoulder, "when you were in her stomach, this woman didn't ask if you deserved to be born or not."

She halts, returns to shout up at Suresh's chest, "And that child Sister Anu took to Shimla—that was your son."

A collective gasp rolls through the crowd.

"He doesn't have your name and you'll never call him Hindu because he came from a Christian woman's koke, but that Moses is two-in-one: Hindu plus Christian. *Han!* And if he was in that clinic, would you allow *him* to come out?"

A man shouts from the crowd, "Hindu father makes it a Hindu baby."

Another shouts, "Christian woman must have been a prostitute."

"Mata-ji, so I slept with a prostitute," Suresh says in a boy-whine.

"Lie to others, not your mother. You just took what you wanted." Damini resumes her march uphill.

Father Pashan and Sister Anu follow her closely.

"Don't you go anywhere," Suresh shouts at Father Pashan. "Understand? Nowhere, unless I say so."

The crowd is snaking behind them on the narrow road, men snickering, gawking and gossiping.

Father Pashan holds up his hands. Suresh prods him forward with a blow to his back.

Sister Anu says, "Don't touch him!"

Suresh leers, "Shall I touch you?" He grabs her arm and yanks. Off balance, she stumbles after him up the drive, swept along with the crowd. At the top of the slope, the men spread across the clearing.

Where did Suresh find so many men? His retinue clumps and throngs by the chapel. Beyond the chapel, she can see Mohan, standing on the clinic veranda, airgun at his side. What security can poor Mohan provide against his uncle?

Damini and Shafiq Sheikh emerge from the clinic, each helping a patient wrapped in blanket. Sister Anu shakes off Suresh's grip and meets them at the gate. She and Damini help the women past Suresh, through the crowd, and to the jeep. Father Pashan's conciliatory, persuading tones fade behind her. She helps the two women into the back seat of the jeep.

"Why didn't you tell me your son is Moses's father?" she hisses at Damini.

"I was ashamed," Damini hisses back.

They race back uphill to the clinic.

Father Pashan is on the ground, hands to his belly, groaning. Sister Anu rushes to him, helps him struggle to his knees. "What happened? Where is Suresh?"

Before Father Pashan can answer, a red monkey comes jabbering and squealing out of the throng of protesters. His tail arcs back and forth, a great big white bandage burning on it. The monkey is jumping up and down.

As it tries to get the bandage off its tail, sparks fly, sparks catch and in a moment the chapel is surrounded by a moat of fire. The smell of burning petrol fills the air.

Father Pashan staggers to his feet. "The chalice!" he says. And before Sister Anu can stop him, he is racing toward the chapel. But already he cannot enter it for the lick and hiss of flames. He turns back, facing the crowd.

Over the crackle and gusts of flame come the red monkey's mad chatter and screams as it zigzags down the clearing. The crowd scatters, but in the corner of her eye, Anu spies Mohan dashing toward the monkey. That monkey could attack the boy, set him on fire too.

And Damini is running toward Mohan, screaming, "Nahin, Mohan, Nahin!" Sister Anu shouts "No, Mohan, no!"

The boy stops a few feet from the red monkey and cocks his head. He reaches out to the monkey with one hand, the gun loosely held in the other. Sister Anu is right behind Damini as Mohan turns to his grandmother. "Monkey hurting." Tears run down his cheeks.

The gun rises to Mohan's shoulder and he aims at the monkey. The air seems to burst, ballooning against Sister Anu's chest. A huge thud in her heart, and happening slows.

The monkey should fall.

The monkey doesn't fall. The monkey dances on, jabbering, screaming.

It takes a long time to happen, yet it happens in a moment, and in that moment so many other things are happening, things she is and isn't aware of, and the moment seems to go on forever, a crumpling and folding moment, a moment in which she is moving faster and faster, but not fast enough towards Father Pashan and the end of that moment is followed by another in which he falls and there is so much blood so much blood from his one blue eye and his side and in his hands and another moment in which he may or may not die and another in which she is holding his bloody head in the lap of her white kameez and knows he did.

PART V

Zindagi Aur Kuch Bhi Nahin,
Teri Meri Kahani hai
Life is nothing more than your story, my story.

(Song from the movie *Shor*)

Jalawaaz
October 1996

ANU

SISTER ANU, STILL TREMBLY AND RAW, TAKES A SEAT before the sub-district magistrate's desk. She has had two hours of sleep, bathed and changed into a clean white salwar-kameez with a black dupatta about her neck, but can't rid herself of the smell of anger, smoke and ashes from yesterday, the sight of Father Pashan running toward the blaze, the feeling of his warm blood-spatter.

The priest risked his life for the symbol of a last supper two thousand years ago. He really must have believed in his own power to transform the wine into the blood of Christ. Would she have been as prepared to die for that tradition? No. Another failing she must add to all her failings.

The owner of the damaged property, Mr. Amanjit Singh, takes the second chair. He seems dressed for a New Delhi dinner party, in navy blazer, grey pants, a tie striped red and black that matches his red turban. His beard, tightly rolled and netted, glistens in the morning sunlight pouring through the single window. Though he nods and smiles ingratiatingly at the SDM, he has an air of confident expectation—past favours are coming due.

The SDM yells to a sub-sub-assistant for tea, and flashes his Chiclet smile. He begins in English, to establish he can speak it, and continues in Sanskritized Hindi that causes both Sister Anu and

Amanjit Singh to strain for understanding. Periodically, for emphasis he returns to English laced with a South Indian accent. First of all, he says, by the Mental Health Act of 1993, he cannot charge Mohan, a fourteen-year-old mentally unfit boy, with murder. It was an accident—

He pauses, gazes at each in turn from under beetled brows. Sister Anu and Amanjit Singh tilt their heads in agreement. "These are the imperfections which mark our civil society," he says, as if he would like to charge Mohan if not for the law.

"I didn't think an airgun was dangerous," says Sister Anu.

"It isn't," says Amanjit Singh. "You don't need a license to carry one."

"The father-ji had no chance, though, because the bullet hit him in the eye," the SDM says. "The police have confiscated it."

Assistants and sub-assistants enter, proffering files for signature and supplications they have written on behalf of people who cannot write. When they have gone, and the sub-sub-assistants have left a tray with tumblers of tea, the SDM continues.

Someone used the red monkey to light the fire with his tail, he says, so that no one could be blamed, as if the monkey was re-enacting the burning of Sri Lanka in the *Ramayan*. "But I feel," he says, "it is verrry wrong to use Lord Hanuman in this way. Isspishlly nowadays during Dussherra, when yevryone is celebrating the burning of Lanka again."

He informs Sister Anu that the police will be transporting Father Pashan's body to the Jesuit residence in Delhi. "But he could be buried in the cemetery here," says Sister Anu. "He loved Gurkot and the people here . . ."

"No—the Jesuit brothers are recorded as his family; it is their dharma to perform his funeral. But not to worry, sister, in the South we say the atman returns again and again to be with people it loves. So your lover will return—of this I am verrry sure." He offers a box of tissue.

Sister Anu shakes her head. "Father Pashan was not my lover."

"Ah, so you say." He takes a tissue himself, to glove his fingers against the heat of his tea.

Amanjit Singh says, "But this was premeditated vandalism, ji. It must be attacked at the source."

The SDM asks Sister Anu, "You know the ringleader?"

"Suresh Singh Chauhan," says Sister Anu.

Amanjit says, "Suresh is the son of our old Damini-amma. We played together as children, every summer. He wore my clothes. He was like a brother. Well, maybe not quite a brother."

The SDM nods, "This woilence and ruffianism is creating a problem in the whole district. Unnecessary. Completely unnecessary woilence."

"Is there such a thing as necessary violence?" A stupid question, maybe, but one Sister Anu asks herself too, when she thinks of Vikas.

The SDM leans back in his chair. He regards Sister Anu as if she's a different species. "I have said to the superintendent of the police that this riot was verry verry wrong, and that ringleaders and ruffians must be punished. But to you I say it could not be helped. You see, you Christians come here, come yevrywhere—yeveryone knows you eat the cow, though she is protected. Why do you never understand?"

"There is no cow involved in this incident," says Sister Anu. "There was no cow near the chapel, no cows were being killed or eaten by anyone."

"Ah, so you say."

"I do not just say. I know. Show me one cow that was involved in this incident."

The SDM looks past her through the doorway, as if a cow might walk in any moment. "Then tell me what began all this—what happened."

"What happened? A Christian dalit woman was raped. Maybe Father Pashan told you?"

"Yes, he came, he told me his suspicions. But what does that have to do with this mamla?"

"Her rapist was Suresh." She's still hurt—no, angry—Damini did not tell her before. But it's not easy to find you have created a son who terrorized another woman, held her down and raped her. At least Damini eventually faced reality, unlike Pammy Kohli who at first denied Vikas could have raped Anu, then said it was Anu's fault for saying no, and later said she couldn't remember Anu ever telling her about it.

Amanjit says, "So he got fresh with the sweeper-woman—he might do that, yes. But she could just accuse anyone. Accusations don't mean he is guilty. What is her proof?"

"The woman would not come forward," says the SDM. "But she was already married."

She asks, "If she wasn't, would you have made Suresh marry her?"

"Usually, yes. But not in this case, Sister. She's a sweeper-woman."

"So?"

"This Suresh Singh is a Chauhan, that is to say kshatriya caste—then how can he marry a sweeper? But again I'm asking, what has this rape to do with yesterday?"

"The Christian woman decided to give up her child for adoption. So I took him to Shimla to find him a good home."

"Him?"

"Yes."

"Sister, you want me to believe someone gave you a boy baby for adoption?"

"Yes—her husband wouldn't accept the child."

"Ah, naturally. And these days you can get fifty thousand for a boy."

"We were not selling Moses, we were placing him for adoption. The woman's husband would have sent her away if we had not helped her. Suresh cooked up a protest, falsely accusing us—me—of selling Hindu babies abroad. He led protesters from Jalawaaz, and they came to Gurkot and burned down the chapel, and Mohan shot Father Pashan by mistake."

"Spontaneous woilence. You see, population becomes provoked by the presence of you people. Then for a few days there is a lot of tokha-takhi—lot of chaos. Then," the SDM stretches out his hands as if playing a harmonium, "all will be normal, all will be happy. This is Hindu tol-ration."

"How can it be spontaneous, ji?" says Amanjit Singh. "You can't bring so many men walking from Jalawaaz without planning."

"Amanjit-saab, this is not Delhi. Here in the Himalayas, people have respect, co-op-ration. Every place is holy, not only churches and gurdwaras."

"Why is it that when riots take place only the property of minori-ties is damaged?"

"Aman-ji, every man in India now says he or she is a minority so he can get a job or some free thing or some small adwontage."

"There is no question, sir: Sikhs are a minority, and so are Christians. This is just like 1984. *Planned* violence against minorities. Your Jalawaaz police had to know all those men were walking and riding motorbikes and taking trucks from here to Gurkot. And the petrol was poured all around the chapel *before* the protestors came."

"The Order of Everlasting Hope would like you to investigate the police report and register a case," says Sister Anu. "We want to bring charges of rioting, intent to hurt, trespass and assault—"

Amanjit Singh interrupts, "Wait. SDM-saab, you are right. Why would Suresh lead a protest and burn down a *chapel?* The Christians never did anything to his family. His mother even works at the clinic. Someone bigger is behind him."

"It could also be a series of unrelated events, ji. Just bo-the-ration. And if it happened, it could also be that it just took place all of a sudden."

"*If* it happened?" Amanjit Singh rises, tucks his thumbs into his belt, dominating the room with his sheer bulk. "Have you seen the damage, sir? The chapel is burned, ji—only the stone confessional booth remains. Both wards of the clinic are damaged. We were lucky it was evening and no children were in the school. Those hooligans just melted into the mountains as soon as they caught sight of my car. But the whole forest could have burned. My home, my new cottages—all could have gone up in smoke. As it is, the gurdwara is blackened and," his voice breaks, "the Guru is badly burned."

"Someone was in the gurdwara? Only one body has been reported to the police."

"No sir," Anu inserts, "he means his holy book—his Bible, his *Gita*. For him, the *Guru Granth Sahib* is a body, a person."

"The police report should have mentioned this," says the SDM. "I will inspect this guru book tomorrow. Please to sit down."

Amanjit visibly controls himself and resumes his seat.

The SDM takes a sip of tea. "This is a tragedy," he says. "Such things happen, but not usually in my district." He shakes his head sorrowfully. "We have to keep an eye on Suresh and what he may be teaching young peoples, because, you know, the BJP could go out of fashion and the Congress Party and their secularism could someday come back—it has happened before. And there is the matter of this sweeper-woman's baby."

"We are still trying to find him a home close to Gurkot," says Sister Anu. "Would you like to adopt him?"

"I?" says the SDM, with a smile and wave of his hand. "I have a blood-son, and can have many more. Adopted sons don't come to your help in old age, Sister, only blood will help you then."

"Most people in this district think as you do. That's why I had to take the boy to Shimla," she says.

The SDM has the grace to look slightly trapped. He sips his tea for inspiration.

"Tell me," he says, "how a woman like you somehow got mixed up with Christians? I mean: we understand rice-Christians, but you? The police are questioning that Muslim driver of yours—he tells us you used to be a caste Hindu?"

Sister Anu says, "Why are you questioning poor old Shafiq Sheikh! Because he's the only Muslim around?"

"Yes, madam. You find me one more Muslim and I will question him as well. These days Pakistanis are yeverywhere, yeverywhere. Coming over the border, posing as Muslim-Indians until they can do some hera-pheri—boom, boom! I say Mughal Empire is gone, but we are left with all these Muslims, more Muslims living here than in Pakistan. At least after British Empire we are not left with British—except for you Christians."

"Where is Suresh, now?" asks Sister Anu.

"In jail," the SDM gestures over his shoulder in the direction of Jalawaaz's police station. "He gave us names at first—now he's giving us true names.

"You see, madam-ji, you must be sentimental. You must have respects for Hindu sentiments, not just Muslim and Christian sentiments. Muslims and Christians have this, this ten-*den*-cy toward intoleration of Hindu sentiments. It's because of your one god, no other gods allowed."

Sister Anu opens her mouth, but Amanjit Singh is on his feet again, his annoyance bristling in all directions.

He too follows one god, no other gods allowed.

"SDM-saab, I will not let this matter drop," Amanjit says. "Even if the padri were alive, I wouldn't let it drop. You may not fully understand, so let me say it again. My Guru, the *Guru Granth Sahib* was damaged." He plants his fists on the SDMs desk and leans over till his turban and beard are inches from the man's alarmed face. "If you investigate who Suresh was working for, you will find the culprits. This follower of Vaheguru swears: I will give you all the help you need."

Sister Anu treads gingerly across hillocks of brick and mortar rubble of the burned chapel to salvage what she can. Images of the terrified burning monkey, the swarming crowd of angry men, Father Pashan's blood on her kameez, the smells, screams and horrors of the church burning replay in her mind and contrast with the peaceful sway of the wind through the pines.

If Lord Shiv, destroyer of worlds, ever manifested himself, this is what our world would look like. If I survived Armageddon or nuclear winter, this is what the whole world would become.

At the far end of the field, the bell tings sorrowfully in the decapitated belfry, surrounded by fragments of metal and glass. She knocks on god's door mentally, but has never felt it more closed. Her hair, still frizzed from the fire, tumbles about her shoulders—she doesn't tie it back. Particles of ash fly through the twilight air, grit in her teeth.

I will carry the memory of this within me the rest of my life.

The chapel's plastered plank walls crumbled like matchsticks, but the structural beams are intact; a rumour circulating among the Christians says the metal skeleton was not weakened but strengthened by the fire. At the heart of the skeleton, the jagged remnants of the altar still stand. But really, the only surviving structure within the footprint of the chapel is Samuel's ornately carved stone confessional.

Birdcall pierces the eerie silence, *kew-kew!* Beneath her feet, the ground is charred, dried and pitted from the footprints of Christians and Sikhs standing together, passing buckets of water from hand to hand to douse the flames. Black particles flutter past.

She should have done more outreach, created friendships, connections. Should have worked as much with the men of Gurkot as with the women.

The Hindu men who followed Suresh must have felt left out, humiliated in some way, threatened by the growing health, education and independence of their girls and women. Because how can calls to nationalism alone justify the anger that created this deed?

Sister Anu grasps the blackened door of the confessional and pulls. She takes one look and a shriek escapes her. She blesses herself, and peers closer. Damini is slumped inside, dark-ringed eyes closed. Is she dead?

Sad old black eyes flick open.

"What are you doing here?" says Sister Anu.

"Using the forgiveness chair," says Damini. "Goldina said I should."

Sister Anu feels on precarious ground. "Is it helping you?"

Damini shakes her head. "Abhi nahin," she says. Not yet. "I have less thoughts in my head than a potato. I don't want to sleep, I don't want to wake up. I don't want to eat or drink. I don't want to talk. I have Dipreyshun."

She closes her eyes, as if she might sit there forever.

Sister Anu doesn't know what to say. She stares at her fingers, blackened with soot from the door handle. Mist is circling, descending with the evening. A cold wind is whistling through the pines. Rain will be next. Damini's despair oozes from the confessional like a miasma.

"After the SDM moved Suresh to a jail far away beyond Shimla," Damini says, "I applied for my pension again. I told the government my son cannot support me from jail. The postmaster told me it will take a few years because I don't know anyone to bribe and fast-en up the process. How will I live in that time? I have sold my silver toe ring, my silver nose ring, even my gold earrings—all that I got for my sister-in-laws' weddings. And after all that my son has done," she gestures at the blackened earth that was the chapel, the damaged clinic beyond it, "you won't want me working for you anymore."

"Not because your son did this," says Sister Anu. "I was going to— oh, jaane do!—never mind." Nothing will be gained from mentioning her intention, even before the church burned, to let Damini go. She tries to sound encouraging, "You know so much about medicinal plants," she says. "You could even work with scientists in Shimla. I remember you gave the ojha's wife a sweet leaf, madhupatra. And you told Father Pashan it was better for him than artificial sugar."

"I gave the ojha's wife a sweet leaf I can't taste myself."

"Since when have you been unable to taste sweetness?" Sister Anu shifts to diagnostic mode.

"I don't know—December, 1992."

Sister Anu knows what happened in December 1992, at the Babri Masjid when that Muslim shrine was demolished by Hindu fanatics. Sister Anu is not surprised that Damini felt the trauma as everyone else, but her reaction should by now be blunted by time. She says gently, "Then think what sweetness is, and how you must find it again."

Damini looks over Sister Anu's shoulder at the devastation. She says, "I went to ask for a phone number in Kasauli jail where I could call Suresh. The police made me wait outside with the sweeper-women for hours. Then they told me he already had one visitor—you! You wanted to taunt him?"

"No, I prayed for him. Lord Jesus teaches us to forgive."

"Ha! It's easy to forgive others."

"No it isn't. I could be angry that you have been selecting unborn girl babies to die. I could be angry because you knew Suresh was Moses's father but allowed me to take the boy to Shimla for adoption. And I could be really angry and hurt because your son burned down our chapel and your grandson killed our priest. Or I can say: you and I must change something in Gurkot."

Damini thinks about this for a moment.

"Was he all right?" she says.

Sister Anu could describe Suresh's squalid 14 square metre prison cell without bed or mattress shared with seven others; the jail superintendent who demanded a "donation" before he would let her visit an under trial prisoner; how Suresh bragged that he was occupying the same cell where Gandhi's assassin, Nathuram Godse, once occupied in 1948; the 400 grams of wheat, 90 grams of cereal and 250 grams of vegetables he is allowed each day. The brutal discipline of guards who follow a nineteenth-century British manual; the lifer convicts who, he said, made his life miserable . . . but sometimes it's kinder not to describe. So she says, "Suresh said to tell you he could come to trial in only four to five years. Three, if he has good bhagya. And he can also be let out of jail for a few days if he is needed to perform your last rites."

"Did you see his food?"

"Yes, he ate rice, daal, and some vegetables in front of me."

But she knows Suresh wouldn't have been given as much to eat if she had not been present.

At the beginning of her visit he said much that was unrepeatable. She had expected to feel anger, even rage, but his fears of annihilation by non-Hindus were so paranoid and his loneliness so extreme, she felt only pity. "He said activists are working very hard to change his conditions, so maybe he will be moved to Tihar Jail in Delhi or a jail run by a private company. And he said to tell you he has been doing meditation and has been given devotional music cassettes. And some discourses of Swami Rudransh."

"*Ooofff!* Is Swami Rudransh sitting in prison with my Suresh? Is Swami Rudransh sending bail for him? When he was still in Jalawaaz jail, Suresh told me not to worry, that his boss in New Delhi will send bail for him." Damini closes her eyes. After a while, she says, "How will I know when the chair gives me forgiveness?"

How to answer?

"The chair works if a priest is with you," Sister Anu says gently. "When he is here, you sit in the chair and tell him what is troubling you. Afterwards, he tells you what you must do to be forgiven by god. But since Father Pashan is no more, would you like to talk to me? I cannot impart the grace of forgiveness as god or Father Pashan could, but maybe my listening will help. We can't change the past, and the present is what it is, but we can change the future."

Damini opens her eyes, "Because of my deeds in this life, I will return as a crow in my next. Or a rat. Or an insect."

Crows and rats and other animals, Sister Imaculata said during novice classes for Sisters Anu and Bethany, don't have souls, which means you can't return as one. But since Christians have so often expanded the definition of animal to cover women, homosexuals, Jews and the colonized, and since Hindus have so often expanded the definition to cover women and outcastes, Anu prefers to believe that if humans have souls, crows and rats and insects must have them too. She tries a different approach. "Father Pashan once told me god loves us even if he does not love our deeds. God is with us in our suffering."

"Even if we commit the worst paap?"

"Even if," says Sister Anu.

And so Damini tells Sister Anu what Sister Anu suspected. There was indeed a baby, Leela's child, a girl child. And Damini sent her back to brahman. And things have gone wrong and more wrong ever since.

"The *Gita* says that if our intentions are good, and we do our dharma, the outcome will take care of itself," says Damini.

"And were your intentions good?"

"Leela said when I left her and went to Delhi, she began to learn not to want what she cannot have." Her voice falls almost to whisper. "She said if Chunilal had not refused the girl a name, she would have fed her. That's when I realized I was doing what Chunilal wanted, not what Leela wanted. So I was angry with Chunilal, all the time he was so sick, all the time I bathed him, massaged him, shaved him, fed him when he could no longer eat. I had stained my karma not for Leela's sake as I thought, but for his. A man has his dharma in each of the four stages of life, but a woman has only one stage: to tend the men of her family, then her children, then her in-laws. So little by little, I got this Dipreyshun."

"Do you feel better now that you've told me?"

Damini looks around. "Even the mountains look deaf, today. Even the mountains are full of accusing eyes. Again and again I see my finger—mine!—pushing the tobacco between those two small lips." Her head drops, she clasps her hands between her breasts.

"Is there more to tell?"

"I feel my strength is falling lower and lower. Any lower, and it will dive into the riverbed of the Meethi Darya. No, this chair has no magic for me. And telling you is not enough."

"Damini," says Anu, "I have seen you help people. I heard you refuse to harm Kiran's baby girl—only a good woman would do that."

"That's what I thought. But how can I be a good woman if the son I made tore down a masjid and burned down a Christian house of god, and raped a poor woman? So when I began thinking all this, Dipreyshun came."

"If you want to feel better all the time, you have to do better deeds."

"What to do?"

"First, don't take any more women to Jalawaaz Clinic for the ultrasound."

"Then *I'll* have to select which soul can stay and which should be returned to brahman." She hides her face behind her hands. "I don't want to do that ever again."

"But parents are sending boys and girls back to brahman before they are born."

"Before birth is bestest time."

"Is it?"

"Yes. Then one power button drives both mother and child, like a radio and cassette player."

"We Catholics believe it is paap to kill even before birth."

"Then you Catholic-types please don't have a cleaning if you don't want it. But a mother who wants a cleaning should not have to walk five hours to get one, or have to explain to anyone why she needs one."

"But surely you see that just because a mother *wants* a cleaning doesn't mean she *needs* one. Or that she will make a right decision."

Damini is silent for several moments. Then she says, "What is right? How am I to know?"

Sister Anu lowers her voice to make her own confession. "All right, I can agree that cleaning an unborn child from Leela would have been better than neglecting the child till she died of starvation or fever, or killing her. And it was cruel of Father Pashan to tell Goldina she will go to hell if she had a cleaning, when he knew she was raped. But we don't know whether the women you took to Jalawaaz wanted their babies cleaned out or whether family pressure drove them to get a cleaning because they were told the child was a girl."

"Pressure . . . yes. My Mem-saab—though I knew her so well, I could not tell if she took her own life by her own hand, or if Aman and Timcu drove her to do it. She was a woman who needed a mirror to see her own bangles—very beautiful, you know, but couldn't believe she was. That's why she got Dipreyshun. A man and his family don't have to say or do anything. We all know what will happen to us if we don't do their wishes. So women in Gurkot say, Either I suffer or the baby suffers."

"Then we should help husbands and fathers understand that girls are gifts from god."

"Girls are expensive," says Damini in a tone of warning.

"Girls and women work as hard, sometimes harder than men. Look at your Leela, and your Kamna. They don't get paid, so people say their work is not worth anything. But tell me, what would have happened to Chunilal and Mohan if they didn't have Leela and Kamna?"

Damini hunches into herself as if racked by internal pain.

Sister Anu says, "Is your life better now than when you were a girl?"

Damini looks up at the evening sky as if trying to see the past. "Yes, twenty paise out of a rupee better."

"Is Leela's life better than yours?"

Damini tilts her head—yes, then shakes it—no. "I don't know, I don't know."

"The only way we can know is to let each girl's story happen."

Sister Anu waits. Eventually Damini presses her sari-pallu to her eyes and says, "What can I do, now?"

"I don't know," says Sister Anu. "But whatever you do must be done soon, because this chair will soon be gone, and then there will be no forgiveness and the SDM will come to know you have been helping women get abortions if their babies were girls ... and he will have to follow the law."

"You'll tell him?"

Never being pledged to secrecy of confessions as Pashan was, Sister Anu has the power to reveal. "Our deeds are karma, Damini. God and all the gods know what we do. You know your own deeds. And look how bad you feel—even the forgiveness chair has been unable to help."

"He'll put me in jail. You know what policemen do to women in jail? And what will happen to Leela without Chunilal, Suresh or me to help her?" Damini's chin quivers. She twists the free end of her sari around her finger.

"Damini, think how many grandmothers, mothers and mothers-in-law live with guilt, as you do? Only you can persuade women of Gurkot to stop 'stopping' girls. Or find a way to stop everyone in Gurkot from 'stopping girls.' You have to help girls and women survive." Sister Anu pauses. "And if you don't show me some effort, some change, yes, I will tell the SDM."

DAMINI

DAMINI EASES HERSELF FROM THE CONFESSIONAL. SISTER Anu reaches out, helps her find footing on the blackened stone. Damini surveys the damage. All caused by Suresh, her Suresh.

Would Sister Anu really report her to the SDM? Would she let her be arrested for homicide and put in jail? She told the Jesus-sister because she wanted to be understood. She shouldn't have. But she needs a cure for Dipreyshun. Couldn't Sister Anu just give her a pill?

She would like to honour some of what Sister Anu believes, though for her life begins when a child breathes, not in its time in the womb.

And true life begins when a child's story begins. But what she has been doing has brought her no peace, only ghosts . . .

Everyone is always finding terrible impossible tasks for her to do, new mountains for her to climb.

"Look!" Sister Anu interrupts her thoughts. Fireflies spark in unison, synchronizing with no authority. They pulse as partners, creating a field of light over the charred ground.

"Why are they acting together?" asks Damini. "Is any more mighty than the rest?"

"No, all the same. But mostly they do as others do. See now there's one who is not following the same taal." Indeed, one firefly has begun flashing at a different rhythm.

A ripple of light swells across the charred field from end to end as the fireflies adjust to a new rhythm. "See? One changes," says Sister Anu. "And the rest follow."

Damini snorts. "It's easy for fireflies. You think if I change everyone will follow me? No, ji! Men have to be told everything."

"Then you better find a way to tell men. Tell them girls have feelings like them."

"But we don't want to be like men. Men should learn to be more like us. But how funny it sounds to say a *manav, aadmi* or *purush* should become an *aurat, istri* or *theemi*. No one will understand. Everyone will laugh!"

"Say *insaan*, then," Sister uses the word descended from Persian. "All of us can try to be humans first. Just beings. All I know is, you better find a way to say it that everyone in Gurkot understands."

Damini steals a sidelong glance—Sister Anu looks determined to do just as she says.

She sighs. "Men, women—all of us have lost our true honour because we think our sons are gold. I tried to indulge my son and son-in-law so they would look after me in old age. I forgave my son the first time he attacked a house of worship, and that made him more bold. I was so afraid my son-in-law would send me away or tell people Leela's baby girl was mine, I did bad things. If you promise not to tell the SDM, Sister-ji, I promise to find a way to heal men and women here."

Sister Anu tilts her head, agreeing.

"But," says Damini. "I can't just tell people of Gurkot straight out. We are mountain people—we don't trust the straight way."

Jalawaaz
November 1996

ANU

THRÉE WEEKS AFTER THE FIRE, SISTER ANU IS BACK
in the office of the sub-district magistrate, summoned to be informed
that a more powerful god, the district magistrate, has issued a stay
order on the operations of Bread of Healing, pending a government
inquiry. The court, unlike the SDM, and perhaps with a little help
from Amanjit Singh's close friendship with the State of Himachal's
chief minister, has decided "such" things do happen in the SDM's
district. And that charges of rioting, intent to hurt, trespass and
"outraging the morals of a woman" can all be upheld against Suresh.
Inquiries can go on for years. The SDM cites the most famous—the
gas leak at the Union Carbide plant in Bhopal, the massacre of Sikhs
in Delhi, both inquiries in progress since 1984, the Babri Masjid
inquiry in progress since 1992. While the investigation continues, he
wags his finger at Anu, "I assured Aman-saab that I will warn you,
you Christians better not retaliate. You tell your Christians to be like
your Jesus. Explain to them that these young men were misguided.
They knew not what they did."

Sister Anu replies, "Those men knew exactly what they did. Since
we have no chapel and no priest, I can't give our congregation the
sermon you want."

"Ah yes, you can't preach. So backward state of affairs. Throughout

India, women can preach—only you Christian women can't. My wife, she is constantly preaching. I don't listen, but I say she can do it."

"It would help Christians believe justice is being done if you arrested more than one man. It took more than one man to bring the petrol from Jalawaaz, and someone other than Suresh set the monkey's tail on fire."

"Only two more witnesses have come forward, so we arrested several bachelors. Now maybe others will speak."

"Why bachelors?"

"Because this is what happens when men have no sex."

"You're saying their brains stop working if they don't get sex?"

"Semen builds up, Sister-ji. As a nurse you should be knowing this."

It's fruitless to argue with the SDM. But at least there will be an inquiry.

"You know this Suresh," the SDM says, "was a social worker and a teacher."

Sister Anu nods.

"He worked for the Bajrang Dal. Excellent Hindus. Little fanactical, but verrry good-intentioned. Inter-related to RSS."

"No I didn't know that." Sister Anu grips the table, lightheaded at the implications. The banana and oatmeal she ate for breakfast churn in her stomach.

"We've learned the several names of Suresh's boss in Shimla. We have learned the name of his New Delhi leader. He even gave us his license plate number."

A bad feeling comes over Sister Anu. "Who is it?"

"A big saab." He reaches for a toothpick holder, slides a toothpick between his fingers, and picks between his teeth.

"His name?"

He gives an exaggerated sigh, and glances at his Timex. "Why you need to know his name?"

"Why are you protecting it?"

"He has a good family—Kohlis."

"It's Vikas Kohli, right?"

His expression changes to interest. "You know Vikas-saab?" A shade of wariness in his tone. "How do you know him?" The wariness has changed to arch insinuation.

The SDM already assumed Father Pashan was Anu's lover, to fit his views on Christian women and nuns. He's now leaping to the same conclusion about Vikas. What would he think of the truth?

"I have met Vikas-saab," she says carefully. "His wife and I are friends."

"Then you can understand the problem I am in."

"What problem?"

"Aman-ji told me he will bring charges in a criminal case. He's accusing Vikas-saab of conspiracy, property damage. He says his lady-wife saw Vikas-ji giving Suresh a large sum of cash in the chai-stall, right there in Gurkot. He says Vikas-ji told his lady-wife that it was a donation, but she is sure it was a bribe. So this is why Aman-ji is alleging involvement in instigating people to riot."

"And?"

"This is one case Aman-ji cannot win. Too much difficult. You see, Vikas Kohli was nowhere near here—he denies any connection."

"But why is that your problem?" says Sister Anu. "Let the case take its course."

"It's that way only. Aman-ji is my friend, and your friend Vikas Kohli is now my friend. The district magistrate is not here, the district commissioner is in Shimla. Only I am here to save the good names of Amanjit Singh and Vikas Kohli. Both are continuously applying pressure, very much pressure."

"And do you find this pressure tempting?"

He looks surprised, then hurt, then wounded. "How could you think so, Sister?"

Gurkot

DAMINI

DAMINI WEARS HER THICK BROWN SHAWL FOR THE climb to Lord Golunath's temple. There are no forgiveness chairs under its conical dome, but everything is alive and when she reaches up and strikes the bell, vibrations echo as if joining a celestial song. The pujari, who was dedicated to the god of justice at thirteen, emerges. His eyes are narrowed against the sunset, his voice firmed by twenty years of chanting at marriages, puja ceremonies and death rites. He is the pandit who refused to officiate at Chunilal's funeral, but the hair on his oiled chest ripples with his muscles today, when no danger is present. Despite the cold, he wears only a white cotton dhoti. He sinks into a slingback chair outside the shrine and nods encouragingly.

Damini sinks to her haunches before him and keeps her gaze on the scuffed toes of her boots as she skims the surface of the story, ending with that part of her problems that he can understand: Suresh is in jail. "Why did this happen?" she clasps her arms around her shins. "Always I thought I could rely on my son in my old age."

"It is plain: you looked at another woman's misfortunes and thought they could never happen to you."

Yes, she had thought that Mem-saab's misfortunes could never befall her. How did the pujari know? She had thought her Suresh a more dutiful son, a more brotherly brother, a more spiritual man than Aman. How did the pujari know?

Some holy men hear the past you carry with you.

The pujari's scent is comforting—sandalwood incense and cannabis. But the beedi he lights is tobacco. Damini takes one from the knotted end of her sari and lights up too.

"No" she says, eventually. "It was my fault. I let my son believe he could do no wrong. I let him believe women exist to do his bidding."

"He was misguided by many, not only you."

"The swami who misguided him is free, the saab who misguided Suresh is free, the men of Gurkot who protested with Suresh are free. Only my Suresh is locked up."

"Those people are not locked up," the pujari says, sucking on his beedi, "but they cannot be free till they escape samsara. Who can be free till he never takes birth again?" He blows hot air and smoke into her eyes. "And you, ji? I have not seen you here before."

"I mostly go to the gurdwara." She twirls Mem-saab's steel kara about her wrist.

"But today you are needing something from Lord Golunath?"

"Oh, no need, ji—I don't need," Damini says immediately. But she does need. If she goes to jail like Suresh, there will be no one left to help Leela. She lifts her chin. "You please tell Lord Golunath, he should come down from his mountain, come out of his temple, and just see, just look: what is happening in his village."

The pujari suggests ceremonies of varying lengths and complexity—he too has to make a living. The least expensive is a jagar, an awakening for those who believe they are awake. Damini says, "Maybe a jagar."

"Don't think it's easy," says the pujari. "The ojha must travel into the spirit world to supplicate Lord Golunath to wake. He doesn't do it often, or for just anyone."

"Tell him it is for Damini who gave him madhupatra to sweeten his wife's tea and make her kinder."

"I will. But you must understand: when Lord Golunath awakens, or when he awakens us, who can say what can happen?"

"Will he punish those who have done wrong?" says Damini faintly.

"He has many ways to bring about justice, most of them unseen."

"Then is there danger?"

"The same as always, behen," he says, calling her sister. "Whenever you open a gateway to the unseen world, other spirits also can enter."

"As in a time of birthing," says Damini.

"Yes."

Damini stubs her beedi beneath her boot heel. She reaches into her bodice, retrieves a pair of gold flower-shaped earrings, the same that Mem-saab gave her.

The pujari rolls them in his palm. He looks away at the snow-clad mountains and shakes his head. "Mountains," he says, "cannot be brought together. Only people can."

Her donation is insufficient. Damini takes a folded khaki envelope from between her breasts. She counts out three hundred rupees more. The three hundred rupees her Piara Singh died for, the bribe that tore his heart open. "Whatever comes," she says, placing the rupees in the pujari's outstretched hand.

"*Jai Golunath!*"

Beginning at dawn the next day, women call the ojha's message uphill from one house to the next. He will invoke Lord Golunath at Tubelight's home midway down the mountain, so that some will have to climb for the jagar, others will have to descend. Lord Golunath will speak to everyone. Even outcastes, even if it will embarrass the upper-castes to sit cross-legged beside them. Bajantris set out, carrying their drums and instruments to Gurkot, walking from two villages away.

Soon after morning tea, Damini lets herself in at the nun's house. Sister Anu is lying on her back on a yoga mat on the terrace in setu bandhasana pose. Shoulders, palms and feet flat on the floor, pelvis lifted like a small bridge. "Where is Sister Bethany?" asks Damini.

Sister Anu lowers her hips and sits up. "Already at school. Actually not at the school—it's padlocked until the stay order is lifted. She's holding classes in a tent on the clearing. I will go and help her later, but I'm leaving for Shimla in a few days time. We still don't know when the clinic can reopen. The bishop says he can't send another priest to Gurkot after what just happened. Aman-ji says he will turn Bread of Healing over to an NGO."

"What will you do when the enjiyo comes?"

"I don't know yet. I want to be where I'm needed."

Damini delivers the ojha's message, telling her that she is needed at the jagar ceremony. "Come tomorrow," she says, "and see me keep my promise."

"I will," says Sister Anu, wiping her face with a towel. "Though there's not enough time for me to get permission from my superiors. We don't have such awakenings in our Church, you see. Even when I was Hindu . . . city Hindus don't observe such ceremonies."

"Muslims don't either. It's we who have the need." Damini picks a book off the table beside the wicker chair, wipes it with a corner of her sari, opens it. It's in English. "What is this?"

"A story book."

"About maharajas."

"No, just ordinary people. A woman."

"Who could be interested?"

"Another woman can be. A man can be."

"Why?"

Sister Anu rubs the towel over her neck. "To compare to her own life. Or compare to his own." She rises.

No one I know has a story like mine, so who would be interested in reading my story?

Damini takes her leave of Sister Anu and continues to the Big House.

She enters via the kitchen. Khansama ushers her into the receiving room, and disappears behind a screen. He'll be listening to every word.

Amanjit Singh is sitting at Sardar-saab's desk in a straight-backed chair, writing in a leather-bound notebook. A beautiful young Mem-saab smiles up at him from a silver-framed photo. Sardar-saab, in a rose-coloured turban gazes steadily from his gilt-edged frame on the wall above the desk. Kiran reclines on a sofa beneath the central skylight. Today she wears a peach cotton kaftaan, no makeup, no sunglasses. The baby girl in the rocker beside her looks up at Damini with shiny brown eyes.

"She is well, na?"

Kiran tilts her chin—yes.

"What is her name?" Damini holds Kiran's gaze, demanding respect as an elder.

"Angad," says Kiran. "Angad Kaur."

Amanjit Singh looks up, "Are you here for the money? I sent the cheque for thirty-five thousand, but Leela sent it back."

"No," says Damini. "I'm not here for money."

"Mohan signed the deed. To whom can the boy sell if not to me? Leela and you can't farm that land. Let's not waste more time—take the cheque, Damini-amma."

"Maybe someday," says Damini, determined that day will come after moksha, when her soul has nothing more to learn, when she's freed from birth and rebirth.

"I'm giving this much because you were my mother's maidservant for so many years. Look, I'm not even holding you or Leela or Mohan responsible for Suresh's actions, because I heard you saved the patients."

Damini drops her gaze to the Bokhara carpet, and says nothing.

"I'm going to build a more modern clinic, you know, as soon as the NGO people persuade the government to lift the stay order," Aman says, sounding as he did when he promised Mem-saab he would look after her. "It will have an operating theatre, a full lab, an MRI, an

EEG, an EKG . . ." He checks off these wonders, moving a forefinger from the pinky of his other hand to his thumb. Now he's back to his pinky, ". . . an ECG and an ultrasound machine."

Damini looks up. "An ultra-soon here in Gurkot?"

"Villa owners will find it very convenient," he says. "We can have some charity cases as well."

"And Sister Anu?"

"Oh, Dr. Gupta will continue to work for us. And if the nurse wants to remain, she and the teaching sister can rent the residence cottage."

Damini delivers the ojha's message. Interest flickers in Kiran's eyes. She looks at Amanjit.

"I'll attend if I have time," says Amanjit. He shows Damini squares covered with small writing in his notebook, to make her understand how very busy he is.

Damini nods, then says, "No notebooks." She does not want Aman to tell cocktail party stories to his pink buyers and fellow Sikhs about Hindu ceremonies. For Kiran's benefit she adds, "And the ojha-ji says no cameras."

"*Leh!* Why, Damini-amma?" says Amanjit.

"You should remember what people do and say, Aman, not only their photos," says Damini. She glances at Kiran, "And with your own memory."

DAMINI

ON THE DAY OF THE JAGAR CEREMONY, DAMINI WAKES
feeling worthless and empty, as if nothingness is her normal state. It
could be grief over Chunilal, over Suresh in jail without bail. Or it
could be her own great paap. She hasn't felt such hollowness since
the day she tried the forgiveness chair.

May the jagar be successful.

Damini's feet feel heavy as her heart, and today even her combat
boots offer no cheer. She wears the violet phulkari-embroidered
shawl Mem-saab gave her, for violet is the color of spirit.

Spending too much on one god can offend another. Could it dis-
please Anamika Devi that Damini asked for a jagar for Lord Golunath
and not for her? But Anamika Devi existed before all 333 million
gods, yet few worship her—who can even try and appease her?

As the sun sinks past the hills of Gurkot, the villagers remove
their shoes and file into the centre room in Tubelight's home. Supari
and Chimta cover their heads with their saris, and take their seats on
the jute dhurrie with all the other women, facing the ojha's unclean
left side. Matki carries a toddler on her arm and wipes his nose with
her dupatta. The Toothless One is helped to the ground by her two
daughters-in-law. Even Vijayanthi arrives, having ridden up the
mountain on her grandson's back. Kamna props a textbook on bent

knees between her forearms and tries to finish her homework. A Petromax lantern flares, turning her bangles to prisms. Goldina squats a few feet away from the rest, the set of her shoulders defying anyone to object to her presence.

Sister Anu places her shoulder bag on the windowsill, covers her head with a heavy black shawl and takes a spot on the dhurrie, beside Damini. Samuel bows over folded hands to the ojha, then retires to an adjoining room, so no one will notice his presence.

Amanjit is ushered to a space where he can sit cross-legged in his white kurta pyjama, and lean against a wall as backrest. A moat of space forms around his lime green turban, though more and more men arrive. Mohan spies Amanjit as soon as he enters, and knocks several knees and toes as he leaps over cross-legged men. When he reaches Amanjit Singh, he leans over and envelops him in a bear hug, as if he were a long lost friend, instead of the would-be evictor of his family, then he takes an open spot a few feet away.

Kiran comes in, looking appropriately solemn. She places a platter of uncooked rice beside the ojha as Amanjit Singh's donation and crosses the room to the women's side. She looks more comfortable than cross-legged Amanjit, one hip on the ground, folded legs to the side. She takes off her sunglasses, polishes them and puts them away.

The dark, wiry ojha sits on his heels, hands on knees. He rocks back and forth, he rolls around his waist. When he holds up his arms, his sleeves fall back and his tattoos change shape. The drummer beats his nagara, the singer calls to Lord Golunath in Pahari. The bow slides on the ektara; its melody resonates in men and women alike.

The ojha begins to tremble. He runs his fingers through greying hair. A voice too large for his slight frame emanates from him. "I come when seen and unseen energies resound." His voice fills the small room. "Why do you ask this poor ojha to bring me?"

The pujari leads the puch-session. "Golunath-ji, this old woman has questions."

No one turns to look, but everyone might as well be staring at Damini.

"Golunath-ji," she says, "I am not very old, but no longer young. I have two children—this daughter, Leela, and one son. I came to visit Leela for a little while, but then I committed a great paap. I have tried to erase it, but all the good deeds I have done are not enough."

"What was your paap?"

She can't speak it. Who can understand her crime, her heinous crime?

"Tell," says Sister Anu, her voice both encouraging and firm.

"Tell!" shouts Chimta as if she'll wrest it out of Damini.

Damini gropes for words in any language: Hindi, Punjabi or Pahari, then tells. About that night, that baby, that beautiful creation of her creation, her granddaughter . . . the cold . . . tobacco . . . "I returned her atman to brahman. I said it was a mistake. I said it should have decided to be a boy." She omits nothing, not even the eyes like twin fireflies; her telling creates the tale. "I did it," says Damini, looking around at everyone, "though I didn't want to."

Damini's story could be the story of other mothers, other baby girls, but Leela cries because it is her story, her mother's story, and her baby girl's tale. Leela tells Lord Golunath, "She did it for me, because I wanted it."

"No, Chunilal wanted it," Damini tells Lord Golunath, in Leela's defence. "He wouldn't even hold the baby. He would not give it his name."

Tubelight says, "Even I, who am not very bright, can read a man's wishes."

Chimta says, "Aren't you ashamed to tell this?"

"No," says Damini. "The time to be ashamed was when I was doing it."

Kamna says to all, "That night my papa sent me again to the cow's room to sleep, and he said he would beat me if I came out before morning—he knew what my nani would do. And," she says to Leela, "the next morning, he didn't cry."

Sister Anu wipes her eyes.

Mohan says, "Men don't cry," as if he understands he is defending his father.

"Of what use is this telling?" says Vijayanthi. "Which woman can do what she wants? The shysh-tem is like this only. We do what men want done."

A man responds, "Mata-ji, we too do what you women want done. You want a brick or cement home, you want a bit of land, you want grain in the storeroom, you want food and clothing for the children. We sacrifice for these. You blame us men for all your sorrows, but all must do our duty, regardless of consequences, as Lord Krishna told Lord Arjun in the *Gita*."

The women's side of the room erupts as each tries to respond. Chimta shouts loudest, "You men don't care if we suffer so long as you do your duty. That way *your* karma stays clean—but what of ours?"

Supari aims a stream of betel-juice at the corner of the room, wipes her mouth on the back of her hand and says, "The taste of anger never leaves me."

The room hushes.

Goldina says, "I'm the one everyone blames when babies die, because I cut their cords and dispose of the Lotus that comes afterwards. But it's not only you, Damini-ji, who does as a man wants. Kiran-ji too, knows what Aman-ji expects and does it—even if it stains her karma, even if another woman will be hurt, even if her own baby would be hurt."

Aman looks puzzled. Kiran becomes very interested in a photo of Lord Ganesh just above eye level.

Leela says, "All of us women do our dharma, regardless of consequences to our karma."

"Any other paaps?" Lord Golunath seems anxious to be gone—maybe because the ojha is gasping and his eyes rolling back. "Large ones?"

"I took women to the Jalawaaz clinic for ultra-soons, and if they were having baby girls, I would help them clean the babies out," says Damini. "I said the machine would now be the selector of souls."

"If they were having baby boys, did you help them have those baby boys cleaned out?"

"No."

"Then it's true, you forgot justice! Yet you call for me to give you justice? Tell me, what punya have you done?"

"Many meritorious deeds, from healing and teaching, to saving a child. But still I have many injustices to be ashamed of. My son broke down a mosque and burned a church," says Damini.

"Your son's karma is his own. He will find it difficult to balance such deeds in this life. But you can't help him, because you are not your son."

"But I *am*. Lord Krishna said in the *Gita* that if Lord Arjun killed, he didn't really kill anyone. He said all forms return to the formless. He said we are all one, we only think we are different."

"Huh!" says Lord Golunath. "After death, not now."

"Not now?"

"If you were all one, with no separation, you would have known what your son intended. But as it is, you couldn't have stopped him. Because you see, right now, you have one body, he has one body. That's two bodies—yes?"

"Yes," says Damini.

"Then you can't be your son while alive, only if you're dead. Are you dead?"

"No, but my son says all Hindus are one," says Damini. "And he says all Christians are one, and he says all Sikhs are one, and all Muslims are one. He says if one Christian does a crime, all Christians are guilty. He says if one Sikh does a crime, all Sikhs are guilty. He says if one Muslim does a crime, all Muslims are guilty."

"Ask him if he would like to stay in jail till he atones for every crime committed by all nine hundred and seventy million Hindus in the world. I can do that for him."

"No, no!" says Damini.

The possessed ojha is slumping as if about to pass from this world.

"Then you stop saying sorry for your son's deeds, and for anyone else's as well. Stop saying sorry for living. Live the life you have been given, and continue to do punya. Many good deeds and donations will be required to overcome what you did."

But Damini's outstretched arms implore Lord Golunath not to leave, "Golunath-ji, I cannot afford to donate more to your temple. And while some say it's unjust to clean out girls from the women, some of us say it is best for the family. So what is our dharma?"

"Do dharma with compassion," says Lord Golunath. "Think of the possible effects of your actions. Try and shape the future for better."

The ojha falls back, closes his eyes, and groans.

"Some say the future will be better if girls are cleaned out, some say the future will be better if they are not. How can we know?"

The ojha opens his eyes wide, as if he's seeing terrifying images.

"Whose future?" says Lord Golunath.

"Ours," says Damini.

"Don't you love your children equally?"

"We do love, of course we love," everyone nods and mutters.

"Not for what they do for you or will do for you, but as brahman formed in flesh," says Lord Golunath's voice.

The ojha claps his hands and trembles visibly. He writhes and twists and rolls from his waist. He runs his fingers through the rice, then over his hair.

"Of course, of course," the men nod at each other for reinforcement.

"Then why are you only cleaning out girls, not boys?" says Lord Golunath.

"Why should we clean out boys?" shouts a man from the back of the room. "That would be like taking a gift and flinging it down a well."

"If you worship me," the ojha booms in Lord Golunath's voice, "you must love each child, no matter which I send."

"*Hah!*" comes a shout from Supari's husband. "Then don't send us girls, don't send us cripples." He half-rises from his squat in excitement. "It's your fault if you send them—we can't love them. We're not gods, we're just men."

"*Haan!*" a great sigh of agreement passes through the men. "Golunath-ji, one girl, maybe two. But you're sending us too many girl children. It is unfair."

"Why?"

"We can't use girl children."

"But you do. They work, they earn. See this woman is living with her daughter."

"Visiting," says Damini, faintly.

"She made her daughter; why should she not live with her?" says the possessed ojha. "I send you both boys and girls to teach you to be fair, not only to provide for you in old age. I send them so you learn to be parents, and become good ancestors. Use? What use is the beauty of the sun or the moon or the grandeur of the Himalayas?"

"Girls cost more," says a voice from the men's side of the room.

"Do you make your sons work as hard?"

"No, ji, no!"

"Without girls, there would be no women, and without women you would not be born, and without women's shakti, you cannot survive. When a man can't farm, a woman steps in to do his work for him, but if a woman can't work, can you do her work? If your mother or wife or daughter falls sick, I see only one or two of you who can cook."

"I can make daal," says Mohan.

Every head on the men's side of the room swivels toward him.

"Only daal," Mohan says.

"The rest of you—if you have to go into the cookroom even for a minute you say, 'Too much smoke!' None of you can clean a baby's bottom, none of you can wash a chai glass."

"Yes, yes—this is very true," a few men agree.

One shouts, "Then what? These are women's dharma. And they do it so much better than we can."

The god says, "Anything you don't like doing, you call women's dharma."

Damini asks, "What is a woman's dharma if her husband refuses to name his girl child?"

"Her dharma is to protect her child," says the god. "Leela should have named her child herself. And if the child needed two names, Leela could have given her family name."

"*Hein!?*" the men shout. "What are we hearing?"

"Yes, hear this. A woman's family's name is just as good as a man's. If any man refuses to give his daughter his name, let a mother's name protect the child. Leela has shakti like you, all she needed was himmat. You, Damini, could have given her that courage. Instead of killing her creation, you could have changed the world for the better. Men have been telling you women how for lifetimes. Why didn't you, a woman, help even one woman ask why and, why not?"

A hush descends on the room. The ojha is still trembling. Tubelight's husband rises and places the first rupee offering on the rice, as if to say, This jagar is over.

But Damini still has questions, "What can a woman do if her son, her own creation, tears down mosques, churches or gurdwaras?" she says, a desperate edge in her voice. "Must a woman please her family, no matter what their expectations?"

The ojha's voice gains energy to embrace all, "Arey-oh, men of Gurkot! You have all forgotten women's shakti. You women as well. Re-dedicate yourself to Anamika Devi! Your goddess has the answers. She can show you the way to lightness, she can give you himmat. You cannot feel fear and courage in the same instant. Respect and embrace the goddess. Don't hide her in a cave! Bring her into your hearts!"

Men squat-walk forward, palms pressed together. Each man folds his hands and looks ardently at the ojha. The ojha marks each of their foreheads with a teeka, the blessing of Lord Golunath. Women hold out their sons, the ojha applies the ceremonial vermilion mark on the child's forehead.

Damini's third eye seems to have split the space between her brows.

Matki stares silently at the ojha, patting her son to sleep. Chimta is plaiting her daughter's hair. Tubelight's knitting needles flash in the lantern light. Supari's daughter is looking at her mother for guidance, Supari's eyes are fixed on her husband across the room.

The women can see what Damini sees. The men won't change. They'll receive teekas as marks of the god's favour and go home. After you get a teeka you don't get sick, whether you change your behavior or not. It's like an injection, which must be why injections are also called teekas.

Men's voices join in praise, "Jai Golunath-ji" but they don't say "Jai Anamika-ji," as well. The ojha's words have perished as soon as spoken. They chant as if stricken with sincerity. Oh, they are adept deceivers of the god, of all gods. Some are touching their foreheads to the ground, bottoms in the air before the presence of Lord Golunath, but any pair of ears can hear their unspoken thoughts and desires: that man in the corner is thinking of his pear tree. The one beside him is looking forward to his nightly beedi and swig of rum. They'll go home and beat their wives or children to feel more like men.

Someone must bring stree-shakti to a world pulsing with the energy of men. Someone must summon the right energy to bridge the gulf between human and divine.

Who can?

I can—I am electricity. I may be husbandless, I may be past childbearing, but I am still the rod that connects the living to jee. I was born to serve as the channel where divine ener-jee breaks through.

What was the incantation her mother-in-law spoke all those years ago? The mantra was a code established in advance, a call only the goddess can answer. What if Damini misremembers it? What if the goddess gives far more than Damini wishes? She could die as Piara Singh did—heart cracking open, unable to contain the divine force of the universe.

Come, Anamika Devi. Damini fine-tunes her ear to hear subtle vibrations. She breathes the mantra, talking to the goddess as to herself. *Come, goddess of the unborn, you who name the nameless—come!*

ANU

SISTER ANU'S BEEN SITTING CROSS-LEGGED NOW FOR over an hour, listening as Damini confesses, the horror of the deed overcoming her again. But confession cleanses, whatever form it takes.

Damini is talking to the ojha, and to Lord Golunath. There's no test to know if the ojha is speaking or Lord Golunath. Which is the human, which the divine?

Everyone seems to believe and know Lord Golunath is here. Have I become so Catholic I can't feel the presence of god in any other form but Christ?

Anyone in this room could report Damini to the SDM—who, she notes, has not been invited.

They won't, because there's enough guilt here to fill the jails of Jalawaaz and Shimla for several years.

Sister Anu will have to confess her presence at this ceremony to some new priest who probably won't understand. Bishop Tutu, orchestrating Truth and Reconciliation trials in South Africa at present, would endorse this event. But neither truth nor pretence will bring back the real victim. That child, that poor infant girl. What does it do for Leela, who may have struggled to forget her baby girl and now may have to begin the journey of mourning again?

Sister Anu's sit-bones hurt. Her salwar is ruched up on her shins. She should have worn socks. Damini said a jagar begins when it begins and will end when it ends. "Anything important should be done slowly," she said.

She is sitting between Damini and Leela, leaning back against the wall beneath the room's single window. Ostensibly so as to be close to her shoulder bag on the windowsill, but really to be near a source of air. This small room smelled of whitewash paint before thirty or forty steamy bodies crowded in.

On the men's side of the room, Amanjit Singh's bright lime turban stands out among the worn white turbans and dhotis of the farmers. He's sitting cross-legged as in the gurdwara, his gold watch shining on his wrist. Kiran has taken her seat as far away from Sister Anu as possible, and does not glance in her direction. She wears her usual expression of bored sophistication, as if doing everyone a favour by her presence. Did Damini's confession crack Kiran's cocoon of certainty?

God and goddess photos make a collage across each wall—just out of reach of a small girl sitting in her father's lap. A toddler crawls from his mother's embrace and stands shakily before the two musicians. The drumsticks of the nagara keep pace with Sister Anu's heartbeat—a mesmerizing rhythm. The second musician plucks at the single string of an ektara as he sings.

Not Sanskrit. Not Hindi. It's Pahari, the language of the mountain peoples. The ojha looks spent. Lord Golunath appears to have departed, now.

Beside her, Damini begins to sway to the music, hands making mudras, gestures like an actress in an old movie. Her shoulder moves. An elbow pokes into Sister Anu's arm.

Damini's head rolls from side to side. She crosses her arms over her breasts. Is Damini having a seizure? Sister Anu glances at Leela. Leela is watching her writhing mother with interest but no hint of panic. And apparently Damini is not in pain.

DAMINI

THE DRUMMING GROWS FASTER, LOUDER.

Damini's bones shift, her spine tingles and curves into the shape of a sitting cobra. One shoulder is rising, rolling back, then the other. She sways, nods, rocks back and forth and moans. Men's faces blur. Will the goddess answer her call?

Blood and spirit open to rhythm. The air vibrates with the billion vibrations that are rising within Damini. An electrifying charge fills the air, and a billion interconnections seem to happen. Damini can see past, present and future at once, as if watching a TV. She can smell them too, along with the spoor of every body in the room.

She is sitting, then standing. Mental and material energies merge. She is splitting.

Is this dying? Her self flows out. No, it's that split state she knew in pregnancy, a shifting inside of herself to make way for another, one who watches unseen.

The energy of reeti, commitments and connections revolves around her. She draws it in, takes in spirit, offers herself as the vortex of maximum energy, energy that impels her to speak. Faltering, strange sounds she does not recognize as her own.

First syllables, then words, then phrases—not her own, not her voice, not her speech, but a lost language from a time before time.

Damini's arms flail. She is shaking, trembling. She does not recognize the voices, but senses sound, intent and a white heat rising from her womb to energize all matter from the very smallest particle to the whole.

Who is it, who comes?

Blood beats at her temples, beats to the drumbeat all around, making connections for which as yet there are no names. The unseen is not asleep or simple, but demonically active. Familiar asuras snap inside her . . . demons with long fangs. Now outside, frothing. They seem to rake her flesh with blood-tipped talons. Unexplored angers,

angers swallowed and digested along with every fear she's ever given herself is incarnated in these hungry ghosts. And they in her. They have lived within Damini from the time Damini was first taught she didn't matter. They have sucked in every need Damini ever suppressed, every want that became Don't Want, every word she ever believed insignificant, every insult received. They swirl up from karma she has not expiated and orbit the room. They roar as they devour the present and the past. They command her breath, speak with her mouth, gesture with her arms. They will touch her future if she gives them power.

She opens herself to stree-shakti, and the asuras of fear subside.

She is receiving a new language now. Not an outer language like English, but a human, inner feeling-sense rising from beyon-sense, from all the knowing she already has. Its gestures are familiar, like that language she spoke with Mem-saab, which had no high and low, no he or she.

One voice is more insistent, struggling up from all the others. Someone laden with gifts is present, someone from a time of abundance. Her head is full and empty, all at once. She feels a great clarity and openness. Thinking, thought, any ideas she brought into this roomful of expectant people fly from her and recede as she allows her body to enact what she witnessed only once before.

Where does the voice come from? From a distance and from nearby. From above, from below ground. From air moving into a pair of ears, opening eyes, opening mouth, mouth so tightly closed.

Beings appear and move through her mind, move fast, too fast. One feels stronger than the rest—its shakti wants to utter itself through her. She's losing her grip on the present. The voice springs from no place ever known, till there's only this moment, ever expanding, ever collapsing and she is the rod bringing it, birthing the voice.

Damini feels a familiar wetness between her legs, and stands. Blood—she is bleeding from the cowrie-shaped place that no longer bleeds! This blood is Anamika Devi's, as she comes through that gateway to the world.

Damini points a finger at the cluster of men in the opposite corner. She clears her throat with a sound somewhere between a growl and a grumble. She's seeing the men, seeing them and the unseen at once. Who taught her to do this? No one. She is seeing visions in her head. And she is saying those visions, doing them.

Is she dying? If she dies now, is it natural or unnatural? By her own choice or by accident? If by accident, will she walk temporarily in the prêt-lok with Mem-saab, or become a sad ghost forever, like her mother?

She is becoming small, very small, like a speck swept away on a reed broom. She is swept away . . . she is amazed and delighted to be swept away. She encloses another being with glee, as she once enclosed Piara Singh, as she once enclosed her children. And delight is trance, and trance is between dreams and reality, between sanity and madness, between illusion and delusion. In trance, fantasy and truth are indistinguishable. In trance, seen and unseen come together. In trance, the strange and familiar collide and new forms come into being. If she were some other woman, some other medium, Anamika might speak differently, but in trance, Damini opens to infinite possibility, no longer steward of tradition but selector of traditions to expand the soul. Here the nameless can be given form, born equally from Damini's ignorance and understanding. In trance, Damini sees—then describes, does, and sings what she sees. What comes through her will answer a question, fill a gap in creation, and encourage more questions. Because trance is the ongoing euphoria of mind and body in tune with a spirit, the spirit, Anamika Devi's spirit. Damini is trembling, trembling but speaking—what is she saying?

For once, Damini cannot hear. She is too small.

ANU

DAMINI SPEAKS IN A HUGE DEEP VOICE. SISTER ANU recognizes a few words in Hindi, but most are in Pahari. Her eyes are half-closed, but this is not a state of consciousness or unconsciousness that Sister Anu has observed in any patient.

"Anamika Devi has arrived," Leela translates helpfully, joyfully in Sister Anu's ear.

It is possible that everyone's presence tonight—Aman's, Kiran's, her own—has changed Damini's consciousness as the observer affects an experiment. Perhaps the audience has caused a shift of consciousness from one plane to the next, much as Anu senses her own state changing in prayer. That mental energy can cause physical events and states can be proven just by lifting an arm, but this . . .

Damini rolls on the floor, shouting in Pahari. Leela lunges forward and picks at her mother's sari. She covers Damini's head, her bare midriff, trying to maintain her modesty. She rocks back on her ankles to translate for Sister Anu.

Now a high scolding voice—not-Damini's, not-Damini's—says Anamika Devi is angry.

"Why, why? Tell us, tell us, Anamika Devi," sing the musicians.

The drums are beating in Sister Anu's heart.

And all the men sing out yes, tell us, tell us what has angered you.

DAMINI

"MEN OF GURKOT! LISTEN TO ANAMIKA DEVI." DAMINI'S voice is huge, deep. Sensations flow through her, to the ground. "Lord Golunath has a full idol and a temple, and all I have is a cave. You think it's enough to worship my form as an earthen pot? Ha! You don't honour me."

"We do honour you," shouts a man wrapped in a blue Kullu-shawl.

"If you honoured me, you would honour my shakti everywhere. In your daughters, mothers, wives, and daughters-in-law—even women from other families, other castes, other villages."

"Even women belonging to other villages?" says a man puffing a beedi. "Why?"

"Because every woman is someone's daughter," says Damini, in the goddess's voice.

"This is true," the man laughs. "Some poor behen-chod was made poorer by her birth." He looks around, acknowledging snickers at the poor sister-fucker.

"A strange woman is also someone's sister, someone's mother, someone's grandmother—every girl and woman is sacred, not only me."

"Why are *you* complaining, Anamika-ji? You are anointed, you are worshipped. Why should we go worshipping every woman? When will we earn a living?"

"Don't listen to him, Anamika-ji," shouts the man in the blue shawl. "We are not all like him."

"Then why do you stop girls from coming, why do you only want sons?"

"What should we do?"

"See what I see," says the voice of Anamika Devi. She who names is describing, sending echoes far into the future to form pictures, speaking a world into being, the world that is here, and a world that will be only twenty years from now. She who describes is explaining a world in which men need to pay bride prices, where men will feel they must abduct women, because violence and competition will reign supreme, where sweetness, giving, sacrifice, nurturing and co-operation will have no place, where men will find themselves sharing a wife as in the days of the *Mahabharat*, sharing with their brothers and sons. She who explains is predicting, showing them a world twenty years from now, when men will trade ever younger girls to other families, just as cows and goats are traded.

"Our sons would never do such things, Anamika-ji," says Tubelight, setting aside her knitting. "Other men might do such things, not ours."

"I too said our men would never do such things," remarks the Toothless One, "but that was before Partition."

"I too said my brother would never do such things," says Leela. "But that was before he and a few others in this room burned down the Christians' church."

Some men try to look innocent, some pretend deafness and look away.

"I too said our Hindu brothers would never do such things," a low growl comes from Amanjit Singh, "but that was before 1984."

"Do you ever tell your sons no?" says the Anamika Devi voice. "Do you explain to them that women can feel? If you keep stopping girls from coming, you only hurt your sons." And she foretells war and more war, bloodshed and anger. "Because men," says the goddess, "pick fights like elephants in musth when they have no sweetness in their lives."

"Anamika-ji." The man with the beedi looks a little shaken. "I tell my daughters, You are the same as boys. I say this is the new age of barabari."

"Yes, you men have learned the talk," says the voice of Anamika Devi. "Girls are same as boys, women are the same as men. But I know you," she says, sighting down the line of her forefinger. The man gulps smoke into his lungs. "Your daughter's name is not painted alongside your son's at the door to your home. You tell people you have a son and a mistake, you tell her she is your burden and your duty, but that your son is a gift. When you die, will your daughter send you to the next life or will your son?"

"My s-son."

"And when your daughter-in-law Supari came to your home, you renamed her, though I, Anamika Devi, had already given her a name."

"It made her feel part of her new family, ji."

Supari grinds her teeth over her betel nuts.

"And is she?" says Anamika Devi. "Then why do her parents feel obliged to send you gifts all her life? If she is so much a part of your family, do your grandsons carry her name or only yours?"

The men begin to shout. "Show us men who do what you're asking!" yells one. "There are no fathers in the world who can be just between daughters and sons. Daughters are not sons, sons are not daughters. My daughter-in-law is better than a daughter, but no son-in-law can help me like a son. "

Another shouts, "Is there any father or mother in the world who does not need sons? I can't take from a daughter. A daughter can't leave her real family and tend to me in my old age. Will the government support me when I am old? Will you look after me when I am old? Ha!"

ANU

SISTER ANU CAN'T STAND SHOUTING MEN, SHE JUST can't . . . she has a flashing sensation of being somewhere else though her body is still functioning. She used to tune out Vikas that way.

Damini is writhing, thrashing, flailing, bending backwards into an extreme arch. She's transformed, unrecognizable. Is the goddess really speaking? Which voice is human, which voice is divine? How is Damini's experience different from Elijah's or Isaiah's or Ezekiel's? Or the Sufi Mansoor Al-Hallaj uttering "Anna al-haq" while in trance? How different can it be from Jesus's vision of the Holy Spirit descending like a dove? What if the heavenly voice, bath qol, the "daughter of sound" truly belongs to nameless Anamika?

In her possessed state, Damini is claiming the authority Jesus, the Buddha, godmen and gurus all claimed to effect changes in traditions. Well, why not?

Damini straightens and crosses to the men's side of the room. She moves along with jerking limbs till she arrives before Amanjit Singh. She circles his little island.

The drumming rises, as if echoing the heartbeat of the universe. Damini leans over and holds Aman, one hand at his heart, one at his back. She holds him this way and says, "Respect everyone." This is a new voice, a voice that bounces up and downhill as if Damini does not hear it. "Protect both daughters," says this voice, as if Damini is accustomed to giving orders, though gently. "And ask your wife why she needed to snatch from her lowly sister when the gods have given her so much."

She moves away, more graceful, swaying strangely at first, then dancing.

Kamna rises and joins her grandmother in her dance, as if the music is within, and each movement rises from some wellspring of shakti. Both seem to be dancing on another plane, linked by trance to a larger world, seeing another dimension. Kamna bends back as if opening her heart, swaying as if echoing the dances of leaves. Can anyone even call this dancing?

When she was near death, Sister Anu had the feeling her consciousness was seeking and linking to an unearthly power. If the bright warm light she had seen could be named god or Jesus—why not Anamika Devi? During her training when she tended patients in coma—Ganga-water couldn't release them from the trance state. Maybe when Pentecostals speak in tongues, they're speaking Hindi or Pahari, and English-speaking listeners just don't know? Physics and physicalism offer no further explanation of what is happening in this room.

But what if Damini's trance-state is mere self-hypnosis? Is Sister Anu's prayer and meditation self-delusion too?

What if a divine spirit really is speaking to Damini and through her? Why not to Anu, who has spent so many hours in prayer and yearning? Why not to Anu who so admires god's creation? Why not to Anu who came here to do the Work? Why can Anu not revisit the bright warm light just one more time? For all her sacrifices and prayers, god or gods or goddesses have all remained obstinately silent. So have Christ, the saints and angels.

DAMINI

DAMINI RETURNS WHERE SHE BEGAN, DROPS INTO LOTUS
position, eyes half-open, still in trance, as if a tree rooted in her yoni
rises to merge with her torso. She rolls her head from side to side
and sways. She can feel her veins and arteries fork and net beneath
her skin, her breasts, and within her arms. Her arms feel like
branches of the tree and her henna-red hair has come loose in a halo
of coiled springs.

She is up on the mountain where the spring begins, down at the
river, swaying on the rope-bridge, climbing the ghost-trail, descending it, gazing down at a baby girl who opens her eyes, gazing up to
the gods. She is inside the chapel before it burns, outside the chapel
as it burned—all places all spaces all times are hers because they are
Anamika's.

Fear demons claw and screech that Damini will remain forever
small, that there will be no going back now that she has been both
outside and inside the goddess. What if she has revealed too much
of her self? Anamika Devi lives in a place where Damini cannot. She
must wrench herself away—separate—cut her cord to Anamika, but
keep the stump growing from her solar chakra.

Fear brings thirst, and she's clawing upwards, reclaiming her own
body, her own voice.

"Water! Water!"

Tiny needles seem to prick her face—water. She smells her own
flesh, alive as never before.

"Leave, Anamika Devi!" shouts Matki. "Leave this woman, now!"
Cold water splashes over Damini's face, trickles down, tickles her neck.

Sister Anu is leaning over her, shaking her. Damini falls forward,
hitting her shoulder but feeling only distant pain. She lies there,
aware of legs and feet passing, devotees leaving, and the tumult of
argument in the next room.

Gentle arms are lifting her. Direction and balance return slowly.

Piara Singh's voice is in her right ear—did she feel a puff of air on her eyelids, almost as if he were breathing again? His diamond eyes glitter in the half-dark. His male energy complements her own, restoring her. Does his beloved presence mean she has done enough to balance the stain on her karma?

Tubelight is before her, bearing a tray of laddoos. Sister Anu takes one of the bright golden balls. "Eat," she says, and a laddoo comes toward Damini.

Damini bites into the laddoo. Saliva suddenly streams to meet the sweetness. Amazing, returning sweetness. Sweetness, always there, no longer inaccessible. Sweetness that calls to her own remembered sweetness. She turns to Piara Singh, to share the other half with him, but he is gone.

A turbaned man with a rolled black beard stands in the doorway, a woman in salwar-kameez silhouetted behind him. "*Dayan!*" he says.

Damini flinches from the malevolent power of the word. She doesn't care what Aman thinks of her, but if other men hear he thinks she's a witch, they could turn against her. It has happened to other women who learned to say what men should hear—some were paraded naked, some expelled from villages. She glances around. Sister Anu, Leela and Kiran have heard him, no one else.

"What happened, Aman-ji?" says Damini, in the bright tone she used when Aman and Timcu were unmarried. "Tell me, what did Anamika Devi say?"

"You don't know?" Amanjit comes close. Damini stares into those lychee-stone eyes. She drops her gaze and pulls the end of her sari over her head.

He can barely control himself. "Your Anamika Devi told each farmer to build a shrine on his farm."

"Then? That is good—like a gurdwara in each home."

"No it is not," Kiran says. "If each farmer builds a temple on his property, we can't buy their farms and build cottages. We can't tear down their temples."

"Legal—illegal—what does Anamika know of the law, Kiran-ji?" says Damini. Memory stirs—Anamika's voice saying the farmers of Gurkot shouldn't be loyal to Amanjit just because they were loyal to his father. There can be honour, said Anamika Devi, only from serving those who have honour. "If you buy their land, I'm sure you won't feel any pain when you demolish a shrine."

"I don't fear Anamika Devi," says Aman to his wife, "not at all." He clears his throat. "I'm not a Hindu—why would I fear her?"

"But if we demolished a single shrine to a Hindu goddess, the Development Authority would never allow us to construct a cottage or a villa in its place," Kiran says, "even if we offered crores of rupees. We could end up in jail, like Suresh is for destroying the church on our property. Oh, Damini- amma is very clever. She knows the authorities would never pardon a Sikh man as they have pardoned Hindus for the demolition of the Babri Masjid. Sikhs don't have as many votes."

Kiran has a point—Suresh was never caught or questioned by the police for his role in the demolition of the Babri Masjid. But a glow of satisfaction comes over Damini to think that Aman might be afraid to continue building his summer cottages, at least in Gurkot.

"Next time," Kiran almost spits at Damini, "tell people they don't have to build shrines."

"I don't know if the goddess will ever come through me again, Kiran-ji." Damini's tone is elaborately polite. "If she does, I will speak no more and no less than the goddess wants. But now that we know what Anamika Devi asked, I promise you her first shrine will be built on Leela's farm. Chunilal's atman is wandering in the prêt-lok, wandering the roads of the Himalayas—may a shrine to Anamika be his final stop."

Kiran tosses her black mane and flings her dupatta around her shoulders.

Amanjit Singh says, "How can we compete with the world when we have superstitious, backward people like you?"

Damini grins up at him. "English-speaking saabs like you will surely find a way."

Aman turns on his heel, almost bumping into Kiran, and they leave.

Leela approaches, a new respect and also trepidation written on her face, "Come, let's go, Mata-ji."

The night is as dark as if the whole world has been sucked back into Anamika's cave. But fireflies dance across the terraces, and a single light shines in Chunilal's old room, guiding Damini uphill as she leads Sister Anu, Leela, Kamna and Mohan home. Sister Anu has accepted Damini's invitation to share their roti and potato-pea curry without any saab attitude of bestowing a favour.

But after they have all washed hands and feet beneath the water pipe, Damini says, "You all go into the cookroom. I'll sit outside."

"Why?" says Kamna.

"I am unclean."

"You?" says Leela. She glances at Sister Anu and titters behind her hand.

"But you just washed," says Sister Anu.

"Yes, but tonight blood came again. I have not felt bleeding for years."

Sister Anu says, "If the goddess sent you your menses, how can you be unclean? And if you are unclean, then I will sit outside with you."

"Oh no, you're a guest. You go in."

"Not without you," Sister Anu says, a stubborn set to her chin.

"I'll stay outside too," says Kamna. She turns to Leela, "Ma-ji, you go in."

"Huh, I should cook all alone like a servant and give you all food outside?" says Leela. "No, you all prepare to sleep hungry tonight."

"Even Mohan?"

"No, I have to cook for him."

"But we're all hungry, Ma-ji!" says Kamna.

And so Damini steps over the threshold, into the kitchen.

Nothing shrivels, nothing dies. Leela checks the milk—it has not soured. It may later, but for now . . .

Sister Anu sits with them in the half-circle around the coal-stove, wiping her eyes in the smoke. "Your body and clothing seemed to glow all the way home," she says. "And your face is still . . . radiant. Do you know why you were chosen from all who were present?"

"You think Anamika Devi should have chosen an English-speaking woman, na? I think Anamika-ji said, 'Here is Damini, she has a pair of ears to listen, she has a pair of hands to work; I can use her.' Goddesses are like saab-log. They think like-that-like-that."

"I thought goddesses only visit other families, not ours," Leela says. She slaps a roti onto the hot iron tava.

"It runs in our family," says Damini. "But not by blood. I got it from your father's mother. Some things are passed down by spirit and example, too." She begins to chop onions to sweeten the daal.

She is not surprised Anamika's voice came through her—the mantra called her. But how did Mem-saab's voice and others she did not recognize come through her? And why? Is this what the goddess meant so long ago when she came in dream? "What comes through you changes you. What comes through you, creates you." How can she know if she has changed? The one who opens the gateway may not remain the same being as the one who has gazed through it.

"You really don't remember, or you were just saying that for Aman-ji?" says Leela.

"I was there," Damini says, searching for human language to describe what happened. "But I could only watch and wonder who was speaking. I had good bhagya that their ears opened."

"Yes, but were they hearing?" says Leela.

Damini sighs. "Whether it means we will treat our mothers, sisters, wives, daughters and granddaughters as if the goddess can come through her anytime, I don't know. Even if those who don't believe Anamika Devi spoke, would hesitate to disobey. Lord Golunath witnessed everything Anamika-ji showed us, and he is the god on the hill, the god men worship for justice. Lord Golunath said we should bring the goddess from her cave." That thought falls like a raindrop onto water, and an idea ripples through her. "But for that, we must make her a body."

"She already has her pot," says Leela. "And that," she nods at the pink poster which has found its way to a corner at the far end of the cook-room, "can be her image. I can put it in our shrine with all the other gods tomorrow. Or I can make her a special temple for her pot and this poster outside on the terrace. Why does she need a body as well?" She reaches for a potato from a sack beside her and begins to peel.

"A carving will tell her how we are now, and what she is for us," says Damini.

"She can see how we are," says Leela. "She knows what she is for us." She looks at Sister Anu for support. "A carving is expensive. I sold the chickens a few days ago, and soon we may have to sell a cow."

"Maybe," Sister Anu says in soothing tones, "she has no form. Maybe she's just energy." Jade-coloured peas spring from their shells into the aluminium bowl in her lap.

"Oh no," says Damini. "If all her forms disappear, she'll be as dead as the spirits. Then who will name and protect us—you saw the world she showed us, the world that is to come if all women's shakti disappears."

"She is everywhere," Leela says, "but her jee must be in that poster. Because she doesn't look like me at all—she's laughing."

"Then I hope one day you'll be like her," says Damini. "But Anamika Devi is not only for us, she's also for men. And men will not see us as we are if they only worship the poster picture. Look how they worship Rekha and Madhuri Dixit in filums, but not the women beside them. It's not only men today—Lord Ram preferred to worship a clod of earth instead of Sita Mata. This is the problem:

men have to be told everything and then shown it again. I say Anamika must have a carving."

Kamna places a pea against her middle finger, draws the finger back and lets fly as if playing marbles. "We should tell Samuel what we want and he'll carve it," she says.

"That's a wonderful idea," Sister Anu says. "He certainly needs the money."

"No money," says Damini. "We'll pay in potatoes, and in peaches next spring. Samuel may do it, or he may not. Anamika Devi did not help him when he suffered, and neither did his Jesus-god. We must ask gently. I'll tell him that if we make no difference between sons and daughters, men and women, Anamika Devi can bring Lord Golunath's ener-jee into the world."

Leela bites her lip. A firefly dances into the room, and circles her at shoulder level. "Real justice?" she says.

Damini nods. The promise will be almost too daunting to speak, and the sweeper could take it far beyond her meaning. He might think all those ordained low can have bhagya like the twice-born.

But if there can one day be justice for girls, there can also be justice for Samuel and Goldina.

"Father Pashan would tell us to work for justice," Sister Anu says fervently. "He too would say we must make no difference between high and low."

Damini looks out at the ridges of the mountains, at the clouds folded between.

There are differences. Sister Anu has lost her clinic but already her employer has another job for her in Shimla. And she has a living husband—what kind of husband is just her bhagya—who may still take her in. Women like her from the city—Hindu, educated, speaking English—always have somewhere to go.

Shimla
November 1996

ANU

A MARIGOLD MAKES A BRIGHT ORANGE SPLASH ACROSS the putty base of Imaculata's computer monitor—placed by the convent's computer technician to propitiate the unseen. He must have exorcised the latest viruses and replenished the daily offering of backup disks, too. The computer file structures are much like the Church's hierarchies, and its inner mechanisms seem governed by a much faster version of Canon Law. Sister Anu opens Netscape and touch-types as if playing a piano.

I refuse to excuse Hindu Nationalists as Sister Imaculata does, simply labelling them evil. Individuals did these crimes, not satan. Each man made his own decision to join in the violence or not. Oh dear! I should believe in satan but instead I have come to believe we each harbour evil within us, and feed it our self-interest and fear.

The Jesuits will be sending a new priest for the parish, but till then Imaculata is leading prayer meetings. She is encouraging people to sing hymns in Hindi and has allowed the harmonium to be brought in— Indianizing the service. Many more are coming to the chapel.

Thank you for the photographs from Halloween. It was strange to see Chetna dressed in a habit. Tell her nuns in our order don't wear those in India! You looked very beautiful in your wedding sari and jewellery, and

Jatin in that brocade uchkan-jacket.

I am learning to grow hydrangeas for Sister Imaculata, playing the piano on Sundays in the chapel and teaching Human Biology to privileged young girls. Even girls of our class and caste know so little about their own bodies! I admit they remind me of Chetna, and that is its own joy and pain.

Dr. Gupta has accepted a position at a private clinic in New Delhi. Amanjit-ji's elder brother came from Canada and built it around the time Amanjit-ji built the Gurkot clinic, just to rile his brother, and now he's hired Dr. Gupta just to rile Amanjit-ji more. The two brothers are still in court, fighting over their mother's mansion. Kiran tells me the case will drag on for at least thirty years. But Dr. Gupta says it will probably finish in twenty because daughters will not have the stomach to fight in court and bribe where needed. I feel sure Kiran will teach Loveleen and her baby sister Angad to prove him wrong. And maybe one will marry a man who can continue the court battle.

No stamps required—email is making stamps obsolete. Rare stamps in Dadu's collection are turning even more rare. Sister Anu points the cursor at SEND, and clicks her mouse-button, staccato.

December 1996

ANU

AFTER EVENING PRAYERS AND DINNER, SISTER IMACULATA draws a Tibetan shawl over her knees and pulls her rocking chair close to the fire in the nuns' recreation room. Sister Anu leaves the others gathered around a game of dominoes and takes a chair beside her. The scent of pine from the red and green tinselled tree in the corner mingles with the deodar wood burning in the grate.

"Are you all right, Sister?" Sister Anu had read the bishop's letter when it fell from Imaculata's hands a week ago: he said he endorsed her prayer meetings and applauded her service and zeal during the temporary absence of a priest but reminded her that no nun should lead a congregation to believe that transubstantiation had indeed happened by her hand. "The wafer and wine do not become the body and blood of Christ by the hand of anyone but an ordained priest." In effect, he says Imaculata has committed fraud, and this led "inevitably" to excommunication. Sister Imaculata is barred from receiving the sacraments and participating in worship, but can continue as lay principal of the convent.

"I haven't lived in India all these years," Imaculata replies, "without learning worse things can happen." Her chair creaks with grim regularity.

"But it's truly unfair, Sister!"

Church tradition is a stream in progress, just as Sister Imaculata said to Anu only two years ago. It changes direction in its own time. But . . .

"The bishop holds the Church and its reputation above the individual," says Imaculata. "It's our fault—we turned our Pope and his priests into gods."

"How can they justify it to themselves?"

"Jesus," says Sister Imaculata, "never said only men can be priests. There aren't even any women chancellors in the dioceses—it's mostly men listening to men. We've let them believe they're infallible."

"I have organized a petition to the bishop on your behalf," says Sister Anu. "Sister Clare is the only nun who refused to sign it."

"Yes, and all this week she has taken her meals at another table," says Imaculata. "The others are disobeying the bishop, I think, since they're not shunning me. They were at my prayer meetings. They know I didn't, I would never . . ."

She falls silent.

"Is it true about your visa?" says Sister Anu. The news flew through the convent today: the Indian government, pressured by the anti-missionary rhetoric of the RSS and its Hindutva organizations, has refused Sister Imaculata's application for extension of her Indian visa. And since VIPs with enough clout to override the refusal have discharged Sister Imaculata from their tribe, sympathy is now all the Shimla congregation can offer.

"'Tis so, yes. I must learn to live in Ireland again. That will be strange after all these years here. I was looking forward to meeting my old colleagues in one of our nun's retirement homes someday. But I can't now."

"Oh dear Sister . . . I wish . . . I mean, I want...How will you live?"

"I thought of renting from one of my brothers. He had a modest two-up, two-down before Ireland became the Celtic Tiger. But it's now valued at more than a million pounds, and he values himself accordingly. I wrote to one of my nieces to see if I could stay in her bed-sit, and she replied today by email. 'Oh, yes,' she said, 'and please could you teach me all about Hinduism?' I don't know anything about Hinduism. What can I teach her? So – I'll have to see."

Will what Anu is going to do add to Sister Imaculata's troubles— or help? "May I read you a letter?"

Imaculata nods. Sister Anu clears her throat, clears it again. In a low, even tone, she reads a letter asking permission to leave before taking her final vows.

In solidarity with Imaculata, she is refusing to serve VIPs' and VVIPs' children any longer, refusing to pontificate about social justice from within the luxury of the convent. But this is not in her letter. If it were, the sister would simply tell her to go and work with Mother Teresa.

And the lines on the page do not say that if the divine appeared to the ojha and Damini, Sister Anu's service and prayer have been irrelevant. They do not say that the bright warm light she saw only a few years ago now seems unattainable, though she has sometimes experienced flashes of connection when she plays the piano. They do not say Sister Anu has been unable to give up her belief in reincarnation and worse, she among all the nuns cannot believe Christ is the only god, the only way.

The lines on the page do not say she must also be the one nun in this order who cannot, does not, believe in heaven and hell because she has seen the hells men make on earth. They do not say she believes that dogs, cats, crows and rats have souls because she knows at least one man, maybe two, who will surely be reborn as animals. And the lines on the page make it no longer necessary to confess her lie or acknowledge she is still married to a man who will be reborn as an ant.

But she knows Imaculata will feel all of this in her voice, her disobedient voice. And when Anu is finished, the older woman is silent a long time. Then she says, "You want permission to leave. Have you prayed about this?"

"Yes, sister." Sister Anu prayed as Amanjit Singh registered a criminal case against Suresh and other rioters. But witnesses are fast disappearing, the SDM has been mysteriously transferred and after only one hearing, one of the judges as well. And between prayers, Sister Anu found herself railing at god.

If you care so much about Christians, to the exclusion of all others, why couldn't you divert a .22 Diana airgun bullet one centimetre to keep your loyal servant alive?

Imaculata and other people of the cloth seem to remember Father Pashan as a soldier who fell in the line of duty. His name is rarely mentioned and prayer has done nothing to bring him back.

Sister Imaculata's anger surges at Anu. "And even after prayer and meditation, you want to send this letter to other provincials and Mother General?"

"Yes, sister."

"Didn't you tell me you were a very adjustable woman?"

"Yes, I did, Sister. But how much should we have to adjust? Can't the Church do some adjustment as well? Look how they are treating you after all your years of service."

Imaculata bites her lip as if holding back a flood. "Don't you be making me your excuse for leaving, Sister. God will provide for me." In a moment, she says, "I had such high hopes of you, Anupam. I thought, 'A young Indian nun. If only we can keep her.' Silly of me, I know, because I always knew you had that little problem: disobedience. Still, I hoped you would grow into my role and take care of our sisters."

"I've been a failure as a woman, a wife, a mother and now a nun," says Sister Anu.

"I wouldn't say that. You have made progress."

"I've disappointed you."

"In some ways—not all," Imaculata says. "So many are attracted by the security we offer—well, used to offer. I just thought you were different."

"I was attracted by security too," says Sister Anu.

A snort of derision. "Shafiq Sheikh said you risked your life trying to save people in the clinic."

Sister Anu gazes into the smouldering fire. "So did he."

"You miss Father Pashan—is that it?"

"Yes." Living without men also distorts the world.

"Did you have feelings for him?"

"Not that way," says Sister Anu, meeting Imaculata's eye. "He made me realize it's possible for a man and woman to be friends. I admired him. I thought everyone would admire all the work we were doing, what he was trying to accomplish. "

"'Tis a shame, my girl." Sister Imaculata sighs. "I regret I never told him how much I admired him. I would have loved to have a wake for him, to celebrate his life, you know. But right now, a wake could be considered a foreign ritual." Her hand covers a tremor in her lips for a moment. Anu's throat constricts in sympathy.

Imaculata fixes her gaze on the gold ring on her left hand, masters herself. "We'll never know what those Hindu men thought they were accomplishing, or for whom. But reconsider, Sister. Surely you're needed once the clinic in Gurkot reopens?"

"I'm no longer the right person for it," says Sister Anu. "I fear I will recommend birth control pills to women like Goldina. I now feel abortion should be available to women who need it because of rape or any other reason. I think a woman must own her own body all the way to the moment a child takes its first breath and gains consciousness at birth. And I believe Damini's daughter, Leela, should have been able to get an early abortion even though I could not have brought myself to have one."

"You certainly have been brainwashed by family planning propagandists."

"Oh, and one more thing. I never want to refuse care to a patient, even one who may have AIDS."

"Not to worry. You've just disqualified yourself from a job with us."

Anu pushes a lock of hair away from her eyes. "Sister Bethany is also an Indian nun—did you consider her as your successor?"

"She doesn't have leadership ability," says Sister Imaculata.

"Bethany? *Bethany* doesn't have leadership qualities?" Anu says. She waits.

"I see I've learned Indian ways too well," says Imaculata.

Sister Anu says quickly, to rescue the older woman from embarrassment, "I asked the project leader of the NGO taking over the clinic how he would fund his work. He said, 'With the x-ray machine.' He said, 'People in Canada and the USA will send their x-rays by email and our doctor will interpret them and send them back the next day.' And he says they have a training programme for young hill women to become nurses and midwives." Maybe that will persuade Amanjit-ji to keep the free clinic going for a few years.

"But do you really believe dalits, tribals and other backward caste people don't need us?"

Sister Anu shakes her head. "There's always more we can do, more we should do. They need the support of touchables of all religions. They need people of conscience worldwide to come together against caste, as people did against slavery and apartheid."

"You don't say."

"We should care as much for the treatment of their bodies and rights, as we do for their souls."

"I admire your passion, Sister." Sister Imaculata says. "Tell me, did we bring any souls to Jesus?"

"Father Pashan said belief is personal. He just wanted to alleviate suffering and set a good example. But it's progress that some women have begun to speak about domestic violence, and sexually transmitted diseases. That we vaccinated children, discussed sex and menstrual problems. Damini is starting a Women's Survival Society—members have to promise before the goddess not to kill, beat, sell or neglect baby girls, girls and women."

"The goddess, is it? Can't even keep the first commandment—no god but god. All that work . . ." Imaculata digs in her toes, her rocker creaks back. "Well, do as the good Lord tells you." Her tone consigns Sister Anu to the devil. "It is not for me to question his ways."

Sister Anu rises and stokes the fire. What kind of god sacrifices his beloved son and then, once the son has saved the world, sacrifices more good people, beloved as Father Pashan? Why did god or Pashan need to reenact any part of Christ's story? Does it not make Christ's death and resurrection pointless? She resumes her seat.

"So you're returning to Hinduism?"

Returning would only be necessary if she had left it. "It's possible that praying to thirty-three crores of gods might bring me closer to infinity than praying to one, but I haven't decided."

"You need a role, Sister. You had a role here with us."

Anu says, "I can either sidestep through life as a daughter, sister, wife, mother or nun or seek my true self. I can't wait till I'm fifty or sixty before I really begin my life. I should choose its shape and form. It shouldn't be something that just happens to me."

Shadows leap and dance across Sister Imaculata's face. Her expression hardens.

"Go back, then. Retrogress to your temples, your idol-worship, your low-or-high-caste ways. Whatever it is you Hindus do."

"Sister, don't say that . . ."

"Then what should I say?"

"Talk to me in your own words, with your own feelings. As if we were just two women."

"Just be a woman, you say? All right, say then—what might you be needing from me?"

"Your blessing—or at least your good will. I can't take my final vows, but I still cherish your friendship. Maybe I have to seek god in new ways, my own way. I must venture out, even if it is difficult. But I am not someone who returns the same way I came. I want to be open to transformation. The world may be all illusion, as the vedas and shastras say, but it's the only one I have." She feels no bravado as she says this, but no shrinking either. "Then maybe I'll feel the deep connection that I seek."

Sister Imaculata seems to master her anger with an effort. "Venture out, then. Venture forth. No one is stopping you."

Sister Anu stretches her arms toward the fire and makes another try. "I want independence and self-direction, Sister. And I don't doubt our Lord can provide them."

"Independence is over-rated, Sister. Obtain it, and you'll trade it away before the cock crows. We create interdependence in life—why not decide to value what you have?"

"If I do trade my independence again, it will be my decision, not that of the Church."

"You'll see, we all need redeeming in our own way, Sister. For our sins."

"We should be responsible for our own sins, rather than foisting them on poor Jesus. Why is he our whipping boy?"

"Hush! You can only ascend to heaven through him—don't you see that, my dear? On the day of judgement, won't it be better to have served Christ, than not?"

"If god is as great as I believe, he will see through such pretences. He'll give me credit for the courage not to depend on the Church's explanations." Anu takes the rosary Imaculata gave her at graduation from her pocket. She holds it out.

Recognition dawns on Imaculata's face. She slowly draws it from Sister Anu's hand. "To love god is to give oneself utterly, Anu. If you cannot do that, then I agree you should leave. Christ can exist without you. The question is can you exist without Christ?"

"I don't intend to. I am a better person when I try to follow Christ's example. I feel I have become more charitable, more accepting of people who are different from me. I can truly say I will still be a Catholic, just with a small 'c.'"

Sister Imaculata stands and stokes the embers. "Huh, small c!" she says. "No such thing. Leave the Church, Sister. Why wait for permission? We're not a cult that will threaten you or try to stop you. Walk out tomorrow, as I've seen a few nuns do. But don't suppose," she taps her forefinger to her temple, "that the Church will ever leave you."

DAMINI

DAMINI, LEELA, KAMNA, SUPARI, MATKI, TUBELIGHT, Goldina and at least twenty other married women ranging from fifteen to eighty years or more, are seated on dhurries spread before Anamika Devi's pot form. The Toothless One is still grumbling about the walk uphill, then down the ghost-trail, (though her daughters-in-law nearly slipped down the mountain as they half-carried her). Chimta and her mother-in-law sneak in, having told their husbands they are collecting firewood.

Flickering diya lights throw shadows on the rocks, a couple of bats sway and stir above Goldina's kerchiefed head. In order for Goldina and other outcastes to participate, this meeting couldn't be held at Tubelight, Chimta, Matki or Supari's home. And if Damini held it at Leela's home, these women would have expected to sit on chairs and Goldina to crouch beside them. But in Anamika Devi's cave everyone must sit on the ground before the goddess. Just entering the cave turns Damini hot and cold, and her mouth dry as Thar Desert sands, but she is determined to carry out the goddess's wishes, bring her out of this cave and honour her shakti.

After they have sprinkled Ganges-water, sung a few bhajan-songs, and made offerings and performed aarti, Mohan looks around, "Where are the other boys?"

Damini explains, "Only men who promise not to kill or beat their daughters, sisters or wives can be in the Women's Survival Society. And since you have not beaten anyone . . ." Mohan seems to have forgotten killing a man by mistake, and it seems kinder to keep it so.

"He's not getting married," says Kamna. "So he can't beat a wife. Neither am I—"

"Why not?" says Tubelight.

"So I won't beat a husband." Everyone laughs and Kamna looks surprised. She was serious.

"Bhaino," Damini interrupts, calling them sisters, "In our first meeting, we must decide how to show Anamika Devi's unforeseeable nature. It's a very small step, but we know it takes small steps to climb a mountain. We could decorate this cave to please Anamika Devi, but Lord Golunath and the goddess have asked us—no, told us—to bring her into the open. And because her form has somehow effaced itself from our hearts, she must be given a body. I have asked you here to say what you want, and decide these matters."

"Yes," says Tubelight. "She wants to be something other than her pot—she should have a face and a true name."

Several women are nodding.

"How many arms should Anamika Devi have?" asks Damini.

"Oh, at least ten," says Leela. "She works all the time, just as we do."

"Das-angulum!" says Chimta. "Even Durga Devi usually has only eight."

"Ten," says Goldina firmly.

Damini asks what should Anamika Devi hold in each of her hands?

"In one, she should hold a conch shell to call all women to her side," says Supari.

"No, a cowrie shell, to show what we have in common," says Tubelight.

Matki raps Tubelight on the arm, and pulls her dupatta across her embarrassed giggles. "The conch, because her spring gives us water."

"Should she wear a mangalsutra?" asks Damini, suddenly anxious. If Anamika Devi receives a wedding collar, how will she speak through a widow?

"No," says Supari. "She's always been untamed by marriage. If she marries, her husband should wear a collar to keep *him* faithful." She grinds her betelnuts.

"And if she's a widow, she doesn't need one," says the Toothless One, pointing to her own bare neck, then Leela's and Damini's.

"A big spoon," says Tubelight.

"Because she cooks for the family?" says Damini.

"No, to spank her children if they need it."

"Not the boys," says Chimta.

"Yes, boys also," says Damini.

"For that, she'll need a very thick slipper," sighs Chimta.

"Maybe a pair of boots," says Damini. "Because she walks beside us—she doesn't have a car. And she's like an unknown soldier, since we don't know her caste."

"Every woman can't wear combat boots," says Tubelight. "Don't think she's just like you. How long can you survive in the mountains if you make enemies of the snow leopards?"

"A broom," says Goldina. "Definitely a long broom. And a small one as well."

After a short silence, the women around the circle nod agreement.

"I can give my umbrella to protect her statue," says Damini.

"No umbrella," says Goldina. "Only you women carry umbrellas."

"She still needs a pot," says Matki. "So boys and men remember where they come from."

"Give her a leaf of madhupatra," says Damini. "She has natural sweetness."

"She needs bangles on all her arms," says Kamna, jingling her own. "And a book, because she wants us to read."

"She needs a drum." says Supari. "To drum us into existence."

"Or at least to drum you awake," says Matki.

"Can she have a cow? She has to look after them."

"How can she carry a cow in her hand? They call you Tubelight because you're so-o bright!" says Chimta. "And she has to take care of brothers, fathers, husbands, mothers-in-law, fathers-in-law, sons, daughters, grandchildren, not only cows."

"She needs a sword," says Damini. "To show she can rise above the rank of major." Major being the highest rank allowed to women warriors in the Indian Army.

"No sword," says Goldina. "A sword means she's for warrior caste women only. Her war is here. She needs a sickle to cut twigs in the forest."

"Yes, a sickle, " says Damini. "That only makes nine."

"One hand should be empty," says Kamna. "It's reaching for a husband's hand."

"Empty so that she can reach for whatever she wants, then," says Tubelight.

"Oh-no-no-no!" says Chimta. "She's reaching for her husband's tail!"

"Achcha," says Damini when the laughter has died down. "Now what shall we name her?"

"What is wrong with Anamika Devi?"

"Nothing, but it means we have not named her."

"No, it means she is without name," says Supari. "She names us, she named the gods—how can *we* name her?"

"All this time, nameless, has anyone paid her attention? We put her in a cave and left her there, gave her a rupee once in a while."

"I've been given so many names," says the Toothless One. "Never liked any of them. I say call her a beautiful name or none at all."

"Yes, she should have a real name," says Chimta.

"Do you have a real name?" says Kamna.

"Of course. But if someone called me by it, maybe I would answer, maybe not. I don't even remember it. How does it matter what I'm called?"

"It matters," says Kamna. "So everyone knows your story will be different from your sisters', mother's, and grandmother's."

And so the ideas and arguments for Anamika Devi's name last till sundown, and begin again the next day when the women meet in the jungle to hack and gather firewood. Suggestions are shouted from terrace to terrace as they water beans, potatoes and onions in the gold light of mid-morning.

Damini hears Goldina shouting, "Calling Anamika Devi by some new name will do nothing. First, we should change our actions. If she wants a new name, let her name herself. But let the word for the goddess remain, and other goddesses—forgotten or to come—can call themselves Anamika."

Damini feels an inner smile. Agreement is desirable but not required. If the Women's Survival Society of Gurkot cannot find a new name for Anamika Devi, she who names the gods can remain anonymous.

March 1997

DAMINI

IT TAKES A MONTH, DAMINI TELLS HERSELF, ONLY because important work should be done slowly, and it is after the Holi festival by the time Samuel finishes carving the ten-armed goddess. On Anamika Mukti Divas, the day the goddess will be freed, Damini leads the men and women of Gurkot to the cave.

Anamika Devi is brought out—how beautiful yet fragile is her pot. Mohan and Kamna hold it up so everyone can admire its roundness, its fullness, the specks and tints in its gradations of brownness. Damini keeps her gaze on its wide mouth and curving wholeness as the procession sets forth uphill, the goddess's pot riding in a sari-sling on the shoulders of Mohan, Kamna, Leela—and Goldina. Shocked expressions, and whispers—*khuss-puss, khuss-puss*—break out at Goldina's temerity. A few sarcastic barbs are launched till Damini says, "The goddess doesn't object, why do you?"

Up the ghost-trail they climb, the pot swinging between them, then downhill to Leela's home, heading for the peach trees on the lower terrace, near the cow's room. The pot goddess is set down gently, beside her new ten-armed form and before the pink poster. Leela sinks to her haunches beside the little mound at the edge of the terrace.

The pujari does a puja of Anamika in pot, poster and sculpted forms, to show equal respect. He paints beautiful half-open eyes on

483

the stone goddess, and does another simple ceremony to waken her. The women break into song, Kamna enters the circle and twirls and sways, glass bangles chinking for joy—Anamika's subterranean existence is ended.

But before the pujari can sweep everyone's donations into his knapsack, Damini leans forward and hands him fifty rupees instead for his service. "From now on, I am her pujari," she says.

The pujari and all the men and women gathered around seem amazed by her audacity—Damini is amazed by her audacity. She knows everyone is thinking, It's bad luck for family members if a widow performs puja. They are thinking, She is doing someone else's dharma, and that is never good. They are thinking, Who does Damini think she is?

But Anamika Devi came through Damini and no one else. No one can object or challenge her.

No one objects or challenges her.

So this will be her new role in the movie of her life.

But how should she worship Anamika? Damini enters trance, consults Anamika and receives the answer: *What has a Name exists; I claim all who are named.*

Name those Nameless who emerge from you. I will give you boys' names, I will give you girls' names. Sometimes I will say names you can use for boys or girls. I will give you new names you cannot say are Hindu, Muslim, Sikh or Christian. If a father refuses his, I will send you new family names and my blessings to any mother who bestows her family's name upon her child.

Worship the Name.

Because the Name can be said—and if not said, then written, sung and danced. What is said and written, sung and danced alters everything, so powerful is the nature of the Name.

A few days later, Leela directs Mohan to put a few planks over the unfinished feeding trough, to make a speaking platform for Damini. She expects her mother to see visions of the future, exorcise demons, foretell world events and heal by touch. Damini ascends the platform, and tries and tries. But the only vision that comes is for Goldina, because Goldina told Damini she and Samuel will be travelling south across the baking plains to Nagpur. There they'll attend a commemoration rally for the conversion to Buddhism of Dr. Ambedkar, the same who wrote Goldina's treasured book, *The Buddha and His Dhamma*. Damini predicts Goldina and Samuel will leave Jesus and the idols he carves to take the 22 vows and turn to the Middle Way. It may take Samuel years but he will overcome the belief that his conditions were ordained by the karma from his previous lives. He and Goldina will be called by Navayana Buddhist names—for a while. And she predicts they will move to a large city where sweepers get second chances and can rise above sweeping. There, Samuel will carve his name on his work and be called a sculptor, and be feted by those who can see past his bloodline.

Damini sees them standing before the flame of the unknown, unnamed soldier, and then at Vijay Chowk, the intersection where the Dancing Policeman dances. The pillared domes of the Presidential Palace and the two Houses of Parliament stand behind them. In her vision, the Dancing Policeman points forward—Go. And because "Chal Chal Chal Mere Haathi, Oh Mere Saathi" plays in her head, she is sure Samuel will become famous in all of Delhi, then Mumbai, then Kolkata and beyond for sculpting triumphal statues of Dr. Ambedkar for dalits to worship. And that Samuel's patron will lead the new party for dalits and other backward castes, the party with the elephant symbol. And his patron will use money and donations from the poorest to build Samuel's statues of Dr. Ambedkar before addressing the hunger of her constituents. Damini cannot say how she knows this but she does, that Samuel will return to Gurkot to buy one of Amanjit Singh's villas, and no one will call him lowborn then.

"When?" says Leela.

"A few years before his atman recombines with the souls of others."

"If it recombines with yours or mine, how will it carry his bad karma to the next life?"

"If it can't, it won't. Anamika Devi says this is how Buddha brings justice, each person starting out clean as soon as he comes into the world."

"Achcha, never mind Samuel and Goldina, can't you foretell what will happen to your own granddaughter?" Leela sounds exasperated.

"No," says Damini, "I'm no astrologer who tells people only what they want to hear. We don't know the future, so that we'll work to shape it. My trances should help women any time, not only when they have a baby. They should tell their stories to their fathers, brothers, husbands, sons-in-law and sons. Men—and even some of us—will be surprised that we have stories. Then maybe they'll see we are not cows just because we make children and milk, or dolls they can dress up and hit, or children for whom everything must be done, but insaan." She repeats it in English for emphasis. "Peepals!"

"What if no men come to listen?"

"Then I will be a pair of ears, listening to women's questions. And I will ask the goddess to answer in her voice, in other women's voices, and in my own. And we will tell our stories to each other. In the end, our stories, not our children, are the only creation we possess in this life."

Other than this one additional faculty, this one special endowment, the goddess has given her no further gifts. Damini cannot cure boils, barrenness, snakebites or the burdens of family expectations. She cannot lighten the weight of family honour that drives men and women to insanity. She cannot exorcise anger asuras—it will be difficult enough for her to manage her own demons.

Leela is disappointed. But truth is often disappointing—and sometimes cruel, and often ugly—but still a beginning.

"Will I ever find Kamna a match? Where will I find a dowry for her?" says Leela.

Kamna comes before them, her hands fisted as if ready to fight. Looking beyond her grandmother and mother, gazing at the roads etched on the far mountains, she says, "Don't worry about arranging a husband or a dowry for me—I'm going to drive Papa's truck."

"Huh! A girl doing bijness?" says Leela.

"I can," says Kamna. "If Papa were alive, I would drive with him."

"I know who has taught you driving, and she is a good driver of cars . . . But this is a truck."

"I can do it," says Kamna.

"You need to know all the roads and maps," says Leela.

"I learned when Papa was teaching Mohan."

"But you can't drive alone," says Damini. "And that truck is old."

"Mohan can come with me," says Kamna. "He can change a truck tire. He can do easy repairs." Her excitement is contagious and she will not be dissuaded.

And having recently broken from the known and taken her own steps in the direction of the unknown, Damini cannot chastise her granddaughter. To Leela she says, "Kamna should make her own story, a story different from yours and mine."

"We'll come home often," Kamna says to Leela. "We'll take you to see New Delhi, Ma-ji."

After hours of remonstrating, Leela throws her sari-pallu in the air and says, "Go, then, but don't come home crying every time you break a bangle."

PART VI

It's a boy!

Pre-arranged message from Trinity Site, New Mexico,
to President Truman, July 18, 1945

September 5, 1997

ANU

The air smells green and cool the day Sharad Uncle comes for Anu in his new white Contessa. He drove eleven hours yesterday, eleven hours on cratered roads and switchbacks, stayed the night at a "luxury three-star" hotel on the Mall Road in Shimla and is ready today to drive another eleven hours to take her back to New Delhi. She should be grateful.

But now that it really is time to leave, memories of the last few months—of accompanying the all-Hindi choir in the chapel; helping the NGO personnel navigate the bureaucracy and reopen the clinic; of working with Damini at the Women's Survival Society; of helping Bethany prepare legal information camps and hold subtitled movie nights to help adults learn to read—all tug at her heart. And this sunny morning, Sister Imaculata shook hands rather than embraced her in farewell after her last meal in the refectory.

Sharad Uncle has retired from the bank with a "decent" Provident Fund. The hair that scuffs his collar is thinned, and salted with unruly strands of white. "Your salwar is too baggy," he says, after greetings. "Your kameez looks as if it's from the eighties." He crushes Sister Imaculata's mauve hydrangeas as he reverses. With a great crunch, he gears forward, around the rickshaw circle, behind the chapel and up the hill to the convent gates. Once outside he takes a hairpin bend.

When he stops for petrol she asks the question she could have asked a long time ago. But she wanted to see his face when she asked. "Uncle, did you send Vikas a newspaper cutting that told him where I was?"

Innocence passes instantly over his features, a look more damning than guilt. He shakes his head. "Chalo, we have a long way to go and your aunty is waiting."

Was it a case of stupidity, or well-intentioned bungling? Who else would have given Vikas the cutting? Purnima-aunty wouldn't. Mrs. Nadkarni certainly wouldn't. Why does it matter now, with her divorce granted three months ago? Anu is a free woman who will now try to be independent as well.

Sharad Uncle stops the Contessa across the state border in Punjab and alights. "Wait," he says.

By the roadside, a gunny sack lies across a tire, creating a trough. A man comes and pours some grain into it. A skewbald horse picks its way to the tire, and noses at the feed. Past the road, two boys in bright white dhotis swing a cyclamen pink turban between them, dipping it to fish in the slosh of a canal.

Sharad Uncle returns and reaches through the window, a bottle of cardamom milk in each hand. The creamy liquid is unexpectedly soothing.

"Anu," he says, "I am very sorry to say, there is no chance of reconciliation for you now. Vikas has married again. Nisha—the daughter of an old friend of mine. Very sweet and kind, very docile." He pauses to let the immensity of the contrast sink in. "He sent us a lovely wedding invitation—saffron and gold, with a swastik design all around."

He offers her his handkerchief; Anu waves it away. "Did you attend?"

"No, no. But I was collecting donations for the BJP, and Vikas came to the charity performance. A variety show—very good show, with nice Hindu girls modelling saris. Very tasteful."

"How much did he give?"

"Fifteen lakhs."

"Fifteen—?!"

"Not to worry. It's like American foreign aid. We have to spend it on advertising with Kohlisons Media. But he does get the credit on his taxes."

"What was the meeting about?" Anu says, like a surgeon cutting to bone.

"Just a lot of talk about getting Christians out of India."

"That would include me."

"No no, not now that you've left the convent."

"I just left the convent today, so I hadn't left whenever you met him. And getting Christians out would include Mother Teresa, who's done so much for the poor."

"The poor, the poor! Look after yourself and family, first. Now you've come out, *shukar hai*! First thing, we must stop at a temple for a blessing."

A fist clenches inside Anu. "No, not right now, Uncle. I'll go to the temple if I want, and the church if I want. But when I want."

"Stubborn girl, you are," says Sharad Uncle. He swings himself back into the driver's seat and slams the door. He starts the car and fiddles with the radio, but every station is playing wistful sitar music. Mother Teresa has died of exhaustion at eighty-seven.

As the Contessa approaches Kalka at the edge of the plains, the music gives way to discussion of Lady Diana Spencer's virginity test; her almost-arranged marriage; her humiliations by her polo-playing Prince Charming; her glamour, charm and compassion; her many humanitarian causes; and the millions of pounds the British will spend on her funeral ceremony. At least Anu was never as desperate for male attention. The princess is being recast as a goddess . . .

The air conditioning strains. Her uncle stops beside a blue tarpaulin sagging above a few tables and chairs. A tripod sign beside the chai-stall reads: *Guru Nanak Number One India Restaurant*.

The restaurant named for the first Sikh guru reminds of Rano, and Rano of Chetna.

Over a lunch of masoon daal, gobi-allu and roti, Sharad Uncle says he's learned to use a computer well enough to get his horoscope delivered by email each morning. He writes to Rano and Jatin and his sons almost every day, now. His mobile phone pings with a quick call of welcome from Purnima-aunty: she is in an NGO meeting with gynaecologists, discussing what can be done about the declining number of girls in the population.

The world whirls past Anu's window again.

Water buffalos stand knee deep in flooded fields, and cranes sit single-legged on embankments. By the time evening tempers sunlight, the Contessa is nearing New Delhi. The outskirts take hours to traverse—the capital has gobbled village land around it for miles. Connaught Place, the shopping circle at New Delhi's centre, mills with people and more people who have not missed a day in the life of Delhi.

This is not the sleepy stagnant Delhi Anu left three years ago, a city of 1970s buildings. Glass-faced high-rises, flyovers, hotels, and shopping malls say its code of frugal restraint has eroded.

Women in scanty attire advertise gymnasiums, resorts, soft drinks and cellphones from towering billboards. Public service ads exhort in huge letters below a photo of a girl in pigtails, "Save the Girl Child!"—Vikas must be making a fortune. Flooring shops displaying huge slabs of Italian marble have sprouted beside roadside chai-stalls.

What is that store selling? Health food? And what's that beside it? A fashion school.

Mercedes and BMWs ride shoulder to shoulder with Maruti Zens, Suzukis and the old 1950s Ambassadors and Fiats. Three college-age girls waiting at a bus stop, book corners poking through their cloth satchels, are not wearing salwar-kameez, or jeans and kurtas, but denim jeans and *T-shirts*!

A woman hitches her sari to pick her way across a rutted side street. Another holds a dupatta over her nose. One steps out of a car, turns and blows a kiss at a man her own age. A kiss in public!

Unrecognizable names adorn gated residential complexes that seem to have arrived directly from Europe. Set down amid the dust and hubbub of cursing, sweating drivers, as clumsily out of place as the gated Tudor mansions erected by the British in Shimla.

The Delhi of her childhood is a vanished landscape, precious but recoverable only in imagination. This New Delhi looks West, and welcomes new colonizers.

Anu pokes her elbow from the window of the Contessa and rests her chin in its crook. And now she smells dung fires beside lean-to shacks, raw sewage from monsoon drainage ditches. And through a greeny-brown haze of smog rise notes of marigold, rose and jasmine from garlands piled for sale to templegoers.

When they arrive, Purnima-aunty rocks and holds her, crying and laughing at once. "Didn't find a community that lives by its principles?"

"The nuns live by their principles—I just couldn't share them."

The centre courtyard of Sharad Uncle's home has been roofed, Rano's old room upstairs has been extended and a second storey added, along with a tenant. The drawing-room has sofas in place of the old divans, and the wall colours are coordinated to match the cushions. Sharad Uncle shows her his bathroom with the new tile and shower and goes to bathe. As Purnima Aunty orders samosas and tea, Anu pages through imported magazines *Glamour, Cosmopolitan, Vogue* and *Ms.*

Sharad Uncle sits down to tea and says, "All this because of Wipro," in explanation of his sudden wealth.

Wipro, Indian partner of GE Medical Systems, the American manufacturer of ultrasound machines. Sharad Uncle is so very proud to be an investor. Well, ultrasound is a great boon that helps every area of medicine from neonatal care to breast cancer detection, even as it helps to unbalance the population. *Ms.* says several southern states in the America require a woman to have an ultrasound twenty-four hours prior to having an abortion. The writer dubs the test anti-choice, but seems unaware that it can also promote selecting by sex.

The old cook no longer lives in the servants' quarters behind Sharad Uncle's house. "He got sick and returned to his village. Then we found we can't compete with the salary offers for factory labour," says Purnima-aunty, dipping her samosa in tamarind chutney. They do have one sweeper-woman, who commutes by bus three hours a day from the Trans-Yamuna river area for two hours of work. And a fourteen-year-old cook-boy who made the samosas.

"Your Mumma's acre in Gurgaon is now worth several crores," says Purnima. "I should have bought it from her when she wanted to sell it after your Dadu died. Please, call her after you've rested, okay?"

After tea Sharad-Uncle and Purnima-aunty show Anu her new room upstairs. It's about the size of her bedroom in the Shimla convent, but with an air conditioner, which, Uncle explains, runs off a private generator. *Panchatantra* and Amar Chitra Katha comics Rano and Anu borrowed from each other till ownership could no longer be determined are stacked on a side table. Anu's books: *On the Origin of Species, Gray's Anatomy, Candide, The Story of My Experiments with Truth, The Discovery of India,* the *Bhagvad Gita,* the Holy Bible—stand on the bookshelf. Her photo of Mumma and Dadu stands on the desk beside Dadu's stamp collection. Purnima-aunty returns the quilted cloth bag with her old nose ring and the rest of her jewellery. Anu finds some Vaseline, but the hole in her nose has closed.

In the adjoining bathroom, Anu, unused to showers, takes the low plastic stool before the bath bucket. She runs her fingertips over her eyes, feels her scar, throat, shoulders, arms. She cups her breasts and actually looks at them. She explores her waist and hips, the slippery softness between her legs, that had from violence birthed new life—Chetna. She looks at her reflection carefully. Her face—her scar looks deeper than she remembers. And she had not noticed a few threads of silver in her hair.

Welcome back to the world, Anu.

Purnima-aunty is beginning a new campaign: for a thirty-three percent women's quota in Parliament. Quotas are needed because men speak fluently of equality for women yet keep them from power. Every political party has listed it in election manifestos since 1996, but it won't happen for several years yet. Still she says, "We have to start now." And she says girl education is working. "Women run NGOs. Women from several respected families have taken to modelling, some are becoming actresses, even learning to dance."

"Are they paid?" says Anu, who must earn as soon as she can but dares not return to Adventure Travel in case Vikas were ever to find her. "Or are they just given pocket money?"

"No, now women are taking jobs in factories."

"Can a woman live on what she's paid?"

"Yes, I think so. Unless she's employed by her father, uncle, brother, or husband. Because then she can't argue, no?"

"And these call centres and programmer jobs—do they pay well?"

"Not as high as for men, but salaries are better than before."

Anu's economics is rusty—food, clothing and shelter were all paid for in the convent, and before that by Vikas. What can she contribute?

"Open a beauty parlour," Purnima-aunty suggests. "They never fail."

"An ex-nun with my face, opening a beauty parlour?"

"Okay-okay, what about a slimming parlour? Sell vitamins and protein shakes? These days people are all wanting to fight age, instead of getting respect from it."

Anu shakes her head, smiling.

"Have your face redone. Now medical tourists come because Indian plastic surgeons do such wonders."

"No, I think I'll leave it."

"Inner beauty—you have that. Always did." She pauses. "Everything is possible, now. Do whatever you want, but with Sharad's okay."

Gurkot
May 12, 1998

DAMINI

AFTERNOON IS LOSING LUSTRE AS DAMINI SQUATS ON the road beside the general store and the chai-stall, finishing a glass of chai and a rusk and listening to a melancholy old song "Kabhi Kabhi mere dil mein . . ." playing on the radio.

She should have journeyed to Allahabad for the Maha Kumbh Mela last month and taken a dip in the Ganges along with fourteen million other pilgrims, the easy way to remove all paaps once and for all. But she didn't and today her heart is very low. It could be she's missing Suresh or Chunilal or Sister Anu—or Anamika Devi.

This morning, devotees came and Damini tried to call the goddess for their questions, sprinkling Ganga-water all around her statue, anointing her poster with vermilion. But the goddess would not come. Eventually, Damini sent the devotees away, saying Anamika must be attending to more important matters. But what will she do if the goddess never comes through her again? Leela has farming, Kamna and Mohan are away in the truck—Damini can't sit around with no donations, just eating.

Maybe Dipreyshun has come again.

She takes a bite of her tea-soaked rusk and hears Khetolai, her birth village, mentioned on the radio. She stands, one palm feeling the hard hot edge of her tea glass through the end of her sari, the other seeking the solidness of the mountain. The All India Radio newscaster's Sanskritized Hindi mentions Khetolai again.

A big-big bumb has gone off in her village. A test of the Atom Bumb, the bumb Chunilal said would end all stories in India and everywhere else.

Damini doesn't own a single square metre of India, certainly not in Khetolai. She has been a guest in every home where she has lived, and will never feel truly at home with Leela, but she scrambles into the chai-stall and gasps out, "Why?"

The announcer is talking about a two-in-one test, using words she's never heard in Hindi or English—Fishun, Litheeyum Deyoteride, thurmo-nyoo-cleyar.

"Was anyone hurt?" Damini yells at the radio. The chai-wallah obligingly turns the dial, and the announcer sounds as if he's yelling back in answer. Gandhi-ji's followers of non-violence are gone, he says. Every prime minister since Nehru, he says, has urged restraint, while secretly urging Indian scientists to help India replace imported weapons with made-in-India ones. But the new prime minister, Atal Behari Vajpayee, decided after only ten days sitting in his new office that he was man enough, strong enough, tough enough, to give the green light to test the big-big bumb.

Damini's third eye sees the Dancing Policeman at Vijay Chowk change his stance: Go.

And matter became ener-jee, says the newscaster in awed tones.

He's probably never seen jee form matter during a birth. But which matter became ener-jee? Where? Loharki, Bharariya, and Mava, the desert villages where her sisters live since marriage, surround Khetolai. She has not spoken with her sisters recently.

The chai-wallah helps her call the sister who lives closest to their old village. Everyone is together, yes, all safe—she shouts her questions, her sisters shout back.

They were all together, visiting Khetolai for their cousin-sister's wedding, they tell her. But soldiers herded them out of the village in the middle of the bride's henna ceremony. "It was one p.m.," says her now-eldest sister. "No, it was noon," says her middle sister from Bharariya. "It was the hottest time of the day in the desert," says her sister from Mava, "because the mehndi dried on my hands in moments."

"There were a thousand of us," says her sister from Bharariya.

"Fifteen hundred at least, if you count the children," says her sister from Mava. "They said there would be a big big bumb, but they wouldn't let us run away! There was no shade—they had not provided tents or water. And here we were, fifteen hundred people in the white desert heat of May. It was forty-seven degrees," she says.

"A hundred and seventeen degrees," says Damini's now-eldest sister from Loharki, who measures by the old system. "We had to stand outside for four hours—old, young, sick, a few women were pregnant—the soldiers looked at us as if we were foreign. I fainted."

"We looked where the soldiers looked. I felt the earth tremble, as if a child were stirring inside," says her middle sister from Bharariya. "A plume of dust rose over a clump of rohida trees, then—*phph-phat!*—it felt as if I had been slapped right across my breasts."

"What breasts?" her sister from Loharki says, in the distance. "Kofta-balls, even after three children."

Which makes Damini and her sister laugh. Sobering, her middle sister continues, "I saw champa flowers tremble, but they did not fall. You know, the kind our papa-ji used to sell. And then, all of a sudden, the earth seemed to move like a sheet. We threw ourselves to the ground over the children. Some tried to run, but the soldiers stopped them at gunpoint. I really thought they would shoot them. When the soldiers cheered, 'Bharat Mata ki Jai!' we cheered as loud as we could, too."

Damini's sister from Loharki takes the phone. "A few seconds and it was over," she says. "They let us go back into the village, and you know what your grand-nephew said?"

Damini shakes her head as if her sister can see her. Her sister says, just as if she had seen Damini. "He said, 'Will there be school tomorrow?' I said, 'Are school children in America taking holidays every time their government drops a bumb?'"

Her sister from Mava is back on the line. "And I had left in such a hurry, I found I had not tightened the tap completely—half a bucket of water went to waste. We went to the well—and do you know, water had drained out of it."

Her eldest sister has taken the phone. "I say, How did they know if it's safe to be there? And there was a big crack in the wall of the wedding hall. I was glad we don't live in our old home anymore, but we live close enough."

"We should protest," says her sister from Mava, in the distance.

Her eldest sister turns away from the mouthpiece, "You—always thinking like-that-like-that. Be grateful it wasn't like 1974."

"It *was* like 1974," says her sister from Mava, taking her turn on the phone. "The soldiers said the PM will be coming to see us—we have to ask for an investigation."

"The PM will just detour around the village," says the eldest. "Mark my words, he's coming to congratulate the scientists. My father-in-law asked for an investigation after the 1974 test. He was given a radio instead. Since then, we have shown health workers the cancers in people's mouths and their throats. We've showed them bone tumours, skin lumps, breast lumps. Today a soldier told me, 'This is a perfect test; nobody will get two-in-ones.' I said, 'We're not asking for radios. We're asking you, because you made us stand in blistering heat for four hours, you set off a blast—your science men must know what more will happen to us this time.'"

"They were just following orders. Doing their dharma. They didn't care about the effects on us," says her sister from Bharariya.

The horizon is a jagged rip between a fiery earth and a platinum sky as Damini hangs up, guiltily relieved her sisters are safe. And relieved Anamika Devi didn't come today not because of any diminishment in Damini but because she was busy tending to more important things. Important things are done slowly and mostly happen unseen.

Behind Damini, the radio begins to play "Vande Mataram." The sons of the motherland are called by the song to worship the slayer-goddess Durga Devi. And what of the daughters?

What do goras like the Embassy-man and his wife think of India now? What does Timcu's gora wife think, what do Mem-saab's Canadian grandchildren think of India now? Now will they think India is important enough to visit?

A few seconds and it was over, said her sister. But anything so big, so important must have taken time.

The government has been spending money on the miltry all these years since 1974 and Madam G.'s Emergency. In that time, we ordinary people have been living from one real emergency to the next. Rats clawing in our bellies, diseases like Chunilal's. Ignorance that makes us trust astrologers and men like Swami Rudransh, and turns our poverty to misery, crime and imprisonment. No miltry has been fighting for women's wishes. Why didn't they use that money for electricity connections, drinking water filters, latrines, clinics and schools in Khetolai and Gurkot?

New Delhi
May 29, 1998

VIKAS

AT 6 A.M., THE FULL FURNACE OF SUMMER SUN HAS YET to focus upon Delhi, but the air still seems to waver and warp as Vikas enters Lodi Gardens. Mr. Kohli is waiting on the lawns beside the Glass House, windmilling his arms, touching his toes. "Buck up, beta, *oy!* I've already done one round."

Vikas smothers a yawn and falls into step beside his father. They set off down the narrow paved pathway girding the ninety-acre garden. Past the palm tree with "Vikas" carved around its grey trunk—he had been trying to impress Kiran.

Which brings to mind her husband and his bloody lawsuit. Game over, Amanjit Singh. India's Hindu bomb turns law meaningless, criticism treasonous and simple crimes—like financing a church-burning or a gurdwara-burning—unimportant. Justice has been saffronized. Let Amanjit Singh pit his Sikh Chieftain money against a leader in one of India's RSS Hindu organizations for a few more years. The nuclear playing field will make everyday violence petty and permissible.

"Saw BBC yesterday?" Mr. Kohli breaks into his thoughts. "Five underground nuclear devices."

Vikas nods. "New Delhi TV showed their PM Nawaz Sharif saying it was 'inevitable' and then the uproar in our Parliament yesterday."

"There they were in Islamabad, lighting sparklers, dancing in the streets as if they'd all had one big Sufi mystical experience."

"Just because we got ourselves a bomb, Pakistan had to set off a Muslim bomb." Vikas turns toward the tomb of Muhammad Shah Sayyid. "Like ours, mated to a missile so they no longer need to shove it out of an aircraft. But these are mini-nukes, ji. Just thirty-five kilotons. American seismologists will minimize that and say twelve, just like they said ours was much less than forty-five.

"But even if it was only twelve each, Pakistan's now in the nuclear club with us," says Mr. Kohli. "And we can't even blackball those fellows." He marches into the shadows, as the path winds between thickets of bamboo.

"We and Pakistan are entangled in a quantum connection," says Vikas.

They fold their hands to greet an acquaintance as they walk past a fifteenth-century mosque.

"How come they were ready just days later? For everything else, it's 'inshallah.' Huh!"

Laughter floats across sun-scalded lawns, from yoga-laughers, standing before the towering sandstone domes of the Burra Gumbad, aspiring for longevity. Past the yoga-laughers, father and son slow to stare at two women in salwar-kameez kicking a football between them. Another woman is doing push-ups a few feet away. Mr. Kohli shakes his head in disapproval and Vikas follows suit.

Parrots and pigeons take wing from a ruined turret, and soar into a blue sky. Over the park boundary wall, Vikas can just see the buildings of the India International Centre. Tongues of academics and diplomats must be wagging in its dining room. Turning northward to the gateway, another mosque comes in his way—is there any place in Delhi where he can avoid them? Muslim architecture, Muslim monuments, Muslim history, the Urdu language. Older and more pervasive than anything left by the Brits.

Father and son walk in silence till Mr. Kohli says, "One commentator started talking about China's test at Lop Nor three years ago, and he kept bringing up that we fought the Chinese in 1962. Eyewash. Why didn't he mention the US test in Nevada last year— underground, mind you, underground. Their President Clinton unilaterally broke a five-year moratorium. Why should they do it, but not India?"

Or Pakistan, but it wouldn't be patriotic to say that.

"Wait while I get us the *Hindustan Times*." Mr. Kohli detours off the Athpula Bridge to the free newspapers stacked by the entrance gate. Vikas amuses himself by flicking stones at ducks and geese swimming in the lake beneath the bridge, and then takes the path that runs along the ruined walls of a fourteenth-century fort. He's almost to the corner turret when his father catches up.

"Listen! 'Even after the fall of the Soviet Union there are still thirty-six thousand nuclear weapons in the world, most in arsenals of the USA.'" Mr. Kohli is reading from his folded paper in rhythm with his stride, "'About five thousand of them are still on alert.' Don't you think any one of them could be misdirected by some Pakistani hand to land in India at any time?" He doesn't say how a Pakistani hand will find its way to an American missile to misdirect it, but there's always a question mark.

Mr. Kohli leafs through a few more pages, then tosses the paper into the bushes by the boundary wall. Passing dog-walkers hush the barking and whining that breaks out.

Women sitting cross-legged on blankets in a shoulder-to-shoulder huddle are listening to advice from a saffron-clad sadhu. The sadhu dangles spindly bare legs from a metal bench before them. From the few words Vikas can hear, they seem riveted to his lecture on ego-annihilation.

Two young women, deep in conversation, pass him without a sidelong glance. Vikas stares after them. "The problem," he says, "is women and gays. Every international agency is full of them now.

They've been pumping money into Pakistan for development, and Pakistan has been spending it on atom bombs." He leads his father in the direction of the Sikander Lodi's tomb.

"And the Americans! Einstein said when America got the bomb that it was like putting a razorblade in the hands of a three-year-old. But do CNN experts bring that up? No."

"Americans want a 'level playing field'—well, India and Pakistan have now given them the battlefield of Kurukshetra," says Vikas.

"They don't know Kurukshetra. All Americans know of the *Mahabharat* is the line Oppenheimer quoted, 'Now am I become Death, the Destroyer of Worlds.'"

"He was right, Dad—a single person can do a lot of damage."

"But my point is: these are not the most important lines Krishna ever said to Arjun in the *Gita*. If I were producing their show, I would quote the most glorious lines."

Mr. Kohli climbs the steps of the tomb and declaims as if to wake Sikandar Lodi:

> *He that thinks of it as being a killer and he who thinks this is slain:*
> *both do not know—it neither kills nor is slain.*
> *this is not born nor ever dies, not in the past present or future*
> *un-born, changeless, eternal it is, primeval;*
> *it is not killed when the body is slain*
> *knowing this is indestructible, constant, unborn, immutable,*
> *how does a man kill anyone, Partha, who does he kill?*

Vikas looks around, embarrassed. When Mr. Kohli has finished, he climbs down the steps and they walk on.

"Did you broadcast Swami Rudransh's reaction to our bomb last week?" says his father.

"Yes, he said Indian scientists must do their dharma, regardless of consequences. And that science is the weapon of spirituality."

"Will he give a statement about this Muslim bomb?"

"Oh yes, he'll say Christians and Muslims have only one life to live, while we Hindus will reincarnate and inherit what's left. And if the world blows up, then what? Every thing is everything. We will all be returned to brahman."

"And if any Americans are left, they can still be furious."

Vikas stops by a row of palms. The dome of the Sheesh Gumbad blocks the whole sky. "Americans have been playing baseball in the Imperial Gymkhana Clubs for so long, they don't realize the game is now kabaddi. And the arena has shifted to the Indo-Pak Line of Control. Now we too can deal death from afar, as Europeans did for centuries."

"With enough power to make mountains fall to pieces," says Mr. Kohli.

The path returns to the entrance and the sign bordered in red: *Glass House*. A few stones still weigh Vikas's pockets. He looks around. By this hour there are so many in the park, that throwing stones would provide public amusement. But laughter still rings in his ears—the yoga-laughers?

He follows his father to the exit, glances back, but can't see them. *What is there to laugh at?*

ANU

THAT EVENING, ANU STANDS AT THE PERIPHERY OF A GAUDY hubbub, in three-inch heels and a sea-green sari with a goldthread border. She's feeling strange, and not only because her midriff and arms are bare. She's here at the invitation of her school friend Shalini and the encouragement of Purnima-aunty. She sips a gin and tonic, hoping it will help her adjust. She smiles uncertainly at strangers.

The men gathered beneath the chandeliers argue and bargain— Vikas would call it "negotiation." They don't seem to like each other, but are united in favour of deregulation and freedom from taxes.

Former schoolmates, they trust each other to keep agreements and secrets.

She gazes around at the collection of Delhi socialites. They look better on Page 3 of the *Hindustan Times* where she can enjoy their plumage minus their mocking tones. Women who live from the outside in.

White-gloved servants sail between them bearing silver trays arrayed with toothpicked canapés.

Shalini comes toward her, trailing several look-alikes. "Do tell us, Anu, what was it like being a nun?" She smooths her shaded butter-silk sari and tosses burnished curls. "I've always wanted to know."

"I don't think I can describe it," Anu replies. Apparently she has been invited as the conversation piece du jour.

"Aren't they all lesbees?" says another, dabbing her lips with an organza serviette.

Anu says, "No more or less than in the general population."

But Lip-dabber's attention has already wandered to someone far more important. She waves over Anu's shoulder.

Shalini says, "I used to tell Sister Imaculata that Catholics are the only group that wants Indians to increase population. Are they still preaching against contraception, Anu?"

"I don't know about other Catholics," says Anu, "but I have come to feel contraception is better than abortion, infanticide or starvation."

"Infanticide? Starvation?" Lip-dabber's attention has returned for a nanosecond. "Only in the villages." A turmeric stain spreads across the organza.

At least she didn't say, Such things don't happen in India.

Anu takes the opportunity of doing a khisko, as Rano would call it, sliding away to another group when Shalini turns to greet a new arrival. There a woman in a halterneck choli is talking about email attachments and downloading. Esoteric terms circle Anu like mosquitoes. Someone clicks a remote control, Anu can't name the song.

She helps herself to a lamb kebab that melts in her mouth. Vikas would have sent it back to the kitchen saying it was undercooked, overcooked, too hot, or too cold.

A tall unctuous man appears at her elbow, leering as if she has veered from nun to prostitute. He vanishes as soon as Anu mentions having a twelve-year-old daughter. Anu moves to a new group now orbiting Shalini.

"A toast to the CIA," says her hostess, raising her glass of champagne. "All their satellite technology and they didn't know."

"They knew, ji," says a gangly young man. "But what could they do about it? And when Pakistan set off its bomb yesterday—the CIA couldn't stop them either."

"They must have known and approved Pakistan's bomb," says a man sporting aviator eyeglasses, "How else could Pakistan have tested a nuclear device just seventeen days later?"

"Abdul Kalam says we can have small nukes with no problem," the gangly young man says earnestly. "He's a nuclear physicist, he should know."

"Does he?" says a greybeard. "How many physicists said Chernobyl couldn't happen."

"Oh, nuclear power is far off, now the US has banned dual-use technology. We can reverse engineer aircraft engines and even Pentium chips, but where will we get uranium?"

"Canada, ji. Canada," says the greybeard. "Uranium comes from Canada. And aluminium for centrifuges. Our first nuclear plant came from there in 1955."

"The Canadians will stick with NATO on sanctions," says the gangly man. "NATO is America anyway."

"No problem, ji. We'll find thorium deposits—one ton can give as much energy as two hundred tons of uranium. Kashmir has thorium," says the man with the aviator glasses.

"Poor Kashmir," Shalini says in a tone of obligatory acknowledgement.

"Nuclear weapons hold all creation hostage," says Anu. "I cannot believe so many religious leaders are silent." Father Pashan would be writing, speaking and protesting. Purnima-masi is writing to women's organizations. Mrs. Nadkarni says other activists are protesting too, but not very many, not enough, and no NGO has been formed yet.

"Because they see how much confidence our bomb is giving us. No one can call us an underdeveloped country now," says Shalini. "Besides, if we Hindus die, we're all coming back in a few days. Muslims won't, Christians can't either. Oh, are you still Christian, Anu?"

"I no longer have a religion."

"You can't *not* have a religion," says Shalini. "Every Indian has to have one. And separate laws for Hindus, Muslims and Christians. Thanks to the British and dear old Mahatma Gandhi."

"It doesn't matter what religion I or you profess, there will be pain, violence and loss if there is nuclear war," says Anu. This brings a great guffaw from the gathering, as if she has said something quaint.

Anu falls quiet, sidles away. Maybe they can't imagine the suffering if they survive a nuclear blast and shockwave. Haven't they heard of Hiroshima? Any nurses who survive will have to care for people dying lingering and painful deaths from failing immune systems, radiation sickness, internal bleeding, pulmonary edema, organ decay, cancers, birth defects . . . these future events are densely contained in the birth-moment of the bomb.

She approaches a group of shapeless women, sitting in the corner, arms folded under their shawls. They are the kind she and Rano used to call the Orange Juice Brigade because that's all they ever drank. A few of them remember her, and expect her to be as they knew her, or to have become like Mumma. She calls them aunty, sits down, discusses the Star TV shows they watch, and dutifully exclaims over their jewellery. It's restful, the only comfortable place at the party. As she exchanges small talk, her mind also moves to the call she just had with Rano.

Rano had news—she is finally pregnant. How Rano cried, Anu cried. How Rano laughed, Anu laughed. "It's a designer baby! The egg donor's IQ was 160, so she'll be intelligent." Yes, it's a girl, so Rano won't have to worry about tying a turban on a boy. There were many embryos to choose from. "Chetna is responsible—she brought us luck!"

Words failed Anu, but because it was Rano, the word outrageous didn't come to mind. But she should have said selecting one soul over another is unjust even if you let technology be your selector, even if you choose a girl. She should have said that if a missing—or present—Y chromosome is now a disability, some could decide that having one blue and one brown eye like Father Pashan is imperfect, or being born under the sign of Gemini is grounds for embryo selection. A few decades hence, physically different but reasonably able people like Mohan will simply not exist. People like Bobby, too. Everything is in the vedas, even eugenics—utilitarian arguments for violence have been around longer than *Mein Kampf.*

But she didn't object—couldn't—in the face of Rano's happiness. And Rano had also said that yes, Anu should come and visit for a few months, or as long as she wants. And that it was up to Chetna if she wants to return to India for awhile or forever—she's old enough to make up her own mind.

Anu had faltered, then. She should have said she wanted Chetna back, right then. But she still has no job and cannot afford to go to Canada or send Chetna a ticket. When you leave your ex-husband Christ, he doesn't have to pay you maintenance—he's out of this world. Her savings amount to nothing. And she won't ask Mumma or Sharad Uncle to lend her money.

Now, sitting with the older women at the party, Anu has a moment of clarity.

The Bomb could end all New Delhi's neverending cocktail parties any minute.

She never belonged among socialites, and never will. And she will not let Chetna become remotely like any of these women who can't see bangles they're not wearing, as Damini would say. Anu yearns to be with Chetna. She must know her. She was the one who named Chetna. Vikas didn't. Names change what they describe—for better or worse. She must begin with that being she created, reclaim her daughter, support her, stand behind her, bring her back from Canada, induct her into the Women's Survival Society, give her whatever she can.

Anu will help Chetna become someone who lives her life from the inside out.

Do it now, do it now, do it now.
Now, before it is too late . . .

ANU

THE MORNING AFTER THE NEVER-ENDING COCKTAIL party, Anu takes a betel-spit splattered staircase to the basement level behind the Ritz Cinema in Connaught Place. The stamp dealer sits cross-legged on a red carpet in his shop. A precarious pyramid of shelves loaded with stamp albums looms behind him. As a shortcut to trust, she introduces herself as she has not in many years, as the daughter of Deepak Lal.

"You've come at a very good time," he says. "Very auspicious release this very day, from the Postal Service. I show you, I show you . . ." He opens a velveteen box to display first day covers for the latest stamp. Swami Rudransh's baby face with its rupee-sized bindi grins up at Anu.

She declines. The stamp dealer looks slightly offended, but offers her Coke.

Anu cups her palms about the chilled bottle as he verifies the health of any relatives and remote relatives he can associate with her. By compliments and inquiries, he tries to place her. Only then does he hunch over the stamps in Anu's mother-of-pearl inlaid box. He remembers the stamps better than he remembers Dadu. His tweezers hold them over the square of the light table before him, then up to the naked light bulb, one by one.

The rarest three: the one with the Indian flag was the first issued after Independence in 1947; the one with the emblem of the Ashoka lions; and the ten-rupee stamp issued on the first anniversary of Independence, to commemorate Mahatma Gandhi after he was shot.

Dadu said, If you are ever compelled to sell or trade them, be sure it is for something vital.

"Independence stamps," says the dealer. "Why you wish to sell?"

"For my daughter's independence."

"Huh!" He names a price.

Anu shakes her head and doubles it.

"If I had so much money to pay for three stamps, why would I be sitting in a shop like this?"

"So no one thinks you need to pay taxes," says Anu.

He smirks as if she has read him. He draws one of the stamps toward him on the light table. Then the second, then the third. The tip of his tongue passes over his lip. "I must show them to another expert . . ."

Anu gently sweeps the stamps back into the box. She writes on a scrap of paper. "Send the money to this address by five p.m." she says. "Or I will show them to another dealer." And she rises, shouldering her bag.

Back on the radial road out of Connaught Place, shapes of taxis look solid and safe—but too expensive. Anu takes a scooter-rickshaw home instead of the bus.

Delhi is full of shadows, as if asuras dance everywhere. Vikas's demon eyes follow her all the way. She must stop feeling as if she will meet him—it's impossible in a city of fourteen million.

In her room at Sharad Uncle's she throws herself on the bed and allows herself ten minutes of tears and a mental lashing that would have made her mother proud:

Why don't you ever accept what you're given? Always, always holding out for better things. Always expecting the impossible. Now maybe you've lost your chance to bring Chetna home.

But that evening, a cycle-courier rings the bell at Sharad Uncle's gate. He passes a thick brown envelope through the bars with Anu's name on it.

June 1998

A N U

SHARAD UNCLE HAS SHOWN HIS NEW LIBERALISM BY
allowing Anu to go to Toronto. He's even driving her to the airport,
using two handkerchiefs as pads on his steering wheel. "Tell Rano
we are thinking of emigrating to Canada," he says, wiping his forehead with one of them.

"To live with her?" says Anu.

"Oh no, no—no need to trouble Rano," says Sharad Uncle. "We
have our three sons—all in Canada."

"I can babysit my grandchildren, save them the cost of daycare,"
says Purnima-aunty in ultra-practical tones. "Rano has her work, her
house, her responsibilities."

Rano will soon have a baby girl who will need babysitting as well.
With all her talk of equality, Purnima doesn't believe in living with
a daughter, even if her daughter and son-in-law would willingly have
them visit.

"But you have servants to look after you here, you have a house,
and investments. Why do you need to go to Canada?"

"Our sons should have an opportunity to do their dharma," says
Sharad Uncle. "And now we're the right age, we can get Canadian
social insurance. It won't cost them anything more—not to worry.
Why should strangers benefit from the taxes they've paid all these

517

years? Nowadays you go for a few months or years, come back." He beams as if the world's problems have been solved by better transport and digital communication. He pulls up at the fringe of the crowd of passengers, families, workers and porters outside the international terminal. "Anu, you have your ticket?"

"Yes, uncle." She has a deeply discounted ticket, courtesy of her old boss Mr. Gurinder Singh at Adventure Travel.

Sharad Uncle hugs her as if she is only going to Bombay—*oops*, Mumbai. But Purnima-aunty holds her tightly and murmurs into her ear, "Email us, call us. Call your mother also—she will miss you even if she doesn't say so. Now you go, my littlest baby, and bring your baby home. Be happy—ja!"

Sharad Uncle prepays a porter to see her through the door, helps with her baggage all the way up to Security. On the other side, Anu strolls the Duty Free. Feeling daring, even reckless, she buys an eau du toilette for herself, opens it, even sprays some on. For Rano and Jatin, she buys a coffee-table book with photos of India. For Chetna, she is carrying her jewellery and the rest of Dadu's stamp collection in her carry-on. She also has a new edition of the *Panchatantra*, several Amar Chitra Katha comics, and two children's books by Ruskin Bond in her suitcase.

Boarding, she notices the flight attendants are not wearing saris or salwar-kameezes, but skirts and blouses—even as Christians try so hard to Indianize for survival in India. The TVs light up as soon as the doors are closed for take-off. "Within a decade," says the American-accented newscaster, "there will be a home kit that will offer a private non-fail way for a pregnant woman to test if she is having a boy or a girl. At ten weeks, when the fetus is still an early embryo." The assumed inevitability of the march of technology is in her voice.

Sleepless in her window seat, Anu sips from a bottle of Bisleri water.

Why should Chetna trust you? So what if you gave birth to her—what have you done since?

Her skin tightens beneath the air draft from the nozzle above her. Her head rolls to her shoulder.

And Sister Imaculata is flying beside her on the wing, black-booted feet dangling below her white skirt. She's just beyond the double oval of the plane window, bearing mauve hydrangeas in outstretched hands.

A rush of euphoria pours into Anu's tiredness. She will learn about Halloween. She will see chestnuts roasted on an open fire. She will taste pancakes with maple syrup, and shop with Chetna at Little India on Gerrard Street.

The plane lands and Anu walks down corridor after corridor, collects her bag from the carousel and loads it on a trolley-cart. A woman wearing a uniform blazer over a sari collects her customs form. Anu pushes her cart through the automatic doors.

A throng of eyes. Raised placards. Maybe Rano hasn't come.

But one face stands out in the crowd, a sparrow face like Mumma in old pictures. A little girl is jumping up and down and calling. Anu drops her baggage, and begins to run.

Chetna, oh my Chetna.

EPILOGUE

Non nobis solum
Not for ourselves alone.

Motto of the Order of Everlasting Hope

Gurkot

January 2005

DAMINI

MIDWAY THROUGH A JANUARY MORNING, CLOUDS SAIL
between the crests of the far hills. Damini locks the storage sheds,
takes up her umbrella, and turns to descend the stone stairs when
Chunilal's purple-green truck comes to a stop beside her. Kamna
descends the ladder from its cab.

"So you've come," says Damini. "Your mother waits for you two
each day as if you were the moon who will break her fast."

"But *you* haven't missed us at all." Kamna teases, embracing Damini.
"I just made a delivery to the Big House," she says. "Amanjit-ji is
building a greenhouse to grow medicinal plants."

"He'll sell them to foreigners." Damini jabs her umbrella into the
ground.

Kamna adjusts her dupatta and kameez and shakes her wrists,
displaying her tinkly rainbow of bangles. "Look!" she says. "Steel,
like your kara."

"You be unbreakable too," says Damini. "Mem-saab said women
and men wear it to remind us we are the keepers of birth and rebirth."

Mohan comes around the truck and embraces her. He rattles off
the towns they have passed through. "Barog, Solan, Dharampur,
Kandaghat, Shogi, Shimla, Jalawaaz . . ."

"Very good, very good," says Damini, turning again to the stairs.

"Wait! Look who I brought," says Kamna. "All the way from Delhi."

A woman in a blue-green printed salwar-kameez with a matching dupatta across her shoulders comes around the truck. When she takes off her sunglasses, Damini recognizes Sister Anu. "*Vah!*" she says, and folds her hands. But the former Jesus-sister embraces her.

Mohan lies down on the ground, sticks out his tongue and catches a few drifting snowflakes. "You said I could eat snow like ice cream," he says to Kamna.

"Maybe next January," says Damini. "There's not even a centimetre this year. Come, come, Sister-ji. We are indeed honoured."

They descend the stairs and find Leela in the cow's room. She almost overturns the milk bucket in delight. Greetings and exclamations take flight on the crisp mountain air. Kamna has brought new combat boots for Damini, and a yellow and red printed salwar-kameez with a matching dupatta for Leela. Anu has brought a Nokia cellphone as a gift to both of them.

"So you can call your sisters or call me in Delhi," she tells Damini. "Kamna can show you how to use it."

"I know how," says Damini. "I've seen Kiran-ji using hers. But I'll only fill up ten rupees at a time."

Chai will warm everyone. Mohan brings a plastic chair for Anu, then helps Leela carry a large pot of water to the cookroom. Kamna and Damini sit cross-legged on Damini's speaking platform, facing Anu.

"It's good that Kamna brought you," Damini says to Anu, "I hope you corrected her driving. I worry about her all the time. A young girl—late at night. Driving on the Grand Trunk Road, brushing against death at every turn. At least she has a brother beside her." But as she says it, she knows the mere presence of a man may not be enough when a policeman's open palm thrusts through the cab window.

Anu says, "We cannot protect everyone we love, Damini."

"Is your daughter still in Canada?"

"No, Chetna lives with me in Delhi."

"It's not too hot, crowded and dirty for her?"

"No. And she enjoyed riding to Shimla in the truck."

"She speaks Hindi only slowly," says Kamna. "But she was telling me on the way that she learns better in English and still misses many things from Canada. And her boyfriend."

"*Haw!* A boyfriend?" says Damini.

"And girlfriends," Sister Anu says quickly. "And she misses peanut butter sandwiches, Nanaimo bars and blueberry pie."

"Those are to eat?" Damini asks.

Sister Anu nods.

"I told her I'm sure her boyfriend's donuts will come to India soon," says Kamna. "Nowadays everything from outside is coming in—Mr. Timmy's will too."

"But you didn't bring her to meet me," Damini accuses.

"We stopped at St. Anne's in Shimla," Anu says. "Not for long, because my old teacher, Sister Imaculata, has gone back to her country, and many nuns I knew have been transferred. I wanted to see you and the new private clinic and Sister Bethany at the school here. Chetna wanted to stay and play basketball with some girls at St. Anne's, so I came with Kamna."

"So young but deciding if she wants to go, where she wants to go—it's good?" says Damini.

"It's very good," says Kamna. She gazes past Damini at the distant grandeur of the peaks. "Chetna liked riding in my truck, and she was so kind to Mohan. She was telling me they have Muck-dun-alds in Canada, too. And Bata. And all the way I kept thinking to myself, 'I still wish I also had a little sister.'"

Damini's throat closes in remembrance and loss; she takes a deep breath. "It's not easy to lose a sister, or a granddaughter."

"Or a daughter," Anu says, as Leela rejoins them. She points down the valley splashed with asphodels, "What are those?"

"Temples," says Leela. "Farmers are competing to build shrines to Anamika Devi. See, all of them have a view of the snow peaks. So much effort have they spent that they would protest in marches and in court if Amanjit-ji were to demolish a single one. Not one would allow his ancestral land to fall into the hands of any man who has not pledged respect to the goddess."

"India is shining here today," Kamna rubs her palms together, then thrusts her fists beneath her armpits. "But I'm surprised Amanjit-ji is here in January."

"He goes back and forth to Delhi every few weeks for his legal matters," says Damini. "One case with Timcu-ji, and one in which he's suing your Suresh Uncle's boss for the damage to the chapel, the gurdwara and the *Guru Granth Sahib*. But at every hearing Lord Golunath denies Aman-ji any favours."

When Anu asks, Damini tells her that yes, people still come to her with questions for Anamika, and when they do, she wraps herself in Mem-saab's violet phulkari shawl and repeats her mantra till she falls into trance. Then the many voices within her rebound on the hills, echoes turn to pictures, and Damini describes the unseen that she sees. "If a daughter is coming to a home, Anamika Devi tells that truth. If a boy is coming, Anamika Devi foretells that too, just like an ultra-soon machine. I don't know how this is. But before every puch-session, before any questions of boy or girl can be asked, I say the women should first tell their stories. Men have to be still and listen at this time."

"What does that do?" says Kamna.

"Men unlearn that thing they learned to call women's stories— 'complaining.'" says Damini.

"And maybe they learn how it feels to be a woman," says Leela.

"I don't know if they can," says Damini. "Even some women can't feel what poor women feel." She's remembering Kiran as she speaks.

"Do the women speak truly in front of men?" asks Anu.

"Once they begin, women soon forget others are listening, and speak from their hearts. And as we listen, all of us compare. And one woman's story is nothing like another's—not even her mother's, her sister's, her daughter's or her grandmother's. When the telling is over, Leela comes forward. She helps me allow only women to ask questions of the goddess. And do you know, their telling then shapes the questions they ask! But sometimes Leela still has to teach those who can speak but not ask, how to ask Why and Why Not."

"What do the men say?" asks Anu.

"Oh, they grumble! They say, '*We* ask the questions.'"

Leela adds, "Then I say, 'Anamika Devi says we women must question, even if questions are disrespectful. Maybe there are no answers, maybe even she can't find the answers, but we have to start from questions.'"

"Do the men agree?" says Anu.

"Oh no," says Leela. "They say questions are dangerous, that questions challenge what is and change what will be. They say questions deprive the world of mystery. We say, 'Yes, but each question invokes respect for Lord Golunath even as we worship Anamika Devi.'"

"Leela tells them many forms of questioning. How to ask, what to ask and when," says Damini.

"The men must be worried you'll misguide the women," says Kamna.

"The women's questions are their guides," says Damini. "Not I or Leela. And men can ask their questions through the women."

"But Anamika Devi won't answer bijness questions," says Leela.

"Like?" says Kamna.

"Like, 'How much will the boy's side ask to take this girl?'" says Damini.

Anu shakes her head. "We need new words to talk with men, maybe even a new language."

"You may be right," says Damini. "We need new words even to talk to daughters and sons. Anamika Devi can bring about reality, but she can't answer every question I have. Once I asked her why Lord Ram or Jesus Christ needed a birthplace, and she said this is a question only a man can answer. I asked, 'Why is *koi* always a man? Why can't someone also be a woman?' This, she said, was a question for Lord Golunath."

Damini teaches women who can speak but not act how to disrupt their own lives with questions. To women who can only do as they are told, she explains how to go on strike by refraining from doing, and gives words to use when any master expects them to work without pay.

And because she is a pair of ears, Damini also hears what supplicating women need to say to men. Don't want to get married to the boy your father has chosen? Damini hears the request beneath your question, and asks Anamika Devi to tell your father so. Want to study and never get married? Damini hears and asks Anamika Devi to tell your father for you. Want your husband to use a topi when he comes to you at night? Damini hears you and asks Anamika Devi to tell your husband so.

"Women can have strange desires," says Kamna.

"Yes, sometimes women come who want and need no children, not even one son. Or women pray to Anamika Devi for a daughter. Anamika Devi can even tell a father or husband such desires."

"Can you speak for all women? Any woman?" says Anu.

"No. Only those with whom my spirit bonds. The Sikh scriptures say, in ancient Punjabi, *dhol dharm daya ka poot.* 'Responsibilities rise not from birth, but from compassion.' If I find compassion, I will think not only of my duty, but of the effects of my actions on others."

"And what if you can't?" says Anu.

Damini wags her head ruefully. "If my compassion fails, angry demons come. Usually, I can discharge them before they harm anyone—but sometimes, yes, they find speech."

Leela gets up, "The water must be boiling over!"

"Will girls be allowed to have sisters in Gurkot?" says Kamna, when her mother has left.

"I think so, yes," says Damini, "When a little sister is coming, Anamika Devi asks for an oath, deep sworn in her presence, that the girl will be named at birth, but not before."

"Not before?" says Anu.

"No. Before birth, she says a woman is two-in-one and must be asked what she wants and if a cleaning is her wish, she should be cleaned."

If Anu does not agree, at least her silence agrees that no rule adequately addresses every woman's story. Leela returns with a trayful of steaming glasses and a bowl of sweet jaggery.

"But after the child is born," says Damini, "I say devotees should remember that the goddess wants no others to remain unnamed like herself."

"And I say you cannot ask and take from Anamika Devi without giving something back." Leela says. She moves around the little group, distributing tumblers of tea and jaggery. "If you do, you will not value her words. That would be stealing without learning or understanding."

"And this is why Anamika Devi asks for an oath-deposit. If a girl is born and dies unnamed, the money will be forfeited to the Women's Survival Society of Gurkot."

"Huh! Do men pay, now?" says Kamna. "I remember when you first said this, they would complain and complain."

"Oh, we tell them an oath-deposit costs less than an ultrasound and cleaning, so they pay. But it's not only men who have to swear."

"*Women* have to swear?"

"Because," Leela says, "a mother or a grandmother should swear that if her husband doesn't allow her to give the child his family name, the woman will give the child her family name." She sits suddenly, knees apart. The empty tray slides from her lap. She pulls her dupatta forward to cover her face a little.

Everyone is silent. Damini pats her daughter's arm.

"I've started using the money," Leela says, recovering her voice, "to make interest-free loans for a few months to people who don't want any favours from Amanjit-ji."

Kamna gives a low whistle. Which makes Mohan whistle. He whistles and whistles till Leela shoos him upstairs. "But don't the men say, 'Give the money to us'?" Kamna asks as the whistling fades.

"Yes," says Damini. "But I say, 'You'll only spend it on rum and lottery tickets.' And I tell them they can ask the women to employ them."

Leela says, "Fathers often offer to bring Anamika Devi a she-goat, but your nani says Anamika could be angered by a sacrificed body or blood. One offered to bury an earthen vessel of money beneath her statue, but we say Anamika Devi only wants flowers and sweetness."

The gift of moving between worlds is emboldening. And a responsibility. In the echoland of altered consciousness to which her gift gives her entry, she sees many futures for Kamna, and also that her own future, now that she is in it, doesn't resemble the one she expected. "Once Anamika Devi has answered the questions of suppli-cants," she says, "I speak in my own voice. I say, 'See how shameless I am, living with my daughter in my old age! Still the goddess comes through me.'"

"And they say . . . ?" Anu prompts.

"All say, 'Hein? Hein?' in surprise. And I have to say, 'Yeh bhi hota hai!' I say it over and over. I even repeat it in English: 'This also happens!' Then only they begin to see that a parent *can* take from a daughter. I say, 'This also happens that your son may not be there to help in your old age. Then if you have not treated your daughter as well as you treated your son, if you abandoned her, starved or beat her, or simply used her strength like a wordless animal—with what face can you turn to her for help?'

"I say, 'My daughter is looking after me in my old age instead of my son. Shouldn't I be proud of her? But no, people say I should feel ashamed to be living with her. But look, I am no longer ashamed of things I should be proud of, and proud of things of which I should be ashamed.'"

Mohan is playing the TV very loud now.

"He must be hungry," says Kamna.

Leela rises to make some potato curry for her son. But then she stops, looks at Kamna. "And you, what do you want to eat?"

Kamna smiles shyly. "For me? I like the peas with cauliflower. I'll help you."

"No, today you sit with your nani and the sister-ji."

Damini, Kamna and Anu look out at ranges upon ranges for a while in comfortable silence. Then Kamna says, "When someone finishes the questioning, Nani, do they go away satisfied?"

"Anamika Devi never gives a complete answer," says Damini. "Nor is there any. We just go to the next life and learn more. But she does say one question can have many answers, and women can find those answers too."

To Damini's ears, at times, Anamika Devi sounds like her mother, at times a friendly mistress like Mem-saab, at times the small girl who walked behind her mother in the desert. At other times Anamika is an unrecognizable mystery. The goddess seems to like the soft glow of oil lamps and lanterns lit at night—at those times, she speaks in Mem-saab's voice.

And one night Anamika spoke in the high thin voice of a ghost-child. Leela laughed and reached out her arms and Damini woke from trance to hold her very close, till both cried. Leela thought she knew whose voice came that day, but only Damini truly remembered the voice of her sister Yashodara, the little girl from Khetolai who fasted to death in the Rajasthan desert, after the water ran out.

Still all the gods and goddesses seem conflicted and undecided about the direction the world will take. Another war with Pakistan happened and both sides could not use nuclear bombs because the destruction of Pakistan would mean the destruction of India. Everyone, including the spirits, including Anamika Devi, agrees there will be yet another war. Expectations of death are fading, annihilation is becoming familiar to a new generation. Many possibilities exist. Few exclude each other and each moment contains the seed of the rest.

Maybe the knot in Damini's heart will always remain, as will the ache and the horrors of dreams.

"Kamna," she says, "No little girl should lose a sister as you did. Never again will I need to become a stone to know what a stone feels like. Never again will I need to become a mountain to know what a mountain feels like. Because I am a person, my heart has melted, like the ice on those ridges that recedes a little farther each year. And because a person can feel, and a person who is a woman can create, can nurture, I have made it known in Gurkot that I will take in baby girls if anyone finds them abandoned."

"And boys, too?" says Kamna. "Boys like Mohan?"

"Yes, and boys. I never told you, but Moses was the first child placed with the Anamika-Yeshu Adoption Centre at the Shimla convent."

"This way, Goldina knows he is safe and near his relatives," says Anu. "We can visit him on our way."

Kamna sits very still at this news of her cousin-brother. Maybe Damini should have told her before, but she couldn't. Damini turns to Anu.

"And you, Anu-ji? Are you still healing others?"

"Yes. I work at Deluxe Hospital in Delhi."

"Mem-saab used to go there. It's a saab-hospital."

"Yes, it's private. But I am also helping Sister Bethany by trying to find couples who want to be parents, not couples who want a child. We have so many children there now, that I said I would return in summer and help her at the adoption centre."

"She'll pay?" says Damini.

"No, I'm volunteering."

"You'll be a bridge between the saab-log and us," says Kamna. "Nani, how is Suresh Uncle?"

"Still an Under Trial in Kasauli jail. Whenever I visit him, I learn again that a pure moment of joy or sorrow is impossible," Damini says. "Every day I ask Anamika Devi to bail him out, because the jail officers are like gods and want more cash offerings than we can muster. But even Anamika-ji must believe he deserves more punishment. I tell her he is one of us. I say no healing can happen without his doing his dharma, being a father for Moses. I tell her he cannot pay for the damage he did, but he can teach people at the temple to be better Hindus. I may not like what your Suresh Uncle has done, but I love him as his mother."

Leela descends to the terrace, with Mohan carrying her sari pallu like a train. He sits down beside Damini, and the pallu becomes his reins. Leela holds out a small bottle, "For you," she says to Kamna.

Kamna smiles as she takes it, then opens the bottle of Fair & Lovely and smooths it over her cheeks. She turns to Anu and holds out a tiny dab for her and Anu rubs it over her cheeks, too. Then Kamna puts a dab on Damini. Wrinkles smoothen beneath her fingertips as she rubs the cream on. Then Mohan wants a dab—and another and another.

Damini takes Kamna's arm on one side, Mohan's on the other. "Come, your story is only beginning. Remember, you two, take joy in sweetness. Sweetness survives—sweetness will exist, somewhere beyond the end of the end."

New Delhi
October 29, 2005

ANU

IT'S THREE NIGHTS BEFORE DIWALI. IN GURKOT, DAMINI
will be lighting shell-shaped clay diyas to welcome Lord Ram back
from Sri Lanka. But there are no clay lamps in the intensive care unit
at Deluxe Hospital, where Nurse Anu is on duty.

She lit lamps the year she brought Chetna home. They flickered
from the windowsills of the rooms she rented from Sharad Uncle and
Purnima after they moved to Canada. And Chetna wept all night
despite them. Her tears began after Anu called Rano's family with
Diwali wishes and Chetna took the opportunity to tell Rano she
didn't care if Lord Ram ever came home. She said she wanted to
celebrate the Sikh festival Bandhi Chhord Divas, and Anu-mama
didn't know anything about Guru Har Gobind Singh-ji and wasn't
letting her. Then she asked Rano if she could please come home.

Nurse Anu leans from a window. Occasionally the honk of trucks
and the rumble of buses bruise the night, but it is otherwise quiet. So
quiet, Anu can hear peacocks calling—*Keyoo, Keyoo!*—from their
perches on rubbish heaps. One storey below, frogs burp from a nearby
pond. The night watchman's bamboo walking stick shocks the night
as it strikes the pavement.

Like the shock on Chetna's face when Rano said that no, she
couldn't come back to Canada—Rano couldn't look after two girls

without servants. After that, Chetna went into what Damini would call Dipreyshun. Until Mumma came to Delhi to meet her. Mumma, who no longer calls widows loose or immoral, made Ovaltine-laced milk for Chetna. She called Chetna "beta" as she used to call Bobby, but wouldn't stay more than a few days in case it made her look bad, living with her daughter. With Mumma, Chetna has forged the kind of bond Anu tried for, yearned for.

Nurse Anu straightens, and draws the window screen tight against mosquitoes.

Life takes strange turns. But is god involved? Maybe not at a personal level. Still she prayed her thanks by habit when some thugs in the mob who burned the church were sentenced—but they were acquitted on appeal. She prayed for help as plenty of money came from somewhere—presumably from Vikas and his RSS friends in the saffron organizations—but found that the Church could bring no corresponding pressure to bear on the legal system. Only Suresh is still in jail.

Cars are honking on the streets outside. A commotion is coming closer . . . Loudspeakers in the hospital corridors blare names of doctors. A doctor's jacket hanging on a hook nearby begins ringing. Down the corridor, another cellphone amplifies as it demands an answer.

"Turn on the radio and the TV!" cries a doctor, shrugging her white coat over her sari as she goes out to meet the ambulances. Anu turns up the volume on All India Radio. Just music. Off the air.

She hurries to the nurses' lounge, flicks channels till she finds New Delhi TV, which shows footage of bloody bodies on the streets. Men are hugging, women are weeping. The wounded are being carried to taxis. Most will be taken to government hospitals. The rich will be taken to private hospitals, like this one. Crowds surround reporter Barkha Dutt, who is questioning witnesses. A motorcycle lays charred, its wheels melted off. Shop fronts are shattered. Bleeding victims are crowding into the back of a tempo.

She flicks to CNN. "No Americans killed." Yes, but what about others?

Sirens wail and wail. A few ambulances are flying up the arterial roads of New Delhi. Finally BBC's Late Night News explains: "Terrorist blasts have torn through Paharganj and Sarojini Nagar—both markets were jammed with holiday shoppers. Another blast went off on a bus." Later, she will learn sixty people have died and two hundred have been wounded.

She recognizes Vikas the moment he is brought in, though his scratched face has the grey-brown pallor of Delhi smog.

Lord Jesus, give her medical distance! Of the billion and more people in India, here's the one person she doesn't want to meet ever again, not even in a next life. Damini would say it was written in her bhagya. Sister Imaculata would say god works in mysterious ways. Professional training says she must deal with him as a patient.

He is dazed and grazed, but must have threatened loudly or bribed the police to get here. Must have shouted, "Don't you know who I am?"

Right femur cracked in the stampede, left clavicle too. Fracture of right radius and ulna requiring bone setting.

Once a cast is on the leg and it is raised in traction, he is moved to a private room. Doctors dart in and out—Vikas is too drugged to notice.

His parents arrive with whisky and a pack of cards for the vigil at the bedside. Vikas's uniformed servants bring ice and soda.

Nurse Anu exchanges room assignments with a younger nurse, newly arrived from Gujarat. Mrs. Kohli may not notice her nurse's cap, white dress and stockings, her slightly grey hair, or her scarred face, just as she never noticed servants, but Anu can't take the chance.

She doesn't have to walk past to hear when the Gujarati nurse is helping Vikas to the bathroom or bringing his pills. And she jumps every time she hears him bark buy-and-sell orders into his cellphone. Once in passing she risked a glance into his room to see the nurse listening to his heart. Maybe he has one.

His sycophants arrive, bow and scrape before him. Nurse Anu would like to chop him to pieces before their eyes.

Around midnight, Nurse Anu enters Vikas Kohli's room.

That fearsome face, innocent in repose. Any minute now, he'll open his eyes and try to charm her again with his movie-star smile. She clasps her wrist. Pulse: normal.

Feelings? Complete detachment, as if she were soaring above, everything two-dimensional below. Here nothing matters, everything is temporary. The larger story is all she can see. She thinks, *This is what Tagore called Airplane Morality.*

If she does what she is considering doing, she will pay. Her soul will enter fish, fowl or insect. What if she returns as a man and Vikas's soul is sent to be her wife? Wouldn't that be karmic justice? Nurse Anu almost laughs out loud.

Only in Bollywood do women turn into avengers. Only the slayer-goddess Durga Devi wreaks havoc. Only in the Canadian novel Rano sent can a woman escape by hiding in the hills while the war against women continues. If she does what she is thinking of doing, redemption will require the appropriate penance ritual, the feeding of many brahmins, donations to the poor, and the full recognition that retribution was not hers to deliver.

And there's that inside little voice . . . that goody-goody voice. It tells her to find a priest right now on this Diwali night, confess and say "through Jesus Christ our Lord" and save herself from sin.

No—visit a priest afterwards.

At 9 a.m. the next morning Nurse Anu is walking out of the hospital lobby after her shift, when she hears a young woman say Vikas's name.

She's dressed in a lemon short-sleeve shirt of a material that stretches tight over large breasts. Spikey sandals below her jeans. Twenty-four? Twenty-five? Straight hip-length hair tied at the nape of her neck. About Anu's height, but a little heavier. She stands at the reception kiosk and asks again for Vikas's room number in a tentative voice.

Even at this distance, Anu can almost taste the fear in that young woman's mouth.

"Your good name, please?" The receptionist demands, looking up.
"Nisha Kohli."

Very sweet, very docile. Mother of Vikas's two sons.

The receptionist's gaze slides sideways. She shuffles her paperwork strangely and looks uncomfortable.

Nurse Anu approaches. "Mrs. Kohli? I was just going to his floor. I can lead you there."

In the elevator, Nisha Kohli keeps her gaze on the ground. Anu's eyes travel from the massive solitaire on Mrs. Kohli's ring finger to the bruises that run between her gold bangles all the way up her forearm to the hem of her sleeve. Are these what caused the receptionist's discomfort?

Anu reaches out, touches the closest bruise. "Were you hurt in the bombing?" she asks.

The younger woman jerks away. "Oh no, no. I—uh—fell." Her gaze drops to the floor again.

"Very bad bruising, Mrs. Kohli," says Anu. "It doesn't look as if it's from a fall. Did someone hurt you?"

"No, Sister," And after a pause, she says, "Dhanyavad—thank you for asking."

One more story. This young woman's parents have sent her into battle without training, weapons or armour. She is locked in mortal combat with no strategy for attack or retreat. "Please tell me, do you need help? Is someone hurting you?" Nurse Anu steals a glance—above her kajal, Nisha Kohli's eyes are rimmed in red and shimmering with tears.

Only a few days ago, thanks to activists and women's organizations, Parliament has declared that beatings, insults, ridicule, humiliation, name-calling, threats, disposal or keeping of a woman's
wedding gifts are crimes against women's human rights. But laws
don't transform society overnight, and Nisha Kohli must be trying
as hard as Anu did to stay married.

"No, no, it's all right," says the younger woman.

The doors swish open. A man in a business suit turns from his
vantage point in the hall. "Mrs. Kohli!" He rushes to the doorway.
Does he not see the young woman's state? A reporter in salwar-kameez rises from a chair, microphone in hand. "Hello, ma'am," she
says, as if the woman she addresses looks whole and hearty. "What
do Mr. Kohli's doctors say?"

The new Mrs. Kohli brushes her forefinger across the corner of
each eye, raises her chin, and strides forward to meet the press.

Three-forty a.m. by the clock above the nurses' station. Pre-Diwali
fireworks crack to life. A car honks, a scootie-horn blows on the
street below. Nurse Anu's inner voice is silent. Her oath. Her vow of
healing. There's a blank spot in her memory where they should be.
This is the test of all her training, the only test that matters.

Jesus says forgive, turn the other cheek. Gandhi taught non-violence.

And look what happened to both of them!

Luck doesn't always come calibrated correctly. It needs manual
adjustment from time to time.

*Do the right thing just because it is the right thing, with the professional's
detachment. Play your role like Dr. Gupta, regardless of who is the patient,
regardless of the effect on said patient, without attachment to outcome.*

Just as Lord Krishna counselled Lord Arjun.

The Gujarati nurse has been fasting almost 37 days and with only
a few days to go before the end of Ramadan, can hardly stand up.

"Go home," Anu says to the grateful young woman. "I'll look after the patient."

What is right action? What is dharma? Is it not to go to the defense of a woman whose soul is being crushed, who cannot act for herself? Is it not to do what should be done for justice to prevail? Not the law—justice! Oh, where is Lord Golunath? She has no idea where to find an ojha in Delhi.

If she does not act, her experience will be of no use to other women. But is this the right act? Nurse Anu can persuade herself it is, even without extensive proof. Still she arms herself with one of the digital recorders used by the doctors.

Could Mrs. Kohli's bruises be caused by someone else? No.

Thy Will be done—but how can I know what is Thy Will and not my own?

She must overcome conscience and empathy to become a selector of souls, and do what must be done.

Nurse Anu takes four potassium chloride ampules from her tray and fills a syringe—50 cc. She enters Vikas's room. The IV-pack is dripping sweetness into his dreams. He sleeps—baby boy innocent, just as he would after hitting her.

An intense act of will brings her forward. Rational anger courses through her nerves like fire. She disconnects the tubing running from the IV to the cannula jabbed beneath his skin.

For the sake of the young woman in a lemon shirt with bruises down her forearms—hopeful young wife, as Anu once was. For killing her love, for robbing the beauty from her life. For the years in which death claimed Anu while living. For the years of Chetna's life that she missed. For a brave man shot in his blue eye, for the many Christians who lost the focal point for their prayers. For the witnesses who disappeared, the judges who were transferred. *Non nobis solum.*

If she fixes her syringe to the cannula and shakes Vikas awake, two slits will open on his face. Thin lines of glittering jet eyes will look into hers. They will light with recognition for one instant.

Memory will pin him forever to that moment, half-risen, mouth a little open, eyes bulging in shock. Hands rising to clutch her throat, then clutching his chest instead. His well-feared face will turn into a cartoon. Two ruby drops of blood will appear where the cannula went in. One swab—they will be gone before they can brown. *Oops, Mr. Kohli—your nurse made a medical mistake.*

Something will leave her when the deed is done. The day nurse will arrive. Nurse Anu will discuss charts, changes in treatments, lab work to be sent in that day, x-rays and ultrasounds to be carried out. She will deal with the pain of others. She will transfer her patients to the next nurse—all will be well.

Nurse Anu will wait so no one will think she left in haste, till the raucous chittering of birds ushers in a blue-tinted dawn. In the nurses' changing area, Anu will remove her cap and apron and make a cup of strong Nescafé. Doctors' rounds will begin. The day nurse will visit patients who need medication, then the nurses aides will do their rounds. Vikas's body will be discovered. The press will descend.

She will be questioned, but the post-mortem will show cardiac arrest. So many bodies are piled in Delhi's morgues, it will take months. And no one will dream of checking potassium levels.

Mrs. Nisha Kohli will be a widow, but at least she will no longer feel the mind-numbing panic Nurse Anu remembers so well.

You want to kill a man, a conscious, living breathing person, another human being. Is this Anu?

Would it be an act of generosity or one of selfish revenge?

For conceit, for lack of empathy. He who has none, deserves none of mine.

You have no right—only his mother had that right, and only before he became conscious. Because it's creating that is difficult.

She should believe as a Christian that his soul will suffer in hell for the suffering he has caused her and Chetna, for the suffering of Father Pashan. When you're Christian, you don't have to be judge or executioner. But she can't help it—she believes as a Hindu that his soul will return. As a rat, a frog, maybe a crow.

Better still, may he return as a Muslim, a Sikh, a Christian, a Parsi or a Jew. Karmic justice, if there is any.

Kill Vikas and he will have won by making her act like him. But . . . kill Vikas and she will feel larger, no longer helpless. Will that change be reversible?

She approaches the bed.

The glittering eyes are open and he is staring at her. "Anupam! What's in that syringe?"

"Could be sodium pentothal, could be potassium chloride." Her voice comes out evenly, as if her heart isn't jumping in surprise at his sudden recognition. "If it's sodium pentothal, you'll talk and talk, and you might even tell the truth. If it's potassium chloride . . ."

She describes how he will die, and how his death will feel. And Vikas yells. He grabs for her but is restrained by his leg still hung in traction. She backs away a safe distance.

"The doors and walls are thick here, Vikas. And I'm the only one on duty in this ward. It seems you have been cruel, not only to me . . ."

Vikas is pressing back into the pillows now, recoiling from her upheld syringe, "Anu, I didn't know your precious padri would die!"

The mistaken confession takes Anu's breath away. "I was referring to your cruelty to your wife."

"Oh—"

"But you've just provided more reason why justice should be done."

"You're still angry about that little church and that padri, after eight years? Burning churches and gurdwaras is just a first step."

"Toward what?"

"A pure Hindu Reich. By 2025 we'll have no more Muslim, Christian, Sikh or Jewish terrorists. No more Muslim bombs like the ones today. Think of it! Frighten non-Hindus enough to make them leave, and eliminate the rest."

He makes it simple enough that it almost sounds profound.

"And women?"

"Oh, mothers shall be honoured!"

"And daughters, sisters and wives? Must they be beaten, as I was?"

"What lies you make up, Anu," says Vikas. "Look at you, so full of anger. Why do you make up such lies? Why do you hate me so?"

Nurse Anu says, "I met your second wife in the elevator. I saw her bruises."

"All these new glass doors in the city. Must have walked into one."

She answers this with silence.

"Aha—you're jealous, you're jealous!"

She stands looking down at him.

"C'mon, yar! You'd kill me just for hitting her once or twice?" Vikas gives a hard-edged laugh. "Why not let me off with a lecture?"

Nurse Anu holds up her recorder. "I could just put your confession on the net and it will become like the stains of your karma. Or I could give it to Amanjit Singh for evidence."

Vikas tries to laugh, but stops in a spasm of pain. When he collects himself, he attacks, that voice hammering at her. "Seven years after we exterminated your lover and his conversion factory, we're still here. RSS leaders said Gandhi would be killed for giving half of India to create Pakistan—it happened. We said the Babri Masjid would be demolished, and wasn't their damn shrine brought down brick by brick? We said that India should be nuclear, and it happened a week after our chaps in the BJP were elected. What we say will happen, happens."

"Justice can also happen, Vikas."

"Ha! Three years ago we exterminated thousands of Muslims and all that happened was inquiry after inquiry. Each time our money and connections move us closer and closer to the magic word. Power. Power suit, power lunch, power drink. Total Power!

"And we will come to power again, because those who go to the polls worship Mother India and don't read English. Majority rules, darling, the majority Hindu community!" He winces, and all of a sudden has run out of energy. He lies back on the pillow, his face grey.

He must be very tired, his whole body must be hurting. How pathetic he looks with his leg suspended, and one arm in a cast. Her gaze drops to the syringe, to her hand holding the syringe. "In a few minutes, the great Prince Vikas might turn into a frog. Or come back as a woman," she says.

"Bloody rubbish." Vikas strains to sit up, to get at her, as monitors of his vital signs arc and flash all around. "Touch a hair on my head, and you'll be in trouble."

"Sometimes," Anu says, "people in intensive care can become paralyzed after accidents. Some fall into a state of coma for long periods. It's a strange feeling, Vikas, like going back to a time before birth. You'll be unable to lift a finger. You'll be dependent on the kindness of nurses, as you were dependent on the health and kindness of your mother. Would it be better for you to die than to live?"

True fear, the kind Anu felt every day for nine years, dawns on Vikas' face.

"Help!" he yells.

Everyone will hear. But most will feel it's Nurse Anu's dharma to answer.

She turns her cheek. The one with the faded scar, in which sensation is not the same as in the other. She could be considering his plea, she could be steeling herself against him.

The needle in her hand approaches Vikas's skin. Her gaze rises for a moment—outside, the sun is lifting off into incandescence. The wisdom of the universe vibrates around her.

Acknowledgements

Demographers estimate that 45 million baby girls were missing in India in the nineties, and 42.4 million from 2001-2008 as a result of prenatal selection. Worldwide, 160 million girls are estimated missing since the 1970s. Those missing girls inspired this novel. Some characters began from *A Pair of Ears*, a short story included in *English Lessons and Other Stories* (Goose Lane, 1996). Readers of *What the Body Remembers* (Knopf Canada, 1999) will recognize Mem-saab as Roop, Sardar-saab as Sardar-ji.

In the US, I am obliged to Dr. Melita Beise, Ron Cesar, Jim Ptacek, Dr. Catharine Malloy and Hari Iyer who gave of their time for interviews. Judy Bridges gave me friendship and working space at Redbird Studios. I appreciated the comments of fellow novelists of the Redbird Writer's Group led by Elaine Bergstrom (pen name Marie Kiraly). I thank members of SAWNET, the South Asian Women's listserv for wide-ranging opinions on issues of contraception, abortion, motherhood and fertility. I am very grateful to Indira and Jit Singh Pasrich for their generous hospitality and a writer's studio in 2008. The Ragdale Foundation awarded me fellowships in 2009 and 2010. I appreciate Susan Tillet, Regin Igloria and the many writers and artists I met during my residencies, for their deep respect for the creative spirit. My greatest debt is to my husband, David Baldwin, whose love, patience and humour over seven years helped me bring this book alive.

In India, Dhanshri Brahme of the UNFPA, social worker Sandhya Gautam, Sister Monica Joseph and the sisters of Jesus and Mary, the sisters of Loreto Convent Delhi, Mrs. Janet Chawla of Matrika, Dr. Sharad Iyengar and Dr. Kirti Iyengar, founders of Action Research and Training in Health, and Firoza Mehrotra of UNIFEM contributed time, ideas, expertise and concern. Dr. Kimberley Chawla of East West Medical Centre scoured Indian newspapers daily for articles that would help me, reviewed several sections of the novel and provided invaluable medical expertise. Any errors thereafter are my responsibility. For warm hospitality, intense discussion on development issues, and the experience of the hills, I thank Aloka and V.K. Madhavan of the Central Himalayan Rural Action Group (Chirag.org) in the Kumaon hills, and Subhash Mendhapurkar of Social Uplift Through Rural Action (Sutra.org) in Jagjitnagar. Conversations with a man of huge spirit and courage, Father Cedric Prakash of Prashant, ranged from issues of fundamentalism and caste to Indian Christianity. I am deeply obliged to Tejinder Singh for his generous hospitality in Shimla, and expeditions to Karsog and Kotgarh. These places contributed, along with Kumaon, to the creation of Gurkot and Jalawaaz. Warm acknowledgement to traditional healer Bhagirathi Devi and her family for a homestay in Sunkiya, India.

Madhu Kishwar's writings in *Manushi* inspired Anamika Devi's ten-armed form. I owe the pink poster image to artist Nivedita Jadhav of the Asmita Collective. I am indebted to the late film critic Amita Malik for many discussions over the years on the subject of motherhood, creativity and their relationship to a woman's self-respect.

In Canada, my gratitude to Brian Brett for his urging to explore paradoxes, and bring more balance to the narrative. Thank you to Satwinder and Parm Bains for most gracious hospitality in Vancouver, and Cindy Birks Rinaldi for her love and steadfast encouragement. Grants from the Canada Council provided a vote of confidence and capital infusion for research exactly when I needed it.

My first readers David Baldwin, Jaya Bhattacharji Rose, Laurel Boone, Judy Bridges and Ena Singh provided valuable suggestions and corrections. They may disagree with opinions expressed in this novel.

I am grateful to my insightful and probing editor and publisher Anne Collins, at Knopf Random Canada, for taking the characters to her heart and sharing my vision. Many thanks to Angelika Glover for her diligent and careful copyediting, and to the managing editor, Deirdre Molina, and to vice president, creative director, Scott Richardson, for designing this book.

My agent Samantha Haywood marketed *The Selector of Souls*, and offered guidance, support and enthusiasm. David Bennett, Meghan Macdonald and the rest of the team at Transatlantic Literary Agency supported her efforts. Attorney Marian Hebb has watched out for me since 1998.

Readers familiar with the works of Madhu Kishwar, Margaret Abraham, Patricia and Roger Jeffrey, and Amartya Sen, will recognize background reading. I am indebted to Rabindranath Tagore's diaries (1932) for the airplane metaphor for two-dimensional detachment ethics.

Among the many books and magazines I consulted, I recommend: the online archives of *The Economic and Political Weekly of India*; *Myths, Rituals and Beliefs in Himachal Pradesh* by M.R. Thakur; *The Power Behind the Shame* edited by Janet Chawla; *Divine Enterprise* by Lisa McKean; *The Body Hunters* by Sonia Shah; *New Nukes: India, Pakistan and Global Nuclear Disarmament* by Praful Bidwai and Achin Vanaik; *Weapons of Peace*, by Raj Chengappa; *Guru English* by Srinivas Aramundan and Anupam Rao's *The Caste Question*. For global histories of sex selection, I recommend *Fatal Misconception* by Matthew Connelly; *Unnatural Selection* by Mara Hvistendahl; and *The Means of Reproduction: Sex, Power and the Future of the World* by Michelle Goldberg.

"Chhoti si Aasha" was written by P. K. Mishra. "Zindagi Aur Kuch bhi Nahin" was written by Lakshmikant Pyarelal. Ramesh Menon's translation from Canto II/16-21 of the *Bhagvad Gita* is used by permission of Rupa Publications. The quote from *Song of Krishna* (5) by Viswantha Satyanarayana translated by Velcheru Rao is reprinted by permission of the University of Wisconsin Press. A more extensive bibliography is available at www.ShaunaSinghBaldwin.com.

SHAUNA SINGH BALDWIN was born in Montreal and grew up in India. *The Tiger Claw*, her second novel, was a finalist for the Giller Prize in 2004 and is forthcoming as a film. Her first, *What the Body Remembers*, was longlisted for the Orange Prize for Fiction and was awarded the Commonwealth Writer's Prize for Best Book (Canada and Caribbean region). It has been translated into fourteen languages. She is also the author of *English Lessons and Other Stories*, the collection *We Are Not in Pakistan* and co-author of *A Foreign Visitor's Survival Guide to America*. Her short stories have won literary awards in the United States, Canada and India. She holds an MFA from Marquette University in Milwaukee, where she currently lives with her husband.

M,